Fiery daughter of
Nancy cannot for

He has everything—good looks, charm, daring . . . and
now Graylings, an English mansion left to him by a father
he'd never known.

George Stein

Nancy's kind-hearted soldier brother, George will face a
dark destiny to possess lovely Annabel Steele.

Annabel Steele

Lovely and gentle, she must defy all those she holds dear
and brave the cruel hand of fate to follow her desire.

Patrick Steele

Born with a chip on his shoulder against the Steins, Patrick
will not rest until he settles the score.

London and New York in World War II

On either side of the Atlantic, two families will face trag-
edy and joy, despair and hope, as the tides of war test their
loyalty and their love . . .

The Dew of Heaven

Charter Books by Caroline Bridgwood

THIS WICKED GENERATION
THE DEW OF HEAVEN

CAROLINE BRIDGWOOD

THE DEW OF HEAVEN

CHARTER BOOKS, NEW YORK

THE DEW OF HEAVEN

A Charter Book/published by arrangement with
Pan Books Ltd

PRINTING HISTORY
Pan Books Ltd edition published 1987
Charter edition/May 1990

ISBN: 1-55773-333-3

Charter Books are published by The Berkley Publishing Group,
200 Madison Avenue, New York, New York 10016.
The name ''CHARTER'' and the ''C'' logo
are trademarks belonging to Charter Communications, Inc.

PRINTED IN THE UNITED STATES OF AMERICA

10 9 8 7 6 5 4 3 2 1

This book is dedicated to all the friends who have helped me so much over the last two years: Irene, Isabel, Clare, Ali, Tor, Genevieve, Boggie, David, Paul and Alex.

With special thanks to David Williams-Ellis and Rebecca Pogrow, who fed me while I was writing this.

"And when Esau heard the words of his father, he cried with a great and exceedingly bitter cry and said unto his father, Bless me, even me also, O my father.

And Isaac said, thy brother came with subtilty and hath taken away thy blessing. And he said, Is he not rightly named Jacob? For he hath supplanted me these two times: he took away my birthright; and behold, now he hath taken away my blessing.

And Isaac his father answered and said unto him, Behold, thy dwelling shall be the fatness of the earth, and of the dew of heaven above; and by thy sword shalt thou live, and shalt serve thy brother; and it shall come to pass when thou shalt have the dominion, that thou shalt break his yoke from off thy neck . . ."

GENESIS 28, 34-40

Part
One

Prologue

Somerset, August 1937

"We may our ends by our beginnings know."

Sir John Denham

THE SUN BURNED down hard from the centre of the sky. One of the labourers straightened himself up and slewed the sweat from his brow, watching the spray fall on gleaming stubble. Then he tugged off his waistcoat, pushed his sleeves back, and fell to with the others, making the scythe bite cruelly into the waiting corn. Only a few yards distant, khaki-clad troops were carrying out mortar practice, squatting on the shorn ground and pursing their lips in concentration.

Nearby was Heathcote House, a grey, stone manor behind a high wall. Sunlight picked at the crumbling brickwork and dust-laden leaves of trailing ivy. There was no sign of the owner of the house, Adrian Steele, or his wife Jennifer, but their three children were out on the unkempt lawn. The baby, Kit, clasped the sides of his pram and rocked his small, fat body to and fro, making the springs squeak. Twelve-year-old Patrick was teasing a dog with a stick. The creature's angry yelps drowned the tuneless humming of Annabel, who was on the swing.

The dog's jaws closed on air and not stick for the fifth time as Annabel eased herself into a standing position on the swing and began rhythmically bending and straightening her knees to set the seat in motion. Her fine, dark hair flapped against her neck. Then her foot slipped and she tumbled to the ground with a shrill cry of shock and disappointment.

"Annabel!"

At the same time, Kit craned his head towards the noise and fell out of his pram to the ground, but his shrieks of pain were ignored as Patrick raced to Annabel's side and lifted her awkwardly into his arms like a piece of broken china. He pushed her hair from her damp face and pressed her head against his chest so that dark strands clung to his shirt, rocking her as he had seen his mother do once, a long time ago.

Kit sniffed quietly to himself as the tears dried on his cheeks and Patrick's dog slunk away with the stick in his mouth.

Less than two miles away, in the grounds of a grandiose white-washed Georgian edifice named Graylings, ten-year-old Nancy Stein and her thirteen-year-old brother George were spying through a fence, giggling.

The sheltered area beneath the sloping roof at the back of the stables would have made the perfect spot for a rendezvous; a rendezvous unseen by the rest of the household, but for a small gap in the wooden fence that ran behind it. It was through this gap that George and Nancy were peering, their cheeks pressed together so closely that both mouths bunched like roses. They were watching Simon, the gardener's lad. Simon rubbed the back of his hand across his stubbly chin, looked at his watch and then started to whistle. Nancy recognized the tune; it was *"Walter, lead me to the altar"*. She had often heard it coming from the bakelite wireless set that Mrs Burrows kept in the kitchen and played until the valves glowed red hot.

Before long there was a rustle and a slight gasp and Simon was joined by the kitchen maid, cursing because she had snagged her new stockings. Simon kissed her.

"Don't look," George said. "It's disgusting."

But Nancy did look and it was not disgusting, it was very tender the way they leaned towards each other with their mouths half open like hungry baby birds.

George turned away from the fence and began to walk down the grassy slope.

"Shall we go to the post office and buy sherbet fountains?" asked Nancy, sensing George's disappointment with their adventure and anxious to placate him.

"We haven't any money."

"I have. I got two lots of pocket money this week."

"What? Who gave it to you?"

"Mummy gave me sixpence and I said, 'When can I have a rise?' So she said, 'Maybe next time. You'll have to ask Daddy.' So I went to Daddy and said, 'Mummy says I've got to ask you about my pocket money.' And he gave me sixpence."

"A whole shilling!"

"I know." Nancy laughed and George stared at her face with outright awe and admiration.

"Well, hurry up then Nan—go and get it!"

Nancy turned and started to run back towards the house. George smiled to himself as her footsteps retreated and the sound of her laughter grew too faint to hear.

<u>One</u>

Somerset, Winter 1942

IN THE VILLAGE of Nether Aston, the Lamb and Child stood squarely on the High Street, at a point where a sharp bend in the road pushed it into prominence and its sign was clearly visible to all passers-by. It was the only public house within a radius of several miles and although its exterior had looked neglected since the outbreak of the war—its solid oak door warped, its windows grimy—it still retained its position as the centre of village life.

It was a sharp, cold night in December, and inside the pub a wood fire was burning in a massive stone hearth. A group of uniformed servicemen from a nearby camp were crowded around the bar, handing out cigarettes and laughing with a big-boned brunette who wore bright red lipstick. Oblivious to the stinging woodsmoke, the elders of the village were sitting near the fire and playing dominoes, slapping their pieces down on the wide stone hearth and muttering amongst themselves.

The heavy wooden door was pushed open and two more people came into the crowded room. One of these was a boy, slight and pale with dark hair and wary eyes. The other was some fifteen years his senior, a portly figure with a chubby face and a florid complexion. His hair was thinning but he moved with a confident spring in his step, while his young companion had the tense, guarded movements of an old man.

"Right then, Patrick . . ." The man rubbed his plump hands together and held them up in the direction of the fire, "What are we having?"

"I don't know, but I know that *I* can't get them. It's against the law. I'm still seventeen."

Greville Dysart continued to smile, despite Patrick's disagreeable tone. "Of course you are, old man! Of course you are! Right, you find a corner and make yourself scarce and I'll get them."

He returned with two glasses of scotch. Patrick pulled a face.

"Oh, come on, old chap, this stuff's like gold dust nowadays!" He took a sip from his glass and swilled it around his mouth. "Nectar! It really is! Your life will be the poorer if you don't acquire a taste for it, believe me!"

Greville spoke with all the assurance of a man who had sampled the world and formed his own conclusions. He and Patrick Steele were distant cousins, and it was Patrick who was the native of Nether Aston, and Greville who was the immigrant in the small community. Patrick's father was Adrian Steele, the only son of a yeoman farmer called Roland Steele who had married into the aristocracy and lived just long enough to regret it before lapsing into senile dementia. Roland's wife, Lady Henrietta Dysart, was the daughter of an earl, a fact which she never ceased to impress upon him. She raised Adrian Steele to share her social aspirations and set her sights on his marrying into the Colby family who owned Graylings, the largest estate in the area. But when Gerald Colby named Adrian as his heir after the death of his eldest son Frederick, Adrian was reluctant to share his good fortune with his mother. She returned in high dudgeon to Castle Cloud, the Dysarts' north country seat, where she acted as housekeeper to the cousin who had inherited the earldom.

Greville was the grandson of one of Lady Henrietta's less distinguished cousins, and he grew up in the shadow of Castle Cloud. He remembered being ticked off by Lady Henrietta when he was Patrick's age and had gone to the Castle to shoot for the first time. She was a sour, scrawny old lady with piercing blue eyes and a chilling voice, and she didn't appear to like Greville very much. But then she didn't like anyone very much, and at least Greville found favour with "Cousin Percy", as he called the earl. When he left school, he moved into the Castle in the role of an unofficial *aide de camp*, and for several years he enjoyed the comfortable life of a hanger-on, gently deflecting some of the estate funds in the direction of his own bank account. When war broke out in 1939, his fortunes changed. He managed to avoid fighting by obtaining bogus medical certification for a small price, but Castle Cloud had been commandeered by the army, and the eighty-year-old earl had moved into a residential home for the elderly. The old way of life was dead.

Supported by the Dysart funds that he had embezzled, and by a relentless opportunism, Greville moved south. He knew that Lady Henrietta had married into a landowning family, and prime agricultural land in the southern counties still brought in money. Perhaps he would find something to suit him . . .

What he found was a decaying house called Heathcote and no money at all. A couple of remaining farms were struggling to survive while Lady Henrietta's invalid son lay in bed and her grandchildren lived like hermits. Their mother had abandoned the family home when they were very young, and Greville couldn't help feeling sympathetic to her plight. Nevertheless, he stayed on as an unpaying guest and family mentor. The children were tractable, particularly Patrick, who had inherited Lady Henrietta's sourness but none of her spirit.

Besides, there were many more comings and goings in Nether Aston than there had been in the wilds of Northumbria, and Greville had no difficulty persuading himself that if he waited patiently there would be situations for him to exploit right there on his doorstep. He had now spent three years listening to local gossip in the Lamb and Child and pushing the Steele children in whichever direction took his fancy. He was fond of them. "My little marionettes" was what he called them privately.

Greville was a familiar face in Nether Aston now, though still a newcomer by village standards. The villagers had been deeply suspicious of him at first, and wary of his sophisticated manner. But Greville had at least been born and bred in the countryside and he exploited this fact to the full. He knew the form, knew which questions to ask. And when the locals realised that he understood the passing seasons and could tell a woodcock from a wood pigeon they relaxed a little.

The Steele children had been objects of pity since their mother's desertion, and many people considered it a good thing that there was a respectable adult in the house to keep an eye on them. The ailing Adrian Steele didn't count. No one really considered the possibility that Greville was using the Steeles, for what did they have, after all, but a couple of worthless farms and run-down house? Those who still mistrusted Greville's smooth manner kept their feelings to themselves. But he was still considered an outsider.

While Patrick toyed with his glass of scotch, Greville was leaning in the direction of the domino players, trying to hear what they were saying.

"Patrick, old man, why don't we go and challenge these old boys to a game. I want to know what they're up to."

"All right."

Patrick followed Greville across the room without enthusiasm, and they were admitted silently to the circle. Greville was too busy keeping an ear open for news to really concentrate on the game, but Patrick watched the old men intently, particularly one who was shuffling the unturned pieces behind his hand.

"Hey, that's cheating!"

There was a murmur of disapproval at Patrick's accusation and one of the old men said in a low voice, "Do you want to play or not, lad?"

"That's all right, gentlemen, we'll leave you to get on with it!"

Greville led Patrick away by the elbow. "Look Patrick, I know the old boy was cheating, but you're supposed to ignore it! You're never going to get yourself liked if you behave like that. People will just reject you. And then how are you going to make the most of life's opportunities? Eh? It makes sense if you think about it . . . Now take that chap who's just walked in . . ."

He pointed to a man dressed in the uniform of the United States Air Force, who was just settling himself down at an empty table. He appeared to be in his late twenties, suntanned and upright, his square jaw creating an unexpected contrast with aquiline features and fine, dark brows.

". . . He's American, and all Americans are loaded, so you and I are going to go and have a wee chat with him."

Greville manoeuvred his plump body around the tables and chairs with surprising agility. Patrick trailed behind.

"Evening sir! Mind if I sit down?"

Greville squeezed himself into a seat without waiting for a reply, which seemed to amuse the American for he smiled slightly as he gestured towards the already occupied seat. "Sure, be my guest. Drink?"

"Well, that's awfully kind. If you're sure . . ." Greville hastily summoned the barman and ordered a double scotch. "Very decent of you."

"You're welcome. How about your friend?"

Patrick shook his head and looked down at his feet.

"American, aren't you?" Greville shot a reproving glance at Patrick and turned quickly to smile at the serviceman.

"That's right. United States Air Force."

After conventional platitudes had been exchanged, Greville began to discourse at length on his intimate knowledge of the area, and the American leaned forward with genuine interest.

"You know anything about a family called Stein?"

"Why yes, 'course I do, old man! Not personally; they don't mix with our family, but they're well known here as the local landowners. Big estate. Several thousand acres. And the house of course. Graylings. Early nineteenth . . . no, probably late eighteenth, though I could . . ." He stopped, unnerved by the

American's intent interest in his rambling, and asked, "Why? Have you seen it?"

"No. Not yet. Tell me about the Steins. What are they like?"

"Middle-aged couple with two children. Pretty girl. Nancy. Son looks pleasant enough, but he's away at university. She— the wife—inherited the house from her family. She was a Colby. But he's the one with all the money. Owns a bank, so there's plenty—"

"Are they happily married?"

"Goodness me, I'm not the person to ask! If village gossip is to be believed, yes. But it's the same with all families; who knows what lurks beneath the tranquil surface! Who knows!" Greville took a noisy gulp from his glass of scotch. "Wouldn't you say so, Captain . . . er?"

"Exley. Guy Exley."

"Of course. Now this may interest you—Stein's an American, like yourself."

"Uh huh. As a matter of fact, he's . . . a relative of mine."

"Good God! Is he? Well, that's a turn up for the books, isn't it Patrick? So you're here to visit them?"

"Well, I—"

"You *have* to visit them. Now that 'We don't get around much any more', as the song goes. I mean, it's in times like these that we need our relatives! That's why I'm here, isn't it, Patrick? You *must* see them, coming all the way from—where did you say it was?"

"Long Island, New York."

"Yes, well, there you are then. If I were you, I'd waste no time in going over to Graylings. Why not tonight?"

"I think it's a little late. But I am planning to pay them a visit. Soon." He looked at his watch. "And now, if you'll excuse me."

The big brunette with the lipstick watched him as he left the pub. So did Greville Dysart.

"I tell you Patrick, he's the one to watch. An American *and*—"

He nodded in the direction of the road that led out of the village to Graylings.

"—one of *them*."

Brittany Stein wrapped her wet thighs around her husband and drove down hard until her insides turned to a thousand tiny candle flames, leaping and quivering, burning and, finally, releasing her. Afterwards they lay side by side, hands touching, like two dolls in a pram.

They did not *have* to talk, though sometimes they did. On this occasion they were silent in deference to the extreme rarity of the occasion. It was mid-afternoon and for once the house was empty but for the two of them. For once they could draw the curtains without blacking out the windows at the same time. The dark-green glazed Holland blackout screens were propped clumsily against the bedroom wall, incongruous in the lavishly decorated room. They were lying on a vast Empire bed beneath a "polonaise": a circular canopy from which heavy folds of strawberry coloured silk fell to the four corners of the mattress. Thin, grey winter light trickled into the secretive, artifically created gloom.

"Darling Brittany . . ." sighed Jake.

She rolled over on her side to face him and began running her fingers through his hair; hair still thick and shiny despite his fifty-four years. He caught hold of her hand and kissed her fingertips, then drew them into his mouth and sucked them longingly, teasing them with his tongue. Brittany pressed closer.

Downstairs in the hall, the front door bell rang.

They both lay still and listened, tensing against what was to come. The bell rang again.

"Damn!" said Brittany, struggling out of bed and into ribbed lisle stockings and a tweed skirt. The mood was lost, and when would there ever be a chance again with Jake in London so much of the time? She had thought herself so clever, giving Mrs Burrows a day off on the same Wednesday that her assistant, Marion, had taken the twelve Graylings evacuees to see the Christmas pantomime in Bristol, and sneaking upstairs with Jake as though he were someone else's husband. But she had forgotten about the necessity of answering the door herself.

Her irritation increased once the door was opened. She had never seen the woman before.

"Yes?"

"Brittany Colby?"

"Brittany Stein."

There was something vaguely familiar about the woman, and Brittany looked more closely, appraising the details of her appearance and trying to make sense of them. She was entering middle age; forty, perhaps older. It was hard to tell because of her worn and rather hounded look. She had a sallow complexion and her hair was very dark and thick: from the way she tossed it self-consciously around her shoulders as she spoke, Brittany guessed that it had once been considered beautiful, but now it was lank and dull. Her outfit was curious, to say the least. There was an expensive mink coat and a ridiculous little tiptilted cocktail hat perched on her head, but the fur hung open to reveal a grubby silk garment resembling a pyjama jacket. In her right hand were clutched a lizard-skin handbag and a gas mask in a satchel of violet velvet adorned with artificial roses. The sort of object that Brittany's daughter, Nancy, and her schoolfriends would have heartily derided as ''genteel''.

''I want to talk to you,'' said the woman abruptly, glancing past Brittany's shoulder into the hall, almost as if she was expected.

Brittany was momentarily taken aback. ''Oh, er, yes . . . Mrs?''

''McConnell.''

Mrs McConnell followed Brittany into the library, looking around with a strange, wild expression in her eyes. She exclaimed when she saw the warm red walls and pale carpet.

''Oh—it's different in here now, isn't it? Much brighter.''

''You've been here before?''

''Yes, once. One Christmas. You probably don't remember.'' She half raised her face towards Brittany and there was something in the hooded grey eyes that stirred a memory, but Brittany could not quite . . .

''I'm Leonora McConnell. Seaton was my maiden name. Your cousin.''

''Leonora . . . of course . . .''

Brittany sank down onto the arm of a leather chair. Leonora. She remembered now. A pretty, rather spoilt child who clung to her mother's skirts. Daughter of Gerald Colby's sister, Georgina Seaton, the aunt that she had disliked so much. But Gerald Colby had been Brittany's father in name only. Years of hushed voices and whispered secrets, and Gerald's puzzling will leaving the estate to Adrian Steele, had led to her discovery that she was the child of an adulterous affair. And that the shooting ''accident'' in which her mother's lover had been killed by a bullet from Gerald's gun had probably not been an accident at all . . .

. . . Suddenly a host of faces, long-since dimmed, filled the room. Her beautiful French mother, Lucienne, and her mother's lover, Charles Teasdale. Her real father. So Leonora was not really a cousin, though Brittany could hardly tell her that now . . .

She opened her eyes again abruptly and saw Leonora staring at her anxiously. "Sorry Leonora. I was just remembering the last time you came here. Would you like some tea?"

"Oh no, I didn't come to have tea. I came to ask if I could come and live here."

The matter-of-fact delivery of this strange reply made Brittany sit up and look closer. The other woman was so still, so composed. Like a sleepwalker. She did not smile as she began to speak, yet seemed quite at ease. It was Brittany who was fidgety, nervous.

"I don't want to stay in London any more, not now. So I thought I'd come here. You know, like an evacuee. My mother's dead and her house has been sold, so . . . since you're my cousin . . ."

Not *my* cousin, thought Brittany, trying to remain patient. Perched there on a chair, with Leonora still in her coat, she felt like an employer interviewing a hopeful candidate, or a headmistress hearing the grievances of one of her pupils.

"But I thought the bombing was all over in London? A lot of the evacuees from this area have moved back there. It seems rather . . . odd to decide to leave now." She paused and bit her lip, thinking abruptly of Jake lying restlessly on the bed upstairs. "You see, it's rather difficult here at the moment. Normally, of course . . . well, there's plenty of room. Only I've still got twelve of my evacuee children, and I run a school for them, here at Graylings. They're out at the moment," she added, explaining the plaintively childless silence. She did not want Leonora thinking she had to invent excuses. "So we're . . . full up," she finished lamely.

Leonora smiled and tossed her neglected hair. "That's all right Brittany, I've got the cottage."

"The cottage?"

Leonora fumbled in her lizard-skin bag and drew out a much-fingered manilla envelope which she handed to Brittany. "It's on the second page. I've underlined it."

The document was an original copy of their grandfather's will. The house and estate were left to his only son, Gerald, but in the paragraph that Leonora had underlined it was stated that ". . . *the two-roomed dwelling situated at the top of the north paddock, hereafter called the cottage, I bequeath to my elder daughter Georgina, with remainder to her heirs.*"

The document was undeniably genuine, though Brittany could not remember anyone ever mentioning the bequest.

"Well," she said slowly, "the cottage is yours, but it's hardly habitable, Leonora. I used to do my painting there, but I haven't had a chance to use it for a while. There's a sink with running water, but only an outside lavatory . . . And what about furniture? Are you *sure* about this, Leonora? Have you thought it through?"

Leonora *was* sure. She *had* thought it through, and now that she had descended on Graylings, nothing was going to make her turn round and go back to London.

And so she came to live on the estate. She caused havoc on the last precious, peaceful day of Jake's leave. She insisted blankly that she did not care about the state of the cottage, but Brittany felt obliged to furnish the items necessary for the minimum level of comfort. What about her own things? Leonora explained that they had all been left behind in London—it was too much trouble to haul them all the way down here with the trains so impossibly crowded and, besides, there were strict regulations about the amount of luggage one carried during wartime.

Brittany was searching cupboards for sheets and pillowcases and towels when the children returned with Marion. Plain, earnest vicar's daughter, Marion Wakeley had answered the advertisement Brittany had placed in a local paper for a "general helpmeet in the care and education of the evacuee children". That had been in 1939, at the outbreak of war, and Marion and most of the children were still at Graylings even though two thirds of all evacuees had returned home within a year of leaving their native cities.

The children billeted at Graylings were aged between six and fourteen, and they all worshipped Brittany. They called her "Auntie". Brittany secretly disliked this title and had tried to encourage them to call her by her Christian name, or "Mrs Stein", but the billeting officer had told them to call her Auntie and in this one thing they doggedly obeyed.

Looking down from the landing, Brittany saw the children flood into the hall like the Israelites crossing the Red Sea, with the patient Marion bobbing helplessly in their midst. The seas parted and they surged up the stairs to find "Auntie" and tell her about the ENSA pantomime and how Derek had been sick on the bus. As soon as they discovered the source of her activity, a "new lady" had come to live in the cottage, their excitement reached fever pitch and they begged to be allowed to help Leonora move in. The older ones were put to good use carrying over a small iron bedstead and mattress, a few chairs and a table; but the smaller ones were a hindrance, dropping things and getting in the way. Overall the process was not speeded up, but Brittany watched them fondly as they danced up the path ahead of a bemused Leonora, tugging at her hands and pleading with her to hurry so that they could give her a guided tour of her new home. The mink coat was the centre of amazed attention and they all wanted to stroke it. One or two even sniffed it. They had never seen a fur coat before.

When they had first arrived at Nether Aston from the East End of London, many of the children had never even seen a cow or sheep, and were equally confounded by Mrs Burrows' activities in the kitchen. "But Auntie," they would protest, "I thought cakes came from shops?" They were very different now, as they ran eagerly in and out of the two rooms of the cottage, carrying saucepans and lampshades and any other bric-à-brac that Brittany had been able to salvage from the main house for her unexpected neighbour. Their clothes were still shabby and patched, but then weren't most people a little threadbare since clothes rationing? And they were clean, their hair shone and their cheeks were rosy. The group of youngsters that Brittany had driven to collect from the reception centre in the village had been a dismal mob; dirty, undernourished and, in some cases, abused by their parents. Brittany, whose own children's less palatable habits had been ironed out by a devoted nanny, grappled bravely with lice, soiled underclothes, and grimy, uncut toenails. There had been bed-wetting too, and an older girl called May pilfered any little treasure that she could lay her hands on. Saddest of all were these glimpses of the other, harder life. May once came to report that she had put the younger ones to bed early " . . . so that you two old geezers can get off to the boozer." When Brittany gently explained that she and Jake had no intention of going out to get drunk, there was general amazement.

It was a bitterly cold evening and Brittany eventually sent the children off to bed, though they pleaded to be allowed to stay up longer. As they left, little runty Jim tripped over a cardboard box of knives and forks.

"Blast the fucking bastard!"

Leonora raised her eyebrows, and Brittany laughed. "That's one thing I haven't been able to improve, I'm afraid—their language!"

Leonora was fumbling amongst her luggage. "I'm very grate-

ful for all your help, Brittany. Here—stay and have a drink."
She pulled a bottle of scotch from her bag and hugged it mater-
nally against her chest. Brittany noticed that her hands were
shaking.

"Not for me, thank you," said Brittany, pushing back a stray
lock of hair from her forehead. "I've got to go and make some
supper for Jake. He's going back to London tonight. And I haven't
put up the blackouts yet." She thought with dread of the fifty
windows which took nearly an hour to cover. "It's quite a task."

Leonora was unscrewing the top of the bottle. "I'll come and
give you a hand in a moment, if you like."

"That would be very helpful, thank you."

As Brittany went to the door, she heard the neck of the bottle
clink against glass. Climbing the path to the house, she saw
Leonora in the unshielded window, lifting the glass to her mouth
with a strange, rapt expression.

Once she was back in the house, Brittany stuck her head round
the door of the library where Jake was sitting listening to the
gramophone. "Sorry about all the interruptions today, Jake."

Jake lit a cigarette with slow, deliberate movements. "I know.
It's this goddamn war . . ."

"I'm just going to do the blackouts and say goodnight to the
kids, then we'll eat."

"Okay, honey."

Brittany set to work lifting the heavy blackout screens, but
there was no sign of Leonora and she finished the task unaided.
The last windows to be secured were the attics, and then she
went downstairs to tuck the evacuees into their row of beds and
hear their prayers.

"Auntie, May says it's nearly Christmas!" said an excited
Derek as she bent to kiss him goodnight. "Is Christmas *really*
coming Auntie? When is it coming?"

Brittany sat down on the edge of his bed. "Soon. About two
weeks. That's why we've been practising our nativity play, isn't
it? Ready for Christmas." Some of the East End children were
Jewish, and a lot of patient explanation had been necessary over
the past weeks.

"Are we going to get presents?"

"Yes darling, you'll have presents, but that's not what Christmas is all about. Do you remember the Christmas story that
Marion read to you, when the star travels through the night sky
and stops over the stable where the baby Jesus is lying? You

remember that, don't you Derek? *That's* the most important part of Christmas.''

''The star coming to see Baby Jesus?''

''That's right!''

Brittany turned the light out and went to snatch a hasty meal with Jake before driving him to Bath to catch the last train to London. When she got back, she switched on the wireless in the drawing room, put her feet on a stool and closed her eyes with a sigh of relief. After she had dozed for a few minutes, there was a knock on the door.

It was Marion, wearing a rueful expression.

''There's someone here who has something to say to you.'' She ushered Derek in his pyjamas, and mouthed, *''He thinks he's seen something.''*

''What is it, Derek? You should have been asleep a long time ago.''

Derek tugged at the waistband of his trousers, which were several sizes too big. ''Auntie, we was looking through the curtains to see if we could see the star coming to see the baby Jesus an' we saw a ghost!''

''What sort of ghost?''

''It was a big black one, all hairy and that, and it was going up and down on the grass, going *'Woooh'* and—''

''That's enough Derek!'' reproved Marion.

Brittany frowned. ''It doesn't sound much like a ghost to me, Derek, but we'll make sure it can't come into the house. You go back to bed now.''

''Perhaps we've got a ''p-r-o-w-l-e-r!'' hissed Marion as she shepherded Derek towards the stairs.

''It's more likely to be one of the boys from the village playing a prank. I'll go and take a look.''

Brittany went out onto the steps of the portico. The blacked out windows sealed in the light, and she had to blink hard before she could see anything. Then she saw a black shadow moving past the wall of the flower garden. She laughed out loud. Derek's ''black furry thing'' was a mink coat.

''Leonora!'' She hurried down the path after the retreating figure. ''Leonora, wait a second!''

She caught up with her ''cousin'' and fell in beside her, slightly out of breath. ''What are you doing? Are you lost?''

Leonora looked straight at her with her strange, hooded eyes. ''No, just taking some night air. I like to walk around at night. Are you OK?''

"Just out of breath. The children saw you and they were frightened, so—"

"Like a drink?"

Brittany inhaled a distinct blast of scotch.

"I know. I've had a few already. Come to the cottage."

Brittany followed her. "I was hoping I might see you earlier," she said, as she sat down on a makeshift chair.

"The blackouts? I know, I'm sorry. I sort of forgot."

Their eyes met over the whisky bottle.

"Look, I do drink—that's obvious, isn't it—but don't worry, I'm not going to make a nuisance of myself or anything. I just like to get on in my own little way, without bothering anyone and without being bothered."

"I see." Brittany took a sip from the tooth mug she had been offered.

"Look, I'm sorry about scaring the kiddies. Honestly."

"Leonora, does anyone know you're here? How about your husband—"

"Dead. Killed in France."

"I'm sorry. Do you have children?"

"One. Don't see much of her though. I'm not much of a mother, to tell the truth. Not my best role. How about you?" She raised her eyes to Brittany's face, waiting for her to speak. The drink appeared to have relaxed her—spirited away inhibition—without muddling her speech or her concentration. Infected by her mood, and by the scotch, Brittany began to relax too.

"I used to be very fond of alcohol when I was young. Champagne, cocktails . . . especially cocktails. We used to drink them when we went out dancing. At the Savoy, the Carpetbagger . . ." She smiled at the memory. "But these days I'm more cautious about what I drink. The pressure of responsibility, I suppose."

"I meant how about your children? Are you a good mother?"

Brittany blinked. "I . . . I don't know." She thought for a moment. "I don't think I am, really."

"I saw you with those evacuees. You're good with them."

"Ah, but that's different! I find it easy to mother them. Perhaps I'm trying to exorcize a sense of guilt over my own children . . . Yes, that's exactly what it is! How strange, I never admitted that to anyone before, not even myself."

Leonora smiled and shrugged her mink coat around her shoulders.

"I think . . ." Brittany went on carefully, "I think that's what it is. They've both been away at school since they were seven, you see. It wasn't so bad with George, because he was always an undemanding child, but Nancy . . .''

Brittany sighed and her breath made a little cloud of steam in the cold room.

''She's spoiled, certainly. She's had all the material things she could possibly want, but in a funny sort of way . . . we're very happy, you see, Jake—my husband—and I . . .''

Brittany's conditioned fear of losing face began to surface and she felt herself floundering. '' . . . But when I say I've spoiled Nancy, it's not as though I've washed my hands of her, or given up, or—''

''You don't sound certain. I remember you as a child, and you always seemed to know exactly what you wanted and how to get it. I was intimidated. And now . . .''

''And now? It looks rather as though marital bliss has changed me, doesn't it?''

There was a knock at the door of Jake's office.

''Just coming to check the blinds, sir.'' It was the desk clerk who was on fire-watching duty that night, a fat, jocund Cockney called Ike.

''I was leaving anyway.''

Ike withdrew respectfully after checking that the blackout blinds were secure and Jake began shuffling his papers together. It was eight thirty. Time for a leisurely walk back to his rented rooms on the Embankment, stopping perhaps for a dreary meal served apologetically by a restaurant that simply didn't have the ingredients to make food seem tempting. And then to bed. Alone.

It was always at this time of day in London that Jake missed Brittany the most. He looked around his office, taking in the heavy, battered partner's desk, the faded horsehair sofa, the too-small piece of red carpet reeking of mothballs. All air-raid salvage. For two long, slow years he had been strangling Hitler's war economy from his vantage point as financial adviser to the British Government's Ministry of Economic Warfare. He smiled to himself as he wondered what his German-Jewish father would have said of his son becoming a Whitehall civil servant, a lackey. Probably something like: ''You've let me down, son.''

His own bank, Jacob Stein and Company, was in the hands of his trusted second in command, a sporter-of-the-right-school-tie called Robert Denholm. Of course, they had long since been evacuated from their premises in Pilgrim Street and were carrying out business to the best of their ability in a small country hotel in Gloucestershire—their second move after Bournemouth had proved too dangerous with the threat of invasion. There was a lot of informality, use of Christian names and high jinks among the junior office staff now, from what Jake had heard. He thought little of the example of banker Anthony de Rothschild, sitting tight in New Court and entertaining his clients during raids with a luncheon of cold tongue and chutney in the basement. Personal bravado was one thing, but Jake felt sure he would never be able to forgive himself if one of his staff were killed.

He caught a glimpse of a grey, strained face in the mirror as he headed for the top of the stairs. For Jake, as for many Londoners, it was impossible to remember a time when he had not felt exhausted. He worked arduous hours at the Ministry's offices in Berkeley Square, slept badly in the empty, high-ceilinged flat on the Embankment which he rented for practically nothing because of its unenviable position in the shadow of the bombers, and spent his spare time hurrying to Gloucestershire to catch up on business, and to Somerset to see Brittany. He had barely seen his children since the outbreak of war.

"Goodnight, sir!" called Ike cheerfully as Jake stepped out into the square, and then continued to exchange views about the likelihood of an invasion with the local ARP warden.

"We'll have Hitler and Goering over here next," said the warden.

"As long as they bring their ration cards!" Ike laughed fatly at his own joke. Jake stood in the dark and listened to their bantering for a while.

". . . Well, have you heard the one about the two Yank GIs who've booked in at the Ritz. They get talking to a limey in the bar, and they ask him, 'Say fella, d'ya think we could take a couple women to our hotel?' So the Britisher asks where they're staying and when he hears it's the Ritz he tells them it's unthinkable. 'Oh,' says the Yank, 'don't get us wrong, fella. We don't mean a coupla women each . . .' "

Jake moved off at this point. He had lived in England for over twenty years, but still considered himself an American. And he was very uncomfortable with the garrulous, promiscuous image of his fellow countrymen who had invaded Britain in large hordes during 1942. He set off down Piccadilly, taking very great care where he trod. It was not only drunks who apologised to pillar boxes since London had assumed its Hades-like mantle of darkness. Yet for Jake the blacked-out city had never lost its fascination. It had an eery and unsuspected beauty—buildings rising like the steep sides of a Norwegian fjord, searchlights weaving patterns in the night sky. He had never really looked at the sky before the war. And the blackout had its music too, the fluctuating high-pitched moan of the air-raid sirens and a soft, melodic whine from the cables that secured the barrage balloons.

Jake passed a bomb-blasted café which claimed with pride that it was "More Open Than Usual". Thus were civilian battle scars a source of boasting and the artefacts of war incorporated into daily life. During the "phoney war" before the Blitz began, Jake had thought the sandbags in the street a nuisance. They merely burst and looked silly. Yet now they were prized and respected as the saviours of many lives. The war has changed the way we think, Jake reflected. The war has changed everything . . .

He decided that he would stop at the café for tea and stew, but his attention was caught by a faint high-pitched crying that was coming from the mound of rubble to the left of the café. There, amidst glass, inverted desks, stools and thousands of pieces of card and paper, was a cat. His hunger forgotten, Jake positioned his tall body on a slanting plank and scooped the cat up in his arms.

"Must have been the office cat, I reckon. Abandoned."

A thin, sad-eyed woman had been watching the distinguished looking man from the pavement. Jake blinked at the darkness, trying to see her more clearly.

"What will you do with it?" she asked.

"Well . . . I shall take it back to my flat, and then eventually I'll be able to take it to the country for my wife to look after. She likes cats."

"Yeah, so did my old man," said the woman, reaching out a tentative finger to scratch the cat between the ears. "He's dead now."

"Oh . . . I am sorry . . . Was he—"

"A bomb. The '41 raids. And the children too."

"What—killed?"

"All three of them."

Jake looked at the woman with a new respect. How on earth did she manage to keep going? Indeed, what was there to keep going for? When he learned that she lived in a government reception centre, he held out the little cat to her.

"Here, you take it. Company for you. I shan't really have time to care for it properly."

Her face was lit with something approaching a smile and she hugged its thin body to her own. "Really—you sure?"

"Yes. Perhaps . . . perhaps we could go into the café for a cup of tea?"

She shook her head and shivered. "No, no. I won't keep you. You be getting along now. And bless you."

Jake thought about the woman as he got into bed that night. He thought chiefly of the contrast between her and his wife Brittany. The woman with the cat had been so thin and faded, while Brittany, who was surely no younger, was straight-limbed and glossy-haired and laughed like a girl. He almost resented his wife for that; for not having suffered as that poor woman had.

Then he forced himself to remember how hard she worked. The evacuees had originally been destined for the village school, but when Brittany learned that overcrowding meant fifty per class, filthy books shared between two or three and essays written on scrap paper and then thrown away, she volunteered to teach them herself.

Jake had watched her move daily through a battlefield of India ink, paint, raffia and kapok. Of papier mâché animals and gardens in baking dishes. When there was not enough government money to buy materials, she spent her own.

And the children were transported into another world, a world of the imagination, not of rote learning. Jake was forced to admit that his wife's teaching methods were a little unconventional. The children were taken outside to make a map of the estate, a real map like the ones soldiers used at the front. History was as exciting as a whodunit, with the children playing the roles of Nicholas Nickleby's pupils, or chimney sweeps from Charles Kingsley's *Waterbabies*. And Geography was a trip round the world, with twelve pairs of eyes widening at Brittany's descriptions of the broad boulevards of Paris and the skyscraper lifts in New York. Her capacity for total immersion made Jake wonder why she had never considered becoming an actress. At any rate, his wife was a remarkable woman, and if he had seen little of his children since their schooldays began, they were at least happy and healthy. And alive.

Jake was smiling as he turned out his light. He had a lot to be thankful for.

Trinity College, Cambridge
1st December 1942

My dearest Nan

I hope you will forgive me for taking so long to write. I did promise to "Write soon", didn't I, and I well remember how a letter can relieve the tedium of the school routine. I wanted to wait until I had got a true impression of what university life was like before attempting to describe it to you. Also I've been very busy!

The first thing we all noticed about Cambridge was how intolerably crowded it has become. I think it has been affected more than Oxford in this respect. There are the usual wartime anomalies—Christ's is swarming with clerks from the Ministry of Food and the RAF use the Backs as a lorry park. But there has also been a huge influx of students from London: mainly medical schools and the LSE; and the town also seems to be swarming with foreigners of every description. Consequently we have to queue for everything, even a lousy haircut. There has been a horrified outcry at the news that members of the public will now be tramping the hallowed ground of the Pitt Club. It's the oldest and stuffiest dining club, but it has been requisitioned as one of those dreary British Restaurants for the duration.

I've been working pretty hard and I'm through the first set of examinations OK, but it's rather difficult to keep it up when we can hardly call our souls our own. I have to do several hours a week military training with the Senior Training Corps (very boring—just a lot of parading up and down, in fact) and the fire-watching rota is pretty exacting. As you can imagine, the university is terrified about all its precious old buildings burning down. They are less concerned, I think, with the safety of the undergraduates! Our fire party includes three Siamese, an Indian, a Turk and a Lithuanian! On Sunday we had a massed stirrup-pump practice and there were forty of us attacking imaginary incendiaries from behind the pillars of Nevile's Court, much to the distaste of the dons. They're a funny bunch of old so-and-so's, who like to pretend the war isn't happening. They never mention it, even in the face of the enormous signs announcing "AIR RAID SHELTERS" in the New Court. They grumble about having such humble fare as sausage and mash served in the Senior Common Room, but I really don't think they know how lucky they are.

There's considerable hostility to students amongst the townspeople. They think we're draft-dodgers, (which is far from the truth), and there have been incidents of brawling in Cambridge pubs. Student pranks, such as removing manhole covers during the blackout are definitely not tolerated with as much humour as they used to be! You can understand why people get so irate with us when you think how hard most of them are working towards the war effort, in factories and government departments.

Student life is certainly not what it was before the war. We live pretty well, I suppose (there's still plenty of claret in the college cellars), but most of us who came up for the first time this term agree that we feel cheated. Ernest Bevin is trying to step up the production of degrees so much with his new regulations that there's a sense of rush overlying everything we do. Our university life is being crammed into such a short time that we are prevented from developing, both academically and socially.

So I'm volunteering for the army. That's one of the reasons that I'm writing to you now—so that it won't come as such a shock in the holidays. Mother and Father will be anxious, I think, but they won't try and stop me. The regiment I'm joining is in the Middle East and I'll be setting off there shortly after Christmas. My subject is agriculture, which counts as a science and therefore exempts me from national service (for as long as I keep passing the exams) but I've thought about it a lot, Nan, and I'd rather be doing something more positive. There'll still be a chance for me to come back and finish my studies when the war is finally over.

I've been pondering over this letter for so long that my roommate, Bill, has accused me of corresponding with a light of love! And since I'm being so secretive about this lady then she's probably married—the lonely wife of a serviceman posted overseas. So I explained that I'm only writing to my mad, bad sister.

I wonder what sort of war work you will be doing, assuming we're still in this mess when you come of age. Your chief skills are twisting people around your little finger and getting away with the most dreadful things, so the resistance movement has probably got you marked as one of its own!

I'll be coming down in a couple of weeks, and I expect I'll see you then. Try and behave yourself!

Your loving brother, George

Nancy folded the coarse, re-cycled paper with a sigh. Dear, solid sensible George. What sweet letters he wrote. Having an elder brother at Cambridge did not count for much these days when it came to impressing one's classmates. But once he was in uniform it would be different. Uniforms were glamourous. All except school uniforms, of course. Her brother's letter had helped her decide that it was time to shed hers and join the war.

She was sprawled flat on her stomach on the narrow bed, her firm, rounded fifteen-year-old limbs bursting with deliberate sensuality from long-outgrown vyella pyjamas. At St Clare's, in the heart of rural Wiltshire, Matron pooh-poohed blackout regulations, so the dormitory curtains let in a pale glimmer of moonlight. The lights were still on and several girls were reading. At Nancy's end of the dormitory, furthest from the door, her henchmen Joan and Dorothy were exclaiming over a precious copy of *Vogue* that Nancy had taken from home.

". . . *'Only dine in a hat that's tiny, ridiculous and becoming,'* " recited Joan in her breathy, sing-song voice, "Oh, and read this, read this. This bit about *'How to greet the soldier home on leave.'* "

Before Dorothy had a chance to follow Joan's stabbing finger, she was reading out loud again. ". . . *'Be ready then, to greet him. Now, if ever, beauty is your duty. Now, if ever, buy with crystal-clear conscience the clothes that will charm him. Remember, none but the fair deserves the brave . . . Take him to the newest, nicest restaurants. Encourage your cook to excel herself . . .'* Oh gosh! Hey, Nancy, what do you make of that? *'None but the fair deserves the brave.'* It sounds romantic, doesn't it?"

They both turned to look at Nancy Stein, for Nancy Stein was their unacknowledged queen.

Her will was stronger, her nerves harder, her courage greater than theirs, therefore she was arbiter of what was good and what was bad. And she was different; half-American *and* (it was rumoured) half-Jewish! Everyone loved Nancy because her laugh was so infectious and when she liked you, really liked you, it made you feel interesting. But the girls feared her too. Those she considered beneath her contempt were sneered at and those who crossed her came face to face with an icy rage. "She's too used to having her own way," her detractors thought. "She only really cares about herself." But they never dared voice these criticisms out loud for fear that Nancy might get to hear of it and take revenge.

She raised one dark eyebrow at Joan and Dorothy and smiled

her remarkable, innocent smile. "It's a load of rubbish, that article. How on earth are we going to find '*clothes that will charm him*'? It doesn't say anything about clothing coupons, does it? And who the hell has a cook these days? She's probably off driving a lorry!"

Dorothy turned the pages slowly. "Ooh look! I like this fox fur! And the little black straw . . ."

Joan was smiling at the ceiling and repeating over and over again "Beauty is your duty. Beauty is your duty . . ." She said it faster and sniggered when the words started to lose their meaning. "Sounds silly, doesn't it? And it's too bad if you *can't* look beautiful."

As if by a pre-arranged signal, all eyes turned to Nancy, who had strolled over to the mirror and was smiling slightly at her reflection. She knew that at St Clare's it was generally agreed that Nancy Stein was beautiful, but privately she doubted it. It was a good enough face—dark grey eyes beneath thick straight eyebrows of the sort that the Edwardians used to admire. Clear, pinky skin and a small mouth. She knew that if there was any single attribute that her friends envied it was that most superficial of claims on beauty, her hair.

Nancy had vivid, lavish hair that begged to be taken in handfuls, to be squeezed and twisted like silk ribbon through the fingers. There was nothing remarkable about the colour. It was that uniform dark shade that looked brown in some lights, black in others. What drew the eye was the rich texture and the way in which it sprang from her head with a wild, ardent life of its own.

The occupants of Dormitory 5 were still watching Nancy as she padded over to the wardrobe and pulled out a small suitcase. She started to pack it.

"Nancy—*what on earth are you doing*?"

"What does it look like?" she asked drily, rummaging in her top drawer for clean handkerchieves, knickers and hairgrips. "Joanie, you'll lend me your cream sweater, won't you?"

She flashed her sweetest smile and received a dumb nod of assent. "Good. Thanks." The much-prized angora sweater was folded neatly into her case. "Pauline, will you lend me your alarm clock? I'm going to need it if I'm to wake up in time to catch the train."

"Oh *Nancy*," moaned Dorothy. "Don't be so annoying. Where are you going?"

"To London. Joining up . . ."

She was not yet quite sure what she was going to join, but she would find something. The two words sounded impressive anyway. The others were silenced by them.

"So, tomorrow when Gladders notices I've gone, none of you say a thing. You've no idea where I am. OK?"

"But Nancy—if Miss Gladstone finds out we knew about it and didn't tell her, we'll be in terrible trouble. They might even threaten to *expel* us!"

Nancy shrugged. Her face closed in behind its tight, self-contained mask. Her expansive mood evaporated and she became the private Nancy Stein again.

"I can't do anything about that, I'm afraid. That's your problem."

She settled herself down in bed and the dormitory fell quiet. Then she opened her eyes again. There was a sound of sobbing coming from the next bed.

She leaned towards it. "What's up, Rachel?"

Rachel Foster was the form runt; a small mousy girl who was bullied and picked on by her peers, and whose only distinction in their eyes was the fact that she slept next to Nancy Stein.

"Nothing." Rachel hastily swallowed her sobs.

"Come on, you can tell me. I won't tell the others, I promise."

The silence that followed was pregnant with disbelief. "Promise," repeated Nancy.

"It's my Geog. prep. Sally Shawcross spilled ink on it and then ripped my exercise book in half. And Miss Brownlow's going to kill me! She said if—"

"Look, don't worry about it." Nancy patted Rachel's hand. "I'm not going to need mine, so you're welcome to it."

"D'you mean it, Nancy? Really?"

"Of course, or I wouldn't offer, would I?" She went on more kindly, "My Geography prep is in my locker. Just copy it out. And if anyone asks you, tell them I said you could."

"Gosh, thanks Nancy!"

" 'S all right."

"You're very kind—"

"*Shhh!* Go to sleep! 'Night."

Nancy's adventure in London was sadly short-lived.

Getting away from school had been easy enough. The alarm, muffled by her pillows, had sounded at five o'clock but she had been awake anyway. It was still dark as she lumped her case down the long school driveway and headed for the village station. She had half expected to be questioned, but the train had been crowded with troops and she was squashed into a corner and politely ignored. She reached Paddington at nine o'clock with the distinct feeling that nobody cared who she was or what she was doing. Which had not been her intention at all.

She had been to London a few times with Brittany to buy school uniforms, but it seemed bigger now, dirtier, disjointed. There were red posters everywhere on the underground, telling Nancy that "Your Courage, Your Cheerfulness, Your Resolution, Will Bring Us Victory." Amongst them she found an advertisement that offered her a first ray of hope.

"The Pimlico Campaign for Women Fireguards," it proclaimed, "Enrol and Train Now."

She found her way to the recruiting centre and walked in smiling as nonchalantly as she could. Her confidence had been much enhanced by a "borrowed" pair of her mother's peep-toed court shoes and a smear of bright lipstick, lovingly hoarded. She was unused to heels and wobbled slightly.

"Your age, love?"

Nancy shrugged with what she hoped was an air of sophistication. "Eighteen. And a half."

"Your National Registration identity card, please."

Nancy hesitated, then pretended to search in her handbag. The buxom woman behind the desk turned her gaze to Nancy's wobbling ankles.

"You're not quite eighteen yet, are you, love?"

"Er, no, but I—"

The woman smiled. "I know you're only doing it because you want to help win the war. In a way we could do with more like you. But you'd better run on home. Your mum will be worrying about you, won't she?"

Nancy bought herself a sandwich and tried to decide what to do next. Where on earth was she going to spend the night if she had failed to join up by the time it grew dark? She certainly did not have enough money for a hotel, and if she went to her father's flat he would certainly send her straight back to school. And that would be too humiliating for words.

She wandered down Elizabeth Street and into Belgravia, chewing and thinking. In Chester Square she saw a church hall with its doors open and a notice posted outside. She drew nearer so that she could read it. "Mechanized Transported Corps. Women drivers needed." Hunching up the case and steadying her position on Brittany's heels, she marched purposefully into the chilly, polish-scented room.

This time luck smiled on Nancy Stein. It usually did in the end.

The MTC needed girls to start on a preliminary training course at once, and they seemed too busy to ask questions about age. They did want to know if she could drive and Nancy, who had played around with the controls of her father's black and red Alvis and had a rough idea of what they were for, said "Yes".

She and the other new recruits were given temporary quarters on camp-beds in a room at the back of the church hall and they suffered cramped conditions stoically once they heard that it was only a matter of days before they sailed for France. The news sent a wave of excitement through the ranks of sensible upper-middle-class girls who were nearly all in their early twenties; ex-debutantes or university graduates. The use of surnames was cheerfully adhered to, and if they suspected that Stein was a little way off attaining her majority, nobody said so. She fell asleep beneath her rough army blanket, dreaming of handsome, moustachioed Frenchmen who all exclaimed over her hair . . .

The next day she was issued with a uniform. The officers, capable of inspiring awe in all but Nancy, were trim and immaculate ladies with small waists and blue-rinsed hair. They looked as lovely in their well-fitting khaki uniforms as the new recruits looked frightful in theirs, young bodies sticking out shapelessly fore and aft, breast-pockets projecting lumpily. Nancy argued shamelessly until she secured a uniform one size smaller than that offered. She liked the way the khaki cloth emphasised her heavy, rounded breasts and strained tautly across her behind. And she could see that all the other girls were looking wistfully at her hair, which refused to be constrained beneath her cap.

After drilling in Chester Square, the new drivers learned some preliminary first aid ("I hope I never have to deliver a baby—how horrid!" whispered Nancy), and were then instructed in car maintenance.

"Carburettor in French is *le carburettor*," said the blue-haired instructor with the faintest hint of a smile, "and to tickle the carburettor is *chatouiller le carburettor*."

"Voulez-vous chatouiller moi?" Nancy mouthed in faulty, schoolgirl French to the other girls. They began to giggle.

"That will do, Stein."

Nancy saw it was her duty to make her comrades laugh, but

the business of dismantling and rebuilding a carburettor was so engrossing that after a while even she fell silent. By mid-afternoon they had forgotten the cold that made their fingers ache and the hall was thick with the sounds of concentration; exasperated sighs, grunts of effort and muttered curses. Nancy was struggling with a bolt that she had screwed too tightly when she noticed that the other girls had ceased their efforts and were staring at a tall, handsome well-dressed man of about fifty, who was standing in the doorway.

It was Jake Stein.

When he saw Nancy in her uniform a flicker of amusement crossed his face. Nancy smiled at him with enormous relief, but then the amusement quite disappeared.

"Get in the car," he said. Curt, American.

He drove her to Graylings immediately. There was not even enough time for Nancy to give back the uniform which was now making her feel uncomfortable. ("She'll post it!" snapped Jake when the instructor remonstrated.) She only just managed to salvage her suitcase and the high-heeled shoes.

"Don't you even want to know how I managed to find you?" Jake barked, his knuckles grey and white on the steering wheel.

Nancy blinked and said nothing.

"Well, I'll tell you. You probably don't remember meeting a colleague of mine from the MEW, called Max Vallance. He had dinner with your mother and me at Graylings once and when he was walking past this morning he recognised you making an ass of yourself in that khaki nonsense . . ."

Nancy winced at his pronunciation. He said it as though the word were "kacky".

". . . Fortunately he's a smart sort of guy and remembered your age, so the first thing he did when he got back to the office was call me and tell me that my daughter was posing as a member of some Home Guard or other. Miss Gladstone couldn't get any information on your whereabouts when she questioned the other girls apparently . . ." (Nancy smiled to herself when she heard this) ". . . so naturally your mother and I have been frantic with worry ever since she telephoned to say you'd gone missing . . ."

Nancy said nothing, staring at the windscreen with her mouth tight and hard. Jake's voice mellowed a little.

"Look honey, I can understand you wanting to do something like this, it's the thoughtlessness of it I can't understand. Surely you knew we'd be wondering where you were? You might at least have telephoned."

"I was going to."

Jake abandoned the conversation. He was as angry with himself as with Nancy. He had given way to her all her life and although he hoped there was still time for her to learn consideration for others, he regretted not having been stricter when she was young. If he had, perhaps they would now be reaping the rewards of such discipline. As it was, Nancy turned every issue into a battlefield.

Brittany certainly did not take the view that it was too late.

She had been sewing tinsel and gauze together for the angels in the nativity play, and cajoling Mrs Burrows into baking a Christmas cake with dried eggs and making her own mincemeat—now unavailable in the shops—from cut-up prunes, apples, and suet. She interrupted her tasks and summoned Nancy into the library.

"Quite a little siren, aren't you?" she said when she saw the uniform, the lipstick and the high heels. "You can take my shoes off in a minute and change into something more suitable. But first I want you to tell me what the hell you were doing frightening Daddy and me like that!"

"I was going to ring—"

"Don't make excuses! You left it too late! If I thought you were really interested in the war effort, it wouldn't be so bad, but it's obvious that this escapade is just another way of showing off to your friends. Well, you're going to have plenty of opportunity because as soon as we've arranged it with the school, you're going straight back there. That's where you belong, young lady, and not—"

"And you'd know all about that, I suppose, Mummy?" Nancy smiled spitefully. "You never even went to school, so how do you know what you're talking about? You don't even—"

"That's enough!"

". . . And anyway, you've always been telling me how naughty you were when you were my age, and how you were always in trouble. You've already told me you got pregnant with George when you weren't even married."

"Nancy! That's enough, I'm warning you—"

"You're just a hypocrite, that's all!"

Brittany's fury, which had been contained until that point, reached an uncontrollable pitch and she caught Nancy by the shoulders. She did not look at her daughter as she was shaking her, and when she opened her eyes she was shocked to see how white Nancy had become.

"Sorry, darling, I—" She released her hold. The door burst open and one of the children ran in.

"Auntie! Auntie! Derek's broke the manger and the Baby Jesus has fell out!"

"Not now, dear . . . that's right, shut the door behind you."

Brittany sank down wearily in an armchair and waited for Nancy to sit down opposite her. "Darling . . ." she began and then stopped, shaking her head. She was determined to try and make Nancy appreciate her position without prompting further accusations of hypocrisy. It was so difficult to find the right words that for a while she was silent.

"Listen . . . I know I never went to school myself, but that wasn't my choice. I would have envied you, do you realize that? As for my past behaviour, I acknowledge I was no saint, and the last thing I want is for you to use me as your example! Most of the time I'm terrified out of my wits about all the trouble you could be getting yourself into."

Nancy was fiddling with the brass buttons on her uniform.

"But Mummy, I'm so bored at school! Let me stay here, *please*!"

"But with the house full of evacuees darling, it's out of the question."

"You mean you're too busy looking after other people's children?"

Nancy flung her mother a defiant look, unaware that her lipstick had smudged. Brittany flushed slightly.

"No, you know I don't mean that. I wouldn't have much time to give you, that's all. And with the children around, you wouldn't get much privacy."

"I bet if I asked Daddy, he'd say I didn't have to go back to school."

"That's as may be, but as far as I'm concerned, you're going back."

"Daddy says—"

"Nancy! Go and change out of that ridiculous uniform and wipe that stuff off your face. You look like a clown!"

Nancy scowled at her mother and flounced out of the room. The door slammed.

Brittany buried her face in her hands and sighed.

* * *

Nancy dodged the children who were playing in the hall and ran up the curving marble staircase. On the first floor landing she paused and looked out of the window at the gravelled carriage drive that swept in a wide arc across the front of the house. The trees around the edge of the lawn looked vulnerable without their leaves and the lawn was pale with frost. Only the cedar tree looked unchanged all year round, dark and mysterious. She leaned her face against the cold pane and watched her breath mist the glass. She felt more frustrated than angered by the afternoon's events.

They don't understand me. They don't know what I'm really like. Not how I behave from day to day, but what I'm really like, deep down, underneath everything. I could be quite a nice person really, but they don't take the time to find out . . .

There was a movement on the other side of the glass. Nancy rubbed the misty patch with her finger so that she could see better. A military jeep had parked next to Jake's Alvis. The door opened and a young man in an American Air Force uniform jumped out. He looked up at the house and Nancy caught sight of dark eyes and a very masculine jawline. She smiled.

Perhaps it's lucky I didn't stay in London after all . . .

Jake knocked at the library door and went in. He saw the look in Brittany's eyes and sighed. "You've just been speaking to Nancy?"

She nodded.

"I'm sorry honey, I feel like it's all my fault." He sat down on the arm of her chair and stroked her hair gently.

"It's not *your* fault, Jake. I'm sure it's not anyone's fault. But what are we going to do with her?"

"Maybe she's right. Maybe school isn't the right place for her. She could stay here, and we could arrange for some private tuition for her . . ."

"No! That's how I was brought up, and it's the last thing I want for Nancy. She needs the company of girls her own age. Besides, I've just told her she's going back to school."

"I see. So the decision's all wrapped up, is it?" Jake's voice became louder, and he stood up to poke angrily at the fire. "Well, *I* kind of told Nancy she could stay here. She hasn't been doing brilliantly at St Clare's—"

"Jake! Her academic performance is not the bloody point! Jake, are you listening to me at all?"

Jake dropped the poker and ran his fingers through his hair.

"Honey, I appreciate how important this is." He shook his head slowly. "The trouble is I'm just so goddamn tired that I don't know when I'm seeing straight any more. I know Nancy has this way of turning everything into an argument, but maybe if we listened to her, really made an effort to get to know her a little more—"

"I see! You want to take the soft option and give in to Nancy every time. Now you've spent all your youthful passion on darling Katherine you're all burned out! So burned out you won't stand up to your own daughter!"

Katherine Exley was Jake's long-dead sweetheart, whom he had courted in America before he met Brittany. She always flung the name at him when she was angry or bitter and always regretted it afterwards when she saw the closed look that came over his face. She would tell herself that it was immature to be jealous of someone who was dead. And this time Jake was *trying* to find a solution, despite his exhaustion from overwork and nights broken by air-raids.

"Jake, I'm sorry . . . But as you said yourself, Nancy's only too happy to start an argument and play us off against one another. She's doing it now! She knew I'd say no, so she—"

There was a knock at the door.

"Oh Christ, not now!" Jake couldn't hide his exasperation. "Come in!" he shouted.

It was Mrs Burrows. "Gentleman to see you, sir."

"Can't he wait a minute? Who the hell is it anyway?"

Mrs Burrows was too excited to be flustered by Jake's uncharacteristic sharpness.

"It's an *American*, sir. He says his name's Exley."

There was complete silence in the room for a few minutes as Brittany and Jake stared at one another.

"Sir?"

"You'd better show him in, Mrs Burrows."

The expression on Brittany's face was so terrible that at first Jake thought she was about to strike him, or even their visitor. She glanced at the square, powerful-looking man in uniform and then rushed past him and out of the room, slamming the door behind her.

Jake was impressed by the young man's self-possession in the face of this display of bad manners. He extended his hand, and Jake was taken aback to see him smiling slightly as though he had controlled the whole scene from its beginning.

"I'm Guy Exley, sir, Katherine's son . . . Your son."

Two

THE HOUSE WAS exactly as Guy had dreamed it would be.

This came as something of a shock. The picture of Graylings that he had carried in his head for many years was of a gleaming fairytale place, the sort of fantasy house that English lords and ladies drawled and trilled about in the novels his grandmother read. And yet it existed; it was real.

It had been easy enough to get time off from his duties. General Royds only needed Guy as a fancy accessory, along with his custom-made uniforms and his chauffeur-driven car, to prove to the other guys that he, Brigadier-General Joseph Royds had gone straight to the top without the aid of any West Point Academy. Guy was dispensed with a week's pass, and had borrowed a jeep from the 8th Air Force base just north of London. A jeep full of petrol, too. That had become something of a rarity in Britain.

For the three days he had been in Somerset, he had played a game with himself to see how long he could last out before he gave way to his curiosity. He had visited Bath and Wells cathedral, looked around the village and spoken to some of the locals. Now he could stand it no longer. He had to see the house.

In the hope of making himself welcome, he had packed the jeep with PX supplies: tomato juice, tinned ham, butter, eggs, candy bars and scotch. The English were as perverse as their food rationing system. They weren't exactly thriving on such deprivation, yet they insisted on making out that it was good for them. They glowed with pride as they boasted of every little victory over the rationing system.

Guy stopped the jeep at the top of the hill that led to Graylings and looked down. He did this instinctively, exactly as his father had on his first visit to Graylings seventeen years earlier. The house rested in a semi-circular hollow below with its lawns spread before it like a green lake, and with trees on either side.

He was pleased to find no marks of war on this sacred place. The neo-classical porch had tall pillars very like the homes of faded Southern gentry in Georgia or Alabama. Some of those Guy had visited were even larger. But compared to this noble white house they had looked stiff and tawdry, as though they only had a superficial hold on the landscape. Guy was amused at the idea that this house would once have been considered *parvenu* and *nouveau riche* by the occupants of crumbling Tudor and Jacobean halls. But that was a very long time ago. This house had matured, taken root; it had lived.

He had pictured Graylings in his mind's eye ever since his grandfather first told him on his eighteenth birthday that he was not an orphan after all. Even now he remembered the June day on Long Island as clearly as if it were yesterday, learning that he had always felt different because he *was* different. And in the background the humming of the motor mower and the polite thwock of tennis balls on the court at the back of the house had continued, just as if nothing had changed.

Hamilton Exley III and his wife Felicity lived in a buttermilk mansion of the type that inspired Scott Fitzgerald, with pin-neat lawn sloping quietly down to the Sound. Guy Exley had always lived there too, and he had called these people ''Mother'' and ''Father'' because they had adopted him when he was a baby.

Why should they want to do that, his schoolfriends had asked once they were old enough to be curious about these things. Why, if they already had two grown-up children? Guy would shrug and say he didn't know, perhaps they liked babies, but underneath he felt the lurking of something dark and forbidden.

They were in the garden room when his grandfather told him. The garden room extended from the main body of the house and its southern wall was composed entirely of curlicued and crenellated glass doors that opened onto the lawn. It was a room that seemed to suck in sunlight, decorated tastefully in wicker and white, with splashes of summer flower colours: sweet pea pink, magenta, mauve and fuchsia. There was a strong sea breeze that afternoon and Guy remembered watching the curtains with the intense concentration of someone trying to take in a momentous fact. Watching them move in the air above his grandmother's elegantly coiffed head, as they were first blown out and rounded and then sucked in hard against the glass panes.

His grandmother smiled and looked on encouragingly from her wicker chair while his grandfather talked, coral-tipped fingers smoothing her white linen sailor pants over her tanned, wrinkled legs. Her lips were a coral arc.

''Guy, your mother and I wanted to have a little talk with you today, since it's such a special day. Your coming of age . . .''

His grandfather's voice was as big and rich as he was, emanating from somewhere in that tanned barrel of a chest, beneath its thick mat of white hair. Guy was on his way out to play tennis. He rubbed the furred surface of a tennis ball, fidgeting slightly.

". . . As you know, we adopted you when you were a tiny baby, brought you up as if you were our own. But you see, Guy, we had a very special reason for doing that. You were our own flesh and blood, an Exley . . ."

Sudden frost gripped Guy's stomach and the room lurched into sharp focus. His grandmother was smiling thoughtfully amid the billowing curtains. He felt his grandfather's heavy brown hand press down on his shoulder.

". . . You know that Felicity and I had another child who was older than Bobby and Ellen. Katherine. We don't talk about her any more, but the others might have told you something about her—"

"She died from meningitis," said Guy and knew with certainty as he said it that there was a link between her death and his growing feeling of unease. Katherine Exley. There were silver-framed photographs of her in his grandmother's dressing-room. A true Scott Fitzgerald heroine; blonde, tanned, smiling.

"That's right. She died not long after you were born. Maybe you thought that's why we adopted you—because we had just lost a child. But . . ."

"But I—"

"You're Katherine's son, Guy, our grandson. Katherine had an . . . *unfortunate* affair when she was very young. Marriage was out of the question. We won't talk about that now—what's done is done. But we decided we would tell you when you were eighteen, didn't we, darling?"

A dazzling coral smile affirmed his grandmother's collusion.

"But what I want to say most of all, Guy, is that it doesn't make a blind bit of different to us. Never has. We love you—we've always loved you—as though you were our very own. And I don't want you to worry about all of this . . ." Hamilton Exley continued to talk as though he were addressing a board meeting, emphasizing that nothing would change, and no one need know.

Guy was only half listening, distracted by a sense of shock. "I'd like to get on with my game of tennis now, if you don't mind."

He shot out into the brilliant sunshine and a world of uncertainty. At first he was angry. He hated his mother for doing this to him. How could *he*, Guy Exley, darling of Andover and symbol of all that was clean-cut and disciplined, the apotheosis of *class*—how could *he* hold his head up if everyone knew that he was a bastard spawned in an undesirable coupling? His father had not been mentioned and that fact alone made it obvious that he was not an acceptable person in the normal run of things. Everyone liked Guy Exley. Everyone admired him for the most superficial reasons; he was a member of the right family, lived in the right sort of house, knew the best people, was in line to inherit a modest fortune.

And he did not want that to stop.

His second reaction to the news of his procreation was the decision to capitalize on it. He felt let down by the Exleys, but now there was another place he could turn. To do this, he needed to know the identity of his father. It was pointless to ask his grandfather, since he had obviously decided on silence years ago. Hamilton Exley III was a man who stuck by his decisions.

Instead Guy picked his "brother" Bobby.

Robert Exley was thirty-six in that summer of 1937 and married with three children. He and his dull, socialite wife lived in Connecticut but frequently visited Long Island at weekends. It would require careful planning to catch him on his own, however. Guy went to him one evening as he stood on the porch, legs astride, looking out to the stars and the dark waters of the Sound. Tonight Guy felt an unaccustomed self-consciousness approaching the bluff and genial Bobby.

He knows what I am . . .

"Guy, old man—come and admire the view."

"Can we talk?"

They sat down on the steps and talked. Their low voices were sometimes drowned by the noise of the water slapping at the sides of the jetty. Bobby was hesitant at first. He was a man who lived his life according to hackneyed old maxims and the one for this occasion was "Let sleeping dogs lie". But Guy was at his most charming and in the end his uncle—since that was how Bobby was related to him—was relieved to be able to talk of something that had lain buried for almost twenty years. It seemed that the young Katherine Exley had not been in the habit of confiding in her brother, but he had inevitably heard gossip. And the gossip stated categorically that she was expecting a child by Jacob Stein, eldest son of New York banker Isaac Stein. A Jew.

That was all Bobby knew of Guy's long-lost father.

Guy was persistent. He dressed in a jacket and tie, took a train down into the city and went into the largest and most important-looking library he could find. It was a very hot afternoon but the jacket and tie made him feel better about what he had to do. Information about Isaac Stein was easy enough to find, but it took longer before he found reference to his son Jacob.

Finally, there it was. In a back number of a banking periodical dated 1926, there was a small paragraph headed "STEIN JUNIOR GOES IT ALONE". It stated quite simply that following his marriage to the English Brittany Colby, Jacob Stein would be settling in London for good and starting up his own merchant bank which would be run independently of Stein and Sons. On Wall Street there were rumours of a rift between father and son.

Guy went back to the weary, overheated librarian and asked her boldly for any information she had on British merchant banks. He found a profile of Jacob Stein in one magazine, with a photograph. He stared at that picture hard for ten or fifteen minutes, willing himself to believe it. The man who looked back was neither hook-nosed nor hirsute. He was a calm, wise-looking man in middle age with Guy's own eyebrows and chin. According to the article, he was also a success. "Mr Stein, who is married with a son and a daughter, divides his time between his London residence and Graylings, his magnificent Georgian house in Somerset."

There was no picture of the house. Guy wished there was. He closed his eyes in that hot, stuffy Manhattan library and he could see it. It was tall and white and imposing beneath shady English trees. A jewel in a green and pleasant land.

My father's house . . .

When Guy stopped the jeep and appraised Graylings, just as his father had done, he thought how glad he was that there had been no photograph in the magazine to distort his expectation. He also thought about his father. There was no doubt that Jacob Stein was unaware that his son was in England and on his way to Graylings. There was no guarantee that he was in Somerset himself. But did he know of Guy's existence? Did he know that Katherine Exley had borne him a son? Guy ran his eye up the line of pillars to the roof and up again to the numb December sky. And if his parents *had* married—what then?

Guy was pragmatist enough to appreciate that whilst his life would have been very difficult, it would not necessarily have been better materially. A gracious home, a first-rate education, plenty of money to spend—he had all of these things. His grandparents were originally from New England but had moved to

Northport, about twenty miles from central New York, on the shores of Huntington Bay. Guy had grown up on Scott Fitzgerald's "long and riotous island" in a cheerful-looking mansion just fifty yards from the sea. On the other side of the water lay Exley Engineering, founded by the Scots born Hamilton Exley I to capitalize on the great rush to civilize the West. It was still prospering, not spectacularly but the Exleys were able to enjoy a couple of Cadillacs, a staff of Negro servants, couture clothes for Felicity and Ellen, and an education at Andover and Princeton for Guy.

The achievement of academic excellence was not in the Exley scheme of things. Guy's intuition was razor sharp, his self-expression effortless, but he toned down these attributes to fit comfortably within the top twenty-five per cent of his class, never too near the top. Intellectuals, his grandmother stressed, made other people feel uncomfortable and were therefore shunned. It was fine to be clever, but only if you were a competent sportsman too, a real all-rounder. Guy duly kept himself straight-backed on the polo field and whipped his strong, sun-tanned limbs around the tennis court with skill and speed. He did well, earning the joint crown of approval for his prowess and admiration for his disarming modesty. He handed drinks to his grandmother's friends at their bridge evenings and smiled a shy, white smile when they told him what a handsome boy he was. In short, he was perfect. ("Not the apple, the whole damn *fruitbowl* of Daddy's eye," Ellen observed wryly.)

Yet inside Guy Exley something dark and ugly seethed. His grandparents had failed him. They had spoiled him. They had given him everything he ever wanted, except the feeling that he was needed. The pattern of their lives was already complete before he was born; ordered and engrossing. They catered for his needs without making any effort to understand the Guy beneath the surface. They didn't *know* him. But he had another family and another chance. So he had used his Princeton connections to get himself a "soft" posting as aide to the 8th Air Force commander. There had been the inevitable jibes about "flying a desk", but hell, Guy Exley did not want to die. He did not try to deceive himself about that.

In America it was all too easy, his skin only had to tan to the right shade of brown and he was accepted. And the challenge he set himself was not just to be liked. How grand it would be to belong forever, to *own* a piece of this England, a burnished old gold England of waist-high stalks and crystal clear voices!

Ownership was a different thing here. In the States it was passing acquisition, cash transaction. Owning England was a noble thing, carved from centuries of being and belonging.

Guy parked the jeep conspicuously on the gravel driveway and rang the bell at the front door of the house. He asked for his father. He was admitted to an awe-inspiring domed hallway with a marble staircase. The smell of baking floated from the kitchen and mingled proudly with the scent of old oak, wet dogs and mud. In the background he could hear a wireless, and childish voices raised in argument. As the housekeeper led him across the hall, he caught sight of a dark girl staring at him with insolent eyes from a first-floor landing. High-heeled shoes gave an inappropriate impression of height. Her mouth was a gash of lipstick. That must be the daughter, thought Guy, only she's dressed like a hooker. It was confusing. Perhaps it's the maid . . .

"The daughter!" His half-sister for God's sake. Nancy . . .

The girl tossed her hair and turned away, as if angry to be caught looking at him.

Raised voices were coming from the room that he was taken to.

". . . Nancy's only too happy to start an argument and play us off against one another! She's doing it now!"

Guy smiled to himself. Naughty old Nancy. A girl after his own heart.

Silence fell as he entered. The room had vivid red walls and was lined with shelves of books and treasures that would have made his grandmother gasp with envy. His father was there—he recognised him from the photo—and a woman, presumably the wife, Brittany. It was a strange name for an English woman, and to Guy's practised eye she looked Continental. She was quite tall and very beautiful, with a lot of toffee coloured hair.

And that was all he saw of her, because she took one look at him and ran from the room.

The American was unloading boxes of food from the back of his jeep.

Nancy watched him from the landing window as he carried the boxes into the house.

So, he's staying.

She could not believe her good luck. He was like a movie star, only better. Better than Clark Gable, better than Cary Grant.

She was already searching for phrases to describe him to the girls next term; the phrases that would have the most dramatic impact and incur the most envy. *"Glistening dark eyes"* was one, and *"heavenly smile"*. She would have to try and describe the way you could see his muscles shifting under the thin wool of his uniform, and how the immense arrogant power of his body gave the impression that he was taller than he really was. How his floppy, nut-brown hair was exactly the same colour as his skin. Nancy reflected on the combination of white, white teeth and black eyes as he carried the last box into the house and disappeared from view. He reminded her of a gypsy, yet to describe him as such seemed wrong somehow. There was nothing coarse about his features.

She still did not know who he was. The reaction that he had caused in the Stein household betrayed the fact that he was somebody important, not just a casual guest. He had gone out to his jeep leaving her parents closeted in the library shouting at one another. For Nancy, this made the mysterious American more compelling than ever. Her parents rarely quarrelled; and when they did it was usually about her. But surely they couldn't *still* be arguing about whether she was to return to St Clare's . . .

Nancy's first thought had been that he might be a former lover of her mother's. She had had very little contact with men apart from her brother and father and found their ages hard to judge. This one was probably too young for her mother though. He looked no more than thirty. She had crept down to listen outside the library door for a while but could only catch tantalizing half sentences. Her father shouted, *"I don't know how you dare when your bastard has been living under my roof—"*

"Don't drag David into this!" Her mother's voice was shrill.

Nancy had crept away, surprised at hearing her father refer to George as a bastard. Of course she knew all about *that*, had done for years. David was Daddy's younger brother who had died in a car crash when he was young and George was the child of her mother's affair with David. They had not been married at the time, but Nancy found this predictable. Her mother was not a "wifey" sort of person, even now that she was married. There was something too fierce and strong about her. She told Nancy once that it was because she had spent too much time alone.

So perhaps the visitor was something to do with David Stein. There was only one picture of David in the house, in her parents' bedroom. That fascinating image had drawn her like a moth, time and time again. It was taken before a fancy dress party in

1923, and showed Brittany and David standing at the foot of a staircase dressed as Venus and Mars.

Her mother's sepia face was solemn beneath its crown of trailing leaves but David Stein was laughing like a young boy. He had nice twinkly eyes. And he had glamour, Nancy reflected, all the glamour of a young and handsome man who would die in a fast car on the way to his beloved.

As much as she loved her brother George, she could see that he would never be as glamorous as his father had been.

Florrie, Nancy's former nanny, had taken the photograph on the evening of the ball when she was Brittany's maid, and it was Florrie who would patiently repeat the story to Nancy every time she visited. She lived in the village now, crippled by arthritis.

"She gave me the evening off, your ma," Florrie would say dolefully, shaking her head. "And to this day I can never forgive myself for going and leaving her like that. On her own she waited for him, all night. Such a nice gentleman was Mr David. Only he never came . . ."

Nancy left her look-out point at the landing window and went up to her room.

It was a small, breezy room that looked out on to the front lawn. Her friends all kept their rooms at home full of the memorabilia of childhood, but this would not do for Nancy Stein. There were no dolls, no battered teddy bears, no clutter. She was fanatically tidy and kept the room pristine. The brass bed wore a plain white coverlet and a pair of clinical-looking pale blue and white gingham curtains hung at the window. There was a plain white bookcase, an antique desk and chair and a dressing table with a picture of George on it. Nothing more. That was the way Nancy liked it.

It had occurred to her that by now the American would be sitting alone downstairs while her parents wrangled, and that she ought to take the opportunity to go and introduce herself.

But first she must change.

With neat, methodical movements, she wiped the lipstick from her mouth and brushed her hair until it sparkled under the electric light. She took Joanie's white angora sweater from the suitcase and put it on. It clung to her breasts and its fluffiness gave a hazy soft-focus outline to her neck and shoulders. She added a pearl necklace and earrings and a plain grey skirt that she knew was tight around her hips. Then she put her mother's shoes carefully to one side and replaced them with a pair of flat pumps.

"*Nancy!*" It was her mother. "Where are you?"

"I'm up here!" trilled Nancy sweetly.

Damn, damn and blast it, she muttered under her breath. I've obviously missed my chance to be alone with *him* . . .

She descended to find her mother standing on the stairs and her father coming out of the drawing room. She noticed that he took care to close the door behind him.

"Brittany honey, *please*. If you say it now you'll put him at his ease and before you know it he'll have forgotten all about it."

Brittany ignored his cajoling. "Ah, there you are darling," she said to Nancy. "We were waiting for you." She led Nancy into the drawing room. The American was looking very much at home, his gypsy presence dominating the room.

"Captain Exley," said Brittany, "I must apologise for my behaviour earlier. I was a little . . . surprised." She smiled stiffly.

Nancy looked at her mother with renewed interest. Why was she apologizing to *him*? . . . "Curiouser and curiouser," she thought.

"Nancy," said Jake, "I'd like to introduce you to Captain Guy Exley. He's a cousin of yours from America and he's going to be staying with us at Christmas."

Nancy met his eyes for the first time, and a look of recognition passed between them, a recognition so profound that she felt she was seeing her own reflection. It was exactly like an electrical charge racing through her body. She stepped back a pace.

Then she smiled the smile she had been practising in front of the dressing-table mirror.

Brittany saw the smile and decided that it was altogether too winsome.

Susannah Stanwycke rose early on Boxing Day. Twenty guests would be arriving at Cleveleigh Farm at noon and there was a lot of preparation still to do. Besides, she had acquired the habit of rising very early since her husband Hugh and the other men had been called up. She was running the farm more or less single handed now.

The undented pillows and smooth sheets on Hugh's side of the bed haunted Susannah as she crossed the dark polished boards, flinching at the cold. Simon, the herdsman, and Bethan, the Welsh landgirl had promised to feed the stock this morning, but she ought to go and make sure that things were on the move.

She struggled into corduroy breeches, a shapeless sweater of Hugh's and thick woollen socks. When she caught sight of her reflection she laughed. Who would have believed that the exquisite, pampered Susannah Langbourne of '20s London, with her trailing lace frocks and pretty jewellery would end up like this— a cowherd? She loved her life though. She had always been happy since she married Hugh. Not happy in the way that Jake and Brittany were, perhaps, but content.

She tiptoed down the dark, narrow corridor to the stairs, anxious not to waken the children. She had thought Cleveleigh a pokey house when she came to live here as Hugh Stanwycke's bride in 1925, a house of dark wooden doorways and low ceilings, so different to the vast carpeted spaciousness of her parents' mansion in Mayfair, or their baronial home in Leicestershire, Ainsley Castle. Eventually its silence had been broken by the sounds of children and as their family grew Susannah came to love the Jacobean stone farmhouse. The gloom was warm and protective, not pokey.

Dawn light was just beginning to filter through the unblacked-out windows of Ralph's empty room. Her eldest son had volunteered to spend his holiday at a cadet camp and had been sorely missed at Christmas.

Two years after Ralph was born, Susannah had given birth to a daughter, Christina, and then another daughter, Mary, who had only survived a few weeks. Her death had been a great blow for the tender-hearted Susannah and for a while Cleveleigh Farm became a dark and miserable place again. But then Johnnie was born and three years later Alasdair, the youngest. She had a secret contempt for the sexual act but it had been well worth suffering. Her children were her greatest joy.

The door of the boys' room was slightly ajar and Susannah could not resist watching their peaceful sleep for a few moments. Only their hair was visible where hair met pillow; the elder boy's sandy like Hugh's and Alasdair's her own white blonde.

The kitchen was a large, square room skirted with wall cupboards painted a cheerful green and dominated by the scrubbed deal table in the centre of the room. Susannah arranged her ingredients in neat methodical groups on the table, frowning a little at their meagre quantities. Then she stood and watched the sun rise on a crisp, clear morning through the east-facing window, uttering a silent prayer of thanks. Since Hugh had been in Burma, Susannah had come to dread the approach of night and the hours spent shivering alone in their bed. In the dark she fell prey to a host of fears and anxieties, and would often lie paralysed and whimpering with dread. Would she ever see Hugh again? Would she have to raise their children alone? By day she was composed and cheerful and told no one of her fears.

Susannah worked quickly and deftly and by the end of the morning she had prepared a modest spread for the neighbours and friends who were about to arrive. There was not much food, but since the war began that had ceased to matter; people were grateful for whatever they could get. Spirits were very scarce, so Susannah had plundered the cellar for red wine and mulled it in a large pan in the kitchen. The warm heavy scent of cloves followed her into the panelled drawing room as she carried in plates of sandwiches made from chopped black-market ham and dried scrambled egg, and a precious pre-war tin of salmon. Pride of place was reserved for a large mound of rabbit cooked with herbs and chilled in aspic. Hours of struggle had been required to remove all the bones.

Fourteen-year-old Christina was on her hands and knees lighting a fire. She looked up and wrinkled her nose when she saw the plate of glutinous rabbit.

"Eugh—rabbit! Mummy, how disgusting. You can't possibly!"

Susannah merely inclined her head in her daughter's direction with a knowing smile and a toss of her greying blonde curls.

"Don't be silly, darling, they'll never know it's not chicken."

"I'm going to tell them it's ferret!" shouted Alasdair, pressing his nose on the cold window and watching his breath make patterns round it. He cleared a peephole with his finger and fixed his gaze on the gate into the lane.

"Mummy! The vicar's arrived! I'm going to tell him we're having ferret jelly!"

And he darted off with the tidings before Susannah could stop him.

Patrick Steele was standing in front of his washstand, shaving. His movements were clumsy and he cut his chin, swearing as drops of blood fell on to his shirt.

He felt nothing but anger and irritation at the prospect of visiting a house that would inevitably be more agreeable than his own, only to return to his cold, damp mouldering home as if it didn't matter. He was sure that people who only saw it from the outside thought Heathcote a fine house, with its quiet grey stone and solid, encircling wall. It was the largest house in the village unless you counted Graylings, which stood over a mile outside it.

The Stein family appeared as cool and *raffiné* as the white pillars of their home—not that they ever had any contact with Patrick and his family. He had seen the girl out riding a few times, mounted on a magnificent chestnut that made him boil with envy, a precocious child with a bright-eyed look about her. She and her brother were close to him in age, but most of the time they were absent at expensive boarding schools. He and Annabel attended the local grammar school in Wells. Patrick had passed their mother on the village street once. She gave him an icy look and turned away to get into her car.

He had asked his father about that.

"Why is Mrs Stein so bloody stuck-up? Annabel says she talks to *other* people all the time."

Adrian Steele laughed. It was the strangest laugh Patrick had ever heard.

"You'd think even she would realise she has very little to be proud about wouldn't you? Ridiculous name, Brittany."

He smiled slightly, but his dark eyes glittered. It was the look he wore before he raised his belt to beat Patrick. "She's never forgiven me, that's why. Gerald Colby and I—that's her father by the way—were good friends. Once. He left Graylings to me in his will, and your mother and I went to live there. Mrs Stein was pretty unhappy about that as I'm sure you'll appreciate."

"*You* lived at Graylings?"

"If you'd arrived earlier, old man, you might even have been born there. But it turned out that Gerald Colby had changed his mind after all, even though she was . . . so . . . she got what she wanted in the end."

At the time, the thing that surprised Patrick most about this exchange was not learning of his father's occupation of the big white mansion that dominated Nether Aston.

It was the mention of his mother.

Adrian Steele had not referred to her once since the terrifying day six years ago when she had left Heathcote House. He behaved as if his children were not the product of a human relationship and had never been nurtured in a woman's womb for nine months, but were part and parcel of the house he lived in like the dogs or the furniture, or the guns rusting in the gun room. Kit was only a baby when Mother walked out, and he and Annabel could no longer remember her very clearly. But somehow at Christmas she always seemed to be missing.

And now he had to go to some ridiculous Christmas party and have the bloody Steins stare at him as though he were dirt. Just thinking about it gave rise to boiling and uncontrollable anger, and he picked up his porcelain shaving mug and hurled it to the floor, where it smashed into several pieces. It had been Greville's idea that they accept the invitation. Well, Greville could bloody well go to hell! He wasn't going.

There was a knock at the door and Greville came in. He was wearing a plum velvet smoking jacket that had belonged to Cousin Percy. The satin frogging strained slightly around his portly stomach.

"Ready?"

"I'm not bloody going!"

"Now look here, Patrick old chap, we've already—"

"You don't have to go! If you're so bloody keen, why don't you go in my place?"

"We've discussed this. Someone has to stay in case your father needs anything. I would very much like to go, but I thought it would be more useful for you two to meet some people of your own age. And Annabel wants you to go with her . . ." A soft persuasive note crept into Greville's voice.

"I don't like parties!"

"How do you know if you don't go to any? Look at Jacob Stein—owning a merchant bank and holding an important government position. Do you think he became successful by turning down invitations?"

"I don't care if I'm not successful! I don't care about anything!" Patrick kicked one of the porcelain fragments across the floor.

"Ah, but you do . . ." Greville's voice was as soft as butter. "You care about Annabel, don't you?"

Silence.

"You once told me she was all you cared about."

"She is."

"Well then, you won't want to let her down, will you? Go and find her and see if she's ready."

Patrick went to look in the kitchen first, kicking one of the dogs out of his way angrily. The object of its attention was the remains of their Christmas lunch, a tough piece of roast mutton—illegally butchered on one of the Heathcote farms—that still sat on the table, iced with a layer of congealed fat. The ironing board had been left standing across the centre of the room, straddling two squares of carpet that did not match. One pink, the other a dingy green. Most of the rooms in Heathcote House were like that, particularly the bedrooms, which boasted beds without mattresses or windows with one curtain. There were some good paintings, but it was so gloomy and the walls were so dirty that the outline of the frames could barely be discerned.

The only room with a welcoming air was Annabel's, and once he had looked downstairs, Patrick went up there to find her.

"Belle—are you there?"

"Come in."

Annabel was sitting at the dressing table that once belonged to Jennifer Steele. Its ruffled skirt of faded chintz fell in heavy folds round her legs. She was lit by the pale winter sun that streamed through the gable window above her head, turning wispy hairs to a crown of fire and softening the lines of her face like a candle flame on wax.

Patrick thought she was very beautiful.

She placed the hairbrush carefully on the glass surface and turned to her brother with a shy smile as though he had been thinking out loud.

"Do you think this lipstick looks all right, Pat? I couldn't think of any other way to make the skirt look less dowdy." She stood up and smoothed her old kilt nervously.

Patrick smiled down at her and she smiled back at him.

Then his smile faded abruptly. "Don't go to too much trouble. They've only asked us because they feel sorry for us."

"That's not what Greville says."

"Greville! I'm sick of bloody Greville! How long's he going to stay here anyway? He only came for a few weeks and he's stayed for years. I wish you'd tell him to push off, Belle!"

Annabel contemplated Patrick's reflection in the mirror for a moment. Then she began to dab at her lipstick with a handkerchief. "I honestly don't think he's got anywhere to go. Anyway, I'm quite fond of him. He livens the place up a bit." She picked up the lipstick and applied some more. "I won't be a minute, Pat. Why don't you go and round up Kit?"

Annabel finished her make-up and went to say goodbye to her father. She found Greville coming out of the sick-room.

"Greville, can I have a word . . ."

"Patrick? . . ."

She nodded. "He's been asking about you leaving again."

"Again? Oh dear . . . He really is unstable at the moment, isn't he? And his temper's getting worse . . . I wouldn't want you to have to deal with that alone, but if that's what you want—''

"Oh no!" said Annabel hastily. "I want you to stay. He *is* getting more difficult."

"You just run along to the party m'dear, and leave the worrying to me." He looked Annabel up and down. "Very fetching! Now don't forget what I said about talking to the Steins. Particularly that American guest of theirs!" He bounced away down the corridor like an over-sized plum.

Annabel opened the door of her father's room. Adrian Steele was propped up against the pillows, smoking a cigar and reading *Sporting Life*. His grey hair was swept back at a rakish angle, mocking the greyness of his skin.

"Daddy, we're going to the Stanwyckes' drinks party now, but we won't be gone long."

"You're just as good as they are," he said, staring into the distance. Then he smiled at her through the cloud of exhaled smoke. "You're sure to be the prettiest girl there."

"Who's that pretty girl over there?" Brittany murmured into Susannah's ear. Steam from the mulled wine tickled her nose as she bent to sip it.

Before the Steins had arrived, the other guests at the party were subdued in the awkward way of people whose minds cannot be free until the awaited person has come. And when they entered the now overheated sitting room at Cleveleigh, bringing in a burst of cold air and talking in raised voices, the others relaxed abruptly as if hearing a secret signal, and the noise of conversation began to bubble and rise.

Susannah smiled gratefully at Brittany.

"Annabel Steele."

Brittany's elegant eyebrows were raised in two dark question marks. "Not—"

"Yes. Adrian Steele's girl."

Brittany turned to look again at the girl who was standing with her back to the fire, shifting her weight self-consciously from one foot to the other.

She was small, with neat compact curves and very slender wrists and ankles. Her hair was a dark red-brown and its simple velvet band framed a square forehead and wide-set eyes. She made Brittany think of a doe. Her face was too artless to be truly beautiful. Or rather it was the beauty of a very young child. She wore a lovat green jersey and a kilt and her fingers wandered self-consciously to a gold locket at her neck as the vicar engaged her in conversation. Mr Nash, the vicar, was very large and his frame loomed over her, forcing her nearer and nearer to the fire so that her cheeks flamed.

Brittany turned back to Susannah and looked at her with the directness that people reserve for relatives or very old friends. Susannah's parents had been her guardians and they had lived as members of the same family for almost a year. And for years now, since her marriage to Hugh, Susannah had been a near neighbour.

"What the hell prompted you to invite Adrian Steele's child into your house? Don't tell me you've forgotten the way he behaved when Maman died?"

"Children. There are three of them. The boys are over there by the window." Susannah was calm and she smiled slightly at her friend. Her dark brown eyes were reflective. "But Brittany, I think it's a little harsh to visit the sins of the fathers on the children, don't you?"

She looked slowly over Brittany's short, draped dress, designed by Mainbocher and made from severe black jersey. She lifted her eyes to the black, beaded cocktail hat and the diamond earrings. She was without doubt the most elegant woman in the room. And Susannah's eyes said, *"You are a fulfilled, successful, attractive woman. Why is there a hard little part of you that cannot forgive?"*

Out loud she said, "You know Jennifer Steele walked out of that place years ago, and who can blame her. They say he used to hit her. But what about the poor children? Stuck in a mouldering old house that nobody ever visits, that's falling down around their ears. There's no money. And he's ill now, apparently—their father. From what I've heard, it sounds as though he's got cancer. So . . ."

Brittany shrugged and smiled to show that she understood. "I see. And it is Christmas, after all . . ."

"Exactly. And there's a war on. We're supposed to bury our differences in order to beat Hitler." Susannah watched the punch bowl anxiously to make sure that there was still plenty to go around. "Look at those crumbs being ground into the carpet. Still, most of the rabbit's been eaten . . ."

"People will eat anything these days," said Brittany, examining the content of her sandwich suspiciously. At the same moment both she and Susannah saw George Stein crossing the room to talk to Annabel Steele.

"So," burst out Susannah triumphantly, "how has your Christmas been at Graylings? You must introduce me to Jake's American relation. What did you say he was?"

"A cousin."

"Another cousin? First Leonora and now . . ." She waved in Guy's direction. "Well, it must be wonderful having a visitor from abroad at a time like this when none of us have the chance to go anywhere. Aren't you going to tell me about him?"

"No."

The tight monosyllable told Susannah that Brittany was troubled, but she knew her too well to question her. Brittany would confide in Susannah in her own time. Instead she excused herself and went to mull some more wine.

Brittany was left watching her son talk to Annabel Steele. Her placid solemn baby, David Stein's illegitimate son, had grown into an even-tempered and affectionate young man with a very stubborn streak. It was strangely thrilling to have borne two children by two brothers, and Brittany often reflected on the genetic prank that made George Theodore more Jake's son than David's, while Nancy's restless, flirtatious nature reminded her very much of her husband's younger brother.

Today there was a look on George's face that she had never seen before, an intent look, a look of pleasure and self-oblivion. It disturbed Brittany, but she told herself sternly that she could hardly begrudge George the pleasure of talking to a pretty girl. It had not been a very happy holiday for him and that same evening he was going to join his regiment at a camp on the South coast before leaving for North Africa. She swallowed the thought that she might never see him again.

Brittany was well aware of the cause of George's irritability since he had returned from Cambridge. Guy Exley's presence had soured him as much as it gratified Nancy. Her usually laconic daughter had been transformed into a giggling, flouncing show-off. At this very moment, in her tight cherry red dress, hair luminous, she was trying to catch Guy's attention, looking first at him, then at Susannah's precious five shillings' worth of mistletoe.

George and Nancy still did not know who Guy Exley was. Having grown up in a fog of mysterious half-truths herself, Brittany hated lying to her children. She told herself that it would cause less trouble in the long run, since the war would soon be over and then Guy Exley would be gone for good. At least, her head told her so. But even now as she looked at the God-like young American who stood amongst the shabby, war-weary inhabitants of Nether Aston like a statue cast in gold, her heart told her otherwise.

He would not just disappear.

George was less than enchanted with Guy for the single reason that he was jealous. Nancy had always lavished special attention on her brother, had opened herself to him as to no one else, but now she scarcely seemed aware of his presence at Graylings. Brittany's own reservations about Captain Exley were more occult. It was not simply that she disliked having the son of her husband's legendary first love in the house . . .

He was talking to an awe-struck vicar's wife now. She listened to him.

"Well, yes, it's been very difficult this year," Mrs Nash blundered on naively. "I managed to find a butcher with a turkey to sell and he was asking more than seven pounds for it! Our neighbours had cod for their Christmas lunch. Can you imagine—cod! Well, we settled for ham in the end . . ."

"Really? Is that so?" replied Guy in his polite, patronising drawl. He kept his eyes wide with interest as he lit a cigarette with a solid gold lighter.

Most disturbing of all to Brittany was not that she did not trust Guy Exley, but that he knew that she did not. She had perceived that he was what the Americans called a phoney and her perception had caught her in a trap. He looked audaciously past Mrs Nash now, smiling the conspiratorial smile of someone exposed as playing a part but who knows he will not be betrayed.

Nancy was at Brittany's elbow, asking when they were going to leave, because she and Guy wanted to go out riding.

"We can go just as soon as everyone is rounded up. I'll leave that to you." Brittany said crisply.

She was suddenly weary of the game of observing and being observed. She saw Nancy coolly interrupt George's conversation with Annabel and could not help but notice the glad expression on the face of Annabel's guardian angel, a thin wiry boy with very dark hair and even darker eyes whom she had recognised once in the village as Adrian Steele's son. He wore a brooding air and when he frowned angrily, which he did often, he looked very much like his father.

Patrick Steele was the topic of discussion as Guy drove the Steins back to Graylings, squeezed into his jeep. Brittany had submitted to this indignity because of the scarcity of petrol for their own cars, but declined to sit in the front seat next to Guy.

"I didn't like Patrick Steele very much," George remarked innocently. "I tried asking him about his school but he was very bad-tempered about it."

"It's hardly surprising, dummy!" Nancy affected the Americanism to annoy her mother. "He didn't like you very much either. You were paying too much attention to his little sister. The possessive type."

"*She* was nice though. I liked her," said George thoughtfully.

"Pretty too, huh?" Guy said to George, who blushed at the remark.

Guy looked at Brittany in the driving mirror and winked.

The whole family was due to assemble that evening to say goodbye to George.

But Nancy had other plans. George was the person she was closest to and she would not be satisfied with anything less than a private audience.

She went up to his room and stood in the doorway watching him pack. Nothing had changed in this room for years. A one-eyed bear looked down from the top of the wardrobe. An army of lead soldiers marched across a dresser. George picked up a photograph of his parents, looked at it for a moment and then thrust it into his knapsack.

"I've come to say goodbye, George."

"There's no need, Nan, you're all coming to wave me off in a moment." He turned his back to her and put a hand up to his eyes.

"George—"

"Nan, I didn't want to do it the other way—see people on their own—because it's too bloody upsetting!"

"Won't you make an exception for me?" Nancy cajoled, creeping up behind him and putting her arms around his waist.

George turned round and embraced her fiercely. "Oh Nan . . ."

Nancy buried her face in his chest. "Don't go, George! You're the only one who understands me. I don't want that to change."

"Silly girl! It'll be just the same when I get back. You're not going to lose me. You'll *never* lose me. Now—" He pulled away from her, ". . . Let me get on with sorting this stuff, or I'll never be ready."

Nancy walked slowly to the door.

"And good luck when you get back to school!"

"I'm not going back!"

"Don't be silly, Nan—"

But she had disappeared.

Nancy thundered down the staircase to the drawing room. Jake and Guy were playing draughts and her mother was sewing a button onto George's battledress jacket. She stood in the centre of the room, waiting, but they were all too preoccupied to look up.

"Do I *have* to go back to school?"

Brittany put down the jacket. "We've been through this before. The subject's closed." She turned back to her work.

"I wouldn't have to stay at the house. I could have the cottage."

"No, you couldn't. Leonora's there, you know that." She looked across to Guy, who was watching with interest. "And we have a guest. You know the rule about not discussing family matters in front of guests."

"Daddy said I could have the cottage."

Jake looked sheepish. "I only said maybe, honey . . . but I thought we could always offer Leonora another cottage, elsewhere on the estate . . ."

Brittany flung down the jacket. "I don't believe I'm hearing this, I really don't! That cottage *belongs* to Leonora. Quite apart from the fact that you had no business disposing of it elsewhere, *I* don't want Leonora to move. I *like* having her here when you're away."

Guy leaned forward and said, "Surely you both ought to—"

"None of this is your concern!" snapped Brittany. "Nancy, do you have anything else you wish to say, or are you going to stand there like a pillar of salt all evening?"

Nancy gave a sigh of exasperation and turned on her heel. She went out onto the portico, shivering at the cold, and leaned against one of the pillars. Guy followed her. She frowned at him and turned her face away.

"Playing a double game with your parents doesn't often work."

"What would you know about it?"

"Believe me, that scene was all too familiar."

Nancy turned and stared at him, still shivering.

"Here, let me give you my coat." Guy removed his mess jacket and draped it over her shoulders. Nancy stroked the braid with one finger. She sighed. "God, I don't know . . . they mean well, but—"

"But they don't know what you're like, right?"

Nancy stared at him. "How did you know?"

"I just know. But your father was sticking up for you . . ."

"I know. He does try to give me what I want. I suppose he's pretty good in that respect."

"Do you ever tell him that?"

"What?"

"That you love him. Stuff like that."

Nancy blushed slightly. "No. Sometimes I want to, but I just can't say it. I don't know why."

Guy thrust his hands into his pockets and strolled to the edge of the portico. He looked up at the sky. "Maybe you're jealous? The two of them are pretty close. I figure that could make you feel left out . . ."

Nancy stared at his silhouetted figure for a few moments. Then she said abruptly, "I wish you could stay longer."

"So do I."

Everyone except Guy and Leonora came out onto the steps to see George off that evening. All the evacuees were there, giggling with excitement and waving a banner they had made saying "GOOD LUCK GORGE". Brittany hugged George and tried not to cry. "Leonora says to wish you all the best. I tried to persuade her to come, but she wouldn't."

At that moment, Leonora was strolling down the path from the beech copse, high and euphoric from the generous amount of sherry she had just drunk. She pulled her mink coat around her tightly and buried her fingers in the pile of the fur. It was very cold and there was a mist settling and swirling around her. And a mist in her head too, a friendly companionable mist that made the stars jump sideways when she looked up at them. There was a light on in the porch, despite the blackout and it showed George climbing into the front of the car next to Jake. The children waved and shouted. Leonora watched them for a minute, then headed round the side of the house to the path that led to the cottage.

Somebody has left a light on in the study—how careless. No, there's somebody in there. The American boy.

He was obviously ignorant of the blackout rules. Leonora blew on her cold fingers and blinked into the brightness. Looking into a lighted room from the dark outside reminded her of being at the pictures. And he looked the part, like a film star. He was pulling out a folded piece of paper and reading it. He obviously did not care for what he read, because he was frowning and shaking his head.

And he failed to see Leonora's white face in the window.

Three
January 1943

"If we beat Hitler, Auntie, does that mean we'll have to go back 'ome?"

Brittany was sitting on the edge of Derek's bed in one of the large bedrooms that she had converted into a "dormitory". The rows of small wooden bedsteads looked quaint clustering beneath the tall windows swagged with heavy velvet curtains in deep midnight blue. Like flowers at the foot of a mountain. Brittany had made bright coverlets for the beds in yellow, blue and scarlet. Furniture was so difficult to obtain that the evacuees' rooms inevitably looked a little spartan, but there were a few faded and dog-chewed rugs on the floor and some of Brittany's own paintings on the wall. The children admired the paintings politely, disappointed that they were landscapes and not pictures of bombers and battle scenes.

Brittany patted Derek's wiry head affectionately. "Of course you'll go home once the war's over, darling. Your mothers and fathers will be wanting you back."

She looked around the room in consternation at the row of blank, disappointed faces. They did not want to return to their homes, any of them, to the hunger and the abuse.

"Those glum faces won't help us win the war, will they? We've all got to hope that Mr Churchill can end it as soon as possible . . ."

She often wondered how *she* would manage when the evacuees were gone. Her days would seem long and empty.

"And anyway, you'll all be able to come back and visit as often as you like."

This was intended to cheer them, but the children knew as well as she did that such an eventuality was unlikely. The silence that followed was broken by Marion's entrance.

"Are we ready for lights out?"

Marion stood beaming in the doorway. Brittany thought—and not for the first time that day—how well the young woman looked, her round cheeks blushed with colour and her hazel eyes bright. She was always happier when it was like this at Graylings; quiet, with just the two of them and the children. Guy

Exley had left shortly after Christmas, Jake was in London again and Nancy had returned reluctantly to school, vowing to join the war effort as soon as she could.

It was Nancy, more than anyone, who made Marion feel uncomfortable. She treated the elder girl with even less respect than she showed the servants, despising her for being "soft" and not caring if Marion knew it. It was true that Marion's lack of spirit irritated Brittany at times, but she was well-meaning and hard-working and her daughter's arrogance always left the rancid taste of guilt in Brittany's mouth.

She followed Marion along the landing and down the stairs.

"It's *Monday Night At Eight* on the wireless in a few minutes," the younger woman said eagerly. "We could go and listen in the kitchen while I make us some cocoa."

This prospect struck Brittany as extremely dull.

"No thank you, Marion," she replied as kindly as she could, "I'd love to but I told Leonora that I'd go down to the cottage."

This was not really true and the white lie made Brittany feel a trifle schoolgirlish as she hurried down the path to the cottage. Blackout regulations prevented outside lighting but she was undaunted by the unrelenting blackness of the winter night. She had made this trip many times in the dark and was familiar with each hollow underfoot and every projecting branch. Leonora was not expecting her, but it had been Brittany's intention to resume her evening visits as soon as Christmas was over. Leonora had been invited to join in the celebrations, but when pressed she had merely tossed her hair and said that she would prefer to be on her own.

She seemed to be pleased to see Brittany, but it quickly became clear that she was agitated by something.

The cottage was very cold. Brittany sat in her usual place on the end of the bed, near the electric fire. Leonora hugged her fur coat around her as she foraged for clean glasses and a bottle of brandy. Her sources of alcohol were a perpetual mystery, but Brittany suspected that her cousin had been canny enough to befriend lonely officers in the army camp in Yeovil. The Nether Aston Women's Institute ran a canteen for the troops and Leonora worked there sporadically, under pressure from the Labour Exchange. As a woman with no dependants she was required to work.

They talked lamely about the canteen until the first glasses had been emptied. Then Leonora pulled closer to Brittany, the bottle clasped firmly in one hand.

"Listen, I've something to tell you. Something I saw."

Leonora was always "seeing" things, observing inconsequential details whilst life's more substantial events trooped past her. But tonight there was an unusual degree of fervour in her eyes. "You remember the night George went off?"

Brittany nodded and held out her glass for a refill.

"Well, I saw that young American guest of yours poking around in the study."

"*What*?"

Brittany sat bolt upright, spilling brandy down her skirt. She dabbed at it. "The study? Are you sure?" she asked as she licked sour liquid from her fingers.

"Of course I am." Leonora's eyes were still bright, indicating that she had more to tell. "I watched him. All the others were saying goodbye to George, that's what made me notice he was there. He hadn't blacked out the window, of course."

Brittany shivered despite the fire as she recalled the look he had given her earlier that day at Cleveleigh Farm. A look at once guilty and boastful. "You said he was poking around . . ."

". . . In the desk," said Leonora. "He was looking at Jake's will. Do you want to know how I know it was Jake's will?"

"Yes I do," said Brittany calmly. She lit a cigarette, hesitating for a second when she realised that it was one of the Lucky Strikes that Guy had brought.

". . . When I first came here and showed you the bit of grandfather's will that mentioned the cottage, you offered to take it from me for safekeeping. You showed me where you were putting it, and you said it was the same drawer that Jake's will was kept in." Leonora glowed with achievement and gulped down her brandy happily. "And then you admired my gas mask case."

"Yes . . . I remember . . ." Brittany stared down at her cigarette for a moment, without speaking. "Look, are you *sure* about this—"

"Absolutely! I wouldn't mention it otherwise. I know I'd had a couple of drinks but I could still recognise the drawer without any trouble. That's what made me wonder what he was doing there. Do *you* know what he was doing there?"

"No, I don't."

"But you don't like it. I don't blame you."

Brittany sighed. "Leonora . . . I want your advice. It's not just this will business I'm worried about. It's Nancy." She sucked hard on her cigarette, groping for the right words. "She's . . . interested in Guy . . ."

"Ah!"

". . . in the wrong way."

"Ah—the wrong way!"

Brittany smiled at Leonora's determination to take everything that was said to her at face value. "It's no good, I'm going to have to explain properly. Guy is Jake's son." She paused to give weight to the words. Leonora nodded. "His illegitimate son from a relationship he had with an American girl. So—"

"Nancy and Guy are half-brother and -sister."

"Yes, but—"

"But Nancy doesn't know." Leonora folded her arms and rocked to and fro. "Hmmm . . . Why don't you talk to Nancy about it?"

Brittany shook her head slowly. "I can't . . ." Suddenly she felt gripped by despair and she buried her face in her hands so that Leonora only got a muffled impression of what she was trying to say. ". . . *Christ! . . . bloody failure as a mother!*" She raised her face and there were damp smudges of mascara around her eyes. "Leonora, d'you remember that time we talked about it before. It was on your first night here. And I made out that everything was OK really. Well, that was a load of bloody rubbish!" She snatched up the packet of Lucky Strikes and felt in her pocket for the lighter. "I was only too happy to shove her away in school and forget about her for weeks on end! What a wonderful way of evading the problem! But you can't put it off for ever. Now I need to communicate with my daughter and I look back over all those years and I just can't see where I went wrong!"

With an angry movement she clicked the button on the lighter and held it up in front of her face, staring into the flame.

Leonora picked up the bottle and poured out more brandy. "You know what I think? I was no good for my daughter because my marriage was a lost cause. With you it's the other way round. Your marriage is a success. You and Jake are very close. And that's like a door shutting Nancy out. End of speech. Have some more of this, it'll do you good."

Brittany smiled gratefully and dabbed at her eyes.

"This thing with Guy—you're going to have to tell her some time, aren't you?"

Brittany nodded.

"And the longer you leave it . . . et cetera . . . et cetera. Ah, another glass for me, I think. My mouth's dry from all this lecturing. It's not something I've ever done much of."

"But you're right though. God . . . I told Jake I thought she wasn't old enough to know, but it's not that. Telling the children who Guy is means admitting him to the immediate family. And I don't want that." She emptied her glass. "Thanks for the drink, Leonora. And for the lecture. You're better at it than you know."

As Brittany walked back to the house, hurrying against the cold, her mind painted a very clear picture of Guy searching through the desk. She knew what he wanted.

Graylings.

Had he still been there she would have gone straight to him and told him that as long as she had breath in her body, he was never going to take the house she had once lost and regained, the house that was rightfully *hers*. That she was not going to let him in to her family . . .

However, he was *not* there, and she had no wish to summon him back to Graylings, so instead she brooded about it.

The advent of Katherine Exley's son was singularly ill-timed. Graylings and the estate had been in Brittany's sole ownership, but only a year ago Jake had persuaded her to make them over to Jacob Stein and Company to avoid death duties raised by the new government to a crippling sixty-five per cent. Jake held a controlling seventy per cent of the company's shares and could therefore decide Graylings' fate. It would never have occurred to Brittany to change this arrangement or to doubt Jake until . . .

He was so very glad that his son had come to find him.

He had tried to hide the gladness from Brittany but it shone out; in his eyes, in his smile, in the lightness of his step. And Guy had seen portraits of Brittany's family on the walls and had asked about her childhood. On the very same evening that Leonora had seen him. Had he rushed off to the study in a flurry of disappointment after his conversation about the Colby family home, desperate to know whether the nest he perched in was the property of the male or the female? . . .

Brittany turned these questions over in her mind the next day as she travelled to London on the train. There were ten or a dozen people and several boxes in the vestibule at the end of the corridor. Some vomited and one woman fainted. Brittany had managed to secure a seat and she dozed, squeezed tightly between a naval officer and a clergyman. Each time she closed her eyes she fell prey to a vision of Guy Exley as a fat cuckoo in US Air Force uniform.

She was going to spend her few days in London looking up

the few old friends who remained there and having some of her clothes altered by her dressmaker, the next best thing to buying a new wardrobe, which was no longer possible. It had been Jake's idea that she have a few days away from the children before Nancy returned for the Easter holidays, and although she had some qualms about Marion's ability to quench riots single handed, she was eager for the opportunity to talk to Jake about his son.

She would try not to spoil it for him completely. Not yet. And she was confident that she would not have to introduce the subject of Guy herself, merely wait for Jake to bring him into the conversation.

They went to the cinema to see Judy Garland in *Me and My Gal* and afterwards they walked gingerly the length of Fleet Street, arms linked. Above them the dark, reassuring shape of St Paul's poised unafraid, like a crouching giant above lesser, lay buildings.

Jake said, "Well, I tend to agree with Guy's appraisal of that movie. A lot of fun, but awfully corny."

"You've seen him recently?"

"No, but he's telephoned the office several times. He always reminds me what a wonderful time he had at Christmas."

Brittany pulled on Jake's arm to slow him down. She turned to him, but could barely discern his features in the darkness. "Jake darling . . . I'd like to talk to you about that. Some place where I can see you, preferably."

"We could go in there," Jake pointed to the Kardomah Café on the other side of the street. Its frontage was entirely sand-bagged and it boasted "Shelter for 250 persons."

"It looks safe, at least," agreed Brittany.

Inside, the café was crowded with theatre-goers, and airless. A hot, pungent haze rose from damp overcoats and curdled in the smoke from innumerable Turkish cigarettes. They managed to find a space to sit, next to one another on a bench against the back wall. Brittany had not imagined having to deliver her speech with her knees and elbows squeezed up against Jake's, but it was better than being crushed against the bar. It was the sort of place with ancient, long-suffering waiters who gave the impression they had nothing new to learn about the human race. There was no brandy, so they drank port.

"Jake, about Christmas . . ." Brittany removed her gloves and twisted them around in a circle on the table.

"I thought we had a great Christmas, didn't you, all things considered. Having Guy there made all the difference."

Why is he being so stupid, thought Brittany angrily. Didn't he notice Nancy making sheep's eyes at her own half-brother? Couldn't he see how hurt George was to return for his last Christmas and find the household devoting its attention to a strange American?

"It was pleasant," said Brittany carefully. "But I don't think it would be a good idea if Guy came to Graylings again."

"Hell, Brittany!" Jake slammed the table hard with the flat of his hand. "He has an open invitation to visit any time he likes. You know that. We can't go back on it."

"*You* can't."

Jake looked at her quickly. "You don't like him, do you?"

"It's not that. It's just . . . I sensed that Nancy could become fond of him. In the wrong way—you know."

"If that's the only problem then perhaps we *should* tell her who Guy is. I know you think she's too young, but she knows about George after all."

The hum of talking in the café dimmed slightly as a sultry-looking girl stood up and started to sing "Don't get Around Much Any More". People pushed back against the wall to clear more space for her, knocking Jake's elbow and slopping his port over the table in a pink stain. He tried to joke lamely as he mopped it with his handkerchief.

"Aren't we allowed one byblow apiece?"

"*No!*" Brittany clenched her glass. The shrill crooning of the singer was grating on her nerves. "It will cause more upset all round. We agreed about that."

"So we did," replied Jake evenly. "But I can't deny my own son the run of my home. I just can't do it."

"You mean you *won't*." Brittany's voice cracked bitterly. "You won't deny your precious Katherine Exley's son anything!"

"Now you listen to me."

Jake held Brittany's shoulders hard so that she was forced to look at him through the haze of smouldering Pashas. She had not heard that hard, angry voice since they had lunched at the Ritz nearly twenty years ago and she taunted him about the failure of his first marriage.

"I eventually discovered that Katherine had given birth to our child after her parents forced us apart, but they wouldn't let me near him, not even after she was dead. All those years I was

married to Miriam when she wouldn't give me a child, I knew
I had a son I had never seen . . .''

Jake's voice was choked with unshed tears, and Brittany remembered Jake's spoilt, unfaithful first wife, and heard herself
telling him of George Theodore's birth over the phone, and heard
his awestruck voice at the other end of the line saying, ''A son,
a son . . .''

''. . . I could have sought my son out and reclaimed him once
he grew up, but for your sake, and Nancy and George's, I did not.
But now that he has come to find me, I am not in a position to turn
him away. Even you have no right to ask that, and you know it. I
raised *your* son as though he were my own. If this situation makes
you feel uncomfortable then I'm prepared to discourage Guy by
saying nothing either way. On the other hand, if he asks to come
to Graylings and be with us, then he shall . . . What's mine is his.''

The air was filled with the nauseating stench of sun-drenched
weeds and there was a thin, hot breeze. The meadows of the
Somerset wet-lands were warm and aching with pollen. Nancy
trudged through the drying grass, swiping sideways at the frothy
white cow-parsley.

She was deeply bored.

She looked back over the empty summer weeks and assessed
the extent of her ennui. It must have reached a critical level,
because the previous evenings she had consented to play ludo
with Marion and had played four games. And one of halma.
And this morning she had visited Florrie. For the first time ever
Florrie had started dropping hints that she would like to be left
alone to get on with her tasks. Usually Nancy's brief visits were
spent looking surreptitiously at her watch for a polite minimum
of minutes to pass.

After leaving Florrie's cottage she had walked and walked,
walking just to kill time. She would have liked to ride, despite
the heat. Captain, her horse, had been lent to the village doctor
to conserve his dwindling petrol ration.

If only Guy would come!

Indecently soon after her return from St Clare's, Nancy had
asked her mother if he would be visiting Graylings that summer.
Brittany had frowned and said dismissively, ''Not as far as I
know.''

Her mother patently disliked Guy, which put paid to her earlier theory that they had been lovers. She closed her eyes now

and tried to see him, but it was difficult to remember the way his features pieced together. "Didn't you get a photograph?" her schoolfriends demanded breathlessly when she had first delivered her starry-eyed description of the American. She poured scorn on their naivety. The *last* thing you should do, she explained witheringly, is to ask someone for a photograph. Men respond more if you seem uninterested.

But she wished she had one all the same.

Nancy was north of Graylings now, and heading towards the Home Farm. She hung her head as she walked and watched the grass being roughly parted by her ankles. There was a gate at the corner of the meadow, separating it from a field of ripe wheat, and when she raised her eyes to unlatch it she saw a curious sight. In the hollow on the edge of the field there were two young women who appeared to be half naked. Nancy looked away, and then looked again. The women were wearing short-sleeved shirts that just covered their knickers. Their legs and feet were bare. A few yards away lay two discarded pairs of thick corduroy breeches and some heavy boots.

" 'Ello."

The girl who spoke had brilliant bottle-blonde hair. She removed the cigarette from her mouth and smiled at Nancy.

Nancy blushed and turned away. "Sorry, I—"

"That's all right, love, don't mind us. Come and sit down." She patted the rough ground next to her. "We took them 'orrible things off 'cause we was so bleedin' 'ot."

"It's bloody daft to expect us to wear winter trousers in this heat," said her friend amiably. Her hair was vivid red and she spoke with a northern acent. "But they're supposed to be like a uniform so that everyone can recognise us for what we are—the handmaidens of the land!"

She grinned at Nancy.

"I didn't know that Mr Waite was taking on landgirls." She sat down between the two girls.

"We've only just started," said the blonde. She was a Cockney, Nancy knew, because she sounded like Florrie. "And it's bleedin' awful," she added, "in case you were going to ask. Waite's a miserable old sod. And mean. I hope no one saw you wandering about here. 'E's got a sort of vendetta against what he calls trespassers. Passersby, I call them." She lit another Woodbine and inhaled on it deeply.

Nancy hugged her knees, smiling slightly. "I hardly think Waite could object to my being on his land. My father owns it."

The red-head gaped. "What—all of it? The whole farm?"

"And several others like it. My mother's family have lived here for over a hundred years."

"You must live in that big white place down the road?"

Nancy nodded.

The blonde gave a cackle of laughter and extended her hand. "Pleased to meet you! You're exactly the sort of friend we need. Here—have a fag."

Nancy bent her head down for a light as she had seen Bette Davis do on the screen, wondering if the others could tell that she had never smoked a cigarette properly before. She had stolen some of her mother's once but threw them away after one puff. The smoke caught at the back of her throat and made her feel queasy. She tried to lean back on one elbow and inhale casually, but she choked.

The blonde girl winked. "Looks like that might be your first. Never mind—I expect we was just the same."

A round of formal introductions followed. Greta had come from London and described herself as a dancer. ("Greta's me stage name—after Garbo. Me mum christened me Olive.") She was small and rounded with a cupid's bow of a mouth and a snub nose. She wore her hair permed into tight curls and her fingernails were painted crimson, though the varnish had begun to flake and her hands were roughened. Greta had worked in the chorus line of a West End show once, but it was years since she had been able to find work as a dancer. ("Once you've said bye bye to twenty-five, they reckon you're getting too old.") Hungry for a uniform, but rejected by the armed forces after failing her physical examination, the Women's Land Army had seemed the next best thing. She laughed ruefully as she related this, grimacing at the discarded uniform near her feet.

The red-head was called Maureen, and she told Nancy that the colour of her hair was natural before she even had chance to enquire. The prize asset was coiled into a long "victory roll", the great hanks of terracotta hair making a V on the nape of her neck. She had one of those square-jawed faces that looks grim when the mouth is set and pretty when it smiles. Nancy noticed that she had little wrinkles at the corners of her eyes.

Maureen was taller and quieter than Greta but told her story every bit as bluntly. She came from Middlesbrough and had been working in a textiles factory since she was fourteen.

"Money in t' factories is good now," she reflected, dragging on her cigarette and patting her hair slowly. "But I wanted an

excuse to get out of that place. Any excuse. It's a bit like out of
the frying pan and into the fire though, when Waite gets a sulk
on 'im.''

Nancy was puzzled.

"I'm married. That's to say, when it suits *him* I am. Married
when I were seventeen. He's run off a few times since then.''

Nancy drew in her breath. "How awful! You must have been
upset?''

"Upset? What've they taught you at your fancy school, cloth-
head? When he took off I got my only break from his drinking
and thumping me! I were more upset when he came back!''

Nancy thought she might have made Maureen angry, but she
smiled broadly and Greta and Nancy smiled too and suddenly
they were all part of the same conspiracy.

"Time we were getting back to work,'' said Greta. "We're
only supposed to stop for five minutes.''

Nancy was disappointed. She wanted to sit and talk to the
landgirls all afternoon and forget about what time it was. She
wanted to hear about Maureen's husband and Greta's dancing.
They were so much funnier than other girls she knew and they
were brave too, coming to work on a lonely farm when neither
of them had ever seen the countryside before, sharing a tiny attic
with only cold water to wash in, humping bales of hay that were
a back-breaking load even for a man.

She smiled graciously and thanked them for the cigarette, but
her disappointment was obvious, for Maureen said, "Here
Nancy, why don't you come up to the farm later tonight and
have a drink with us. Oh—'' She clapped her hand to her mouth
and giggled. "It's *Saturday!*''

She looked at Greta and they both snorted with laughter.
"Shall we?''

Greta nodded.

"There's a special treat provided up at the farmhouse every
Saturday,'' continued Maureen with mock gravity, "and Miss
Fryer and myself would be honoured if you would come and
partake. Ten o'clock.''

Brittany stopped Nancy in the hall as she was going out that
night.

"Nancy, where are you off to, darling? It's a little late for a
walk. It's almost dark.''

Nancy thought the truth might deflect her mother's attention
from the bottle of vintage claret that was sticking out of her bag,

so she explained at exhaustive length, describing her walk to the Home Farm and her subsequent acquaintance with Greta and Maureen.

Her mother frowned. "I'm not sure how your father would feel about you gallivanting around on one of the farms. It looks as though we're abusing our position of landlords. If you wanted an evening out, surely you could have taken the bus into Wells and gone to the pictures or something?"

"I did that last week, Mummy."

Nancy used the cold, distant voice that made people afraid to cross her.

"And if a five-mile bus ride to the nearest town is the wildest dissipation that I can hope for, then you ought to feel sorry for me."

Brittany shrugged, knowing full well that Nancy would do exactly as she wished, even if it meant letting herself out of her bedroom window on a rope of sheets. In fact she would probably have enjoyed that even more.

"Off you go then." She walked to the front door and held it open for her daughter. "And please don't come back too late. I do worry, you know."

Nancy ran all the way to the farm, clutching her precious burden to her chest. They drank it in the girls' garret room, sitting on a circle of upturned packing cases with an ashtray in the centre like a sacrificial offering. Nancy was shocked by the meanness of the room. The floor was bare and dusty and there was no shade over the bare bulb, no curtain at the window to prevent the moonlight streaming in and blending eerily with the electric light. She was even more shocked at Maureen and Greta's apparent lack of concern with their surroundings.

"This stuff's good," said Maureen happily, blowing smoke into a ring above her Titian head and resting her elbows on corduroy clad knees. ("We've decided to keep our trousers on in future," Greta said. "The sun burned our bleedin' legs to bits, didn't it, Mo?") "I've never had proper wine before. Only the paint stripper they served in this restaurant in Middlesbrough that I went to once. The works manager took me there one night. Wanted to impress me before he tried to get into me knickers."

They finished the wine quickly as though drinking were a mere preliminary and not to be lingered over. Greta looked at a little clock by her head.

"Right, time to go."

It was half past ten.

Nancy followed Greta and Maureen into the yard behind the farmhouse. It was a still, clear night and the moon was yellow as butter. They clambered onto the back of an empty cart and from this platform they had a good view of the upper half of the house. A dog barked uninterestedly.

"What are we supposed to be looking at?" hissed Nancy.

"Shhh!" Greta put a finger to her carmine painted lips and pointed at the window on the left. A light was switched on, but as in the girls' room there were no curtains to draw.

"Too tight-fisted for curtains," muttered Maureen, reading Nancy's thoughts. Mrs Waite had come into the bedroom and was sitting at a dressing table opposite the window, removing her curlers. She was a large, square woman with dark brows and mannish arms. Nancy watched, fascinated, as the farmer's wife applied powder to her face with a puff and outlined her lips with a stick the colour of rotting roses. She was breathless with curiosity about what the Saturday ritual entailed, although she had a sneaking suspicion she already knew.

Mr Waite came into the room. He said something to his wife and then stood waiting while she brushed out her hair, rocking his small, sinewy body up and down on the balls of his feet. He seemed impatient.

Mrs Waite finally stood up and moved over to the bed and lay down in a poor imitation of a temptress on a tiger skin. She was wearing nothing but a thin negligé through which her breasts were visible, like huge white moons, like the pale cheeses she kept in the dairy that Nancy had visited once as a child.

Mrs Waite parted her large blue-white thighs.

Nancy stared. Maureen sniggered.

Mr Waite had been forgotten, but suddenly he stepped forward to the end of the bed like an actor following a cue. The deep sunburned red of his face and forearms was bounded by an abrupt line and the rest of his skin was white, except for his member which bobbed darkly out in front of him. He lowered himself down onto the bed and then, after a blur of movement which seemed to Nancy to last for only a few seconds, he straightened up and stepped back a few paces. Nancy looked for the thing that she had seen before but it was gone. With precise, neat movements, he donned a pair of shapeless striped pyjamas and combed his fearsome grey moustache.

The "ritual" was over.

"It's the pyjamas that kill me," whispered Greta, "I always expect him to salute when he gets to that bit."

"It's exactly the same every Saturday, ten thirty sharp," said Maureen, daring Nancy to doubt her. "And there's nothing else to entertain us, so . . . They ought to get some curtains or a blackout. Anyhow, that's it until next week, folks!"

She swung her long legs over the side of the cart and the others scrambled down after her. The dog barked a warning.

"I ought to be getting back," murmured Nancy. She brushed cobwebs from her cotton dress, bleached white by the moonlight.

"First we're going to show you our den, Nance," said Greta firmly. They took Nancy to a disused Dutch barn on the edge of the farmyard and proudly showed her to the corner that was theirs. And she understood at once why their bedroom looked so unlived in and lacked personal touches. Pictures of film stars torn from magazines plastered the walls, there were two armchairs with rugs thrown over them and a gramophone. A small table had been draped with a lace-trimmed cloth and crammed with hoarded hairpins, nail polish and a bottle of *Evening in Paris*. There was even a primus stove.

"Mrs Waite snooped around in our room back in the house," explained Greta, "so we moved our precious stuff out here."

Nancy pointed to a photograph on the wall. It showed a brawny young man with his shirt sleeves rolled up. "Who's that?"

"My husband," said Maureen, lighting a Woodbine.

"Why on earth d'you keep a picture of him in here? I thought you hated him."

"I never said that, did I?" Maureen's face wore its grim look.

"But he treated you badly, and—"

Maureen shook her head slowly. "She's got a lot to learn, hasn't she, Greta?" She tapped Nancy on the shoulder, not unkindly. "Come on, we've got to be up at the crack of dawn, carting bales."

"Even on a Sunday?"

"Even on a Sunday."

As they crossed the farmyard again, Nancy said, "I wish I could help you. It's awful having nothing to do. Mummy doesn't trust me enough to let me go to London." She shone her torch and illuminated the two smiling faces beneath their haloes of brass and copper.

"Well, why don't you come and give us a hand?" asked Greta. "No need to ask Waite's permission. You own the bleedin' place."

Nancy was struck forcibly by Greta's logic as she trudged back to Graylings, shaking her torch to revive its ageing batteries. She had decided not to return to school in September, but that meant finding some sort of work. The idea of working with Greta and Maureen all day made her smile with sheer pleasure. The three of them would be able to act just as they liked and nobody would be able to tell them otherwise.

The next morning she returned to the Home Farm and told Mr Waite that he had acquired a new landgirl.

It was clear that the idea displeased him, but he was unable to refuse her because she was Mr Stein's daughter. This fact buoyed Nancy, as did the knowledge gleaned at the ritual.

"The girls are new to this part of the world," she reasoned. "Who better to show them the ropes than someone who's lived here all her life? And the government keeps appealing to us to 'Lend a hand on the land'. You won't have to provide me with lodging. You won't even have to feed me . . ."

She smiled her most demure smile at Mr Waite and thought, *I've seen him without his trousers on.*

George shared his mother's view that anything capable of keeping his sister out of trouble was a godsend.

When he returned to Graylings on leave that autumn, Nancy had been working as an unofficial member of the Women's Land Army for two months and professed to be perfectly satisfied with her lot. She rose at first light each morning and George sometimes caught sight of her sauntering down the lane in the greying dawn dressed in jodhpurs and a thick sweater, her lustrous hair cascading from a restraining ribbon. She returned late, too late. Long after the farm labourers had left the fields and darkness had fallen, there would be a crash as the front door slammed and Nancy kicked her boots off, singing. Usually she had been drinking.

At any other time, George would have been sorry that his sister spent so little time at Graylings, but not now. Not after what he had seen. She had been afraid that things would be different when he came back, and she had been right. He would not have been able to talk to her as he used to in the old days. Some days there was not much to do except sit in the library and read, but hard as he might look at the black print on the white paper, George still saw night battle in North Africa. Even the old toys in his room were tainted. When he looked at the proud battalion of lead soldiers frozen in formation as they marched across the top of a tall-boy he remembered the plumed dust thrown up by enemy shell-fire. The desperate scurrying of trucks trying to free their wheels in the sand. The flickering of scarlet fire where wrecks burned and glowed in the dusk. A corpse dangling from the turret of an armoured car like a doll with no sawdust.

And if he shut his eyes he could smell the war: mingled sweat and spices in a Cairo bazaar, the choking human stench of blood splashing onto sand.

He had escaped the Italian assault on Mersah Matruh. Others had been captured and taken to camps in southern Italy. As he ran to the jeep waiting to carry him out of the firing line, he had stopped to help someone who had been shot, a boy no older than himself. The jeep revved its engine impatiently as shells exploded all around it. George had thrown the boy's arm around his shoulder and began to run again, half carrying, half dragging the boy.

"Stop, stop," he had screamed, *"I've got to go!"* His eyes were wide and pleading.

George remembered being told that a bullet in the guts produces an unbearable urge to empty the bowels.

"There's no time you stupid bastard!" he gasped, but the boy still screamed and dragged his heels.

So George had loosened the boy's trousers and supported the damp, clammy body while the others screamed for him to hurry and the dying soldier strained his empty innards over the cold sand.

Cambridge was as distant as a nursery rhyme. Even his brief holiday at Christmas seemed lost and faraway as though behind a veil. A dark veil woven out of other men's deaths . . .

Christmas hadn't been such a happy time anyway, he told himself, so there was no use idealizing it. Jake had seemed driven by the need to impress his American cousin, his mother had been unnerved by him, Nancy rendered irretrievably silly. None of them had been true to themselves in front of that smiling reptile with a gold watch. There was just one thing from the holiday that stood out and made him long to return home.

Meeting Annabel Steele.

He had thought of her endlessly in North Africa, conjuring up her calm face each time he needed to still the terror in his stomach. And he had relived the Stanwyckes' party as many times, replaying it like an old, worn reel of film. The things they had talked about and the pauses in between. In the dust and the heat he could see the soft, cool colour of her green jersey and the way it set off the translucency of her skin.

The Egyptian sun had become the heat from the carved fireplace against the backs of their legs as they compared subjects they liked at school and found they were the same. Then George told her that he had been studying agricultural science at Cambridge and was touched when she responded by telling him about her flower garden at Heathcote. He even remembered the words she used to describe it: "The only lovely thing about the place."

"Not quite the only thing," he had replied gallantly and she gave him a bashful smile. How odd that Annabel was the same age as Nancy! Behind her child's face lay a person far older and wiser than he was, yet he could not rid himself of the strange urge to protect and somehow comfort her. When their conversation ended he went on looking at her. His mother had looked at her a good deal, too.

George had ten days to spend at Graylings that autumn. On the sixth day he almost collided with Leonora as she drifted into the driveway and he walked briskly out of it to exercise Nancy's spaniel.

Leonora smiled up at him, her thick, dark hair lifted by a strong wind. She liked George. She did not think him handsome, exactly, but his sea-green eyes were kind and the way his hair waved back from his forehead gave his face an open look.

He noticed that she was wearing an apron under her coat. "Just got back from the canteen, Leonora? I hope the hungry masses were suitably grateful for your efforts."

"I don't know what I'm going to do about the potatoes."

George was accustomed to Leonora's non sequiturs. He clutched the lead tightly in his gloved hand. Amber leaves scurried over their feet.

"I told Annabel I'd bring them—"

"Annabel?"

Leonora brushed a strand of ebony hair out of her eyes, which had taken on the faintest glimmer of slyness. "Annabel Steele. Do you know her? She helps out in the mornings. The potatoes—"

The spaniel whined at a leaf and started tugging at the lead. "Which potatoes?" asked George patiently.

"Your mother said we could have a few sacks of potatoes for nothing and I've said I'll bring them, but I don't know how to get them down to the village. I don't know if there's a car available, or how you're managing for petrol—"

"We've still got the Citroën on the road," said George quickly. "I could drive them down in the morning if you'll show me where they are."

The next day he carefully arranged to drive exactly half way through the morning to maximize his chance of finding Annabel Steele there. The canteen was run from the village hall, a long, low one-storey building with grimy windows, smelling of damp khaki and stew.

She was there.

Perhaps she won't remember me, he thought.

"George! How nice to see you!" The sleeves of her jersey were rolled up and he noticed the fine, golden hairs on her forearms.

"I've brought the potatoes," he said solemnly, and they both laughed. The other women turned to look in their direction and Annabel's childlike face flushed. She looked down hastily and started to chop the carrots that were heaped on a board in front of her.

"Look, I mustn't keep you from your work. I'll see you again Annabel—"

"No, it's all right, I—"

He started to speak and then closed his mouth. He wanted to tell her everything, but how could he? She waited, knife poised in the air, for him to speak. As if she knew. So instead he told her that he only had a few days' leave and would she care to meet him for a drink one evening.

She blushed again and said, "Yes." In a tiny voice so that no one else could overhear.

"Greville!" shouted Patrick, "Greville, will you bloody well come here!"

Greville went into the kitchen and found Patrick sitting at the table, pulling off his mud-caked boots. He had left school in the summer to work on one of the Steele farms which had had its work-force decimated by the war.

"Don't tell me, old man, let me guess . . . you've decided to renounce agriculture and join a monastery?"

"Stop pissing about, Greville—"

"You're about to cook dinner for us and you need my help?"

"Annabel's already done that. All we have to do is to heat it up." Patrick nodded towards a large pan of stew and a heap of peeled potatoes on the draining board. "That's what I want to ask you about. She says she's going for a drink with a girl from school, but I don't believe her. I thought you would probably know what she's up to, since you know bloody everything.''

''Well, as a matter of fact I don't. But I'm sure there's nothing to worry about. A sweetheart—''

''She's too bloody young for that stuff! I'm her brother and I'm supposed to look after her! I want you to stop her!''

Greville patted his shoulder. ''You know, you're not making sense, old boy. Why don't we let her have a wee bit of fun? And if it looks as though it's going to develop into something, we'll sort it out. OK?''

He went into the hall and found Annabel undoing the bolts on the heavy front door. She blushed when she saw him.

''Oh! Greville . . . I'm just off now.''

''And very bonny you look too, my dear. Blue is very becoming.''

''There was a couple of letters for you today, Greville. I left them in the kitchen. One from the Inland Revenue and one from the Crown Agents. They looked terribly official.''

Greville paled slightly. ''Just boring old business matters, I'm afraid. Run along now and enjoy yourself.''

''You haven't told Patrick—''

''That you're meeting George Stein? No, don't worry, your secret's safe with me.''

''It's just that I'm afraid he'll follow me. You know what he's like.''

''I'll keep Patrick out of the way. You just concentrate on making a good impression.''

Before he left Graylings, George sat on the edge of his bed for a long time, thinking.

The house was still, resting. Nancy was not yet back from the farm. His mother was with the children, trying to settle them for the night, and downstairs Marion was helping Mrs Burrows clear up after the children's supper. From the kitchens the still air carried a faint metallic scraping and the pungent smell of leftover cabbage. The evacuees had made a difference to the smell of the house. It now reminded George of his preparatory school. You could almost smell their dirty fingernails.

He was worrying about making a good impression on Annabel. As it grew dark, he had realised with a strange, fluttering panic that he had no experience of this sort of thing, none at all. He did not know if he was attractive to the opposite sex, he did not know what to talk about; he did not even know what to wear.

In Cambridge it was easy. Girls had always been there to make up a group, and George had simply taken his cue from his friends. One followed a sort of code.

He had also failed to plan where they would spend the evening but Annabel did not seem to mind. In fact she seemed as lost as he was. They had arranged to meet in the lane outside her house, rather than have George come and call for her, and he stood waiting in the dark until he heard her footsteps echo on the stone path.

"I've told Patrick I'm going for a drink with a girl friend," Annabel explained breathlessly. "Otherwise he'll only try and come with me." George nodded to show that he understood and remembered Nancy's verdict on Patrick Steele. The possessive type.

She was wearing a sky-blue sweater and looked very happy. George led the way to the village pub, the only place within a radius of several miles where they might sit and drink. The Lamb and Child had been short of beer for months and the place smelled sour and disused as they pushed open the heavy wooden door. Underfoot, the flagstones were greasy with damp. George went in first. His gaze fell instantly on Nancy and the two land-girls, bright and brittle with their dyed hair and harsh voices. They were still in their muddy uniforms, huddled around a circular table and gesticulating with lit cigarettes.

He stepped back and let the door swing shut.

"We can't go in there—Nancy's in there with her friends."

"Does it matter if she sees you?" asked Annabel patiently.

"Not exactly. It's just my sister. She's—"

What *was* Nancy? Selfish? Unapproachable? Mocking? Nancy could not be defined. George shrugged helplessly.

Annabel touched the sleeve of his coat. "That's all right. I understand." She still seemed happy. "I've got a better idea anyway. Somewhere we can be alone. I'll have to go back to the house for a minute first, though."

George smiled after her gratefully as she disappeared into the night. She returned a few minutes later with a torch in one hand and a flask in the other. "Brandy," she said with satisfaction.

Even with the torch lit, the darkness was suffocating. Annabel took George's arm to guide him, leaning on him slightly as she did so. He imagined her warmth reaching through his coat to his skin and the thought excited him. At the end of the village, the high street began to widen where it joined the main road to Wells and the distances between houses grew greater. Set back a few feet from the road was a small, concrete building with a door and no windows.

"It's a shelter," whispered Annabel. "Local government were provided with some money to build one, but nobody ever uses it. Kit and his friends come and play in it sometimes."

They went down a steep flight of steps and into what George would have described as a concrete cave. Their shoes crunched the loose grit that covered the floor and the sound echoed. Annabel flicked the thin beam of the torch around the walls.

"There are some candles somewhere." She was still whispering.

They lit five candles and the shelter was filled with a muzzy, yellow glow. There was a bed against one wall, covered with coarse blankets, and a bucket behind a partition. Nothing else. They huddled close on the bed, still in their overcoats, and drank the brandy and talked until their breathing warmed the room.

They talked for a very long time. George told Annabel everything. He was going to spare her the tale of the soldier who could not "go", but in the end he told her that too.

"How awful," was all she said. Then, "That poor, poor boy." And she pressed her cheek against him so that his tears mingled with her own.

Much later, she said, "George, I like being in this place much better than I like being at home."

"So do I."

Her head was resting against his shoulder and she squeezed his hand. "I expect you don't feel as though you live there any longer."

He looked at her face and her wide, innocent eyes. They were grey, not in the way that Nancy's were grey, but mingling blue, grey and purple. "How did you know?"

"I just do." She stroked the top of his head with one finger and the silver hip flask slid out of her grasp and rattled onto the floor. "George . . ." She hesitated a little. "Can we stay here tonight? I mean all night."

He felt his whole body waken and tingle with longing. The candle flames quivered against the wall, shading a halo from intense gold to grey. "Yes, but . . . won't they notice that you're not at home?"

Annabel's eyes were defiant. "It's so late that if I wake them up coming in now, there'll be hell to pay. Better if I go back in the morning and pretend I was there all along."

They climbed under the blankets with their clothes on at first, but it seemed silly now the room was no longer cold, so they shed them in layers. There was more shyness on George's part than Annabel's. She pressed close as though she wanted him to absorb her small body in his . . .

He had not meant to do it, but his flesh grew hot against hers and he felt himself pushing into her. It was a lot easier and a lot more comfortable than he had imagined it would be. His body was telling him to move his hips rhythmically and he did so, but really he wanted them to lie still with their faces pressed cheek to cheek as though they were dancing, as though they were still innocent. They fell asleep like that with their bodies joined, warm and wet.

In the morning George felt overwhelmed by a sense of loss as he watched Annabel step quietly from the bed and prepare to leave. He wanted to cry for her as a child cries for its mother, and have her take him in her arms again. Then he remembered his own leaving, and felt desperately afraid. Only two more days.

He reached out and caught hold of her fingers, pulling them until she was forced to sit down on the bed.

"Annabel, will you marry me?"

Greville Dysart had forgotten to put up the blackout, and the thin grey dawn light woke him earlier than usual. He glanced at the alarm clock by his bed. Seven fifteen. Not really worth going back to sleep. He would go down and make some tea.

He fastened his paisley dressing gown around his ample waist and went down to the kitchen. It smelt stale and unwelcoming. The kettle felt cold to the touch. Strange, thought Greville, Annabel's usually been down by now and made herself a pot . . .

He carried his cup of tea upstairs again and stopped outside Annabel's door.

"Annabel?"

There was no reply.

Inside, her bed was neat and untouched. Her silver-backed brushes were arranged precisely on the top of the ruffled dressing table. The curtains were drawn back.

Greville looked at the undefiled bed and laughed softly to himself.

Four
February 1944

"*I'LL BE SCARLETT!*" Nancy insisted.

She had been inspired by her recent trip to Wells to see *Gone With the Wind*. She jumped down from the back of the trailer and pulled a parsnip out of the soil. She crammed a corner of it into her mouth and then waved the remains of the vegetable skyward in a German salute. "As God is my witness, I'll never be hungry again!"

Greta clapped her gloved hands together slowly. "She should have been in cabaret, shouldn't she, Mo? Completely wasted out here."

Maureen nodded. "Selznick might at least have tested her for the part of Scarlett. She's got the hair for it if not the seventeen-inch waist."

She was sitting on the back of the trailer hitched to the tractor, drinking cocoa from a thermos and eating sandwiches. Her legs, clad in boots and gaiters, dangled down. Round her shoulders she sported a mackintosh lined with rabbit fur that gave her an incongruous air of chic. Behind her, and clearly visible above her apricot hair, was a large mound of manure.

"Come on lazy bones!" called Greta. "There's a lot of parsnips to be pulled and a lot of muck to be spread before we get out of this place."

She stooped over her hoe again, singing cheerfully:

"*You are my sunshine*
My double Woodbine
My box of matches
My Craven A . . ."

Maureen jumped off the trailer and fell to. Soon all three of them were singing, warbling their adulterated version of the popular song.

The friendship between the girls was one of complete equality. Maureen's stolidity and Greta's more vivacious nature were complementary and neither dominated the other. Nancy's status as squire's daughter did not place her above the others nor did her swift wit, as it had done at St Clare's. They shared their tasks equally, and any sharp words prompted by exhaustion were always forgotten by the next day. A common language evolved: a language depicting the ill-assorted Waites, their never-ending toil and the hardships of war, and as it grew richer the different shadows cast by their former lives were honed down to the smooth fit of three component parts.

The only disparity that remained was wages. Nancy was un-paid for her work, but as Greta pointed out, the twenty-two shillings and sixpence left after they had paid for board and lodging was hardly enough to start a revolution.

Nancy had just celebrated her seventeenth birthday. Months of hard physical work had thickened her body with a layer of muscle, a development that was all the more marked since her height had stopped increasing. She was resigned to the fact that she would never be tall, but in her view the neat, hourglass figure was now too stocky. Ridges of muscle squared her shoulders and her gait. She took for granted a daily level of exertion that she would never have dreamed possible as she waved a lacrosse stick langorously across the playing fields of St Clare's, and it showed in her stance.

From a distance she looked much older than her seventeen years.

"You remind me of me mam these days," Maureen had said, looking reprovingly at Nancy's chapped, purple hands. But though she was unpaid, she was better fed than the other two and had avoided their continual winter colds. Her hair could still trap and tease the February light like dark satin.

Nancy marched the furrows in her boots and ill-fitting canvas gaiters, kicking parsnips from the frozen soil. She made a bleak figure against the snow-powdered landscape and bare trees, her outline rendered even more square by the army overcoat she wore. It had been worn by her grandfather Gerald Colby during the Great War and returned to Graylings in a brown paper parcel that Nancy had found torn open and discarded in a corner of the attic. The coat was caked with mud and stained with dried blood. Whose blood, Nancy wondered? Brittany hated her wearing it and winced whenever she saw it, but Nancy wore it anyway. That was how she was.

She straightened up and watched Maureen and Greta moving separately across the field, gathering the detested parsnips. From a distance they resembled two large crows, pecking at the ground. She thought about her mother, more distanced than ever since Nancy had been working at the farm. Brittany watched her daughter with mistrust, as though she were an alien being. And why did her mother insist on giving the impression that there was no situation she had not met and dealt with before, no facet of human lore untried by her, no secret remaining in the universe that she had not probed? Her wisdom was a mantle of smugness that Nancy felt a contemptuous urge to tear down.

But she was too content to give much thought to her mother's early life. Her existence on the land did not require her to look either forwards or back. She arose every morning and sang on her way to work because she knew that the day ahead held nothing more threatening or unpleasant than cold fingers or chilblains, but there was a good chance it might also contain a great deal of laughter.

Such a day had been the Day of the Pig, when Greta and Maureen had dressed the Waites' prize sow in a frilled pinafore and let her loose in the high street. And then there was the Day of the Signposts. Village signposts had been blanked out with white paint when German invasion threatened in the summer of 1940. The blank spaces that had once proclaimed ''Wells 4'' or ''Wedmore 3'' proved too tempting to the disruptive spirit, and armed with a pot of black paint Nancy, Greta and Maureen spent a Sunday afternoon directing strangers and Nazi spies to ''Shangri-La'' or ''Eternity'' . . .

They returned to Home Farm at dusk. Greta drove the tractor with Maureen and Nancy squatting in the trailer on top of the parsnips, and during the journey they continued the endless debate on how to take short cuts with the running of the farm and minimize the effort required.

''There must be a quicker way of gathering the wretched parsnips than walking up and down with a bucket and going back to the trailer every five minutes to empty it . . .''

Maureen laughingly suggested that one of them drove the tractor slowly up and down the furrows while the others threw the parsnips onto it as it passed in conveyor-belt fashion, ''—like 'Plough the Fields and Scatter' in reverse.''

On that evening they had a particular reason to wish for more time at their disposal. All three girls were to attend the twice-monthly dance in Nether Aston, an event whose appeal was much enhanced by the patronage of American servicemen from a local camp. The marathon of bathing and dressing up, dancing until midnight, walking home and rising again for work at five o'clock was greeted as a way to score a small victory over Hitler. Greta already had her hair set in steel clips under her turban.

If Nancy was to be at the village hall for the start of the bun-fight she had to begin her preparation as soon as she returned to Graylings from the farm. She tossed the offending greatcoat over the newel post, flung a diffident greeting to her mother and Marion and raced up the carved marble staircase to her room, dodging several evacuee children impatiently. They stared after her, their hands raised to their mouths.

The hordes of servicemen who flocked to village dances had revolutionized them. Nancy could remember creeping down to spy on the proceedings with George one Saturday night before the war and seeing, to her disgust, *girls* dancing with *girls*. Now there were never enough girls to go around and an "excuse me" system had to be introduced for most of the dances. Nancy smiled ruefully as she looked down at her black satin dancing pumps. Their soles were worn thin and rough after only a few months, from the delightful penance of being continually in demand.

"There's only one time when they'll let you take your feet off the floor," Maureen commented ruefully when she could see daylight through her own soles, ". . . and you know when *that* is."

To spare her shoes further torture, Nancy drove into the village in her mother's Citroën Light 15. Brittany had been reluctant to lend the car at first, on the grounds that petrol was too scarce and that Nancy would probably have drunk too much to complete her return journey safely. Nancy had given a careless shrug, wrapped Gerald Colby's blood-stained coat around her and stalked to the front door, her hair gleaming silkily as she passed beneath the domed skylight. Like everything else she did, it was a calculated move: her appearance had quickly weakened Brittany's resolve.

They struck a bargain.

Nancy would leave the greatcoat behind and wear her mother's fur instead, and in return she could take the car. Nancy sniffed reluctantly at the fur. She had made a point of eschewing the trappings that would make Greta and Maureen look poor or shabby. But on this occasion, she reflected as she pressed her satin-shod foot down firmly on the accelerator and sped up the great sweeping arc of the driveway, it would be useful in scoring points off Maudie Lester.

She raised one eyebrow at herself in the driving mirror. The crowded, smoky hall would be dimly lit, and a generous application of cosmetics was essential to prevent one's face fading

entirely into the gloom. Greta had tutored Nancy in the art of
self-enhancement, but had failed to persuade her to pluck her
generous dark eyebrows into fashionably thin lines. Her eyebrows could give her a stern look which was useful. The grey
eyes that looked back at her were subtly outlined with eyeliner
and her small, determined mouth daubed boldly with Carnival
Red.

Tonight no one will think I'm only seventeen, thought Nancy
as she sailed down into the village, no one. Not in this dress.

It was a gift from Jake, the sort of dress that could no longer
be bought in England. He had had it sent from New York, a
knee-length shift of steel-grey jersey. From the padded shoulders, delicate fronds of silver sequins pointed to Nancy's plump
bosom and neat, ruched waist. Truly a dress with which to taunt
the Maudie Lesters of this world.

"Blimey Nance, you look like a bleedin' film star!"

Greta had seen the rough wooden doors of the village part
with a curiously sultry movement. She wove her way expertly
through the tightly-packed, swaying couples to Nancy's elbow,
sniffing enviously at the luxurious silver fur. "Where d'you get
that, then?"

Nancy shrugged off the coat and smiled down at it mockingly.
"Mother's."

And in her heart she knew she mocked herself too, for was
she not secretly every bit as vain as her mother, and had she not
that very evening spent a considerable length of time staring
arrogantly into the mirror in her clean, spartan bedroom and
assessing what she saw with a conceited eye?

"Maureen's gone and got herself fixed up already . . . with a
darkie!" Greta hissed, signalling frantically with her eyes.

Through the smoke haze that hung beneath dimmed, naked
light bulbs, Nancy saw Maureen pressed close against the front
of a tall, vast-chested negro, a resigned look in her eye and a
green ostrich feather tippet fluttering defiantly against her red
hair. Then she slowly took in the rest of the room. The blackout
screens nailed over the windows had been swathed with colourful drapes and the effect was one of being enclosed in a hot,
secret cave, a fairyland after the bleak, open fields. There were
uniforms of every shade of blue and khaki; jiving, jitter-bugging,
waltzing and even attempting the rumba, and the walls swelled
with brash, enthusiastic laughter. A makeshift bar had been
erected in one corner of the room, serving, beer, cider, and

lemonade and, for those who were clever enough, paper cups full of PX scotch.

And leaning against the bar, surrounded by tipsy GIs, was Maudie Lester.

It had taken Maudie an hour and a half to squeeze her frowsy auburn hair into an interesting pyramid of permed curls, thirty minutes to iron her old, faded print dress and forty minutes to dull her too-rosy complexion with pancake foundation. Plus five minutes to cram her feet into her younger sister's shoes.

And then Mis Nancy Stein walked in, her hair bouncing lightly and smoothly on her shoulders like a raven-haired Veronica Lake, a fur floating around her, for all the world like an expensive cover girl.

She counted the men, just as she'd counted the precious minutes of preparation. She counted the men who turned to look at Nancy Stein, including Sergeant Johnny Randall, and a familiar resentment dug its fingernails deep into the wall of her chest.

Maudie Lester was one of the few people in Nether Aston who had greeted the war with delight. September 1939 found her flouncing down the village streets with new vigour, a song on her broad lips. Now, with any luck, she told herself, I'll have a chance to get out of this dump . . .

The Lesters managed Coombe Farm. They were tenants first of the Colbys, then the Steins, and during the period when Adrian Steele lived at Graylings, Maudie's aunt Phoebe had worked as his secretary. There had always been Lesters in this part of the world and they carried themselves with a sort of slovenly pride. After all, local people respected such continuity. The farm thrived, though more as a result of the prime, fertile land than Mr Lester's haphazard methods.

Over the years Daniel Lester and his vague, dishevelled wife had watched the sprawling, ramshackle farmhouse fill with a brood of noisy children, of whom Maudie was the eldest. At twenty-four she still swayed through that same house, high heels clacking on the tile floors, puffing vengefully on a cigarette with painted lips, nothing to do and nowhere to go. There was a girl like Maudie Lester in every village in England, a frustrated Lorelei wasting her song on hoes and hayricks, the petals of the bud opening, ripening and blowing over quite unseen.

Maudie had quite a voice, or at least, that's what she told herself. She could have been a singer or a dancer, if only she weren't *here* . . .

When she was eighteen she had run away to London for a

while, but returned three weeks later in a state of near starvation. She had failed to take into account that in quiet, backwater Nether Aston she was *Maudie Lester*, the object of male cat-calls and female gossip, but in London nobody knew who Maudie Lester was, and nobody cared. Nobody looked twice, mostly they didn't even look once. After her return, the slowly churning years turned her shame into a silent, sulking anger.

And then the war came.

Maudie hastily signed up for war work, but the factory in the Midlands to which she was assigned was hardly the opportunity she had been longing for. There weren't even any men, only more women; so for the second time in her life Maudie returned disgruntled to Coombe Farm. But if anyone had asked her class-mates at the girls' high school in Wells what they would have predicted for Maudie Lester, it would have been a lot more than this. Maudie Lester was bright and, more importantly, Maudie Lester was good-looking. Everyone thought so. Her rich auburn hair could look a little frowsy and untidy, but she had unex-pectedly prominent Slavic cheekbones and a big, hot mouth.

When her hair was in place and she looked her best, Maudie would pout at herself and say, "Hey girl, you could be *anything*. Even a movie star . . ."

For a while Maudie had the consolation of knowing that *here*, at least, she was the greatest marvel nature could boast. The arrival of the landgirls had changed all that. They were in the Lamb and Child most nights, making a spectacle of themselves, laughing and joking with the men; and the men liked that, they even started to look out for them. And naturally they did not spend so much time looking at Maudie Lester, or whispering about her; why should they when they had the high-and-mighty Miss Stein to gawp at, busting cutely out of her tight breeches.

And then the Americans had arrived.

Tonight there were plenty of them to go around, and that meant Nancy Stein would be kept out of the way and at a safe distance from *her* Johnny Randall. Well, he wasn't hers, not really. Johnny was from California and he had an uncle in the movie business, and he promised to mention her to him, *her*—Maudie. Leastways, that's what he said.

She turned back to the bar and pressed possessively against Johnny, sliding her lips back and forth over one another.

"Shall we dance, honey?" she asked. The "honey" sounded silly, but that was the word they used, she knew that.

"Sure." He took her hand nonchalantly and led her on to the floor. "You ever jived before? 'S easy. Just follow me."

Maudie copied the steps that he made look so effortless, swaying her hips and smiling up at his bright blue eyes. Johnny did not appear to be looking at her. He was chewing gum.

"Hey, perhaps I should come out and visit you in California," Maudie said casually. "You know—when the war's over."

The tempo changed dramatically to a slow waltz. Maudie glued herself to Johnny. She fingered his epaulettes, caressing the brass buttons, and ran a large tongue over her lower lip. The scent of sweat and cheap perfume broke over him in a wave.

"Yeah, maybe you should do that." He was looking over her left shoulder, lower jaw working the gum rhythmically. "Who's that girl?"

Maudie stiffened in his arms. "Which girl?"

"Over there—the small dark one that looks like a fashion plate." Johnny's eyes, jaw and chewing gum pointed in the direction of Nancy Stein.

Nancy was in the arms of a freckled farmer's son from Oklahoma who called himself Skip. The excuse-me system did not seem to be in operation that evening so she was stuck with him for the time being, but Nancy was quite gratified that she had time for reflection and observation and besides, it was easier on the shoes. Maureen and the negro with the flashing smile had both disappeared and Greta was dandled coquettishly on the knee of a United States Air Force officer, dropping cashew nuts into his mouth one by one. The uniform reminded Nancy of Guy Exley.

"Excuse me fella," said a voice at the back of her neck, "d'ya mind if I dance with your girl?"

"Sure, why not," said Skip. "As long as I can exchange her for this pretty lady here." He smiled cheerfully at Maudie Lester's rigid face.

Johnny Randall quick-stepped Nancy away, spinning her around so fast that they both laughed and bumped against other couples, provoking frowns and murmurs of "Careful mate!" When they had stopped laughing they slowed down and talked.

She found him pleasant enough, but then they all were, these boys. They all seemed the same to Nancy. She wished this one would not hold her quite so possessively but she allowed the familiarity because Maudie Lester's eyes were burning into her back and that amused her. Sergeant Randall was overjoyed to hear that she was half American and as she had expected, this

piece of news prompted the usual refrain. "You must come and
visit me in California when we're through with this." He tried
to pin her down with his ingenuous blue gaze but she averted
her eyes slightly. He persisted, "No kidding, Nancy—I mean
it."

The borrowed gramophone bumped and scratched its way
through *Lili Marlene*, notes muffled and lost in the thick, stinging cigarette smoke. The air in the crowded wooden hut was
close with body heat. Greta and her officer had disappeared into
the shadows and Nancy suddenly wearied of the desperate gaiety
and the hasty coupling. She steered Johnny Randall back to his
rightful place.

"I'm tired, I think I'll go home now," she said vaguely, dismissively. "See you in Hollywood."

Maudie Lester's teeth ground behind her scarlet lips. She
grasped Johnny firmly by the wrist. Her eyes were hostile above
her belligerent cheekbones. Nancy lowered her eyes very slowly
to where she could glimpse a bulge of mottled lilac flesh.

"Oh Maudie," she said, "look—you've laddered your nylons."

And with the faintest of smirks, she was gone.

That year Somerset enjoyed several weeks of rare, enchanted
summer weather, a blessed salve to war weariness. Each day
opened in a golden haze with birds calling shrilly like phantoms
in the mist. And each day ended in the dark, rapturous green of
fading light and intolerable loveliness.

One Friday Brittany stood in the french windows, inhaling the
drowsy scent of roses and musky wallflowers, of baldock and
lavender and clove-scented pinks. Most of Lucienne Colby's
walled flower garden on the left-hand edge of Graylings' classical facade had been given over to the cultivation of extra vegetables and the raising of hens, but Brittany had kept her precious herbaceous borders. She watched the butterflies jumping
and flirting above the warm petals, pressing and opening their
wings ecstatically, then starting off again. The air was very still.

Before the summer came Brittany had feared she was growing
old. The cold reached probing fingers into her bones, her face
felt tight and drawn, her mouth thin and dried out. But the sun
had streaked her bronze hair with topaz and she wore it loose in
a long page-boy that belied her forty-six years. With the cold
had gone a diet of potato and bread and now her waist was
thinner. Her face was thinner too, accentuating her extraordi-

narily long blue eyes. Nefertiti's eyes, David Stein had called them, in the days when they were lovers.

The warm, dry weather was the perfect excuse for Brittany to relax the evacuees' timetable of lessons and let them spend most of their time out of doors.

They had been set to play croquet in the garden that afternoon, or at least their own version of the game which involved using the balls as bowls and sending them hurtling through the hoops by hand. They had no use for mallets. Occasionally they met with success and the ball cleared the hoop with true aim. But more often the ball went wide, or it struck the hoop, either ricocheting into the air or stopping still in its tracks beneath the arch. When this happened a little group would gather, bending and prodding in an attempt to decide whether or not it was allowed as a "goal." Brittany thought they looked like little old men, so many miniature Francis Drakes bowling while England burned.

Now Leonora had come to sit on the lawn in a deck chair, and she proved an unwitting disruption to the game. Although Leonora was completely uninterested in children—indeed, she was not very interested in anything but her own thoughts—the children remained fascinated by her, especially the younger ones. And in the way of children, they were not in the least discouraged by her repeated attempts to ignore them or repulse their advances. Leonora had sunk low in the striped, canvas deckchair, her eyes closed, her wrists dangling limply over the end of its arms. It *must* be hot, thought Brittany. Leonora had finally abandoned the fur that trailed her everywhere, come rain or shine. Two of the boys, Arthur and the runty Derek, approached quietly and cautiously, their hands behind their backs.

"Miz Lea *Nora* . . ." Leonora started slightly and opened one eye. ". . . Miz Lea Nora, Derek's got five goals!"

"Oh. Good." She closed her eyes again.

"Miz Lea *Nora*, will you come and play *croaky* with us?"

"Go away, Derek. Can't you see I want a few minutes peace and quiet?"

The boys looked at one another, puzzled. Brittany smiled, relishing their innocence. She remembered George at that age.

Do all mothers feel this way, she wondered, longing to put the clock back and see them young again. George was troubling her. He was back at Graylings again, on a week's leave. She had driven to the station to collect him, bursting with excited anticipation like a child. He was standing on the platform with his back to her and she ran to him, laughing and crying and chattering with relief. She had expected him to laugh too, but he only gave a brief smile.

The expression on his face had reminded her of Jake when he was sad. It was the look of Jake's face on the night in 1924 when he had told her he was returning to America and she had realised she was in love with him: sad and closed off . . .

Has it been so terrible, she wanted to ask George, that you can't even feel glad to be home? George had always been so even-tempered, so placid, so open that she had expected him to adapt better than most to the experience of war. He put his arm around his mother's shoulders as he walked to the car, then took it away again abruptly. And she noticed as she drove that he was looking at her out of the corner of his eye, almost slyly, as if he were trying to guess what she might be thinking. She decided to say nothing.

But the longer George was at Graylings, the clearer it became that it was not only his experiences in the Middle East that preoccupied him. He had always been a doting brother, too doting, Brittany thought at times, interested in everything Nancy did and everywhere she went, but now on her rare appearances in the house he was different. Nancy invited him to Home Farm to help the girls bale hay, but he did not go. He spent a lot of time in the village and he often went to the canteen where Leonora worked. Brittany visited the cottage one night for brandy and advice, and Leonora said she knew why he went there.

To see the Steele girl.

One of the girls was tugging at Leonora's hand, and the hand swatted her absently as though she were a fly. The girl was delighted and prodded Leonora again, eliciting the same response. Several other children joined in, clustering like bees round honey. They poked at Leonora's arms with grubby fingers and jumped back with hysterical shrieks of laughter as they dodged her back-handed swipes. She still would not be provoked into opening her eyes. Brittany turned from the window and lit a cigarette. Streaming sunlight bleached the drawing room's china blue and cream walls to milky white and she moved into the shade to rest her eyes. She was glad that Jake was coming to Somerset for the weekend. He might be able to offer some help with George.

There was a tap at the door and Marion's cheerful face appeared. "Mrs Stein—telephone call for you."

"Honey . . ."

Jake sounded apologetic and she knew already what he was going to say. It had happened so many times since Jake had been promoted to the Special Operations Executive, the Ministry of Economic Warfare's engine of subversion and sabotage.

"I've just been told there's an emergency SOE meeting down at Woburn this weekend. I'm afraid I can't duck out of it."

"I see." Brittany puffed furiously on the cigarette.

"Guy telephoned me this morning and I told him I'd bring him down to Graylings with me."

Brittany waited, saying nothing. For the second time she surrendered herself to the irritating inevitability of what was to come next.

"Brittany honey . . . I couldn't spoil his weekend plans just because mine are spoilt, could I? I rang him and told him about the meeting and he said he could get transport and drive down anyway."

"Very well."

"Look Brittany, I understand that you're not crazy about the idea, but there's nothing I can do about it, believe me. You don't have to welcome him with open arms, just be polite to the boy. Anyhow, he said he'd be happy to amuse himself . . ."

I bet he would, thought Brittany as she hung up, I just bet he would.

Mrs Burrows had laid tea on the trestle tables on the porch, which was serving as an informal dining room. As soon as the plates of sandwiches were set down, small hands emptied them and glasses of orange squash were drained with vacuuming noises. Marion hovered ineffectually above the din, crying, "Derek—where are your manners, dear?"

Brittany went to the bottom of the staircase. *"George—tea!"* she shouted.

She half expected there to be no response, but he appeared in army regulation bush shorts and cricket shirt and bare feet and strolled after her into the drawing room. He had inherited his father's olive complexion, turned so dark by the desert sun that it made his teeth and eyeballs alarmingly white. The sleeves of the flannel shirt were rolled up and the concentrated force of his naked brown skin made his limbs seem suddenly larger. Brittany was more aware of her son's physical presence than she had been since he lay as a baby in her arms.

She went out onto the cool, columned porch and poured two cups of tea, but George hesitated. "Mother," he said from the relative quiet of the drawing room, "There's something I'd like to talk to you about. Alone."

"Very well," she said placidly, as a child dodged round her knees. "We'll take our tea upstairs to the sitting room."

The small north-facing sitting room on the first-floor landing was little used in summer, and smelled of old dust and dated magazines. There were blinds drawn to protect the unchanging, and by now traditional, scheme of hesitant lemon and gold. Brittany moved to raise them, but George put up a hand to stop her.

"Don't bother with that, Mother—it's nice and cool like this."

It was not cool at all, but hot and stuffy, so Brittany concluded that whatever he was about to say, he did not want her to see his face too clearly.

"Mother, I'm getting married."

He paused expectantly. Brittany gave a quick smile. "I'm sorry, darling . . . you've rather taken me by surprise . . . Give me a minute to collect my thoughts . . ."

He raised a hand to his mouth and chewed the corner of a nail: an un-Georgelike gesture. "To Annabel Steele," he said.

Brittany was suffering from a distinct sense of shock. She didn't think of George as a man, old enough to marry, but as a child. And the prospect of his marrying Adrian Steele's daughter filled her with alarm.

Although Brittany's mother had not liked Lady Henrietta Steele, the two families had been on superficially friendly terms, and Brittany had suffered a mingled dislike and fascination for their only son, Adrian. And then her elder brother, Frederick, had died from epilepsy at the age of eighteen, and Brittany and George, the brother for whom her son was named, found themselves passed over. Graylings was left to Adrian Steele, for some strange, dark reason that was never completely understood. Was it extortion, or was Adrian's impatient opportunism simply more attractive to Gerald than the failings of his own children? One thing was certain, the decision had played a part in George Colby's suicide at the age of twenty-two . . .

But her son George and Adrian's daughter Annabel belonged to a new generation.

She tidied the back numbers of *Vogue*, feeling numb. "You're both very young," she said carefully, "I wouldn't advise such a step, George, honestly."

"Mother, I know you're not very fond of the Steeles, but Annabel's—"

She raised a hand to silence her son. "It's nothing to do with

Annabel. I'd say the same whoever your choice of partner. Even if she were Princess Elizabeth herself, I'd still say it. You've still got a lot of growing up to do, and growing up changes people. I do wish you'd wait darling.''

George thrust his hands into the pockets of his shorts and said with all the dignity of committed youth, ''We're going to wait until after the war, or until Annabel's eighteen anyway. Perhaps a bit longer. So—''

''Good—then we can talk about it again later.''

Brittany drained the last of her tea and stood up. She had no wish to prolong the discussion while she was still in a state of shock. The sincerity of George's feelings for Annabel was not in question. But how could she possibly begin to explain how she felt about his intended bride's family?

Many years earlier she had decided not to tell her children about the ugliness and wrangling of 1922 when her mother died and Adrian Steele came to Graylings to claim it as his own, leaving Brittany and her brother, George, effectively homeless. Or about the guilt that she and Susannah Stanwycke still felt over George Colby's suicide, because even when Graylings was confirmed as Brittany's, her brother still felt that he had lost both his home and Susannah, the person he needed most. She had wanted George and Nancy to inhabit a clean, sunlit world, un- corrupted by her bitterness.

But fate enjoys playing these tricks on us, she mused to herself as she carried the teacups downstairs and recalled the sight of Annabel's unhappy, neglected mother, Jennifer, hurrying away from the Nether Aston graveyard after leaving flowers on her father-in-law's grave. Who would have imagined then . . .

Outside the children were still playing on the lawn, their small figures indistinct in the hazy light of summer dusk. One of the girls had taken the white cloth from the trestle table and had draped it over her head. Then, as Brittany watched them, it dawned on her what they were doing. They were playing at wed- dings. The bride and groom linked hands and walked across the grass, followed by a flock of attendants, each holding a corner of the tablecloth.

They stopped underneath the cedar tree and Derek, apparently in an ecclesiastical role, opened a book and read from it. The ceremony was sealed with a bashful kiss and the presentation of a tightly closed daisy that the groom had picked from the lawn.

Brittany turned away from the window with a lump in her throat. George had been trying to communicate something very important, and she had been so dismissive that she had probably hurt him. She had let him down.

Oh God, I've failed him. First Nancy and now George . . .

"George!"

She ran to the foot of the stairs and called to him. "George!"

There was no reply. Overcome by a burning need to talk to someone, Brittany went out of the kitchen door and ran and ran. She ran until she came to the cottage and hammered on the door.

"Leonora?"

But Leonora was lying on her bed, snoring, with a half-empty bottle of cooking sherry beside her.

"Damn you, Leonora!"

Brittany hurried back to the house and went to her escritoire in the sitting room. Taking out a sheet of paper, she began to write.

"My darling George,

When we talked today, you may have thought that I was being flippant, or dealing in platitudes. Whatever happens, you must know that . . ."

She hesitated. ". . . That I don't much care for the idea of you marrying a Steele?"

". . . that I just want you to be happy."

After dinner on Saturday, Guy sat in the drawing room and pretended to read a magazine while he observed his companions.

How fascinating this family was! They shared the same casual way of behaving as though they had always belonged in this place, when *she* was the daughter of a Frenchwoman and her offspring the descendants of immigrant Jews. With his father absent he could observe them more acutely. It was as though a lid had been removed that allowed their true feelings to float to the surface. There was none of the enforced joviality laid on at Christmas.

Brittany was sitting in the armchair nearest the fireplace, one leg crossed neatly over the other. She was embroidering. *Bandwagon* crackled away companionably from the wireless at her elbow. Every now and then she would push her hair away from her eyes and glance up at Guy, then look quickly down at her work, vexed to be caught looking at him.

In front of the children she wore an air of perplexed politeness, but he could feel the hostility beneath this glaze. Her air of suppressed energy intrigued him, and he found himself wondering what she had been like as a young woman. She looked often and meaningfully at the portraits of her family as if to say, "This is *my* house, and don't you forget it." Earlier that morning when he had announced his intention of walking to the village to take a look around, she played that curiously English trick of saying, "What a super idea!" with her voice while her eyes expressed complete disapproval. He was becoming quite a familiar figure in the Lamb and Child, and Brittany did not appear to like the idea.

George stood up and switched off the radio. "Nancy, I thought you were going out with the girls tonight."

"I was," said Nancy coolly, from her position near the open french window, "but I decided not to."

George glared.

She's changed her plans because of me, thought Guy, and he knows it. Straightlaced George refused even to pretend to be polite to him and behaved in a way which Guy imagined was a shocking departure from normal. At every attempt by Nancy to attract Guy's attention, George looked as though he would like to snarl. A guard dog on the defensive. Jake had asked Guy to continue to present himself as a cousin and apparently George thought a cousin was a threat. They had taken lunch on the porch, sitting at the trestle tables with the children. When one of Brittany's brood said something that amused Guy, Nancy would catch his eye and he would know from her expression that inwardly she was laughing too. He's jealous, thought Guy, and smiled as he flicked the page of the magazine.

Which brought his thoughts quite naturally and comfortably to the enigma of Nancy Stein. There was something madly exciting about the way she flirted with him, in ignorance of their close blood tie. It made him feel hot at the back of his neck, even now as he thought about it. She was sitting on a low, petit point stool, teasing her spaniel half-heartedly. The thin fabric of her dress was pulled tightly between her legs, alluding to the inviting outline of her crotch.

And yet her pose was childlike. It was this strange contradiction that tantalized Guy most. The sheer unsubtlety of her attitude towards him, her swaggering and showing off, proclaimed youth and inexperience, but there was something quintessentially *knowing* about the seventeen-year-old Nancy Stein.

Again and again these contrasts stopped him in his tracks. She carried her well-developed frame with a fastidious consciousness of its maturity, putting one foot down carefully in front of the other so that her slim ankles almost brushed in passing. None the less she could not disguise the grave, unheeding grace of youth, the urgent forward tilt of the body.

Nancy did not smile often. Her more habitual expression was a wry, decisive turn of the mouth which declared that Nancy Stein was not one to care what other people thought. But when she did smile . . . how could a mere girl have a smile like that? *Oh Nancy, when you smile, you smile with your wrists, shoulders, feet and ankles in a divinely shameless fashion . . .*

She was shameless, and when she smiled, he knew it.

A hot wind blew in through the open french window and gently lifted Nancy's hair. Earlier that day she had bent over Guy to point out Nether Aston's position on a map, and he had felt the faint, silken contact of her hair on his wrist. Rather than flinch or move quickly away, he had stayed still and relished its touch as though it too were trying to arouse him. The cool hair burnt his skin.

The strength of these incestuous thoughts frightened him. He had been attracted to Nancy because they were alike, but his awareness of her sensuality had given rise to a terrible tension in him. He would have to go elsewhere to relieve that tension. Nancy could never be his. The only way he could maintain a link with her was through this place, this house . . .

Guy flung the magazine down on the carpet and wiped his sweating palms lightly over the tops of his trousers.

"It's so hot tonight," he said, "I think I'll go out and take a stroll."

Nancy's nerves tensed when Guy spoke, but she looked steadfastly down at the spaniel, pulling and tousling its ears as though she had not heard him. Only a moment ago he had been looking at her very hard as though he were thinking about her. Perhaps this was a signal for her to follow him?

She knew she could not get up and go after him directly; on the other hand, he must not be allowed to get too far ahead or she might lose him. The ticking of the clock slowed to an agonizing pace. Then Nancy looked at her watch, yawned and sauntered out of the room with the dog at her heels. She did not say where she was going. Her mother peered at her suspiciously from over her embroidery.

She did not dare look at George's face.

The warm night air caressed her skin with a lover's touch. Nancy dodged around the side of the house, keeping well out of sight of the drawing room windows, and squinted into the darkness. A voice spoke faintly behind her. She jumped and spun round, and then laughed at herself. It was only the sound of the radio, carried clearly in the still air. George had risen to switch it on again. She waited for his large, dark silhouette to pass across the window again, then set off up the drive.

She had seen Guy's compact, athletic frame almost immediately, climbing the bend that passed the beech copse. This was disappointing; she thought he might have been waiting for her outside the house. Whatever his destination, he intended reaching it alone, since he was walking quickly and not turning to look back. She would follow him anyway.

Nancy was perplexed by Guy. In some secret, indefinable way they were the same, she was sure of it. Moulded of the same stuff. Although the idea was as yet abstract, Guy seemed to know it too but would not acknowledge it. She kept waiting for some piece of self-revelation, a baring of the soul to the joyous recognition of pitch and tone, and it never came. He used her with the same smooth care that he expended on every other person he came across, and showed her no special favours.

But why did he look at her so often with his gypsy's eyes, and so probingly?

There was a roar and a flicker of light at the top of the lane and Nancy stumbled back into the hedgerow, almost winded with surprise. The car sped past her, hardly slowing to negotiate the bend, so that branches trapped and scraped on the paintwork. It was a small, white car with an open top, and its driver was a woman. Nancy did not wait to see where the car was going, for if she looked back too long, she might lose sight of her prey, but as it passed her she had the impression of a young, calm face and pale hair beneath a chic little beret. Certainly Nancy had never seen the woman before, but she was reminded of the sentimental depiction of Resistance heroines in war films.

Perhaps she was a spy? A member of the Fifth Column?

It was now clear that Guy was headed for the village itself. At first Nancy had intended to walk fast enough to catch up with him, but as his pace became more purposeful she hesitated and hung back. He would probably be angry. He did not want her. She was a small child again, unable to get her own way and it was an unfamiliar, frightening sensation, for Nancy Stein was not used to being thwarted. She brushed a tear away from her eye with the back of her hand and followed him angrily up the High Street.

After a while she forgot her temper in sheer curiosity. Where on earth could he be going? They had passed Heathcote House on their right, but Guy would have no business with the Steeles anyway. They had even passed the pub, and he did not go in. Guy continued until the very end of the street and then stopped to look hastily around him. Then he descended the steps of the disused air-raid shelter and disappeared from view.

Nancy stood in a doorway and waited for him to re-emerge, but he did not. She waited a little longer: still he did not come. Puzzled, she went to the top of the steps. There was something, or someone, down there that she was afraid she might not want to see. She might regret it. Or perhaps . . .

A tiny candle of hope flickered in her mind. Perhaps he had known she was following him all along and was waiting for *her* down there. She ran quickly down the steps and pushed open the heavy door. She was immediately engulfed in cold, damp air that made her skin contract beneath her thin poplin dress. And there were candles, as though she were in a crypt. Like the final scene of Romeo and Juliet, Nancy thought immediately.

''Guy?'' she called weakly.

A faint moan came from a corner and as Nancy stepped nearer her foot caught on something. It was Guy's shirt. The next thing she saw was his naked back, shining with sweat in the candle's gleam. And then Maudie Lester's rocking, rising body and her long, wet mouth opened in an ecstatic scream.

Meanwhile the blonde stranger had turned the nose of her car down the hill and descended to the beckoning Corinthian columns, cupped like a white egg in a deep green basin. She parked on the gravel forecourt and walked briskly up the steps to the front door.

Five

FAYE'S INTRODUCTION TO her mother's relatives was hardly what she had expected.

"Nancy darling, this is your cousin, Faye McConnell," Mrs Stein had said on Saturday evening, but the girl ran straight past her and up the stairs, slamming a door behind her.

The same girl, Nancy, was there at breakfast on Sunday, shooting poisonous looks at the American officer from time to time and maintaining an intent, furious silence. Her brother George, who was allegedly returning to the Middle East that afternoon, was also scowling at the American. And when Faye had arrived late on the previous evening, Leonora had been in a drunken sleep from which no one could rouse her.

Faye was not accustomed to letting a little tension ruffle her, but even she was forced to admit that she had picked a bad time to visit her mother. It was a little like being Alice and stumbling on Wonderland. She had even been surprised to find that the chimerical cottage did indeed exist. After doubting this for so many years, seeing the place exactly as described was a little like having a fairytale come to life.

As she ate breakfast, the American was looking first at Nancy, then at Faye, then back again. He seemed amused. Perhaps he was enjoying the contrast in their looks. Faye's straight butter blonde hair fell in a smooth bell around her face, Nancy's dark curls beckoned the eye. Nancy's mouth was small and neat, Faye's wide and sleepy-looking as though perpetually on the end of a yawn.

If Faye could have read Guy's mind at that moment, she would have had the satisfaction of knowing that her intuition was correct. Guy was indeed assessing Faye, and reaching the conclusion that her features were ordinary, plain even, with the exception of her eyes. They were cat's eyes, slanting and pale greyish green.

And she was not alone in her familiarity with Lewis Carroll, for he was also read by the sons of Anglo-Saxon Protestant New England. As he reached for a second slice of toast, Guy Exley was casting Faye not as Alice, but as the Cheshire Cat.

As the dishes were cleared away, Faye took a long cool look around the dining room, taking in the darkening oil portraits of her Colby forebears. They looked hard, square-jawed: like her grandmother Georgina. She then tried to imagine Georgina Colby as a girl, sitting in this same room, but she could not. Grandmama had surely never been young.

There was a chorus of childish laughter from the other side of the dining room and a squeaking of rubber-soled plimsolls as small feet raced up and down the polished wooden floorboards of the corridor.

Brittany sighed. "Nancy, I'm about to round up the children and take them to Sunday school. Will you show Faye to the cottage, please?"

Nancy continued to stir the sugar round and round the sugar bowl. It spilled at ever-shortening intervals over the rim of the bowl and onto the seersucker tablecloth where it lay among the ridges and bumps.

"She went there last night," said Nancy, without looking up, "she must know where it is."

Faye took in the wasted sugar and the exasperated look on Brittany's face, even though she maintained the same even tone. "Yes, but that was in the dark. You know what it's like on that path at night, you can barely see a thing. Faye will hardly be able to remember the way."

Nancy looked at Guy's face. He was watching Faye's reactions. She looked at Faye, who stared blankly ahead, her slant eyes betraying no hint of dismay at the demonstration of bad manners.

"Come on then," she said, "I'll take you over there now, on my way to the farm."

The girls walked up the path behind the house in silence. It was a hot, cloudless morning and the sun glanced from the dark head to the blonde, bestowing a coronet of silver, then one of gold. Faye was Nancy's senior by four years, but only taller by virtue of her high-heeled, peep-toed pumps. She had a long, low-waisted body and wide hips.

She stopped suddenly in the path and turned to Nancy. "You were very rude to your mother this morning. Why?"

A broad, dark eyebrow shot up. Clearly Miss Nancy Stein did not expect her behaviour to be questioned. She looked at Faye with new interest and something that might have been bordering on respect, but did not reply.

Faye linked her arm comfortably through Nancy's and continued the ascent of the path, bracing her rounded calves slightly as her spindly heels sunk into the ground. "Do you ever give her a hand with the evacuee children?" she asked.

Nancy shook her head. "No time."

Faye considered this for a few paces and then said neutrally, "I thought she looked rather tired. She must be working hard."

"We're all working hard." Nancy noticed Faye's hands which were long and slender, with beautifully manicured nails. Each was a perfect oval of glossy pink polish. The toenails that peeped from her white shoes were exactly the same.

"I don't know what sort of work *you* do," she added slyly, "but it can't be very hard if you can keep your nails like that."

And she flourished her own hands in front of her, tanned and roughened, with broken nails.

Faye gave a sleepy smile. "I can assure you that it's a place where hard work and varnished nails are not incompatible! Besides, looking one's best in spite of everything is considered good for morale."

Nancy abandoned her attempts to perturb her cousin and smiled back. "Did you bring the polish with you? Perhaps I could borrow some—for my toes."

They had reached the cottage and Nancy sauntered off in the opposite direction to bale hay. Faye knocked at the door and entered without waiting for a reply.

It was so gloomy that at first she could barely see her mother. She identified her whereabouts by letting her nose follow a trail of cigarette smoke through the cool, damp air. Leonora was sitting on the edge of her bed, smoking a cigarette with one hand and shelling peas with the other. With the skill of an expert she built up a rhythm—a puff, then a "ping" as her thumb squeezed out the pea and it rattled into the bowl. Guy's visit had given her supplies of cigarettes and alcohol a welcome boost and she was determined to make the most of it. By her side was a half-empty quart of scotch concealed in a brown paper wrapper.

She looked up.

"Oh—hullo Faye," she said, and catapulted a particularly large pea into the basin.

This was how Leonora McConnell greeted her only child, as though they had been separated for a week, not two years.

But, as Faye reflected when she descended the path again after the interview was over, the complete absence of surprise at her arrival had been largely compensated for by a degree of pleasure. Leonora *had* seemed pleased to see her daughter, and had even questioned her about her own life, which Faye interpreted as a favourable indication of her well-being. However, she had been at pains to point out that if Faye intended to spend a few days at Graylings, she would have to remain up at the house as the cottage was far too small.

Faye understood what this meant. Mother's become used to carrying on in her strange way undisturbed, she thought, snatching at a piece of browned grass and poking it between her teeth. She doesn't want anyone to start watching her and criticizing her, least of all me.

The idea that her mother might have bolted to the cottage that she had boasted of came to Faye quite soon after Leonora's disappearance from London, but at first she had no inclination to follow her. Theirs had hardly been a conventional mother-daughter relationship. But with the hot weather Faye began to dream of escaping from the stuffy, broken city to green fields and open spaces. She applied to the Ministry of Labour and they confirmed that a Mrs Leonora McConnell was indeed registered with the Labour Exchange in Wells, Somerset. Reluctantly they supplied her given address: Graylings, Nether Aston, Somerset.

Faye had borrowed the smart white car from her landlord Stephen, and had taken a few days leave from work, her first since she had started in the job.

She worked for the Ministry of Information and, despite Nancy's jibes, she worked hard. Her employers were the favourite butt for war time comedians' jokes. "If you ask the Mystery of Information about that," they would say, "they'll tell you they don't know, and if they did they wouldn't tell you."

Faye had chosen the Ministry quite deliberately because of its reputation as a haven for bright young graduates and professional writers. She saw no point in working with dull people if a place like that would have her and her aim was to make some sort of mark, get herself noticed.

The element of glamour was elusive at first, as she spent long hours typing up releases to send to the Press Association, visiting the printers to collect posters proclaiming "Freedom is in Peril, Defend it with all your Might" or "Go to It!" She trudged on cheerfully through the tedium of distributing the same posters to branches of Woolworths, transport companies and Food Offices, compiling and checking figures over and over again until finally her perseverance paid dividends.

She was promoted to Films.

All the girls wanted to go to the studios and help make the propaganda "shorts" that accompanied every cinema feature; but Faye was probably the only one prepared for the fact that it was not an opportunity to chat and joke with actors and secure a small part for herself. She started by making the tea.

Steely determination that formed the bed-rock beneath a calm feminine exterior proved invaluable, however. She was now a production assistant, doubling as a clapper loader and intoning, "Take Three" in a voice as smooth as honey.

And wielding a clapperboard did not damage the fingernails.

As soon as she was recruited by the Ministry, Faye determined to leave her parents' house and find a place of her own. A girl at work sent her to Stephen Willand-Jones. Stephen was thirty, had dabbled in painting and poetry and café society and inherited a house on the bank of the Thames, at one end of Lindsay Place. At first he lived in the house with his elderly mother, then, when she died, he began to take paying guests. He acquired two adjoining houses in the terrace, filled them with more boarders and began to live the life of an urban squire.

Faye was given Stephen's name and address, and with this precious information on a scrap of paper in her best lizard-skin handbag, she went to visit him one day after work.

The outside of the house pleased her. She liked the muddy, oozy smell of the Thames and the little grey patches above the tide that looked like beaches and were frequented by seagulls. Below the house was a neat line of houseboats. The house itself had a small wrought-iron balcony that possessed the jaunty air of a nautical look-out and an old twisted vine that grew to the upper windows.

Stephen Willand-Jones greeted Faye at the door. With great satisfaction she noted that he was exactly as she had already pictured him: wearing a spotted silk cravat and holding a pipe. His colourless hair was thinning.

He showed Faye around the premises himself, explaining, as they climbed flight after flight of narrow stairs, that the ballroom on the first floor was let out for balls and parties and that the whole establishment was supervised by his formidable former nanny. The tour ended with the attic floor and a room that had been the nursery. It was a large room with a sloping ceiling and a heroic view of the river. This was the only space available, Stephen told Faye—did she want it?

Faye went to the window and looked out. The boats were clearly visible, as well as the factories and warehouses on the other side of the Thames. She turned to Stephen and nodded, her cat's eyes narrowed with pleasure. And so Faye was "taken on."

Now, at Graylings, the scattering of children on the lawn, playing tag in their Sunday-best dress and white socks, told Faye that Brittany had returned from church. She went in search of her hostess to ask if she could stay on at Graylings for a few days longer.

Brittany was in the kitchen, preparing sandwiches for George to take on the train. She greeted Faye with a broad smile.

"Ah Faye, there you are. Come into the library will you? I want to talk to you."

The library had become Jake's domain since he had lived at Graylings, and to Faye it looked like an Aladdin's cave. Arched alcoves in the walls were subtly lit and filled with Chinese lacquerwork, porcelain and precious pieces of jade. Another displayed Fabergé curios and some French enamels. The walls themselves were painted a dusky geranium red.

Brittany wandered to a tobacco velvet chaise lounge with the delicious unselfconsciousness of one accustomed to ostentatious wealth. Faye curled up, catlike, in a chair and looked around her in wonder.

"It's about your mother . . ." Brittany began. Faye smiled a wide, lazy smile.

"It's hard to believe, but she's been here nearly two years, and we know absolutely nothing about her circumstances. She just arrived here, with no luggage, saying she'd been evacuated. But that was long after they'd stopped sending people out of London. You see, she's quite happy to talk to me about *me*, but she never tells me anything about herself."

Faye nodded and gave a small sigh. "I didn't think she'd tell you what really happened. Daddy threw her out."

"Your *father*? She told *me* he was dead, but I did wonder . . ."

"He's very much alive. They were still living together at the beginning of the war, but Mother had already gone strange by then."

Brittany thought of Leonora's passion for drink, her "haunting" of the grounds and wearing a mink coat even in summer. She could not help laughing a little. "I suppose some people would call her strange, but I've grown very close to her. Perhaps 'close' isn't the right word in your mother's case . . . Very attached to her."

"I think she's happy here," said Faye gravely. "And I'm sure she never was before.'' Her voice trailed away, but she felt a quite irresistible urge to go on talking. It's this place, she told herself, it's making me behave out of character.

And then, quite naturally, she began to tell her life story.

''The trouble all begin with Grandmama. Your aunt Georgina Colby—Georgina Seaton, I should say. She died just before the war . . . Anyway, my mother was completely dominated by her. It was most unnatural.''

Brittany moved one hand thoughtfully up and down her forearm. ''Yes,'' she said, ''that's how I remembered her as a child.'' A sober look came across her face as she remembered Christmas 1912, and Aunt Georgina fussing over Leonora's ringlets. It was the same evening that Brittany's elder brother Frederick had died after an epileptic fit, and both she and Leonora had witnessed his collapsing, unconscious during a seemingly innocent party game.

''. . . When she was nineteen, Mother got it into her head to marry Daddy. She met him at a dance in Yorkshire I think, but by all accounts they hardly knew one another. She was absolutely set on the idea though, and nothing could dissuade her, not even Grandmama, which is the strangest part of it all. It seems that for the first time in her life, Mother had made a decision on her own, and for that reason she wouldn't change her mind, even if was the last independent thing she ever did. It amazes me to see her in that cottage now. To look at her you'd think she had always been independent of other people . . . However . . . where was I? Yes, Daddy. My father's a Scot, as you might expect with the name Sandy McConnell.''

''You must take after him,'' mused Brittany, ''because there's nothing of Leonora in you.''

''That's right.''

Faye laughed, and it was a pleasant sound that reached into the dark corners of the solemn, over-decorated room; a low, musical laugh. Her yellow hair swung about her cheeks.

''I think Grandmama suspected the nurses at the maternity home of switching her daughter's baby with somebody else's. Then, as I began to take after Daddy more, she began to loathe me, though she used to pretend not to in front of Mother. Daddy's what people think of as a typical Scot; small and wiry and sandy-haired. Grandmama detested him. She used to call him a vulgar little man, to his face. 'The trouble with your husband Le'nora' . . .'' Faye was a clever mimic and Brittany laughed when the wide, pussycat mouth uttered in Georgina's clipped, nasal warble, " '. . . the trouble with your husband is that he's a bit *middle class*.' To Grandmama that was the most insulting thing you could say about anyone. I suppose it was true in Daddy's case. His father was a sort of minor magnate in the Glasgow area. He owned several houses in the centre of the city, and a few small businesses. Well off, but nothing grand—you know.''

Brittany nodded. It was fascinating to see Leonora's past fall unhappily into place, as though she had only possessed half a jigsaw and was now presented with the missing pieces. ''Go on, Faye—what happened after they were married? Your mother once described her marriage as a lost cause.''

Faye chewed her lower lip and looked up at the moulded plaster rose on the ceiling. ''I suppose it was like a marriage between three people. My mother, my father . . . and Grandmama. She was widowed not long after the wedding. As you know, Mother had a brother, Arthur, but for some reason Grandmama was never very interested in him. So Daddy found himself not only with the pretty, shy girl he married but with this overpowering virago as well. It must have been dreadful. She moved down to London, to be near them. She was around at their house every day. Mother couldn't even buy a new lampshade or traycloth without Grandmama's permission. She vetted their friends. She made sure she knew everywhere they went and everything they did. *Everything*—even the bedroom bits I shouldn't wonder . . .''

The feline eyes twinkled slightly. ''. . . And all the time she was constantly criticizing Daddy and running him down. You're probably wondering why he didn't leave. He needed her money for a start. Grandpa McConnell's businesses were largely running at a loss and Daddy had used some of Mother's money to set up a small import-export business in London. The house was paid for with her money. Even so, we never seemed to have enough. Daddy was one of those rare creatures—a thriftless Scot.''

Faye sat quietly for a few moments and remembered it all. The tall, shabby house near Kensington Gardens. Life at the second-rate boarding school where she never had the things that the other girls had; holidays abroad, new clothes, a pony. The sort of disadvantage fourteen-year-old girls look down their noses and sneer about. How she would have envied her cousin Nancy then, with everything anyone could ever want for, right here at her fingertips!

''. . . And I think Daddy was genuinely fond of Mother too,

in those days. She could be great fun. Because of Grandmama always being around, she was never really like a mother to me. Perhaps she wasn't allowed to be. She always had to play the role of daughter, without ever growing up. So she was more like a sister. Anyway, Grandmama's health was never very good (that was another thing she used to make their lives a misery) and I think Daddy was just waiting for her to die. Poor Daddy . . .'' Faye's voice softened slightly, "it's just . . . well, *ironic* that when she did finally die, the problems between the two of them really started.''

"The drinking?''

Faye nodded. ''It was one of two phenomena, and I've never quite made up my mind which. Either having her decision-maker and her prop, her personality even, suddenly vanish, made her crumble—or she found it so wonderful to be herself again that she decided to do what the dickens she liked and never listen to anyone ever again. Either way, she became pretty impossible. It wasn't just that she drank: she used to wander all over the place, wherever took her fancy. In her fur coat usually. Daddy bought it for her years ago, but Grandmama had decided it was 'common' and wouldn't let her wear it. The house became like a slum, she couldn't be bothered to go and queue for food, she came and went when she pleased. I'd moved to Chelsea by then anyway, but with the strain of the raids, and fire-watching, Daddy lost patience with her. He told her to go. And she did. I think he was quite surprised.''

Brittany was curious. "How did you know she'd be here?''

"She started talking about how she'd inherited a cottage in the grounds of Grandmama's old home. She must have found the thought of it a great comfort, knowing there was always somewhere she could bolt to. I suppose after all those years of being tagged by a shadow, she's enjoying just being alone. Anyway, her address was on her work records, so . . . here I am.''

Brittany leaned forward and put a hand on Faye's shoulder. "After all that, I think you deserve to be considered one of the family.''

Faye thought her smile quite dazzling and her blue eyes the largest she had even seen in a face of that width. She had heard her mother's cousin gossiped about often as the Brittany Colby of the Roaring Twenties, whose reputation for unconventional behaviour was legendary. The charm and the beauty remained in this warm, contented woman.

"You must stay as long as you like, and come again, too. But I must beg you to excuse Nancy's shocking manners."

"Please don't worry about that," said Faye calmly, with a tremor of pale gold hair. "I'm sure Nancy and I shall get on very well indeed."

It was the first time since the summer that Guy Exley had left the Eighth Air Force base to visit the centre of London.

He was struck by the change in the mood of the capital. It was something unseen, a sense of menace. All through the summer flying bombs had fallen on London, giving the streets an eerily autumnal look as the blast stripped the branches bare and heaped the leaves on the ground. There was a pungent smell of sap in London parks when V1s tore bark from the trees. Londoners became remarkably blasé about these summer raids, nicknaming the V1s "doodlebugs." "Here comes a doodlebug," they would say and diners in restaurants would freeze, knives and forks poised in midair. Then, after the bang, people carried on eating and resumed conversation without reference to what had happened. The V1s could be heard approaching at some distance and this seemed to diminish their threat on a sunny Sunday morning. Taxi drivers would sound their horns as a warning.

But in September, the V2 rockets started falling, and Guy saw quite a different look on the faces of the people in London's streets on that clear autumn evening. The men looked tense, haunted, the women like tired brood mares worn out with lack of sleep and food.

These new bombs attracted no nicknames and inspired no jokes. They were preceded by no warning, just a bright flash in the sky, a supersonic bang and the roar of an explosion. This time Londoners knew, when they heard the flat, enormous crack and echoing rumbles, that somewhere nearby there was a deep crater and total destruction all around it. The sound of the explosion was the first anyone knew: after that you were either alive or dead. Many of the people Guy passed in the street looked as though they scarcely believed which of the two states they were in.

Guy was going to have supper at his father's flat.

He strolled towards Picadilly Circus, hugging a large brown paper parcel of food to his chest. He had left plenty of time to walk down to the Embankment with the express purpose of taking a good look at his surroundings and absorbing the atmosphere, but even Guy was growing exasperated with the war. This proud city was tired and demoralized and no longer seemed to care. A reformatory school with regulations designed for the protection of inmates who only wanted to escape.

He passed the Ritz, and when he saw the supper menu offering dried egg omelette and cold apple tart he found himself dreaming of the beach on Long Island Sound. The saliva began to flow in his mouth as he smelled charcoal-grilled prawns and clam chowder, and heard the echoing *chock* of tennis balls on asphalt. He shook himself and walked on.

There were muffled strains of jazz from Rainbow Corner, the large American club in Picadilly, and a thin gleam of light now that the blackout restrictions had been relaxed.

Guy quickened his pace considerably, for Rainbow Corner was the traditional rendezvous of GIs and London's prostitutes. Even so, he could not avoid drawing attention to himself.

"Wot you got there, love?" called one, "the crown jewels? Or was you bringin' me some new nylons?"

"I didn't think you Yanks knew how to walk," commented another, reaching out of the gloom and pawing his uniform. "I thought you went everywhere by car."

In the newly instituted half-lighting, they all looked a little pathetic, a little disappointing. Streetwalkers had adapted to the blackout in their own way, and Guy had found it exciting when they stalked their prey unseen, identified only by the special loud-clacking heels they employed, and shone their torches down at their stocking-clad legs.

When Guy had first seen the interior of his father's London residence, he had been dismayed.

He had always thought of powerful merchant bankers as the princes of city dwellers, and the elaburate four-storey mansion on Fifth Avenue, where his father spent his boyhood, was well known. When he learned that Jake had voluntarily given his Regency town house beside the canal in Little Venice as a reception centre for bomb victims, his irrational irritation was mollified and he felt an increased respect for this quiet, caring man.

Yet despite this and despite Jake's lengthy explanation that rented flats were as scarce as gold dust and this one only available because it was on the river facing South, and therefore dangerous—he still felt (when he visited him there) that Jake was in the wrong milieu. Indeed, it would have been difficult for the flat to do justice to anyone. The two main rooms were large and cavernous, with walls painted canary yellow above the dado and off-white below. There were some dismal prints of sunsets in cheap frames and a threadbare brown carpet that stopped six inches short of the skirting board.

After he had greeted his father, Guy went into the kitchen to unpack the food.

"Ham and eggs OK?" he shouted.

"Sounds fine," said Jake. "I'll come and give you a hand."

The high-ceilinged echoing sitting room played tricks with sound and for a split second Jake could not tell whether it was Guy who had just spoken or himself, their voices were so alike. He went into the kitchen with two glasses of scotch and stood in appreciative silence, watching Guy slice the ham. He worked with quick, neat movements, his hands broad and short-fingered with very white, very well manicured nails.

"I'll fry the eggs," said Jake, "but first let me fetch a sweater. It's getting colder in the evenings."

Guy shivered a little. The feeble heat from the gas fire in the sitting room did not penetrate as far as the kitchen. When Jake returned Guy said, "Some men at the base are saying this is going to be the last winter of the war."

"I hope so." Jake broke four eggs into a frying pan and dodged the spitting fat. "I'm getting kind of tired of the bachelor life, and I think Brittany is too." He poked thoughtfully at the egg whites with a fork. "She's worked damn hard, and had no holiday since 1939. Not a single day, unless you count a quick trip up here to visit the dressmaker. And this place hardly scores as a holiday spot. First thing I'm going to do when this war's over is take my wife on a cruise. A cruise around the world."

Guy took another frying pan out of the cupboard and arranged the slices of ham in it. His fine, ash brown hair flopped over his eyes.

"You know Guy, we never really talked about your plans for after the war. You're not intending to stay in the Air Force?"

Guy shook his head. "I know running around after the stuffed shirts and making their theatre bookings doesn't really count as a taste of the serviceman's life, but I'm pretty sure it's not for me anyway. Whether I'm flying a desk or a plane."

"So what will you do?"

"I don't know, Dad."

Jake still felt surprised at the informal epithet that dropped from Guy's lips whenever they were alone. George addressed him as Father, Nancy as nothing at all.

"I guess I'll go back to Long Island and work for Grandfather's firm again. It suited me OK before."

"I'd be real sorry to see you go so soon. I can easily fix you up with a job in the bank, if that's what you'd like. Think about it."

They sat down to eat at the kitchen table, which was covered with a red oil cloth. There was a comfortable, unselfconscious lull in the conversation as they ate, tearing at their food and munching it noisily without regard for manners.

Guy was thinking about what it meant to have a father, a *real* father after twenty-seven years without one. He tried to decide how he could best compensate for all the lost time. After looking at it from every angle, he decided that he would have to try and take the love and care that was his by right in a concentrated form, to tap it and let it flow out like maple syrup from the trunk of a tree.

"One of the things I'm looking forward to most at the end of the war," Jake was saying, "is spending some time down at Graylings again."

Guy nodded slowly.

"Say, I never had a chance to ask you. Did you have a good time when you were down there in the summer?"

Guy hesitated.

Jake was looking down at his plate. If he could have seen his son's face at that moment, he would have recognised the expression creeping across it as one that Nancy frequently wore when she was about to attempt to manipulate him. As it was, he only heard the rather wistful sigh. "I don't know Dad . . . It was great, I guess, but—"

Jake looked up, and it was Guy's turn to look down at his food. "But what?"

Another sigh. "I tried real hard to fit in and please everybody, but I sensed they didn't really want me around."

"*They* didn't? Who?"

"It doesn't matter Dad, I—"

"Yes it does matter, it matter to me. Who?"

"Well, Brittany, a little . . . and George."

"You mean they were hostile?"

"Yes, sort of. I don't like to criticize your wife. She did *try* not to act like she didn't want me there. George acted like he couldn't stand the sight of me."

Jake flung down his napkin. He drained the scotch from his glass and slammed it down on the table. "I'm sorry Guy, I really am. I don't feel my apologies are adequate.'' He pulled his lips into a thin line, until they almost disappeared. ''I'll speak to them about it.''

''Nonsense Dad, it doesn't matter. I'm heading back to the States soon after all. Here—have a doughnut.''

Jake shook his head. He was watching his son's face. Distress registered in the twitching mouth, just as it used to in Katherine's before she began to cry. In fact it *was* Katherine's mouth, the same exquisitely sensual lips and even, white teeth.

''I feel now like maybe I shouldn't have contacted you. It seems to have made trouble in your family . . .'' He looked sideways at Jake, measuring his reaction, ''. . . Only I thought that's what my mother would have wanted.''

Jake was standing now, gripping the edge of the table with one hand and the back of his chair with the other. Then he moved forward and made a strange gesture: placing his hand on his son's head as if in blessing.

''Of course she would,'' he said fiercely. *''Of course she would.''*

After Guy had gone, Jake sat without moving for more than an hour. There was no light in the room save that from the battered gas fire. He buried his head in his hands and thought of Katherine. When he did that, it was as if he was very young again. He remembered the sense of wonder when he first kissed her, and she kissed him back. When he loved her, and she loved him back . . .

There was one scene which dominated his memory. It was a summer evening and Katherine had told her parents that she was spending the night with a friend at Cape Cod. Instead she met Jake at a party held on a Manhattan roof garden. They danced in the open air and then sat on the parapet and counted the stars above them and the street lights below, hundreds of feet below. They talked of the future. When Katherine was happy she would forget, or pretend to forget the obstacles in their way and would say, ''When we do this'' or, ''When we have that.'' On that evening, he remembered, she talked about how it would be when they were married. ''We'll have to make sure we die on the same day,'' she said. ''Because neither of us could bear to go on without the other. And we must have children, or a child at least, so that we'll be joined together even after we've gone.'' She looked down at the tram cars, a dizzying distance below. ''If we have a child, whatever happens there'll always be a part of us that's together. Let's do that Jake, please . . .''

Jake closed his eyes and groaned with pain. He must not let Guy down. He thought about what he might do, and then decided to do it. He would keep his promise to Katherine and bind their son to him forever.

The garden seemed refreshed after a shower of autumn rain. The heavy drops still trembled on blades of grass, trapping the sun and turning the whole lawn into a sparkling carpet of light. An insouciant breeze blew across a sky washed clean and blue.

Annabel Steele saw how the garden beckoned through the kitchen window. She pulled off her rubber gloves, slowly and deliberately, finger by finger.

Work at the canteen had finished for the day and there was one precious half hour free before Kit would return from school and want his tea. Her mind made up, she went to the back door and donned a pair of outsize wellingtons. They made soft, squelching noises as she trudged across the grass and leaves stuck to them like wet, brown plasters.

The old swing still stood in its place beside the tall stone wall. Annabel sat down on it. The wooden seat was damp and the dampness penetrated through her skirt, even through her underwear. She leaned back, taking her weight on her arms and kicked her legs out until the swing gained its carefree momentum. One of the boots flew off and landed on the wet grass but it lay on its side unheeded as Annabel swung on, flinging her chest against the air, her reddish brown hair flying out like a flag.

The she halted the swing abruptly, retrieved the boot and headed for her room.

My dearest George,

I've just been on the Swing. What a foolish occupation for a person of my age!

I'm writing to you now, as it's just about the only free time I get in the day. When I'm not working, the other three are making constant demands on me in one way or another. I try to bear it patiently, like you said, but—

Annabel paused, sucking on a strand of fine, dark hair. The pupils in her grey eyes widened, making them look almost black.

—but I sometimes think it's no wonder poor Mother left. In your letter you asked me what happened to her. I was sur-

*prised that you didn't know my parents used to live at Gray-
lings for a while when your mother was away. Then they came
back here, and Grandfather died, and then Patrick was born.
Mother couldn't stand it. She hated it here. I've never been
inside Graylings, but I imagine this place must have been a
comedown after that—dirty and damp and smelly. Father was
rotten to her sometimes too. When Kit was born mostly. I think
he was a Mistake. They used to fight at night after Patrick and
I had gone to bed, and we could hear them. They shouted at
each other and sometimes we could hear Mother screaming.
Then she went, just like that, without telling us where she was
going. Father wouldn't tell us either. He said that by running
off she had forfeited all her Rights as a Mother and he
wouldn't let her see us. I think she had a Nervous Breakdown,
because she was in a Nursing Home for a while. She used to
write to us, but she doesn't any more. You also ask what we
thought of her. Sorry for her, I think. She wasn't very kind to
us, but it must be hard to be kind to people when you are very
unhappy. Sometimes she was strict, sometimes she didn't seem
to care what we did. I think I did like her. She could tell
wonderful stories and she was very pretty and ladylike.*

*Father's very weak, and he sleeps most of the time. It's
years now since the Doctor said he only had a few months to
live, but he's still here. Patrick's hard at work on the Farm.
He's never forgiven the Army for failing him on Medical
Grounds. He's furious that people like you are out there de-
fending King and Country and he can't go. Another reason
why I daren't mention our plans to him. I have no idea what
he would have done with the Farm if he had joined up. As it
is, he's very short of Labour and his application for a Landgirl has been turned down. And there's another reason for
him to be extra bad-tempered. Greville has gone. (I told you
about him, he's the cousin who's been living with us for five
years.) He said he was being called away on an Urgent Business Matter and he left in a terrible hurry. Patrick was always
calling him names, but he needed Greville to tell him what to
do. So Kit and I are just trying to stay out of Patrick's way.*

*I do love receiving your letters. They are so interesting! I
wish I could write as well as you. I do pray to God to keep
you safe. Is it still hot where you are—*

Downstairs the front door opened and slammed shut. Annabel
wrote hurriedly:

*Kit has just come back from School, so I must forget my own
life for a while. All my love, your Fiancée, Annabel.
P.S. We haven't heard anything at all from Greville. Don't
you think that's odd?*

"Now gentlemen," droned Lord Selborne, Minister for Economic Welfare, "if I might just draw your attention to the minutes of our last Ministerial Committee Meeting . . ."

Jake looked at his watch. The meeting was dragging on and
he wanted to get to the City by five o'clock. He looked hope-
lessly around the boardroom, at the set jaws above the leather-
topped table, and sighed.

The Minister leaned forward. "Do I take it you're in agreement
Mr Stein?"

"Oh—er, yes. Quite," said Jake.

He was lost in thoughts of what he was about to do. It would
be easy enough, but he was still not sure whether it was right.

He turned it over and over in his mind until the meeting finished. It was half past four. If he caught a bus or a taxi straight
away, he could be at Mr Gabin's office by five o'clock. He could,
of course, telephone, and Mr Gabin would be only too happy to
keep his offices open for such an important client, but that was
not Jake's style. He did not like to throw his weight around,
especially now that people were all trying to pull together. With
a few minutes to spare when he reached Cheapside Jake wandered slowly along the pavement and reflected. He still used the
solicitor he had had in his early days in London when he worked
for Stein and Sons in Ironmonger Lane. He passed Ironmonger
Lane now; and stopped to stare at the brass plaque on the door.
His father had been dead for years and there was no one with
the name of Stein here now. How disappointed Isaac Stein must
have been that his youngest son was killed in a car crash at the
age of twenty-eight and produced a bastard, while his eldest son
fell in love with women he found unacceptable and produced no
male heir.

Except Guy.

The City no longer looked like the City that the young David
Stein had prowled lazily in his dark suit and stiff collar. It had
sustained enormous damage in the air-raids and some of the
sights around Jake now would have appalled even the unsenti-
mental David. The building in King William Street that Jake
entered stood alone and unscathed amidst the wreckage of its

neighbours, which were reduced to rubble and broken glass. A domino that had refused to fall with the rest of the pack.

Mr Gabin was waiting to welcome Jake personally. "Ah, Mr Stein! Welcome, welcome!"

And as a mark of his high esteem he sent his secretary to fetch coffee from his private supply.

It had all been extremely simple, Jake reflected afterwards as he took a bus along Fleet Street. Brittany had mortgaged Graylings, both house and estate, to Stein and Sons in 1925 when she was in financial difficulties. By 1933 the estate was thriving and she had completely repaid the loan, so that she was sole owner again. Then, at the beginning of the war, when death duties rose to sixty-five per cent and the tax on large incomes doubled, Jake had persuaded Brittany to transfer nominal ownership of Graylings to Jacob Stein and Company, to stay in trust for George and Nancy during Brittany's lifetime, or until they were old enough to decide what to do with it. But since Jake owned the controlling number of shares in his merchant bank, in theory he could change the fate of Graylings without consulting anyone. Which was precisely what he had done. He had changed the clause in his will which disposed assets of Jacob Stein and Company after his death.

Graylings would belong to Guy.

Jake decided to go to the pictures and join the other people who were sitting in the dark with an organ dropping lush gouts of sentiment on their jaded nerves. His concentration ebbed and flowed between the screen and his thoughts. As the lights went up after the film he wondered how many of those around him knew what the picture they had just seen was about. Scenes, incidents, flashed into perception and were then blotted out in the dark, fulminating contents of the watcher's mind.

During the war, cinemas had become places to sit down in, to weep in, even a place to escape into a world of romance from a world of unpalatable reality. Jake used the hour and a half to justify his actions to himself.

Nancy and George had already had all their lives to enjoy Graylings, Guy had not. And what was more, he was made to feel that he did not belong there. Even if Guy owned the place in name, it would still be home for his half-brother and -sister, whilst Nancy and George would inherit ample capital to buy their own homes, if that was what they preferred. And anyway, if the situation changed over the coming years, if Guy returned to America and showed no further interest in Graylings, then he could change his will again. As Mr Gabin had been swift to point out, there was plenty of time to reconsider.

Satisfied with this explanation, Jake let himself into his flat. He made himself a tray of supper and sat down to listen to his favourite recording of Puccini. Then, with a burst of nostalgia, he put the oldest and most scratched record in his collection onto the turntable.

It was the "Modesty Rag," the same tune that had played as he and Brittany sat by the fire in her house in Chelsea on the Christmas Eve before George was born. It was at that moment that he realised he was irrevocably in love with the pregnant, unmarried Brittany Colby and the quirky bittersweet melody had lived in his memory ever afterwards as a seal on the emotion. When they finally married in 1926, Brittany jokingly presented the record to him as a souvenir.

And then Jake began his usual evening occupation, thinking of what Brittany would be doing at that very moment all those miles away. The evacuees would all be in bed and Brittany would be sitting quietly by the radio or sewing, relieved to have another day of the war behind her. In the house she loved so much . . .

Oh my God, he thought, what have I done? Brittany really loves that place. What's more, she has *suffered* to keep it. He felt crushed by guilt, and sickened by what he had just done to his wife. Sure, he felt guilty about Guy too, but could Guy possible need Graylings as much as Brittany did?

He sat for an hour with the two of them in his thoughts; his wife and his son. Two needs. Two obligations. And perhaps, after what he had done, two enemies. He would call Gabin in the morning to see if they couldn't find some other way that would allow Brittany and Guy to benefit equally.

He picked up the phone and dialed.

"Nether Aston 231."

"Nancy honey, it's me."

"Oh, hello." The response was cheerful, if non-committal.

"Everything OK down there?"

"The same as ever. Nothing's changed since you last rang, if that's what you mean."

Nothing's changed . . . "Well, I wonder if I could have a quick word with your mother. Is she about?"

"Hang on."

Nancy came back to the phone several minutes later. Jake could almost hear her nonchalant footsteps, determined not to be put out by breaking into a run. "Hello? She's in the bath. She says she's only just got in."

"Oh well, no matter then. Tell her I'll speak to her tomorrow."

"Daddy . . ." Nancy was hesitating as if she had something important to say.

"What is it, honey?"

"Nothing . . . It doesn't matter."

"OK then. Bye."

He hung up.

There were a few seconds of expectant silence, then came the disconsolate wail of the air-raid siren. Jake stood up wearily. It had been like this almost every night for a month now. When the siren sounded, the half-lighting was to become full blackout. He fixed the screens up over the windows and wondered as he did so if all other Londoners were also asking themselves how many times they would have to perform this joyless chore. He sat down and waited for what would come next.

There is was, the timid knock at the door.

"We're going down now, Mr Stein," said Miss Cameron, one of the spinsters who occupied the flat on the other side of the hall, "Are you coming?"

"In a minute," replied Jake, as he always did.

But he had never yet followed the other residents down to the basement that served as a makeshift shelter. Perhaps I should give it a try one of these nights, he mused. And why not tonight? You never knew what these doodlebugs were going to do after all. Jake went into the bedroom to collect his gas mask.

Then it came.

The residents who had already reached the windowless basement did not see the blinding flash of light, they only heard the accompanying noise, like the rushing of an immense, macabre wind. When firemen finally dug them out, they discovered that the dignified mansion block that faced the Thames was a mere heap of stones. The unlucky few who failed to reach the shelter had been killed outright.

Six
February 1945

"I'M NOT GOING through the formality of summoning the family solicitor to read out the will," said Brittany, "while we all sit and listen politely like spinsters at a village concert. But there is something important to be said."

Something important to be said . . . Her mind raced back to the mundane events of the day that Jake died. She had taught the children history in the morning, but they had been excited about the advent of Christmas and had asked to sing carols instead. She had gone for a walk and bumped into Leonora. After supper she'd had a wonderful hot bath, flouting the wartime regulation of five inches in the tub. And when the phone had rung she'd been so comfortable that she couldn't be bothered to get out.

And she would live with the guilt of *that* for the rest of her life, that she couldn't be bothered to speak to Jake. For the last time. She'd said those words over and over as she raged against herself, clutching at her sheets with tormented fingers and drenching them with her tears. Then she raged against Jake. How could he have been so stupid? Why didn't he go down into that stupid shelter? He'd promised her he'd be careful, he'd *promised* . . . Then came a tunnel of despair, then anger again—this time at Hitler's war and its pitiful waste of human lives. Then weary emptiness. The four seasons of grief . . .

And after grief, outrage. She had to formally admit Guy Exley to their family circle. She had to tell the children who he was.

Brittany had chosen the upstairs sitting room to break this piece of news. She could not bear to go into the library. The red walls that had once been so cheerful seemed to be bleeding at her. Jake's life-blood oozing away . . .

There was a fire burning in the sitting room grate and Brittany crossed the room to warm her hands on it. Then she went to close the curtains, almost as if she had forgotten what she was going to say. George and Nancy waited expectantly. A dead leaf dropped from a potted cyclamen on the table and drifted to the floor next to Brittany's feet. She stared down at it and a look of recognition crossed her features as though the frail, dead leaf had reminded her of what she was about to say. She adopted a schoolmistressy pose; half leaning against, half sitting on the table under the window.

"This isn't the sort of thing that I would normally be in a hurry to tell you, but since you're about to go back to Egypt, George, I really have to do it now. It wouldn't be fair to tell one of you and not the other . . ."

Nancy and George exchanged baffled glances.

". . . You already know about the sums of money your father left you, to be available on your twenty-first birthdays . . ."

George's body tightened suspiciously. "He left money to Guy. That's what you're going to say, isn't it?"

"Not exactly," Brittany's half smile melted away and the whole house echoed her anguished silence. The evacuees had been despatched to their respective homes and now Graylings was like a boarding school in the holidays, its empty classrooms leering at passers-by.

"He left Graylings to Guy."

George turned pale, then flushed angrily. "To *Guy*? But he's only a distant cousin!"

"I was just getting to that. Daddy was Guy's father. He's your half-brother."

As she spoke, Brittany watched the expression on Nancy's face, but it remained inscrutable.

She talked to her children at painful length, relating as much as she knew of Jake's affair with Katherine Exley. Nancy's face remained impassive throughout. Her eyes stared ahead, her lips curved upwards, and her feelings—whatever they might be— were hidden away.

George wanted to know if they would have to move out and live somewhere else. Unable to keep the acid from her voice, Brittany explained that Guy had no wish for things to change and that they could all go on living there as long as they wished. As things stood at the moment, he fully intended to return to Long Island when the war was ended. She did not speak of the bitterness she felt now, that was added to her back-breaking load of grief and guilt. To be treated like a tenant in her own home, the home that she had scrabbled and scratched for at an age when the Guy Exleys of this world would be enjoying the carefree repast of youth. George, she knew, would feel the bitterness with her, but Nancy's assumed neutrality angered her.

Brittany stopped her daughter as she left the sitting room.

"Nancy . . ."

She put a restraining hand on her wrist. "I do hope you *understand* what I've been saying."

"Understand?" Nancy pulled her wrist free.

"Yes. Now that you are aware that Guy is your brother, I hope you will tailor your attitude accordingly."

Nancy raised one eyebrow. "I don't see what difference it makes," she replied with her most infuriating blandness. "Cousin, brother—it's all the same with me."

She put her hands in her pockets as though she meant to stroll off, but her gait was urgent, hurried. She had consistently refused to share her grief with Brittany, as if her mother was in some way to blame for what had happened.

"The children are leaving in a minute!" Brittany shouted. "I'd like you to be there to say goodbye."

Nancy disappeared.

According to the authorities, Brittany's evacuees had long been due to return to their homes in the East End, and when the Welfare Officers heard of her bereavement, they arranged for the exodus to take place. Brittany had remonstrated, pleaded, offered any number of testimonials that she was still capable of taking care of them, but the Welfare Office was adamant. The evacuee programme was being wound up. Marion had found a job elsewhere. And today was the day that the children were to leave Graylings for ever.

Brittany stood in the hall and watched the sad little procession as they came down the stairs one by one, each lugging his or her small suitcase. Those that had come without suitcases carried their belongings in brown paper parcels. They were silent with misery; as far as they were concerned, *this* was their home and "Auntie" the person who looked after them. They stood huddled together on the gravelled carriage drive where the bus was due to pick them up. Full of dread, Brittany went to perform the ritual farewell. She walked slowly down the steps of the portico. One of them spotted her with a plaintive wail of *"Auntie!"*, and within seconds she was in a sea of unhappy faces.

"Auntie, where are we going?"

"Auntie, why can't you come with us, *please*!"

"Does this mean we'll never come back?"

"Of course you'll come back!" said Brittany. But her voice cracked and she had to swallow her tears as she bent to kiss them. It was a relief when the bus came into view.

Nancy and George stood on the steps with her, waving as the

bus disappeared. As they turned to go inside, Brittany gave Nancy a brave smile and said, "Well . . . at least now there'll be a chance for us to spend some more time together."

"I suppose so. But I've still got the job at the farm." Having brushed aside her mother's overture, Nancy disappeared.

George had been on the point of offering some comforting platitude, but when he saw the look on Brittany's face he thought better of it. Instead he hugged her tightly, silently, before following Nancy up the stairs.

Brittany flung open the door of the library, saw the red walls that Jake had chosen and burst into tears. She felt completely alone. She was crying so loudly at first that she didn't hear the timid knock at the door.

It was Leonora.

"Brittany, I knew the kids were going today . . . I thought you might like some company. I brought you this." She put a bottle of martini on the library table.

The thought of this sacrifice brought fresh tears to Brittany's eyes. She hugged Leonora, burying her face in the moth-eaten pelt of the mink coat. Leonora was never comfortable with physical displays of affection and she extricated herself on the pretext of looking for glasses.

"Don't you think you ought to go away for a while?" she asked as she bent over to search the shelves of a cabinet.

"Susannah's been trying to persuade me to visit Cleveleigh, but I don't know . . ." Brittany sighed. "I don't like leaving the house."

"Why, because of the will?"

"Exactly. I'm afraid it's going to vanish like Cinderella's finery if I turn my back."

"Then ask Susannah to come here. You need to have people around you . . ."

And entertaining guests will make me feel as though Graylings is my own . . .

"Darling Susannah, I have missed you," she wrote after Leonora had left. *"Please come and spend next weekend here . . ."*

The house was so silent without the evacuees. And George was joining his regiment again . . .

". . . I haven't seen any of the children for what seems like years. Do bring as many of them as possible . . ."

Faye McConnell stood in the window of her room at Lindsay Place and frowned at the muddy banks of the Thames. Her job at the Ministry had been especially tiring of late and the air-raid sirens had kept her awake, though she didn't often bother to go down to the basement shelter these days. She was glad to be leaving the city behind her for a while.

But to reach her destination in Somerset she needed transport. On her first trip to Graylings she had arrived in some style at the wheel of Stephen Willand-Jones' sports car. She didn't intend to take the train this time if she could possibly help it.

She sauntered down to Stephen's room and knocked.

"Come in." He was sitting at the desk in horn-rimmed spectacles, fidgeting with piles of paper. "These wretched accounts," he said, chewing on his pipe. "Hate doing them."

"Stephen, could I borrow your car this weekend?"

"Yes, of course. Going somewhere special?"

"Down to Somerset again, to visit all my crazy relations." She flipped her blonde hair off her face with impeccably polished red fingernails.

"Should be an amusing weekend then."

The smile faded on Faye's lips. "I don't think so," she said gravely. "My cousin's father was killed a few months ago in an air-raid. I'm not expecting to find a very cheerful gathering."

"Well, the keys are over there on the dresser," said Stephen. "But when it comes to petrol, you're on your own I'm afraid. You'll have to buy some on the way down there."

Faye stopped at a garage near Swindon and bought two and a half gallons of pool, which was all the garage attendant would allow her. Still parked in the forecourt, she took her compact from her handbag and powdered her nose. Her lips were thickly outlined with rose-coloured lipstick, her hair combed so that it framed her face with two neat arcs. Then she drove on to the road and continued in the direction of Bristol, smiling calmly into the wind as though the breakneck eighty miles an hour were a mere twenty. She loved to drive.

Brittany was on the steps waiting for her. She looked thinner and older and her hair had lost its toffee-coloured sheen, but she greeted Faye with a bright smile.

"Just in time for lunch, darling! Come into the drawing room. I have some guests I'd like you to meet."

Faye found herself the focus of a roomful of strange faces.

She was introduced to Susannah Stanwycke, a gentle-looking woman with pale gold curls, and her four children. There were two young boys; Johnnie, all scabbed knees, red hair and freckles and Alasdair, a small replica of his mother. Christina Stanwycke was seventeen; round-faced and homely, recoiling awkwardly behind her mother.

The member of the family who most interested Faye was Ralph. She judged him to be roughly her age (which was twenty-two), and experienced a curious thrill of pleasure, when, as she appreciated how well he looked in the dress uniform of a second lieutenant, he greeted her with a beaming and uninhibited smile. He was tall, with the long-backed, short-waisted figure of the English sportsman. His hair was dark blonde and the stubble on his chin gleamed ruddy gold. That fresh, open smile on the pink and gold face proclaimed two things: good health and a good nature. Ralph, it was explained to Faye, was enjoying time off after completing an intelligence mission in France.

The atmosphere in the drawing room was awkward, formal, as though everyone was waiting for something which might not, in the end, happen. Lunch provided little scope for improvement. All but Nancy were intent on making easy, cheerful conversation with the result that two people always seemed to start speaking at once. An "I say, have you heard about . . ." would lock horns with a "Don't you think it's funny how . . ." and both parties would lapse back into an unhappy silence during which they all pretended to be very busy with their food.

Faye was beginning to fear that the afternoon's entertainment would be more of the same, with the dialogue simply transformed to a different set elsewhere in the house, but mercifully this was not the case. Brittany, it seemed, had plans for them.

"Susannah and I are going to go into the kitchen and help Mrs Burrows," she announced. "You boys can go up to the attic and see what you can find of George's toys. And I thought Nancy could take you others out riding, if you would like."

Nancy's horse, Captain, had recently been returned from his temporary employment with the village doctor, and two further mounts had been raised from outlying farms. Predictably, it was Christina who elected to stay behind.

Faye had been born and bred in London and was unused to horses, but Nancy brushed her objections airily aside. Both she and Ralph were experienced enough to look after her, she said, and they wouldn't go too fast. She took Faye up to her room and helped her to squeeze her broad hips into a pair of jodphurs. The result was less than flattering, but Faye was pleased with the way her yellow hair swept out from below the black velvet riding hat and covered her neck like a shawl.

It was a fine day and the earliest itchings of spring were just beginning to vitalise the air. There were no outward signs, save hesitant snowdrops cowering in the damp earth and a freshness in the wind, but the birds could tell that spring was not far off and their song was loud and boisterous. Nancy led her guests along the lane to the west of the house and up the far side of the hollow. The steep wooded lane broke out onto the crest of the Mendip hills, and below lay the flat green patchwork of Avalon, with the Tor protruding like a warm, grassy breast from its surface.

Faye's fat grey pony ambled slowly along its own preferred route, while her weight shifted jerkily from one side of its back to another. Just when she thought she had maintained a degree of equilibrium, there would be an unexpected movement, a bending of the pony's knees, that interrupted her new-found rhythm. And unlike when she was seated behind the wheel of a car, she could not seem to achieve any degree of speed while at the same time maintaining her feminine calm. There was a lamentable contrast between her inelegant display and Nancy's skilled, straight-backed seat, and Faye was relieved when Ralph kicked his horse into a canter and left the two girls behind. Nancy reined in Captain and waited until Faye was alongside.

"You're doing very well for a beginner," she said kindly, leaning out of her saddle to correct Faye's posture. "You're taking all your weight on your toes; move your stirrup back towards your heel, you'll be more comfortable . . . Don't tug on the reins like that . . . that's better. There should be no daylight showing between your leg and the horse's flank. Keep them in tight. And sit further back."

"Do you and Ralph know one another well?" asked Faye.

"Not really. I haven't seen him for years. We met occasionally as children, that's all." She added breezily, "He's rather nice, isn't he?"

"Very," agreed Faye. She looked thoughtfully across the hills. "I've been thinking about Mother living at Graylings. I wondered if it would be different now that your father's dead. Does the house belong to your mother, or to George?"

"Neither. It belongs to Guy."

"Guy?" Faye's mind was blank. Then she remembered the handsome, predatory American who had watched her eat breakfast on her first visit. "Why to Guy? I thought—"

"He's my brother. My half-brother, I should say."

"Oh, I see, then . . ."

Her voice trailed away when she saw the glint in Nancy's eye.

It unnerved her. She brushed her fine, blonde hair back and looked harder at Nancy's face. "That must feel very peculiar," she said sharply, "now that you have to behave like a sister towards him."

"I don't see why," Nancy replied sulkily. "It's not as if I've been brought up with him. He's just like any other man."

"Nancy, don't be a bloody fool!" said Faye, but she guessed correctly that the inquisition would be allowed to go no further.

Nancy glanced crossly over her shoulder, raising one heavy dark brow in her cousin's direction, then kicked Captain savagely forward, urging him first to a canter, then to a gallop until she caught up with Ralph. They were now a hundred yards or more distant, but if Faye screwed up her eyes she could see that the two were engaged in a brief exchange and that Ralph's movements indicated a decision to wait on the spot until Faye joined them. Taking her courage in both hands, and a few large clumps of mane, she bounced her heels against the grey's barrel-shaped sides. There was a sudden forward movement and a heavy, rhythmic thump-thump, which turned out to be her buttocks slapping the saddle. She steadied herself, and though she could not put into operation all the techniques Nancy had advocated, she managed to reach the others at a passably brisk trot.

The lane opened out onto a rough track over windblown scrub, enabling them to ride three abreast, with Faye at the centre. The wind whipped roughly across the rocky ledge and snatched their breath, leaving them half gasping, half laughing. Ralph did not address Faye, but smiled warmly at her each time she caught him leaning forward to look past her and let his eyes feast on the pink-cheeked Nancy. Nancy feigned oblivion of this attention, but a certain perkiness in her carriage betrayed her relish.

"Faye, Ralph went on a mission for the SOE!" she exclaimed. "Isn't that exciting?"

Ralph's florid complexion brightened still further. "I was only there in a very junior capacity," he mumbled. "Not half as glamourous as it sounds."

"Oh yes it was!" Nancy contradicted him. "It was industrial sabotage, Faye! Blowing up German munitions factories, I expect."

Ralph laughed, pleasure at this flattery vying with embarrassment. "It wasn't that at all, I'm afraid."

"What *did* you do?" Faye turned her cool green cat's eyes to Ralph, "are you allowed to tell us?"

"It was really very simple. We were playing about with the

destination labels on railway trucks. You can cause a great deal of chaos when the wrong goods end up in the wrong place.''

''What fun!'' exclaimed Nancy, and Ralph beamed.

They continued in this fashion for a while; both girls addressing questions to Ralph and Ralph replying to both with his voice but to Nancy with his eyes. He demonstrated his loud, hearty laugh at every quip that Nancy made, throwing his head right back. He's certainly smitten, thought Faye grudgingly.

''Come on,'' said Nancy suddenly, ''let's have a race, all three of us. Last one's a sissy!''

''I'm certainly not racing,'' said Faye coolly. ''But you go ahead. I'll watch from here.''

''We'll go as far as that big patch of gorse over there. Ready Ralph?''

''Ready.'' He grinned.

''1—2—3—go!''

The horses surged joyfully forward into a gallop, their hooves echoing dully on the greyish grass. Faye watched them carefully. Ralph turned back repeatedly to look at Nancy, but his horse was larger and more powerful than Captain and he quickly took the lead. Then Faye saw Nancy's feet loosen from her stirrups, and her right leg slide lower and lower down Captain's side until her foot was almost level with the ground and she was hanging around the horse's neck.

Nancy was losing her balance, but why didn't she pull herself up again before it was too late? Captain sensed his rider's predicament, slowing suddenly to a trot, but Nancy's arms released their hold around his neck and she fell to the ground. She lay on her back with her eyes closed.

Faye tried to use her legs to spur her horse into movement, but found that she could not move. Something was wrong . . . She simply sat and stared. A long time seemed to elapse before Ralph saw what had happened.

''Faye! Quick! Nancy's fallen!''

Ralph ran to Nancy's side and knelt on the ground, cradling her head on his lap. As Faye approached, she heard him saying over and over, ''Oh my God, oh my God!''

The extent of his distress disturbed her so much that at first she barely looked at Nancy. Then she bent slowly and reached for Nancy's wrist. The pulse was strong and her cheeks were still pink . . .

Nancy's mouth twitched suddenly and her ribs heaved and she laughed and laughed. It was helpless, self-indulgent laughter, as though she were being tickled. Then her eyes flew open. Ralph looked back at her in consternation. Faye smiled to herself, a wise smile.

"I had you fooled for a moment, didn't I?"

"Not me, you didn't," said Faye lazily. "I saw you fall, remember. I wasn't sure that it was genuine."

Ralph was silent. Then he burst out, "Nancy, how *could* you! I thought you were seriously injured! I was bloody terrified!"

He realised that he was still holding her head, his fingers buried hungrily in her slippery curls, and he released her abruptly. Nancy twisted her head to look up at him.

"What, as much as in France, on your mission?"

"Much more than that! It's a damn foolish trick to play."

"What, really?" persisted Nancy. "You were more frightened when I fell than you were in France? Oh Ralph, you're not serious!" She laughed guiltily. "I had no idea you'd feel that way. It was just a joke! My goodness, if I'd known that it would upset you like that, I'd never have dreamed of letting go of Captain . . ."

This was a much baser pretence, Faye decided, than falling off a horse and playing dead. Pretending that she had not noticed how much poor Ralph already cared for her and was prepared to betray those emotions. She burned with indignation for Nancy's sweet-natured, straightforward dupe.

Nancy finished her mock-innocent protestations with a playful, "There's more than one way to win a race, Ralph!" She let the weight of her head fall back and torment his lap a while longer, then leapt to her feet and sauntered back to her mount, quite unashamed. "Time to head home and get some tea!"

They rode back to Graylings in subdued silence, with Nancy cheerful, Faye vigilant and Ralph bewildered.

He'll forgive her very soon, thought Faye. He'll be laughing like a jay at everything she says before the day's out . . .

As they untacked the horses in the stable yard, a jeep drew up on the semi-circle of gravel in front of the house and sounded its horn.

Before she had a chance to identify the driver, Faye recognized the expression on Nancy's face. Her mouth quivered and her eyes widened dramatically. She was unable to suppress the tremor in her limbs. The curry comb she had been wielding fell to the ground with a clatter as she made for the kitchen door, and the tension within her sparked her into a nervous run. She flung the door open wide and stuck her head inside.

"*Mummy!*" she shouted, "*Guy's arrived!*"

* * *

I am now the owner of this corner of England, Guy had thought as he stepped over the threshold between the porch and the cool marble hall and stood staring up into the blank eye of the domed skylight.

Now, several hours later, he did not feel as though the house was his at all. After dinner he sat hunched forward in one of the drawing room's blue linen-covered armchairs, wrists on knees, and tried to understand why this was the case. As waves of smothered giggles and loud, yeoman laughter broke over him, he decided that it was Nancy's fault.

When he first set foot in Graylings, he had enjoyed a sense of belonging because *she* had made him belong. She had given her home to him, as though conferring a special honour.

But this time she behaved quite differently. She withdrew behind an angry curtain with a press of the lips and a turning of the back, and the secret, joyous essence of the place snapped shut like the petals of a daisy when the sun sinks behind the horizon.

Brittany had behaved from the start as though he did not exist.

He had expected that. He had expected anger, too, when he exercised his prerogative to arrive without prior notice, but she welcomed him with the indifference appropriate to someone she had never met before and would never meet again. A casual observer might conclude that she did not care about the house or who owned it, but Guy sensed a concern; something deeper and blacker than unhappiness. He took care to stay out of her way. She and Susannah were sitting next to one another on a sofa to the right of the french windows, conversing about people and places they knew of old. Brittany had one leg wound tightly around the other, ankles wrapped, while she puffed continuously on cigarettes, never quite extinguishing one before she started another, so that the heap of crumpled butts smoked ominously.

At the other end of the room, near Guy's feet, a small card table had been erected and Faye, Nancy, Ralph and Christina were playing Scrabble. The younger boys hung at the table corners in fascination, every so often sliding coyly to a fresh vantage point and another player's counters.

Guy had no knowledge of the game and had therefore not volunteered to make up the four. Their vocabulary and pronunciation were still largely alien to him, and he had no wish to make a fool of himself. Christina, it seemed, had no notion of spelling, while Nancy was intent on cheating with words that did not exist. And there was much argument about scoring.

"I scored double on that letter," murmured Faye indignantly as Christina wrote down an incorrect score.

"But I've already used that 'double' square on my last go, with QUEEN. You can't use it too."

"Yes I can, if I use the 'Q' to make my word."

"No you can't, you can only have the amount on the counter . . ."

The argument raged on. Nancy silenced it by gathering up all the letters from her wooden stand and putting them down in one word. The others craned into the centre to read it. Faye smiled sleepily, but said nothing.

"ENARPH?" said Christina plaintively. "That's not a proper word! Come on Nancy, stop cheating!"

"Yes it is!" retorted Nancy. "My nanny used to say it to me all the time." She adopted Florrie's Cockney twang, *"Oh Miss Nancy you enarph naughty!"*

Ralph tipped his head back and laughed with relish until his skin glowed bright pink against the fine, yellow flecks of stubble. Barely able to control his irritation, Guy stared fixedly at the patch of wall opposite him, his eyes narrowing. But Nancy had not finished yet. She took away one counter and arranged the others.

"PHANE?" said Christina, with disbelief.

"Yes, you know—it's Shakespeare. *'Fain would I dwell on form, fain, fain deny What I have spoke.'* "

Ralph roared again and even Faye laughed at Christina's consternation.

"Nancy, old girl," Ralph hugged his ribs. "You'll have to stop doing this or I'll suffer internal injury!" His eyes were shining with ill-concealed admiration.

Nancy looked back at him with wide-eyed mock innocence. And then she smiled.

She smiled her richest, most luscious smile, running like electric cable from head to foot. Sparks of voltage from that smile burst into the air and exploded. Guy felt his stomach turn over. He saw, with belated clarity that she had intended to make him jealous and that she had succeeded. Nancy had not smiled one of those smiles at *him* all weekend, and to watch someone else receive it was like receiving a blow from an ice-cold fist.

He would have to try and get her on her own, but how?

Once, if he had got up and walked out she would have contrived to follow, but not now. After she'd caught him consoling himself with that much-enjoyed broad, Maudie . . .

The word "broad" had come into his head as soon as he saw her and had been irreversibly associated with her since. Broad or not, Nancy still hadn't forgiven him for it.

After several more verbal hilarities, punctuated with guffaws and squabbles, Guy got up and left the room. He wandered into the library, drinking in his dead father's benign influence. After the library he toured the billiard room, handling the cues thoughtfully, lifting and weighing them. Then he went to his room and waited while it grew dark. Footsteps passed his room at irregular intervals as the revellers retired to bed one by one. When he went down to the drawing room again, only two remained.

Nancy and Ralph.

They were sitting at the card table, talking in low voices. Ralph started and flushed guiltily when he saw Guy. He stood in the doorway without moving, his dense square frame blocking all but a fine outline of light from behind him. Within this blindingly brilliant silhouette the rest of him was obscured to one shade of brown; brown hair, brown skin, brown eyes, an intense, arrogant monochrome presence dominating the room. He said nothing.

Ralph got to his feet, mumbling that it was time for bed, and left the room, waiting almost apologetically for Guy to step out of the way.

The trick of the light was over. Guy was debonair, smiling, his teeth a hygienic white.

"I thought I might go for a drink," he said to Nancy, once Ralph was out of earshot. "Care to join me?"

"A *drink*? Now?"

"Yes, why not? Come on." He walked to the table and allowed his warm, brown fingers to close around her wrist. The contact subdued her. With the lightest of pressure he pulled her to her feet and led her from the room. And out into the cold, starry night.

They walked to the Lamb and Child in silence. Then Guy said simply, "Don't be mad at me, Nancy."

She did not reply at first, but as she looked up at his face she felt something uncoil inside her, something deep and tight and knotted, and she was flooded with warmth.

"Let's get drunk, Guy," she said and gave him the smile he had been waiting for.

There was a fire in the grate at the Lamb and Child, filling the room with sharp, choking wood smoke which was prevented from ascending the chimney by ancient blocked flues. Two sheepdogs basked ecstatically in front of the flames.

"I'm going to have some perry," said Nancy. "Have you ever tried it before? It's like cider, but made of pears."

Guy shook his head.

A surreptitious hush had fallen when they walked into the room together, and now several pairs of eyes were sliding sideways to watch them.

Nancy leaned closer and lowered her voice. "Let's buy plenty and drink it as fast as we can, so we can go somewhere else."

She went to the bar and ordered two glasses of the pale yellow scented liquid from the oldest and simplest looking barman. She removed the drinks to their table while he was attending to someone else's order, then went and stood in the same position and said in an identical tone of voice, "Two perrys please."

She received them with an innocent smile and handed over a few coins. Guy surveyed the four pints of perry jostling for space on the small round table.

"I bet you didn't pay for all of these did you?"

She laughed. "How on earth d'you know?"

"Because I've done exactly the same thing myself. The guy gets confused and thinks he forgot to serve you the first time, right?"

"That's right." Nancy smiled with satisfaction.

"Before we leave, we really ought to be good children and own up about the other two. But d'you think we're going to?"

"No, I don't."

"Neither do I."

Guy drained his first glass with satisfaction and started on his second. The room warmed and closed around him and his head swam slightly so that when Nancy smiled her shameless smile and said, "I think tonight is a good night for lying and staring at the stars," he could not be absolutely certain that he had not imagined her saying it, or at least heard her say it before.

By the time they left the pub her smile had grown looser and she swayed towards him as they walked. They reached the ridge above Graylings with the house a clear, ghostly white below, and began to descend the drive, but before they reached the bottom, Nancy altered their course and led them up a narrow path to their left. It climbed to the beech copse which stood on a small hill looking over the house and the trees behind it. The steep, grassy slope of the hill was muddy and icy cold to the touch, but when Guy lay down on it beside Nancy, he barely felt it touch him or penetrate to his skin, as though he floated slightly above it.

They lay on their backs, a few inches apart, and when they looked at the sky, the perry sent it veering in a circle and the beech trees behind their heads swam in and out of focus as though the pair of them had just stepped from a rapidly revolving carousel. They were out of breath, even though they were not moving.

Nancy laughed.

"What do you think of our father dying then, like that?" Guy asked.

If anyone else had asked the question it would have sounded odd, flippant even, but because it was Guy, Nancy understood at once what he meant.

"There's something very complete and definite about it being an air-raid," she said, watching her breath make clouds against the inky sky. "No one has time to think or feel. I'd rather he died like that than some other way. It doesn't seem fair that it was Daddy and not somebody else, but if it had been another person, then someone else might be lying where we are now and thinking, *'It isn't fair.'* Do you see what I mean? When you look at it that way, death's not something you can argue against."

"No, it isn't."

"How about you, Guy? How did you feel?"

"I guess I just wished I'd known him better. I felt as though we'd had so little time together."

"Oh Christ . . . and *I* wasted all the time he and I had together! D'you remember asking me once whether I ever told Daddy I loved him? Well, the last time I spoke to him was one of the occasions I wanted to. He rang up to speak to Mummy and I was just about to say it . . . and then at the last minute I chickened out. And half an hour later he was dead—gone."

"Why didn't you? What stopped you from saying it?"

"Perhaps it was pride."

"Pride?"

"I wanted to be completely self-sufficient, and I was too proud to show that I wasn't."

"Because you felt shut out?"

"Yes. My parents' relationship was such a success that I didn't feel they needed me. Particularly Mummy."

"But she needs you now."

Nancy picked a handful of damp grass and let the blades fall between her fingers. "It's too late, Guy. I can't go back . . . It was always much easier with George somehow."

"Because he admitted he needed you."

Nancy laughed. "Right again, *mein Professor*!" She tapped him on the forehead. "Where did they teach you to be a mind reader? But even with George, things have changed. I've lost him somehow. The war's brought about so much uncertainty. Look at you getting Graylings. I bet you never expected to own a house like that . . ."

Guy smiled to himself.

". . . Your whole life can be changed by one air-raid . . . I've never been in an air-raid," she continued dreamily, "I do wish I had. I want to find out what sort of a person I am, whether I'm really brave or whether I just think I am. D'you know Guy," she leaned on her right elbow so that she was facing him, "I read an article in the newspaper once about a millionairess from Torbay—that's a place on the South coast. I read it over and over again; I can even remember her name. Miss Ella Marion Rowcroft. She spent twenty-four thousand pounds on having her own private air-raid shelter built. And there was a huge bronze plate on the bed-head and d'you know what it said? It said, *'Angels are watching overhead. Sleep sweetly then. Goodnight.'* Isn't that incredible? Can you imagine—there is this fat old sow climbing into her bed every night . . . But when I read it, I sort of admired her and I wished I'd thought of something like that, a sort of grand gesture . . ."

"That's very fanciful," said Guy quietly.

"Fanciful? Is that a bad thing?"

"Well, where I come from, you're kind of discouraged from being fanciful, but I think it's a good thing to be once in a while. In fact I'm going to say something fanciful now, if that's all right?"

Nancy laughed. "Go ahead."

Guy looked straight up at the constellated heavens and the huge, unblinking spring moon.

" *'All the stars made gold of all the air, And the sea moving saw before it move, one moon-flower making all the foam-flowers fair.'* That's Swinburne. English."

"I don't like poetry much," said Nancy. "But that's pretty. And fanciful."

They fell silent for a while. Nancy thought that it would be rather nice to lean over and kiss Guy on those Too-Perfect-For-

This-World lips, but she hesitated. Swinburne had made her remember English lessons at school, and George Gordon, Lord
Byron. She had read the letters he wrote to his half-sister Au-
gusta. People had said that it was wrong that he loved her like
that, but what could be wrong about loving someone in every
way, with a love that encompasses even the most distant echo of
the beginnings of one's existence?

But she did not kiss Guy, contenting herself with leaning
against his shoulder and soaking up his warmth with her cheeks,
her nose, her ears.

Guy sighed so deeply that she could see the outline of his
chest rise and fall. "So old George doesn't seem to need you so
much right now. And how about you?" He clenched her hair.
"Do you still need him?"

She shook her head. "I need you. That's the difference. I need
you now."

It was a warm evening in April, and Nether Aston basked in
the lingering light that brought a promise of summer.

Patrick Steele parked his dilapidated truck outside the Lamb
and Child and went in. Since Greville had left the village he felt
a distinct sensation of unease every time he set foot in the place,
convinced that everyone was staring at him, but he'd had a hard
day drilling sugar beet and he was desperate. He didn't care if
nobody liked him and nobody wanted to talk to him, he just
wanted a drink. He scowled at the dogs that came to greet him,
ordered a pint and took up his position in the corner of the bar.

Business was slow in the Lamb and Child that night. Maudie
Lester was sitting at the bar with one of her brothers, smoking
one cigarette after another and watching the door. One or two
of the domino players were dozing in a corner, and another of
them shuffled over to speak to Patrick. He was called Mickey
Padbury, and in the past he had worked on the Steeles' farms as
a casual labourer.

Patrick nodded a greeting. He didn't mind old Mickey. Harmless old boy.

"Still no sign of that cousin of yourn? Old fatty?"

Patrick shook his head.

"Reckon 'e came to a bad end, 'im."

Patrick shrugged.

"Boys on the farm say that sister of yourn got a sweetheart.
Who'd he be then?"

"Shut up, Mickey!"

"Reckon it'd be that young George Stein. 'Course, he's fighting in foreign parts. Africa, they say.''

"Yes, and with any luck he won't bloody well come back!"

Mickey nodded his head with an exaggerated movement and gave a toothless grin. "Ah, but he will! I know see, 'cause my Annie's boy's in the same regiment. The Royal Signals Corpse, they call 'em. And they're due back any day now, Annie says."

Patrick felt the ale churn in his stomach and his gorge begin to rise. He slapped his glass down on the bar and clenched his fist to stop it trembling. "What the hell would you know, you half-witted old bugger?"

He pushed Mickey aside and ran to his truck. The ignition was slow to fire and he swore out loud as he flung it into gear and drove the two hundred yards to Heathcote House.

"Annabel! . . . Where the hell are you? . . . Annabel!"

She was in the kitchen, her hands covered in flour. "What on earth's happened?"

"Nothing . . ." Patrick fought to get his breath back, letting his arms go limp at his sides.

". . . I just wanted to make sure you were still here, that's all."

On 1 May, George's regiment was de-mobbed and he set sail from Port Said to Marseilles.

From there he took the boat-train to London and on 8 May stepped exhausted and dazed from Victoria Station into a crowd of shouting, laughing people. Picking his way through throngs of Londoners dancing the Hokey-Cokey and the conga, he eventually found an elderly man who was willing to stop for a few seconds and explain that Churchill had announced Victory in Europe earlier that afternoon. As soon as he had finished speaking to George, the old man returned to his Hokey-Cokey, gravely putting his right foot in and out and shaking it all about.

Everyone seemed eager to add to the hubbub. Children were banging dustbin lids and dragging empty petrol cans across the pavement. George headed for St James's Park in the fading light and was caught up in a vast throng of people who had gathered in front of a floodlit Buckingham Palace. Coloured rockets exploded in the summer sky, but this crowd was respectful, almost silent. The tense expectancy affected George too, and he put his bags down on the ground and waited. Then the King and Queen and the two princesses appeared on the balcony and waved, and the crowd erupted in a roar. A group near George began to sing

"Land of Hope and Glory," others clung to each other or danced on the spot. A fat, floral-clad woman threw her arms tightly around George crying, "You lovely lad, we've won the war, we've won the war!"

He submitted to the sweaty embrace, then pushed the woman away, irritated.

They were supposed to be celebrating peace, but where was the peace amid all this noise and movement? He just wanted peace, real peace . . .

He walked on to Piccadilly, trying to find a taxi, but there were none to be seen, and besides, the streets were far too crowded for traffic to move. He trudged wearily to Paddington and arrived exhausted to find that there was no train due to depart to Somerset for another four hours. It was a national holiday and services had been severely curtailed. Stupid with exhaustion, he sat down on his suitcase and laughed at himself. I must be the only person alive in this city, he thought, who's missing the bloody war.

George was asleep when his train pulled into Bath station very early the next morning. A sympathetic guard woke him, then asked to shake his hand, a subdued gesture after the agitation that he had seen in London. Taking advantage of his uniform and the man's good-will, he asked if there was a telephone he could use. He telephoned Graylings from a tiny office decked in hand-dyed buntings and a faded portrait of George V, who looked out, surprised, from the fronds of some elderly Christmas streamers.

Nancy answered the phone.

She sounded pleasantly surprised, but not jubilant when George announced that he had returned. He thought she looked very beautiful as she drove into the station forecourt, hooting imperiously for other cars to get out of the way. Her thick brown-black hair waved back from her forehead and she wore a short-sleeved white shirt that made clean lines across her tanned forearms. George slung his suitcase and knapsack into the back seat of the car, and then noticed the boots and rolled-up canvas gaiters on the passenger seat beside Nancy.

"I'm going up to the farm directly after I've dropped you," she said in explanation. Then silence.

"So you're still working up there?" asked George lamely.

"That's right."

Nancy snapped her naked brown foot down on the accelerator and the car swung left onto the main Bath to Wells road. May sunshine filtered through the brave new leaves and made stirring dappled patterns on the bonnet of the car as it passed beneath them. Light bounced from the windscreen.

George shaded his eyes. "What are you in such a bad mood about? The war's over, remember. You're supposed to be glad."

"That's exactly it," snapped Nancy. "It's all over. The men are coming back to the farms. Greta and Maureen will be leaving when the harvest's over. I'll be on my own again."

"I was just coming to that . . . What are you going to do next, Nan?"

"I don't know—what are *you* going to do?"

George smiled slightly, reminded of similar circular conversations from their childhood. "I haven't decided yet. I have to think about it. But first I need some rest."

Nancy flung a charming smile in his direction. "I'm sorry—I keep forgetting. I know that it doesn't show, but I'm damn glad you're back safely." She took her left hand from the steering wheel and hung on to his arm. George basked in the warmth of the moment and watched her face adoringly. This was his old Nancy.

They screeched to a halt outside the fastidiously white columns of the porch, but George did not move.

"Aren't you going in?"

"I don't want to, Nan," said George. *"I can't."*

He sat looking down at his knees for a while. "It may sound silly to you, but I'm not quite ready to go back to it all just yet. It's normal life, isn't it?" He looked up at her face anxiously, and all the weariness of three years' fighting shone out.

"Come on then . . ." Nancy flung the gear stick into reverse and turned the car back in the direction it had come from. "I'll take you up to the farm with me."

Greta and Maureen were standing in the farmyard, hands on hips. "What's this then, eh," demanded Greta shrilly, tapping the bonnet of the car with a disapproving finger. "Lost the use of yer legs?" Then she caught sight of George. "Oh, I see."

"So this is your brother," said Maureen. "We've often wondered why you kept him hidden away, and now I understand why. He's far too nice-looking to be let on the loose."

She ran her eye over George's long legs and waving brown hair, his broad, square brow. Her shrewd glance also took in the fatigue in his eyes and the feeble way he was holding his heavy kit-bag. His wrist was trembling. "You look as though you could do with a cup of tea. Come on."

She marched off to the barn that housed the girls' "den" and George followed her as trustingly as a dog. After drinking several pints of chocolate-brown tea from a cracked mug and eating a plateful of dried eggs, he was left to rest on a camp-bed covered with a mangy horse-blanket. Maureen's husband watched over him belligerently on the wall above. Gratefully, he closed his eyes and slept.

When he woke, it was late afternoon. His limbs were stiff and cramped, and a fly buzzed persistently on the ceiling above him.

He thought he was in Egypt, but the contents of the room said otherwise. A pair of stout boots in the corner. A hair net on the table. Some recordings of Nancy's favourite dance bands. A copy of *Gone with the Wind*.

He rinsed his face and mouth under the cold tap to a symphony of scrapes and bangs and giggles that floated through the open window. Then he went to find his sister.

The girls were engaged in cleaning the tack room at the opposite corner of the yard. George offered to help, but they refused him briskly, so he squatted on his haunches with his back against the cool stone wall and watched them.

Maureen was sweeping the floor, Greta scrubbing down the large butcher's block table in the centre of the room, while Nancy was lifting down the bridles and harnesses from the nails on the wall and dismantling them. She worked methodically with quick, neat movements, sucking in her lower lip pensively.

Would he get her back, George wondered? All his thoughts, his ideas and hopes had been spilled out into his letters to Annabel. Supposing he had written those letters to Nancy instead. Would he have lost her? Would she have that old interest in him, that she had clearly abandoned? When he was young, the summit of George's ambition was to make his younger sister laugh. Nancy was so proud, so scornful, yet there was something in her that made others long to please her. Her smiles and laughter were so contained that they made a rich reward. For a brief spell you felt that Nancy Stein had shared something of herself with you, and the sense of achievement and privilege was wildly exciting.

When the light began to fade, Nancy finished her tasks and George reluctantly allowed himself to be driven home. He had enjoyed being at the farm, in a safe neutral place and alone with his thoughts. Again he hesitated when they came to a halt outside the house.

"How's Mother taking things?" he asked.

"I think she's lonely—but that's to be expected, isn't it?"

"No, I mean about Guy, about him having the house."

Nancy swung her head sharply to look at George. "Is that why you didn't want to go home this morning?"

"Partly."

"Well, Guy's not there. But I don't think it makes any difference anyway. He's probably going back to America now."

"Is that why *you* were so bad-tempered this morning?"

Nancy shot her brother an angry look and slammed into the house without replying.

As soon as he was inside the house again with his shirts folded away in the drawers and his shoes in the closet, George felt angry too.

Because he was back for good, disbelief at Guy's inheritance hit him with a new shock. At night he was visited in his dreams by a bloated, voracious Guy with gnashing teeth. His mother exuded blank acceptance of the situation, and a complete lack of desire to discuss it. It was the same when he came to tell her he was leaving. He had reached a decision quickly, as soon as he had slept sufficiently for his fatigue to leave him, and after several phone calls it was all arranged.

He rehearsed the speech he would make to his mother. *"Mother, with things the way they are at the moment, I don't want to live here any longer . . . ."* But when he made the speech, she did not argue. She said she thought it was probably a good idea.

He expected more resistance from Annabel, however.

He decided to go and visit her at Heathcote, unannounced. Frankly, he was curious. She had assiduously avoided letting him cross the threshold of her home, and he wanted to know what it was like. What lurked there, beside the disagreeable Patrick? He rang the front doorbell several times but there was no reply. His first thought was that Annabel must have gone out somewhere; shopping, or to the library, but if that were the case she would have locked the front door, which was slightly ajar. He went inside.

"Annabel?" he called, but there was no reply.

The house seemed sunk in a gloomy lethargy. He looked in the kitchen first and was shocked by its gaunt slovenliness, despite obvious efforts by Annabel or some other person to keep it tidy. The heterogeneous patches of carpet were the only cheerful touch; a coat of many colours. The square drawing room was tidy but dull and dark, its furniture spare and lumbering. After Graylings George found the house colourless, as though any colour it might have had had been drained away by long-gone sunbeams and absorbed into flowers and the wings of butterflies. Ceilings were clouded with smoke and dust, and the large rooms housed dead, cold hearths.

He looked in the dining room. It had once been quite a grand room. There were two oval mirrors built into the walls at either end of the table, surrounded by black cupids carrying garlands. One of these funereal sprites had swung around on its own axis so that it hung upside down. Another had fallen off altogether.

As he closed the dining room door, George was aware of someone behind him. Patrick Steele was standing at the foot of the stairs staring at him.

"What the bloody hell are you doing here!" he shouted.

His brows were pulled down angrily over his eyes and his fists were clenched so tightly that the veins stood out on top of his hands and on his inner arms. George was surprised by how old he looked, how tight and narrow. His skin was grey and lined.

"The front door was open," he replied coldly. "I'm looking for Annabel."

"Well, she's not in! And you're not to come here, d'you hear? You're not to bloody come here!"

George glanced up the staircase, but Patrick did not move from his position on the lower step. He was trembling visibly. "In that case, perhaps you'd ask her to ring me at Graylings."

As he turned and walked to the front door, there was a scuffling on the upstairs landing and Annabel appeared.

"George! Wait!"

"I thought you'd gone out," said Patrick. His pale face was sweating.

"You knew I hadn't. I was washing my hair!"

Annabel's face was flushed, and damp strands of hair clung to her neck and her cheeks. She darted an accusing look at Patrick and he ran up the stairs without a word.

"Come into the kitchen. I've got to make Kit's lunch."

She took a saucepan down from a shelf and threw some unappetizing mince into it. "It would have been easier if you'd said you were coming," she said, shaking salt vigorously into the pan. Her childlike eyes, like pools of blue-black ink, were mildly reproachful.

"I know—I'm sorry. I just felt like coming now. I came to tell you something."

"Oh?" Annabel reached for the pepper.

"I'm going back to Cambridge." He shifted uncomfortably from the green carpet to the pink.

The vigorous shaking of the pepper pot halted. "When?"

"In a few weeks. Term doesn't start for ages, but I want to catch up on some background reading first."

"But George—you never said when you got back and I saw you . . . you never said . . . I thought you'd stay here. How long will you be gone?"

"About three years. I want to finish the agriculture course I started."

"Three years!" Annabel wailed. "But George . . . Three years is . . . for ever! When you asked me to marry you, I thought it meant you were staying here. If you're in Cambridge—"

"Come with me."

She wiped her hands on her apron and her child's mouth set in an adult line.

"You know I can't do that. I have to look after Father, and Kit. And anyway . . ." She cut herself short, shook her head and began stirring the mince vigorously.

George tried to decide what she had been about to say. "Patrick wouldn't let me," perhaps. Or even, "I can't leave Patrick." Clearly Patrick still needed her, in the way he once thought he had needed Nancy. But there was more to it than that. He had never seen such fear and hatred as he had when Patrick faced him on the stairs. He turned these thoughts over in his mind as he left the house and walked down the front path.

From an upstairs window a pair of dark, angry eyes watched him go.

Seven
August 1945

NANCY WOKE WITH a start when her alarm clock rang. She lay gazing at its apoplectic brass bell, wondering what she had woken herself up for. This was the time when she usually lay cradled in a womb of early morning light, in the blissful border country between sleeping and waking, thinking of all the things she might turn into, all the lives she might lead. It was a time when she could indulge her imagination until anything was possible without the slightest effort. Without even rolling over in bed she could be Nancy Stein, star of the West End stage, Nancy Stein, mistress to royalty, Nancy Stein . . .

Then she remembered.

It was 15 August—VJ Day—and she was holding the biggest party Graylings had ever seen.

She dressed in the oldest clothes she could find: an Aertex shirt from her days at St Clare's (now woefully tight around her chest), a pair of George's bush shorts and a spotted red bandanna knotted on the top of her head.

"You look just like Minnie Mouse," she said out loud to the mirror before she left her room.

In the kitchen she made a cup of tea and sat down to write out a list of the tasks she had to do. It began with "Take up carpets" and ended with "Blow up balloons", and the length of entries in between was daunting. She wanted people to have more fun than they had ever dreamed possible, even if she had to beg, steal and borrow to do it. She wanted to be queen bee again: the powerhouse, the impulse, the inspiration behind the activities of the herd.

There was less national interest in Victory in Japan than there had been in Victory in Europe in May, and less celebration was expected, but Nancy had a good reason for holding her party on that day. For the first time in her life she had the house to herself.

George was in Cambridge, Guy in London somewhere—no one knew exactly where—and her mother was staying at Cleveleigh with Susannah Stanwycke. Susannah's husband Hugh had been taken prisoner in Burma and died just after the end of the war, and when Brittany heard the news she had reacted even more violently than she had to the news of Jake's death. It wasn't fair, she had shouted. Susannah, of all people, deserved better. Her friend's suffering seemed to jolt her out of her lethargy and she volunteered to go to Cleveleigh Manor for an extended stay to help look after the youngest children while Susannah decided the fate of the farm. And she had given Mrs Burrows, the faithful cook-housekeeper, a few days holiday so that she could visit her latest grandchild.

The only person in addition to Nancy, who remained at Graylings, was Leonora, and Leonora didn't count.

At half past nine, Greta and Maureen arrived.

" 'Ello Minnie!'' said Greta cheerfully, tweaking the spotted bandanna. "Blimey Nance, that blouse don't 'alf squash yer wotsits! It's like one of them things Japanese women wear.''

Maureen had her amber hair rolled up in anticipatory curlers.

"How's the progress with our leaving do then?'' she asked, sitting down at the kitchen table and lighting herself a cigarette. "What's the plan of action?''

"It's *not* a leaving party,'' said Nancy firmly. "It's a VJ Day party.''

"Yes, but we're leaving though, aren't we?'' Greta's round painted mouth smiled, unrepentant. "And you're just going to have to get used to the idea, girl,'' she added more kindly, reaching out to put a hand on Nancy's shoulder.

"I don't see why you have to go, you could stay here—I'm sure there would be jobs you could do, you could even—''

"Look Nance, we've been through all that before. We can't hang around here forever. Mo's got to get back to that bleedin' lump of an old man, and I've got to . . . well, who knows. Go back up the Smoke, I suppose.''

"You'll be all right without us,'' said Maureen briskly. Her eyes narrowed slightly as she dragged on her cigarette. "Your sort always are. And you've got all that lovely money coming to you when you're twenty-one. World's your oyster, my lass.''

Her tone of voice left no room for argument.

"The Plan of Action then . . .'' said Nancy bitterly. "It's called Operation Beg, Steal or Borrow . . .''

She began to work her way through the list, pointing to each item with her pencil in what she hoped was a business-like manner.

"Now. Flags. I want us to have a Union Jack and Stars and Stripes draped across the walls as a centrepiece. That comes under 'Steal'. They have the flags flying outside the Crown Hotel in Wells. I want someone to volunteer to drive into Wells and get them.''

''Bloody 'ell, Nancy, we can't just go and nick 'em in broad daylight!''

''Well, we'll call that one 'Borrow' then,'' said Nancy crisply. ''We're not going to need them after tonight, so they can always be returned. Next, buntings. I want the whole house covered with buntings. Does anyone know what happened to the ones that were up in the high street on VE Day?''

''The WI made them,'' said Maureen. ''I expect they're at the vicarage with Mrs Godwin.''

''In that case, buntings are a 'Beg'. We'll go and ask her if we can borrow them. That leaves music. We need to get hold of some of those big loudspeakers, like they have at the dances. Any ideas?''

''As far as I know, they're still in the village 'all.'' Greta was looking at her reflection in the kitchen window pane as she spoke, pursing her lips and patting her peroxide blonde curls affectionately. ''So I suppose that's another 'Borrer'.''

''Sounds like 'Thieving' to me,'' grumbled Maureen.

Nancy ignored her.

''And now we come to the most important item of all. Lights. I want us to get hold of as many as we can.''

''What sort of lights?''

''Any lights. Table lamps, bicycle lamps, spotlights, torches. There used to be some floodlights at the front of the house when my mother was young, but I don't know if they work any more. They were probably operated by gas or something. But we can take a look . . . I want the whole house to be one big blaze of light, out of every window. No curtains . . .''

''No rotten blackout!'' cried Greta, excited.

''No more bloody Hitler!'' shouted Maureen. She started goose-stepping around the kitchen table with one arm raised high and a finger across her upper lip as a makeshift moustache.

'' *Rule Brittania!* '' sang Nancy, and the others joined in.

''. . . *'Brittania rules the waves! Britons never, never, never shall be slaves!'* ''

And the three of them collapsed, laughing, onto the kitchen table.

In the afternoon, Greta and Maureen returned from their scavenging with a third person in tow.

Nancy was standing, precariously, on a step-ladder in the ballroom, dusting the chandelier. From this great height she could see the top of Maureen's flame-colcured head and a large red and blue bundle in her arms, which obscured her face. At her elbow, a small unfamiliar flaxen head was just visible.

"We've got the flags!" shouted Maureen.

"Yes, and damn nearly ended up in the nick!" squawked Greta. Her blonde curls were dishevelled. "You've no idea how hard it is to get those things off the flagpoles. *And* a copper nearly saw us, not to mention the hotel manager. I hope you're bloody well grateful!"

Nancy climbed slowly down the ladder.

"And who's this?" she asked.

"This is Kit," said Maureen. "We found him in the sweet shop and decided it would be a laugh if he came along. Thought you could use an extra helper."

Kit was chubby and fair with the eyes of a sad dog, sloping down at the corners. He wore a patched and darned grey jersey and his shoes had been scuffed so much that their toes were white. He smiled up at Nancy uncertainly.

"Honestly, Maureen!" she said irritably. "What a stupid idea! Don't you realise how much we've still got to do? What the hell use is a little kid? He'll only get in the way."

Kit's dark grey eyes drooped slightly and he blinked.

"Here Kit," said Nancy kindly, reaching in the pocket of her shorts. "They've dragged you all the way down here for nothing, I'm afraid." She handed him some crumpled pieces of paper. "I haven't spent my sweet ration for ages. Why don't you go down to the shop and see what you can get with these coupons?"

"I can help!" he piped up. "I really can! I won't get in your way, I promise. I can carry things and . . . and I'm very strong."

He pushed back the frayed sleeve of his jersey and showed her a small, rounded brown arm.

Nancy laughed. "All right then, you can help for a while. But as soon as you get in the way, that's it!"

Kit beamed at her. She turned to the others.

"Did you get the buntings? And the loudspeakers?"

They nodded.

"Good. Would you put the gramophone and speakers at one end of the room, and a table with glasses at the other? Kit—you come with me."

Nancy carried the heavy cardboard box containing the buntings into the hall.

"This is a nice room!" exclaimed Kit, staring up at the pale blue central dome with its round skylight, and the curving marble staircase that swept up to the first floor landing.

Nancy looked at it with new eyes. She had never really thought of the entrance hall as a room before, but in a way it was. There was a large low oval table made of highly polished satinwood and laden with books and flowers. At the edge of the floor stood the two silk-covered Empire sofas with gilt legs, though as far as Nancy could remember, nobody had ever sat down on them.

"Yes it is rather nice," she said, looking at Kit's eagerly smiling face with renewed interest. "And we're going to put these little flags up all over it. Now, I'll stand on these steps and you hand them to me please."

Kit did indeed prove very useful. He had a sunny, imperturbable temperament and did not seem to mind when Nancy had a different idea every five minutes about where the buntings should hang.

For Kit it was all very simple. He was used to being told what to do from dawn until dusk, and at nine years old had a very mature appreciation of the futility of argument with one's elders.

But he had never met anybody like Nancy Stein before. She was as pretty as a princess in a storybook. His sister was pretty too, but Nancy *behaved* like a princess. Kit could quite easily imagine her sending wicked subjects to have their heads chopped off. Within minutes he had become her devoted slave. If Nancy said, "I think it looks right there, don't you, Kit?" he would nod vigorously, and if she later lost patience with the same arrangement and ripped it down saying, "Oh, no, that's *awful*!" he would echo, "Yes, *awful*!"

When the task was finished, Kit hovered hopefully.

"The other lady said that if I was good I might be able to come to the party . . ."

"I don't see why you shouldn't come for a short while. Is there someone you can ask? Your parents?"

"My sister," said Kit.

"Well, perhaps she'd like to come too, and anyone else who's at home."

"Can I telephone Annabel and ask her?"

"Annabel?" The light dawned on Nancy. "Oh, I see. You must be Christopher Steele, then?" She remembered the little boy who had been sitting shyly in the window seat at the Stanwyckes' Christmas party. But that had been nearly three years ago, and she had been concentrating on Guy . . .

Kit nodded vigorously.

"I'd forgotten about you . . . Ask your brother and sister if they'd like to come then. They already know my brother George, I believe."

Kit hurried off to Heathcote House, anxious to relay the message and return as soon as possible to Nancy's side.

He did not want to miss a moment more of her than necessary, but Annabel said he must ask Patrick, and Patrick would not return from the farm until dusk. Kit hopped impatiently from foot to foot, fearing that Patrick would say "no". He did say "no" at first, but when Annabel declared that she fully intended to go, since everyone in the village who had been de-mobbed would be there, Patrick capitulated. Kit noticed that he often changed his mind like that rather than let Annabel go somewhere by herself. He wondered if Annabel was glad.

They would *all* go, Patrick said, but Kit could only stay for the first half hour.

Kit hurried back to Graylings, leaving the others to follow on later, after Patrick had finished his supper. He knew as he half walked, half ran down the long drive on his sturdy brown legs, that he wanted to climb straight up on to that sugary white porch, pass between the columns and go straight into the entrance hall that he had decorated.

He did not quite know why he wanted to do that until he opened the heavy front door and put his head cautiously round it. Then he knew at once why the place had seemed to beckon to him.

To his wild delight she had chosen that very moment to descend the gleaming white staircase.

Her dress was like sweets. He wanted to run to her and sink his teeth into it. It was pale cream, gossamer thin and shimmering with opalescent beads, like tiny sugary crystals. And there were coloured beads too, sewn into the shape of large flowers; rasberry and strawberry, sherbet yellow and parma violet. Her dark hair was caught up in a top-knot that rippled and shimmered under the skylight.

"Kit!" she exclaimed, and her eyes reflected the rays of bright colour from her dress, "I do believe you're my very first guest! Let me get you a drink."

She took his hand and led him to a large table covered with rows of cups. As she walked the heels of her shoes made a cool, echoey sound on the bare floor. Next to the cups were plates of tiny biscuits covered in red, white and blue icing.

Kit looked at them longingly.

"Have a biscuit," said Nancy as she poured him some government-issue orange juice.

"Are they to eat?"

"Of course they are, silly!"

Kit looked down at his shoes. He didn't want Nancy to think he was silly. "I've got my best clothes on," he said hopefully.

"Let's have a look." Nancy held him at arm's length and ran a critical eye over his grey flannel shorts, white shirt and white socks shrunk from boiling. "You look very smart," she said. "And now Kit, I'm going to put some music on, and I hope you will do me the honour of the first dance . . ."

She took both his hands in hers and walked him slowly around the centre of the enormous ballroom that blazed with light, beckoning Nether Aston like a triumphal beacon. Kit lumbered at her feet like a baby elephant, his head at the level of her waist. Then she bent and kissed him on the top of his head.

Kit thought he was in heaven.

He tried to stay near Nancy, but people came, and more people, and more and more . . . She seemed to evaporate into them, to be swallowed up and disappear like a diminishing speck on a vast, over-lit landscape. The noise grew surreptitiously louder; from a murmur to a hum and finally a roar as tipsy voices struck up competition with the music of Glen Miller's band.

Kit danced with himself for a while, then wandered disconsolately into the hall and fell asleep on one of the Empire sofas, beneath the buntings that had laboured to erect.

He was woken by the sound of voices arguing.

Opening one eye, his field of vision was filled with a haze of primrose yellow organdie. He recognised it at once, it was Annabel's party dress.

"Look at poor Kit!" Patrick was saying. "That Stein girl's probably got him drunk."

"*Sshh!*" hissed Annabel. "Don't be so rude, Patrick! It was nice of her to ask us when she barely knows us."

She cast an admiring eye upwards at the imperious dome. So this was where her dear George lived. It was beautiful, just as she had always imagined it would be . . .

"There's no chance of anyone hearing us in this racket! I don't think much of the reception she gave us either. Cool as a cucumber. Bloody arrogant. Like that brother of hers."

Squinting upwards, Kit could see the purple red flush on Patrick's pale face, and the saliva that bubbled on his lower lip.

"Patrick, stop shouting! You've had too much to drink. Your bow tie's coming off."

Patrick ripped the bow tie angrily from his neck and thrust it into his pocket. Trombones and cornets blared unsympathetically from the record player. Kit closed his eyes.

"Bloody arrogant, that's what they are. They think they're too bloody good for us, all of them—"

"No, they don't!" Annabel's voice was unusually shrill. "That's just not true! They don't . . . because George has asked me to marry him!"

"He *what*? Don't be so bloody stupid, Annabel! How on earth are you going to go off and get married with Father so ill? What do you think it would do to him, eh? It would kill him, that's what. The shock would kill him. And what about Kit? You're the only mother he's ever known. You were just planning to bloody dump him on me, were you, you and your . . . ."

Kit opened his eyes again. They both had their backs to him now. He got up quietly and crept away.

Nancy was taken aback to see Maudie Lester on the arm of one of the hands from Coombe Farm, but she quelled all unpatriotic thoughts and forced a tight smile.

Maudie stared at Nancy's dress with blatant envy. Then her cavernous red mouth curved up smugly at the corners.

"Where's that cousin of yours then, Nancy? He around tonight?"

"My cousin?" replied Nancy innocently. "My cousin? Which one?"

"You know the one I mean. The Yank."

"Oh—you mean Guy? As a matter of fact he's not my cousin. He's my brother. He owns this place . . ."

She waved at the chandelier. Maudie stared.

"Unfortunately he can't be with us this evening, so you'll have to make do with what's here, Maudie . . ."

Nancy had been unable to resist the intoxicating sense of power, but as soon as she opened her mouth, she knew that it was a mistake. Maudie would spread gossip in the village. Pushing the thought to the back of her mind, she gave her most dazzling condescending smile and swept past, making her way to the makeshift wooden platform at the end of the ballroom, where the loudspeakers had been erected. She picked her way carefully over the empty cups and glasses, the puddles of spilt beer and the cigarette ends, and found herself a vantage point from which she could watch the proceedings. The village librarian was dancing a sombre two-step with one of the church sidesmen, while around them a few remaining Canadian airmen jitterbugged at a faster pace, whooping and shouting until the sedate chandelier trembled. Greta was moving dreamily across the floor in the arms of a brawny young man in an ill-fitting demob suit. Nancy recognized him as the village gravedigger.

Maureen appeared at her elbow.

"Queen of all your survey, eh?" she observed drily.

"Something like that. I do find it rather satisfying knowing that all these people are having a nice time and enjoying themselves because of me . . . Look!" Nancy pointed. "Over there, Maureen. The Waites!"

Mrs Waite was clutching her foxy husband to her generous bosom, her mannish arms locked firmly around his shoulder blades.

Nancy and Maureen had the same thought at once. Maureen voiced it.

"No more Saturday nights!"

"Do you think they'll go on like that without us? Every Saturday . . . even though we're not there to watch them?"

"Doesn't seem possible, does it?"

Nancy adjusted the pins in her gleaming top-knot. "You know Maureen, I read a book once that opens with some people lying in a field and looking at a cow. They're discussing whether or not the cow will still be there when they've left the field. Because if they can no longer see the cow, they can't be sure that it still exists, can they? I feel a bit like that with the Waites."

"But," said Maureen, inserting a Woodbine in the corner of her mouth and lighting it. "*You* can still look at the cow, can't you? I mean you can go and check that the Waites still do it every Saturday night. You'll be here."

Nancy thought for a moment and sighed heavily. "God, Maureen, do you and Greta *have* to go? I can get you a job here, or in Wells or wherever you like. I'll ask my mother to help. She knows loads of people. I'm sure—"

"No. I mean it, Nance. And Greta does too. We don't belong around here. Not like you do."

"But Maureen—"

"No, Nancy." Maureen patted her shoulder. "I'm afraid you're going to have to run Nether Aston single handed." She laughed at her own joke, exhaling little clouds of cigarette smoke.

"Well, you needn't think I'm staying on here after you two have gone."

"Where are you going to go?"

"To London maybe. Like Faye."

Or maybe I'll go and visit America.

Nancy felt her mouth trying to form the words, but the idea was only just taking shape in her head, so she checked herself. "Time for the fireworks, I think . . ."

Finding the fireworks had been a true victory, since factories had stopped producing them for the duration of the war. Nancy had found a box of them in a cupboard while she was searching for lights; dusty, but dry and serviceable.

As she went to fetch them, she caught sight of Kit, slumped in a chair, fast asleep.

She shook him gently. "Kit, wake up. It's time for the fireworks."

He blinked and stretched. "Fireworks?"

"Don't you remember? I said you could light the first one. Come along."

She took Kit's hand and led him out onto the portico, where she showed him how to put the fireworks into milk bottles and arrange them in an arc on the front lawn.

Maureen and Greta had been instructed to round up the guests, and they began to crowd onto the portico, peering around pillars, huddling in excited groups on the gravelled carriage drive. Nancy lit a match and held Kit's hand, guiding it to the touch paper.

The night sky burst into a symphony of colour.

Nancy beamed at Kit, whose upturned face was a picture of joy, and then turned to acknowledge the cheers and gasps of delight which accompanied the explosions. And then there was another sound, faintly at first. Car wheels on the gravel.

The brash, expensive-looking car came to a halt at the edge of the lawn, in the blinding light of the fireworks. Guy Exley jumped out, slamming the door roughly.

Until he spoke, nobody paid much attention to his arrival, assuming that he was a tardy and impatient guest. When they heard what he said, they all stared.

"What the hell are all these people doing in my house?"

Nancy ignored him, turning her back to light the last touch paper. The firework fizzled, sighed and toppled from its milk bottle. A few people began to clap, then thought better of it.

"Right, that's it everybody!" shouted Nancy. "End of fireworks. But the dancing will continue."

The guests began to drift back into the house, glancing back uncertainly at the three figures that remained on the lawn. Nancy, Guy and Kit.

Guy stepped closer and reached for Nancy's elbow, but she jumped back as though she had been scalded. Kit looked horror-struck.

"What the hell is this, Nancy? What the hell are all these people doing here?"

"It's a pagan ritual, Guy, called a party."

Nancy was smug, full of bravado. It had occurred to her at once that Guy had come to Graylings hoping to find her there alone. It was a dangerous thought, some would even say a sinister one, but it flickered inside Nancy like a hot little flame and made her feel bold and daring.

"We're celebrating our great Allied victory over Japan. The war, Guy. That's what you were wearing that fancy uniform for, remember? Or were you just wearing it to look cute?"

Guy's face was contorted with anger.

"And who in Christ's name gave you permission to hold your jamboree here? I own this house, you know—"

"Oh yes," said Nancy quietly, stepping closer. "I'd forgotten. Well, let me tell you something, Guy Exley . . ." She raised her voice a vicious half-octave. "These people have worked bloody hard and suffered for six long bloody years. They deserve a party, a bit of fun, a celebration. And *I've* worked bloody hard to give it to them."

"Yes, she has!" piped up Kit stoutly. He darted out from behind Nancy's legs. "She's worked all day, and I've helped her, too."

". . . And I'll tell you something else, Captain Smartarse Exley. It's a tradition here in England that the people in the best position to give a party like this, are the people who do so. That means us. Only you wouldn't understand that, would you? You don't understand how these people work. You don't understand England and the English. You may own this house, but you're a bloody American and you don't belong *and you never will*!"

She spat the last words. Kit stared at Guy defiantly.

Guy felt completely deflated. A smooth, clever reply would have been useless. The things that she said were true. He had been angry because he wanted to find Nancy here alone and he had been disappointed. And now he had succeeded in turning her into an angry, spitting little cat.

"Very well," he said. "Let the party continue. But when it's over, I'd like a word with you, alone."

At the bus stop in Nether Aston, there was a solitary figure with a suitcase.

Annabel Steele had trudged up the high street with her suitcase, singing to herself in the dark to raise her spirits. She stopped now, straightening her beret and looking at her watch a little wistfully. It was, of course, too late to catch a bus. There would be no more buses tonight. Her only hope was hitching a lift. People had been very good about offering lifts during the war, and with petrol still so scarce . . .

If only she could get as far as Wells, then she could wait in the bus station until it was light, and catch the first bus to Cambridge.

Since leaving the house, she hadn't seen a single car. When they eventually came, she would have to make sure that they saw her. Perhaps she should walk up the street a little further?

She picked up her suitcase again, braced herself to steady its weight and walked on, trying to rid her mind of the picture of Kit, fast asleep with the covers flung back and his flannel-clad legs dangling over the side of the bed.

At Graylings, Leonora McConnell was weaving her way through the moonlit garden. Her dark hair fell forwards over her face, making shadows against her skin.

The doors to the ballroom were open, and someone was still dancing. She moved closer, drawn by the music. Hadn't she and Sandy danced to music like that once, at their first ball together? In Yorkshire. And Mama had sat on the side and watched them. Watched the way he held her. Watched for the tenderly spoken words that had thrilled her so much. Like a spider in a corner.

These two were young, as young as she and Sandy had been. They were dancing close and slow in a shaft of moonlight, and his face was buried in her lustrous blue hair . . .

It was a few moments before the fog of brandy cleared in her mind and she saw that it was the moonlight that was making her hair look blue, along with the shadow of his jaw, and the skin on her arms and the back of her calves. All blue. And that was what Glen Miller was singing too, his voice clear and full above the record's scratches, so close that he was singing in Leonora's ear. He was singing *to* her.

"Blue evening, after a lonely day . . .
Blue evening, spent in the same old way . . ."

It was frustrating. She could see their lips moving, but she could only hear Glen Miller. She moved closer to the open window.

Now she was close enough, but they weren't talking. He was kissing her. You could tell from the expression in his eyes that he was kissing her exactly as he wanted to kiss her. That it was an act of sheer selfishness. Leonora watched his strong, sensitive fingers moving over her blue skin and imagined the feel of them.

They were talking again. She could hear them.

"Is this making you feel guilty, Guy? Do you feel guilty?"

"No."

"No, neither do I."

Silence. More kissing.

"Nancy, do you know what I'm thinking?"

"Of course I know. I always know what you're thinking."

"Come on. Let's go upstairs now."

"Guy, I've never . . . but it's not just that, it's wrong, isn't it? We can't—"

"Sshhh . . . No more talk. I can't wait any longer. Christ, I want you so badly . . ."

Leonora turned away. Her heart was beating violently.

I don't want to think about what I've just seen. That's what Brittany was afraid of, and I've just seen it. I ought to tell her . . . I can't tell her. . . .

Without realizing it, she had broken into a run. She stumbled down the path and then stopped, gasping for breath. But she could still hear the music. It was following her down the path.

She put her head down and ran and ran, until she could no longer hear that terrible music.

George Stein stood in front of the mirror, shaving.

Outside his window, Cambridge was waking up and beginning to bustle. Green Street filled with bicycles; undergraduates peddling their way to some romantic liaison, delivery boys in white aprons, dons cycling sedately on their ancient machines. On the other side of the street, a window was flung open to admit the sunshine, and the sound of a piano spilled out into the summer air, then a woman's voice practising an Italian aria.

George left his tiny attic room and thundered down the stairs of the house where he had his lodgings. He passed Desmond Perkins on the landing. If he came down the stairs at this time, he always passed Desmond Perkins, a swarthy, secretive Welshman who occupied the room below his and read Physics at Caius.

"Off to the library then?" Perkins asked, as he always did.

He always used the same tone of voice too, as though the words themselves had no meaning. He made George think of a wooden toy that his mother had been given when she was a child. It was a carved figure of a negro, a grotesque caricature, and if a ha'penny was dropped in a slot in his head, he opened his mouth on cue. What would Perkins' greeting be once term had started? "Off to your lecture then?"

George turned right at the end of King's parade and strolled down to the edge of the river, to walk along the Backs. King's College shone in the distance, stately and magnificent. Graceful willows bent over the willow bank and trailed their pale leaves in the water. A church bell started to chime the hour. How beautiful it is, thought George, and how peaceful!

He thought these things, because they were the required response to such an idyllic scene. But somehow he could not connect these emotions with himself. He was alone in this place. He was lonely.

And the war got in the way. He could no longer see Cambridge for what it was. Or perhaps he *was* seeing it for what it was. Which was the reality, and which the mirror image? It was impossible to tell. The Cambridge that George saw was a glittering toy-town of a world, one where people only played at real life and pretended that there was no other existence outside this narrow, snobbish academic haven. The serene Fenland city was a dangerous mirage on a desert of blood-stained sand. If he closed his eyes now, he would still see the blood and the mess, and then he would open them again and see these glittering, beckoning spires. It was a trick. He could not trust its Gothic prettiness, its beguiling green expanses.

He walked back to Trumpington Street, to the little café where he usually ate a late breakfast. It was crowded with small tables whose red gingham cloths were always stained and dirty, and condensation ran down the windows. He was served with watery tea from a hissing urn, and a plate of sausages and eggs in a lake of fat, which he carried to his table. He always sat at the same table, in the corner furthest from the door, pressed against the steamy window. No one ever offered to share his table, and he was thankful for the sense of anonymity.

As he swallowed his first mouthful of sausage, the door opened and a girl came into the café. She ordered a pot of tea and sat down at the table next to George's. He watched her as he ate, spinning out his food as long as possible, and eventually ordering another cup of tea, just so that he could go on looking at her. She was very slim and very pretty, with curly dark hair that reminded him a little of Nancy's. By the time he had drunk half of his second cup of tea, he realised with a pang of alarm that he had started to think about sex. He wondered what she looked like without her clothes on. Would her breasts be large or small?

She looked up, and when she saw that George was staring at her, her expression was puzzled, as though she felt she ought to recognise him and didn't. George's burgeoning fantasies were doused with shame. He blushed violently and stared down into his cup of cold tea. When he looked up again, she smiled tightly. Perhaps she was lonely too? Perhaps she was waiting for him to join her.

George reached his decision in a hurry. He would count to ten, and then he would get up and stroll over to her table and say very casually, "Do you mind if I join you? . . ."

The door of the café opened again and a tall man came in.

The girl recognised him and waved shyly, and as he sat down at her table, he paused to kiss her on the lips. He wore a brand new sports jacket in a loud check that could only have been American. George turned away, blushing again. Then he paid his bill and left, resenting the sense of disappointment that he felt and walking faster than usual down Trumpington Street, as if to shake it off.

When George passed Desmond Perkins on the stairs, he hurried past to avoid the inevitable response, but he could not help noticing that Perkins seemed unusually animated. *No need to put a ha'penny in the slot this time* . . .

"Stein—wait a minute, you've got a visitor! A young lady. I showed her to your room. She said she'd wait for you there."

She was sitting on the edge of the bed with her suitcase at her feet, looking forlorn.

"Annabel! My God! . . ." He rushed towards her, breathless with shock. "Has something happened? Is there something wrong?"

"I suppose you could say I've run away from home."

She made an effort to smile.

George sat down next to her on the bed and took her hands in his. "Well, this *is* a surprise . . ." They both laughed at the platitude. "Are you here for good?"

It seemed too much to hope for. If Annabel was here, perhaps Cambridge would relinquish the ghosts of war. He would be able to share the place with a living person, and dead memories would be pushed aside.

"How did you get here—on the bus? Listen, you must be exhausted. What time did you get up?"

"I caught the bus at five."

"Come on then . . ." George removed her beret and smoothed her hair tenderly. "Why don't you get into bed and sleep for a while? Then we'll have to go and find somewhere to live. I'm afraid the landlady wouldn't hear of you staying here with me. Not at all the done thing."

George and Annabel spent the afternoon combing Cambridge for a flat or a house to rent. It was Annabel who hit on the idea of looking on the notice-boards of all the colleges. Eventually they found a typed card offering a flat to let in one of the broad, tree-lined avenues on the outskirts of the town. It was in the house of an Indian colonial officer's widow, a very stiff and proper lady called Mrs Mather who wore a lorgnette and a lace jabot. The house had been too big for her since her son's death in 1943, and she had partitioned the attic floor into a separate flat that was reached by the iron fire-escape.

"Mrs Mather, it's lovely . . ." said Annabel, awestruck by the immaculate parquet floors and mahogany lavatory seat.

"We'll take it, if we may," said George, adding firmly, "We are engaged to be married of course."

"Of course. Otherwise you would have been wasting both my time and your own." said Mrs Mather obscurely, retreating behind her lorgnette.

They moved into the flat that evening. The next day, when George returned from the library, there would be no Desmond Perkins to greet him, just Annabel with her newly washed hair and an Irish stew bubbling on the stove. As he sauntered down the tree-lined avenue, his heart soared at the thought. What more could he want? He was so happy he felt positively vivacious.

The flat was clean, tidy and welcoming. Annabel's vivacity matched his own, and the stew was washed down with a generous amount of claret that George had bought on impulse, to toast their new home.

But when he looked closely at Annabel, he could see that

there was something wrong. Her smiles seemed to be costing her a great effort.

"Would you have preferred champagne?"

"No, no." Annabel swept the suggestion aside with another of the gay little smiles. She began to clear the table unnaturally fast, and to wash up with the same distracted energy.

She noticed George watching her and smiled again.

"I love our little flat, don't you? I had such fun here today, putting it all in order. Would you like me to iron a clean shirt for tomorrow?"

"To hell with clean shirts!" said George. "Come here."

She laughed because her hands were still wet from the washing up. He carried her to their high, lace-covered bed and made love to her with infinite care.

The following evening, Annabel smiled a little less and cleared away the supper dishes even faster.

"I think I'd just like to go out for a while, to get some air . . ."

"Fine. I'll get my jacket."

". . . by myself."

She came back an hour later and sat down on the edge of the bed in her coat, and cried.

"Sorry . . . I'm sorry. I wanted to be grown up about this whole thing."

"What is it? What's happened?" George tried to prise her hands from her eyes, but she shook her head.

"I went to the telephone. To ring home. I just had to ring Kit and see if he was all right." She cried harder. "I'm sorry. You must think me such a baby. I didn't want you to think that."

"Just tell me what happened."

"Patrick said Kit had been crying all the time."

George took out a handkerchief and handed it to her. "Well, he would tell you that, wouldn't he?" he said evenly. "Of course he said that. It's emotional blackmail. He wants you to feel bad."

"But it's true, George! That's what's so awful. I asked to speak to Kit and when he came to the phone he was in tears, poor little thing. I felt so mean."

George was silent.

"I'll have to go back, George. I've got to go."

George closed his eyes and saw his new-found happiness draining away like water into sand. Like blood soaking into sand . . . "Please don't go. I want you to stay so much."

"But Kit needs me! I'm the only mother he's ever had and I've left him!"

George was aware that he was being selfish, and felt horribly guilty. Annabel was looking wildly around the room as though she was searching for someone who wasn't there.

". . . I can't let him go through that just because I want to play at housekeeping in a flat of my own with a mahogany lavatory seat! I know how it feels. *My* mother left *me*."

"Well, bring Kit up here then. There's room for him too."

"How can he?" wailed Annabel, winding the sodden handkerchief through her fingers. "He's due back at school in three weeks—"

"He can go to school here. There. Problem solved. End of argument."

Annabel looked at him and burst into fresh weeping. "Patrick said something else too. He said Father was worse."

"Look," said George. He ran his fingers through his hair and turned his eyes up to the ceiling, as though praying for patience. "I'm not going to have this, do you understand? Christ, Annabel, Patrick could ruin our chance of happiness if you let him—"

"Who's going to look after Father? What if he dies?"

George felt stubborness gaining the upper hand over patience. "Never mind *'what if'*. Go back to Heathcote now and judge for yourself. Pack up Kit's things and bring him up here. See if your father's well enough to be moved. If so, we'll have him put in a nursing home up here. If not, find a private nurse in Wells. I'll pay."

"But—"

George would allow no argument. Annabel went to the wardrobe and started removing her clothes.

". . . And you can leave those there. You're coming back, remember?"

Greville Dysart walked down the Pentonville Road with all his belongings in one small suitcase.

He walked slowly, reading the signs above the shop fronts, until he found what he was looking for. "E. BERG, TAILOR".

A small, dark man approached him, brandishing a tape measure in anticipation.

"I'd like a decent grey wool suit," said Greville, "a couple of shirts—sober stripe—and a tie, if you've got one."

The tailor flung a knowing look at Greville's shapeless blue

suit, which looked something like a de-mob suit, and his collar-
less shirt.

"You just got out of nick, then?"

Greville looked surprised.

"We get a lot of 'em coming in 'ere. First thing they want to
do, usually, buy themselves some decent clothes."

"Well, don't worry, I'm not an axe murderer," said Greville
cheerfully.

"What you in for then?"

"Fraud. Twelve months."

Greville tried on the clothes that the tailor fetched for him and
assessed the result in the solitary looking-glass that stood at the
back of the shop.

The man who looked back at him was less portly than he had
been in 1944, but his face was still chubby and his complexion
healthy. He smoothed back his thinning hair with plump fingers.

"Hmmm, not bad."

"Look quite the gentleman again, don't you, sir," said the
tailor who had noticed the signet ring bearing a family crest on
the little finger of Greville's left hand. "You'll have lost weight
of course, but I've left the suit a bit loose in case that changes."

Greville wrote a cheque for the clothes with a flourishing hand,
feeling that the tailor demonstrated less respect than was due
when he saw the name. *Greville R. Dysart Esq.* In fact he even
asked, "You sure this is good? Fraud, and all that . . ."

"Of course," said Greville stiffly. "You may telephone the
bank and confirm it, if you wish. And I would be grateful if you
would get rid of these for me." He pointed to his old clothes.

The next thing on the agenda was refreshment and a pause
for thought.

Greville walked towards King's Cross, and found a café that
was still serving breakfast. Over a cup of strong tea and a plate
of bacon and egg he took stock of his life. Forty years of cheerfully deceiving and exploiting other people, and he had been
caught out once. That wasn't a bad average.

Since he had no other immediate plans, he would go back to
Heathcote. The problem was what to tell the children. (He still
thought of them as children.) When his harmless little bit of
embezzlement had come to light, and he had been invited to
spend some time as a guest of Her Majesty, he had succeeded
in shielding them from this ugly piece of reality. (And the poor
dears were not exactly *au fait* with the ways of the world.) He
would have liked to write, but it would have been impossible

without revealing his whereabouts. So what should he tell them now?

As he sipped his tea, he hit on "a top secret job with the War Office" that had prevented him from making contact. Yes, he rather liked the idea of that. With a smile on his face he paid the bill and set off for Paddington to catch the train to Bath.

"Annabel, Annabel! You've come back!"

Kit wrapped himself around her knees, tugging the bags from her hand as though he was afraid she would change her mind.

Annabel smiled. "Yes, sweetheart, I'm back. But not for long . . ." She took her coat off and flung it over a chair in the hall. "I'm going to take you to Cambridge with me. Would you like that?"

Kit stared, uncertain.

"There's a lovely river with lots of ducks on it. You'll be able to feed them with the crusts of your bread, if you like."

Kit nodded vigorously.

"Good. Now run along upstairs and pack your things. Not all your toys, just one or two. And be very quiet. Let's pretend it's a game and we don't want anyone to hear us. Can you do that?"

Kit nodded again and tip-toed up the stairs. Annabel glanced into the kitchen, forcing herself to be brisk and business-like and ignore the piles of greasy dishes that were piled up around the sink.

She went into her father's room.

Adrian Steele was leaning against the pillows with a book in one hand and a cigar in the other. Ash floated onto the sheets in fine drifts. His skin was grey, chalky.

"Father? How are you feeling?"

"Well, well, well . . ." Adrian pulled his thin lips into a sneer. "Our young Juliet has returned. What's happened then? Is Romeo sick of you already? I gather you've decided to get away from this god-forsaken place and shack up with your beau . . ."

Annabel went out and closed the door behind her.

I don't know what to do. For the first time in my life I really don't know what to do and there's nobody who can tell me. Why can't they each have half of me? . . .

She went up to her room, clean and tidy, just as she had left it. By now she felt breathless from the sensation of being torn in two. Ripped down the middle. She went and sat at her ruffled dressing table, to see if she looked any different. The mirror confirmed that she was whole and in one piece, but the grey eyes that looked back were anxious, the face lacking all colour.

This is ridiculous, she thought. I'm only eighteen years old and I look thirty.

She reached out and knocked the mirror back hard on its hinges, so that she could no longer see herself.

Patrick Steele leaned across the bar of the Lamb and Child and demanded another pint of beer.

The landlord hesitated, calculating how much Patrick had already consumed. "All right, but that's the last one, lad. You've had a skinful already."

Maudie Lester extinguished her cigarette, lit another one and sidled over to Patrick's corner. "Patrick Steele, isn't it?"

She smiled her hot, inviting smile. Her lipstick was smudged slightly at the corners of her mouth.

"I gather your sister's been seen around with George Stein."

"Mind your own bloody business!"

Maudie shrugged. "Suit yourself. If she were *my* sister, I'd want to keep her away, that's all."

"What the bloody hell d'you mean?" Patrick's speech was slurred and beer spilled from his lips. He wiped his hand across his mouth.

"That American who's been hanging around. He's their brother. Leastways, that's what little Miss Nancy told me. And she's living up there with him now . . . alone. I'm sure you get my meaning. So what about the other brother, that's what I say."

"*Christ!*" roared Patrick. "*The fucking perverted little sod!*" His glass flew to the floor where it broke, splattering beer over Maudie's nylons.

"All right, that's enough! Out with you!"

The landlord seized Patrick by the collar and hurled him into the street.

He did not hurry to get home. He swerved from one side of the pavement to the other, kicking at stones and cursing out loud. There were lights on in the hall when he unlocked the front door and slumped against it, belching. The lights made him feel dizzy. He blinked.

And he saw her standing there with the suitcases.

"Patrick, I'm taking Kit back to Cambridge with me."

"*Little bitch!*" He leapt across the hall and caught hold of her arm. "Little slut! D'you know what they do, those bloody

Steins? Hmm? *They fuck their bloody sisters, that's what they do!"*

Annabel struggled wildly to free herself. Kit looked on in terror. "Kit, go upstairs at once!"

Patrick would not let go. "Nancy bloody Stein's up there with that American who pretends to be her cousin. But he's their brother and they bloody well do it together. That's what they're saying at the pub tonight!"

There was a knock at the front door. Patrick tightened his grip.

". . . How could you mix with those vile . . . d'you think George has been having her too? I'll tell you something, I'm going to ask him if he has and then I'm going to knock his bloody block off!"

There was another knock, more insistent this time.

"Patrick, let go of me! I'm going to answer the door."

Struggling free, Annabel ran to the door and flung it open. "Greville! Oh my God . . . it's you . . . thank God."

Greville and Annabel sat at the kitchen table with the bottle of cooking brandy. Annabel blew her nose and rubbed her eyes, which were red from crying.

"But Greville, I told George I was going back. I've *got* to go back!"

Greville took her hand in his. "Look m'dear, I really don't think you can just now. I doubt that George knows about this . . . Nancy business—"

"Pub gossip! It probably isn't even true!"

"Supposing it was. Just think how devastated he'd be. And Patrick's sure to tell him, old girl, if you go. You know that as well as I do." He poured some more brandy for her. "And even if it's not—true, I mean—poor old George is still going to think your family are nothing but trouble. He may have second thoughts about you."

"He'll have second thoughts anyway, if I don't go back!"

"Tell him it's a problem with your father. Look, Patrick's very upset. Why don't you stay here a wee bit longer, just to humour him. Then we'll sort something out, I promise."

Brittany left Cleveleigh Manor feeling that she had experienced the worst that life had to offer.

Susannah's grief had been appalling. When Brittany arrived, she had found her friend roaming about the kitchen in her dressing gown, unable to stop herself crying, in a state of near collapse. The two youngest Stanwycke boys were hovering in the background, uncertain and afraid. Brittany had despatched them to stay with relatives and then devoted herself to Susannah.

For several weeks they had been incarcerated in the drawing room, eating scratch meals from trays, talking and, very frequently, crying. Susannah was withdrawn at first, and angry, but Brittany had persevered. She had forced Susannah to talk about Hugh, and soon she was reminiscing about their courtship and the early days of their marriage, using the memory of his love for her to revive her strength. Eventually she was able to do what was necessary: to tell the story as one that had a beginning, a middle . . . and an end.

Susannah was grateful. God could no longer help her, she said, but Brittany had. As she watched Susannah's crucifix glinting in the firelight, Brittany reflected that it was those who had the strongest beliefs and convictions who felt the bitterness of betrayal most keenly. And she mourned for Jake once more, watching her own bitterness seep out like poison from a wound.

At the end of three weeks, Susannah declared herself to be on the road to recovery, and started to clean the house from top to bottom, the boys were fetched and Brittany found herself standing on the front steps saying her farewells. All around the house the corn was standing high in the fields. Susannah had been too distracted to hire men for the harvesting, and the stalks seemed to bend reproachfully under the weight of the grain.

Brittany shaded her eyes with her hand and looked out at the horizon. It was humid, and leaden storm clouds squatted on the skyline.

"Will Ralph be coming down to give you a hand with the harvest?"

"Ralph? No . . ." Susannah sighed. "He's in London, looking for a job. Just like everybody else."

"I'll put him in touch with someone at the bank if you like. They might be able to help him. Give me a ring about it and remind me."

Brittany carried her cases to the Citroën, then clasped Susannah in her arms and kissed her on both cheeks.

"Brittany . . . how can I thank you?"

"Don't. It was nice to be able to do something useful."

She felt a tugging at her heart as Susannah's small, blonde figure retreated into the distance and disappeared. She gritted her teeth and drove faster. The twelve miles between Cleveleigh and Graylings were so familiar that her thoughts settled on herself rather than the road. The landscape flashing past looked dry and faded, but in the way that a favourite article of clothing looks faded. Its gentle colours were still pleasing.

Brittany felt drained, exhausted, old. She glanced in the driving mirror to confirm her suspicions. There were more grey hairs showing, and she was *sure* that she had more lines around her eyes than three weeks ago. The air was thick with chaff and pollen making her eyes smart and her nose itch. If only it would rain! That would make her feel less tired . . .

But most of all, she needed to rest. At least when she got to Graylings, she would have some peace.

Nancy was having the most wonderful time of her life.

She and Guy *were* exactly alike. She had guessed as much at the beginning, and it was a triumph to have her theory confirmed. They were the same *inside*. If someone were to cut them open, they would both have *Don't Care* written through them like a stick of rock. They agreed about everything. They laughed about everything. Their tastes were identical.

Graylings became their playground. Guy's fierce delight at owning it was matched only by Nancy's pride at being able to show it to him. She took him to the top floor of the house, to the room that had once been the schoolroom, and showed him her mother's Edwardian dolls, her uncle Frederick's tin soldiers, and her uncle George's wooden animals. They behaved like children and raided the attic for old clothes. Guy dressed in Gerald Colby's scarlet and gold mess kit and Nancy donned one of her grandmother's fuchsia silk tea-gowns and they stood in front of a full-length mirror, striking suitably stiff poses, and sniggering. Then Nancy tried on plus-fours and Guy an ancient bathing dress and they succumbed to howls of laughter. After they had calmed down a little they went to the conservatory and plundered the carefully tended vine of all its fruit, taking it in turns to lie on a chaise longue and catch the grapes in their mouths.

Sometimes they just jumped into Guy's newly-acquired Rover and raced up and down the drive in it, just to see how fast they could drive. During the day, they were very happy.

It was at night that Nancy gave way to fear. She would wake, sweating slightly, and then sit bolt upright, gripped by terror and haunted by the knowledge that what she was doing was wrong. She was not religious, but one night when she sat shivering and staring at Guy's moonlit form she was prompted to crawl from the covers and go down on her knees beside the bed. She closed her eyes and clenched her hands.

"Please God . . . If I can only have this one thing . . . just for a little while . . . I promise I'll *never do anything wrong again*."

It was a relief when morning came. They slept in her mother's bed, under the polonaise, and despite the terrors, Nancy couldn't help feeling pleasure at finding Guy there when she woke up. She happily surrendered her favourite day-dreaming time, the time when she would lie in bed and feel she could be *somebody*. She didn't want to be somebody any more. She just wanted to be with Guy. And every morning he was there, smiling at her, reaching for her and pulling her into his arms. Holding her.

Like a baby. Like a very fragile piece of china . . .

Nancy giggled at this image, thinking how she would have scorned it if one of the girls at St Clare's had used it, or how Maureen and Greta would have dismissed it as "daft".

She had hardly thought about Greta and Maureen at all since the party. As far as she knew they had gone now, back to their respective homes. But she did take Guy over to the Home Farm on Saturday night, to watch the "ritual".

He roared with laughter.

"Were you *really* sitting here every Saturday night, watching that?"

"Of course!" said Nancy hotly, afraid that he was about to make fun of her, or think her a fool. But he laughed again and admitted that he had been mesmerised. They made love in the Waites' Dutch barn and then drove back to Graylings at midnight, holding hands over the steering wheel and singing *"I've got you under my skin"*.

The next day, her mother came back.

As soon as she came into the house, Brittany could tell that something was wrong. She could almost smell it in the air.

Since the length of her stay at Cleveleigh had been uncertain, Brittany had told Mrs Burrows to stay at her daughter's until she was sent for. There was no need for her to come back just to wait on Nancy. Nancy could take care of herself . . .

"Nancy?"

Brittany dropped her cases at her feet and stood beneath the domed skylight. A scrap of red, white and blue bunting fluttered against the wall.

"Nancy?"

The curving marble staircase beckoned her gaze upwards. On the first-floor landing, the door of her own bedroom opened. Nancy and Guy came out.

Brittany stared at her daughter. There was a rumble of thunder in the distance and rain began to fall in hurried drops. She went to the cloakroom, closed the lid of the lavatory and sat down on it, staring at her feet. Above her, she could hear the rain on the roof.

She would have cried, but after spending three weeks crying for Jake and Hugh it seemed inappropriate. Instead she retched and shivered. Jake should be here to help me sort this out, she thought, only Jake's gone and left me to it . . .

Brittany washed her hands and face and tidied her hair, her mind whirling like a rat in a cage. She knew that she needed to make a decision. Just one decision, any decision, and then she would feel better.

She decided that she would have to deal with them separately.

"Nancy!"

This time her voice was authoritative and purposeful.

Nancy reappeared.

"I want you to go to your room and pack a suitcase. And stay there until I tell you to come down."

"But—"

"I shouldn't argue if I were you." Nancy recognised the threat in her mother's rigid calm. "I don't want to speak to you at the moment. What you have done is simply unspeakable. Where's Guy?"

"In there."

"Tell him to come down to the library."

Brittany hesitated in front of the telephone, then lifted the received and dialled.

"Faye? It's Brittany Stein here . . . Sorry to disturb you on a Sunday, but I have a bit of a problem . . . I need your help. Can you take Nancy off my hands for a while? . . . You can? Faye, you're a marvel. Listen, I'll put her on a train this evening. Will you be in? Good, I'll tell her to ring from Paddington . . ."

There were footsteps outside the library door.

"Faye, do you mind terribly if I don't explain now? . . . . I'll ring you tomorrow. Bye."

She shook visibly as Guy came into the room. Had he been defiant or distraught, she would have broken down. But as ever he was bland, apologetic, inscrutable, allowing her to remain calm.

He received her invective without comment. Without offering an innocent explanation. Without lying. Only when she demanded that he never saw Nancy again did he falter. There was a flicker in his dark eyes, some unknown quantity. She realised that that was what she had wanted. Not just shame or regret. She wanted this separation to cause him pain.

She paused briefly, to give weight to her demand, then pressed on.

". . . And you had better not underestimate me either, Guy. I'm not a soft touch like your father. I'm sure your elderly grandparents and your WASPy Long Island friends would be very unhappy if they heard about your incest with your half-sister."

No more Guy Exley, clean-cut American hero, perfect allrounder . . .

"I can assure you that you won't have to descend to blackmail, Mrs Stein . . . If I speak frankly, will you hear me out? I guess I've got a speech to make, too."

She gave a curt nod.

"I know that what I've done is a terrible thing. And I've always known that if I did it, I'd have to give her up. Before I came down here I'd already made arrangements to travel back to the States—"

"You can hardly expect me to thank you for that! Think of the damage you've already done! God, I wish I'd—"

"If you're thinking that you shouldn't have told her who I am, you're wrong. This would have happened anyway—"

"And I would have thought even less of you!"

"Think about it, why don't you? She might even have followed me out to America, and the shock would have been terrible when she . . . in the end. At least this way we both had our eyes open and knew it couldn't last."

Brittany stared at him. "God Almighty! Why did you have to let it happen at all?" she shouted.

"We loved each other too much . . . Jesus, what's the point in this? . . ." For the first time Guy's distress came to the surface and he thumped the arm of his chair. "What the hell chance is there that you'll understand what I'm saying? I hardly even understand it myself . . . We are mirror images, Nancy and I," he held up his hands to try and illustrate what he was saying, "and the more we recognised ourselves in each other, the more we loved. I suppose you could say it's the penalty of being vain and egotistical. For both of us. That's the only explanation I can offer you . . ."

He rose from his chair and stretched as though they had been gossiping for hours about old acquaintances.

"But please . . . you must feel free to stay on here. As my guest."

So Guy Exley knew how to hurt *her*.

"I can assure you," Brittany replied through gritted teeth, forcing a sugary smile, "that there's only one way I'll be leaving this house behind. In a coffin."

She came into the hall to find Nancy walking down the marble stairs. Her face was grey and puffy.

"Has he gone?" she asked. There was an unnatural stillness about her, as though she was drugged.

"As far as you're concerned, he's gone." Brittany kept her back to the library door.

"Has he gone?" Nancy repeated with terrible urgency. She reached for the door handle, but Brittany moved quickly and blocked her way.

"Please. I have to say goodbye."

For the first time in her life, Nancy Stein was pleading with her mother.

Brittany stepped back, moved, despite herself, by the wide, staring eyes.

He was standing near the window with his back to her, but he turned when he heard the door opening, and she crossed the room so fast it was as though she fell and he caught her.

"Oh Guy, just . . . hold me, just hold me!"

His arms came up around her waist but she said, "No, *hold* me!"

He wrapped his arms round her back with his chin in her hair and rocked her gently to and fro. She pulled in tighter and tighter, as though she were trying to feel him in the depths of her bones.

"Take me with you," she pleaded.

"I can't. It's not right. You know that, don't you?"

She began to weep, but it was as if she were angry rather than sad. Eventually she looked up at his face, sniffing.

"What am I supposed to do?" she demanded.

"What I'm going to do. Pick up what's left and try to forget."

"But I *can't* forget, Guy! And why should I?" She heard the echoes of childhood arguments, and her frustration increased. "I don't *want* anybody else. I'd rather die."

"Come on . . ." he said gently, "this is pointless, Nancy. I have to go. And I want you to promise you're not going to blame your mother for this. It's my decision, not hers.''

Nancy looked away.

He took hold of her hands and began to prise her away from him. They had fallen back into their appointed roles with the breaking of the spell, he the responsible elder brother of twenty-six and she a girl of eighteen. She submitted to this finality, but as their bodies separated and they stepped apart, a ghastly look came over her face, as though she were indeed dying. And he knew then that though she had let go with her hands and her arms, her soul itself was struggling to maintain its hold, just as his was, and that some dark, sad part of her would never let go.

Nancy closed her eyes tightly as his footsteps traced their path to the door so that she would only hear, and not see, their parting.

Part
Two

Eight

London, February 1947

FAYE MCCONNELL OPENED her eyes and smiled, glad that it was Monday morning. She liked to work.

She stood beside the window in her neat, white negligé and brushed her hair. Outside her attic room in Lindsay Place, the morning mists were clearing to reveal driftwood littering the muddy banks of the Thames and barges pulled by small tugs, ducking their funnels under bridges. Factories and warehouses were visible, right down to Battersea Old Church and the power station in the distance.

Faye dressed and went down to the second floor, pausing to look into Nancy's room on the way, but as always, Nancy was up before her. Years of rising at dawn to work as a landgirl had not lost their influence. She found Nancy in the workroom, sitting cross-legged on the floor and reading the *Sunday Pictorial*.

"Listen to this, Faye—" she said without looking up.

"Nancy," Faye interrupted her. "It's Monday morning. You're supposed to be working, not looking at the Sunday papers."

"I am working!" protested Nancy. "I'm reading yet another article on 'Make Do and Mend'. Listen to this: *'Why not turn that old bedsock into a snazzy little hat?'* " She laughed aloud at the idea. "This could be our new line, Faye. I can just see the promotions . . . 'Footwear to headwear in one step' . . . Or how about *'Hats: what's afoot this season?'* "

She snorted with laughter and ran out of the room, returning with an old grey school sock perched rakishly on her sable curls. Mincing across the room like a mannequin, she intoned again, this time in a pinched, nasal voice, "Ladies, why not turn that bedsock into a snazzy little hat?"

Faye joined in her laughter at the joke, then reached for a copy of *The Lady*, asking in a more serious tone, "Is our advert in here? They were going to run it this week."

"Yes, I checked. Under 'Classified'."

Faye found the page and read the advertisement out loud. " *'Last season's dresses, coats, etc. made to look new'* . . . Do you think we've said enough Nancy? We really need more customers . . .''

Nancy and Faye had gone into business together in 1946. Nancy had been staying with Faye at Stephen Willand-Jones' house since her hasty departure from Graylings in the summer of 1945. She rented a room of her own with the interest from Jake's legacy, and wandered around London at a loose end, got in the way of the other tenants and provided Faye with a constant source of anxiety. She was clearly miserable, but refused to speak about Guy, or what had happened at Graylings. Faye already had the facts from Brittany, but she longed to hear Nancy's own version of events.

Both Brittany and Nancy's former teachers at St Clare's ventured the suggestion that Nancy might apply for a university place that autumn. She might like to go to Oxford, or to Cambridge, where George was still studying for his degree in agriculture . . . But Nancy dismissed university as ''dreary'' and the life of the undergraduate as ''dismal''.

In the spring of 1946, Faye lost her job with the Ministry of Information. She had known that it would happen. Since the end of the war, the number of propaganda films being produced fell dramatically, and the staff of ''Films'' was whittled away. They no longer needed a honey-voiced blonde with immaculately polished nails to wield a clapperboard. Faye was offered a clerical post in a different ministry, but she declined. She had an idea.

The Board of Trade had run a ''Make Do and Mend'' campaign during the latter years of the war, encouraging women to combat the privations of clothes rationing by repairing, renovating and transforming existing clothes. The war ended, but clothes rationing did not and Faye, who was a clever dressmaker, was continually in demand to alter her friends' clothes. After years of smiling submissively at Whitehall bureaucrats, Faye was drawn to the autonomy of self-employment. She decided that she would set up a dressmaking business, with Nancy as her partner.

One of Stephen Willand-Jones' tenants worked for the Board of Trade, and she agreed to help Faye get started by bringing home a generous sheaf of minutes and memoranda about the famine in sock suspenders and the washability of wool. Nancy and Faye pored over them religiously, gleaning ideas and giggling at solemn tracts headed ''The Problem of Pyjamas''.

The Board of Trade officials who taught the doctrines of Make Do and Mend offered their services free, but Nancy and Faye fully intended to be paid. They decided that their clientele would be gathered from the regiments of rich women who had nothing better to do with their time than worry about their wardrobe. "Or rich, *fat* women . . ." Nancy had mused when she read an article that opened with the revelation that *"Clothes are difficult for outsize women"*.

Their first task was to find premises where they could both work and receive their clients for fittings. Stephen listened sympathetically when they explained the problem and offered them a large, airy second-floor room at a very reasonable rent. They had found their "salon", and set about furnishing it for its role. A pink velvet chaise lounge was rescued from the attic and arranged under the window, for the fat ladies to sit on and feel pampered. The work table stood discreetly in a corner with Faye's sewing machine on it, and a set of nineteenth-century engravings representing "Faith", "Hope" and "Charity" were hung on the walls.

"The content's completely irrelevant, but they will add 'tone'," declared Nancy firmly.

The final touch was a dressmaker's dummy. In the end it was never used, but it helped to give the right impression, standing headless and impassive in a corner.

At first they worked on the recommendation of friends alone, then started to advertise cautiously. Business flourished. Faye dealt with most of the sewing, while Nancy conducted the fittings. This job was ideal for her particular brand of bossy charm; the charm of a highwayman who winks at his victims before he robs them. Faye had been afraid that her cousin would drive away customers by laughing at an inappropriate moment, but when she saw a pofaced Nancy kneeling at the feet of a client, rolls of fat rippling beneath her fingers, saying, "Perhaps if Madam would wear a foundation garment for her fittings, things would be easier and safer," she recalled Nancy falling from her horse and playing dead, and wondered how she could ever have overlooked her consummate skill as an actress.

After they had discussed ways of improving the wording of their advertisement, Faye set to work making a baby's layette from old lace petticoats, while Nancy tidied and dusted the room in preparation for the first fitting of the day.

"It's Mrs Harmsworth," she said glumly; "letting out and letting down for maternity wear. I expect she'll want me to talk all morning."

Many of the women who used their services came to the salon

on the flimsiest of excuses, for the chance of interspersing the pinning and tucking with gossip about their friends and fellow customers.

There was a knock at the door.

"Oh no, that can't be her already! I'm not ready for the old witch."

"Ssshh, Nancy!"

The door opened and Nancy stood on the threshold. The housekeeping was still carried out by Stephen's former nurse, a redoubtable figure in a black dress and toupee, who grudgingly acted as receptionist for the dressmaking business.

"A gentleman to see you, Miss Stein." Nanny ushered in a pale, tired-looking man in a suit.

Faye and Nancy stared at him in surprise. They had never had any male customers before. He held out a card.

"Vincent Fosdyke. Board of Trade. I understand that you ladies are running a business from these premises . . ."

Surprise turned rapidly into alarm. They had been working for a year "unofficially", with no government registration or declaration to the Inland Revenue. How could they have found out, Nancy wondered, except through our advertisement? She pictured poker-faced civil servants thumbing through *The Lady*, then she began to think, very quickly.

"I'm afraid you could easily have got the wrong impression from our advertisements," she said, with her most breathtaking smile. "It makes it sound as though we're running a business, when really we're just passing on renovation tips. It's an extension of the war effort I suppose, isn't it, Faye?"

"Oh, yes." Faye nodded. "Volunteer work. Part time."

"Can I be indiscreet, Mr Fosdyke?" asked Nancy, leaning closer and blinding the young man with an indiscreet smile. "One doesn't really like mentioning it, but Miss McConnell and myself . . . have private means. You understand." She sighed, as though wealth were a heavy burden, and Vincent Fosdyke looked suitably embarrassed. " . . . So you see, our work here isn't providing our income. Would you like to see some of the things we do?"

Vincent Fosdyke was given no chance to refuse as Nancy veritably skipped across the room to the work table. "This is a boy's windjammer made out of a father's mackintosh . . . A child's outfit made from a travelling rug . . . Oh, and I bet you can't guess what this is going to be turned into?"

Nancy waved her grey school sock in Vincent Fosdyke's direction with another wicked smile.

"A glove?" he asked hopefully.

"No, a hat! Isn't that wonderful? It's Miss McConnell's idea, not mine. So I'm afraid I can't take the credit for it, but it's a stroke of genius, don't you think? . . ."

Faye stuffed her fist in her mouth to prevent herself from laughing.

Vincent Fosdyke fled.

Nancy related the story of her triumph over the Board of Trade to Ralph Stanwycke, who came to have dinner at Lindsay Place that evening.

With Brittany's influence, Ralph had been given a job at Jacob Stein and Co., and was now a successful fledgeling banker and a constant companion of the two girls. He often dined at Lindsay Place, praising the lively atmosphere of the dining room, which had undergone a revolution when Nancy moved in. Stephen Willand-Jones owned four houses, inhabited by forty paying guests, and every evening at least twenty young people assembled in the dining room for supper, sitting at two or three large tables.

"Why are they so silent?" Nancy had asked loudly on her first evening. A few people who were talking in earnest whispers about Bach's masses looked up and frowned.

"Everyone talks quietly," Faye whispered back. "I don't know why, they just do."

But Nancy didn't. She insisted on making them all jump by talking loudly, and addressing herself to the most banal topics she could think of, incurring the disapproval of Nanny who supervised the proceedings and was nicknamed "the eye of God" by Faye. *"We don't do that in this house, Miss Stein"* became her favourite utterance.

But Nancy did. She organised a ball to which everyone in the house could invite ten friends, and it was a wild success. Nancy was queen bee after that, and the noise level in the dining room rose, although an inner circle still remained faithful to the old regime. Nancy herself had been happier after the ball, but she still refused to talk about Guy.

When he heard of the taming of Vincent Fosdyke, Ralph threw back his head and roared with laughter.

Just as he always does when he hears Nancy's escapades, thought Faye with a trace of bitterness.

"But seriously, girls," said Ralph, as the violent pink of his cheeks began to fade a little, "you ought to think about making yourselves official. You might evade the Board of Trade inspector once, but you can't expect to go on doing it forever. The Vincent Fosdykes of this world will catch up with you." He laughed heartily at his own joke. "Look, can I make a suggestion?" He blushed slightly as both girls turned their attention to him. He went on, toying with peas on his plate. "I've been learning quite a lot about financing small businesses, and—"

Nancy yawned. She always put on a show of ennui when Ralph talked about his work.

"No, listen, Nancy, this is serious. With a bit of capital you could expand, start selling new clothes. You ought to, really."

Faye nodded. "And how are we going to go about it?"

"Leave that to me." Ralph ignored Nancy's yawns. "I'll do a bit of research, play with some figures and come up with some sort of financial plan."

Ralph returned to Lindsay Place several weeks later, on a fine spring evening when the seagulls circled and mewed against a rosy sky. He was in a state of great excitement.

"Have you seen this?" he demanded, stabbing a finger at a newspaper that he was carrying. "This! This is where your future lies!"

"You had better come upstairs and tell us about it," said Faye quickly. It was unlike Ralph to be so melodramatic. She led him up to the salon.

"Dior's 'New Look'," said Ralph, spreading out the newspaper so that they could see the photographs. " *'The look that's causing a sensation in Paris,'* " he read, " *'Round-shouldered, wasp-waisted jackets, voluminous ankle-length skirts. An extravagant revolt against the war . . .'* It's catching on like wildfire apparently. Everyone's demanding the New Look. So there's your chance. You can start providing it."

"It's not as easy as that, Ralph," Faye replied doubtfully. "Some of those skirts have about eighty yards of material in them. They'd be terribly expensive to make, and not many people could afford them. Not with rationing set to continue."

"I'm sure you could cheat though?" Ralph gave her an appealing smile. "You could cut down on the amount of material, and still make the 'New Look'. And your customers must be so sick of the 'Old Look' by now that they'd do anything for the new."

"I don't know . . ." Faye was still doubtful. "If the look is so new, then where are we going to get our ideas from? We need more than these pictures.''

''I've already thought of that,'' said Ralph. He drew out a sheaf of papers from his briefcase and displayed them proudly. ''I contacted a colleague in New York, and he sent me some copies of *Vogue* and *Silver Screen*. Apparently they're full of new ideas. And he sent me the official magazine of the New York Fashion Fair. Here.''

''Let me look at that . . .'' Nancy snatched it from him and soon started to laugh. ''Listen to this Faye . . . *'Artistic Foundations is the maker of Flexees girdles and combinations, Flex-air brassieres and the Corsees step-in and pantie girdles . . . the world's loveliest foundations.'* I wish some of our fatties would wear those! Oh, hang on, wait a minute, listen to this . . . *'Bustees are flesh-like sculptured moulds . . . not simply for the flat figure, but will hold the line for all women.'* I can just see Mrs Harmsworth holding the line with some of those!''

''Here, let me see.'' It was Faye's turn to snatch the magazine. ''There must be something other than underwear. Hats . . . *'Exciting new padre-style hats'*—''

''—made from an old sock.''

''Nancy!'' Ralph did not attempt to hide his exasperation. ''We're taking this *seriously*, remember? If you decide to go ahead, you'll need to invest some of your own money.''

Nancy looked surprised. ''But I thought it was tied up until I was twenty-one. That's not until next January.''

''I'm sure we can get the trustees to release some of it. But first you've got to decide whether you're going to go ahead and do this. Become the queens of the fashion industry.''

Nancy looked at Faye. Faye nodded.

''Yes,'' said Nancy. ''We're going to do it.''

The new business venture was a success.

Nancy invested some of her capital in bolts of material in bright, vibrant colours. The cloth was made up by Faye into spring suits with neat jackets and full ballerina skirts, and within weeks they had been snapped up by regular customers.

They bought greater quantities of material this time, and more variety. Lawns, twills, drills, broadcloths, poplins, muslins, batistes, chambrays . . . Faye hired three women to help with the machining, and they made more suits and jackets and a line of very feminine summer dresses.

The clothes sold instantly. The salon at Lindsay Place was

full to bursting with cloth, paper patterns and racks of finished garments. There was no room for fittings to be carried out. By the summer, the search had begun for larger premises.

One evening in August, Ralph burst triumphantly into Faye's room, holding aloft a bottle of champagne.

"Tonight we're celebrating! Where's Nancy?"

"In the bath."

Faye was not sure whether she was annoyed at being discovered standing over the ironing board in her petticoat, or because Ralph's first thought was of Nancy.

"I've found your premises!" he announced, when all three of them were dressed and assembled on the edge of Faye's patchwork-covered bed. "A lovely little shop in Knightsbridge. The ideal place."

"Won't it be—"

"Expensive? Quite. But you'll easily cover the overheads after you've started selling, and I'll arrange a loan for you in the meantime. There'll be quite a lot of paperwork to do, but basically it's perfect." He beamed at the two girls, pink and self-conscious with pleasure. "I propose we go out to dinner tomorrow night after you've signed the lease and celebrate properly."

The invitation was addressed to both girls, but he looked at Nancy as he spoke.

"I'm afraid I can't," lied Faye, suppressing a shiver of envy. "I already have an engagement tomorrow. But Nancy will go with you."

They both turned to look at Nancy.

"We'll see," she said, with a strange little smile.

That night Faye was woken by an unfamiliar sound coming from the half-landing where the bathroom was situated. She followed the noise, which sounded like someone crying. The bathroom door was locked.

"Hullo? Who's in there?"

It was Nancy.

Faye was shocked. She didn't think that Nancy *could* cry. Or at least, if she did, it would be the crying of a small, spoilt child who had had her doll taken away. But this was different. The tortured look in Nancy's eyes spoke of a deep and private anguish.

"I don't even know where he is," she sobbed. "He could be anywhere."

"Who could?" asked Faye, already guessing the answer.

"*Guy*. I don't even know if he went back to America. But if he did, he must come back here sometimes. He's a shareholder—"

"But Nancy—"

"Oh, I know what you're thinking. It's *incest*. Such a terrible word most people don't even dare say it. Well, it didn't *feel* like incest, Faye, it just felt like being with someone I loved. And I didn't just *do* it either. It's not the sort of thing you just do. I agonized over . . . sleeping with Guy. I thought about the implications then and I think about them now, and I still can't be happy without him. I just know I can't."

"Of course you can. You've got all sorts of things to make you happy—"

"But it's not the same, Faye!" Nancy came out of the bathroom and almost slammed the door behind her. "It's not the same sort of happiness."

"Nancy . . ." Faye put her arm around the younger girl's shoulders. "The cost of that sort of happiness is very high. *Too* high. You'll just have to settle for an ordinary sort of happiness, like everyone else."

"You mean Ralph?"

Faye went silent for a moment. She withdrew her arm. "Is that why you're so hard on Ralph? For not being Guy?"

"Yes." Nancy sounded bitter. She turned away abruptly and started to run downstairs to the salon, with Faye following at her heels. The door was flung open, and Nancy rushed like a frenzied animal at the bales of material that stood waiting to be used; unraveling them, tearing at them, scrunching them between her fingers and then kicking them angrily until the floor of the room was a shifting sea of coral and cerise and taupe. And as she tore at them, she shrieked at the top of her voice, *"Why can't I have him? Why can't I have what I want?"*

For the first time in her life, Faye was at a loss for words. She crept away and lay awake, haunted by the picture of Nancy tearing through the rainbow of colours like a malicious whirlwind, and by the angry despair in her voice.

But the next morning, Nancy seemed to be her confident self again. As she came down to breakfast, Faye overheard her on the telephone.

"Of course, Ralph darling, I'll remember," she gushed, "and I won't be late . . . goodbye."

Faye shook her head at the contrariness of human nature, and continued down the stairs.

Graylings glittered in the autumn sunshine, its outline hard and white against the mellow tapestry of red, gold and russet. Guy Exley stopped his car in the lane and sat for a long time looking down at his house.

My house.

But despite Jake's will, he did not feel as though he owned it. It was over two years since he had been in Graylings, and it seemed to have slipped away from him in some indefinable way. Those two years in America came between him and his house now; the noises and the bright, brash newness of post-war America had followed him to this place.

He had intended to come back to England sooner, but shortly after his return to Long Island, Hamilton Exley III had suffered a massive stroke, and Guy found himself looking on rather helplessly as other people began to take charge of his life. He became the president of Exley Engineering. The job was offered to Bobby too, and while neither of them wanted to fill the position, the short straw fell to Guy as the younger man with fewer responsibilities.

Guy continued to live in the buttermilk mansion on the shores of the Sound, and to escort his grandmother to cocktail parties, golfclub dances and whist drives, while his grandfather lay paralysed and silent in an upstairs room. Once again, he was there to play favourite, to hover behind his grandmother's chair on her bridge evenings. The blue-rinsed matrons that he handed drinks to did not seem to notice the cynicism that played round the edges of his perfect smile. They showered him with invitations to debutantes' coming-out balls and other social functions where he might meet nice young girls and drive them home afterwards in order to earn the privilege of kissing a cool, suntanned cheek or, on some occasions, to enjoy a chaste fondle.

All he knew was that Nancy had been sent away, but surely she might have come back by now? Perhaps she would be there today?

His heart beat faster at the thought and he steadied his hold on the steering wheel as he drove down the slope of the drive. They were two years older now, and more mature. Perhaps they would be allowed to meet, on that basis, if not on any other. As two adults.

The front door was opened by a small, white-haired woman, whom Guy recognised as the cook-housekeeper, Mrs Burrows. She disappeared to announce his arrival, then returned to tell him that he would have to wait, as Mrs Stein was not ready to see him yet. Guy had expected this. She would need time to prepare herself.

Brittany received him in the small upstairs sitting room. Guy was struck immediately by the clutter in the room, as though she had barricaded herself in there with everything she might need for survival. Besides the tea-tray, there was a large biscuit barrel, a wireless set and an old-fashioned gramophone, piles of newspapers and magazines, several articles of warm clothing and a mending basket. There was a fire burning in the grate, even though the October afternoon was mild, and the room felt stuffy and uncomfortably warm.

She was sitting in a low chair beside the fire, darning with lovat green wool. She had become so thin that her clothes looked as though they belonged to someone else, and her tawny hair was peppered with grey. At her elbow, on the table, was a silver-framed photograph of herself when young standing next to a handsome man with dark, curling hair. The contrast between this smiling, willowy beauty and the ageing widow before him struck Guy as peculiarly ghoulish.

When she looked up, the long, almond-shaped eyes were unchanged.

"You might have let me know you were coming . . ." her voice was sharp, ". . . instead of just showing up uninvited."

When Guy reminded her gently that he did not need her permission to visit Graylings, she said, "I understand that absentee landlords are apt to lose their privileges." Her darning needle flashed in the firelight.

"I expect you already know why I'm here."

She said nothing.

"I came to ask after Nancy."

Brittany still did not reply. She picked up the ball of lovat green wool and began to wind it with furious movements.

"Look, I'm not going to try and see her. I could have seen her already in secret, but I haven't. I really meant it two years ago when I said I was giving her up."

"Don't expect me to pat you on the back!" She threw the wool down on the table with a defiant gesture, where it lay at the feet of the radiant, elegant twenty-five-year-old Brittany Colby.

Guy picked up the photograph. "This is you, right?"

"It was taken a long time ago." She gave him a wry smile. "I think in those days I was a little like you. I knew what I wanted and I didn't care about breaking society's rules."

"But you've changed, huh?"

"Yes. I changed when I had other people to worry about besides myself." She picked up her work again, indicating that the subject was closed.

"Perhaps if I wrote Nancy a note, you'd be kind enough to pass it on to her?"

There was a tablet of deckle-edged paper and some envelopes amongst the clutter on the floor. Brittany offered no resistance, so Guy picked them up and settled his square, muscular frame on a spindly chair in front of a French inlaid escritoire.

The note was difficult to compose. There was very little he could say, since it might be unsealed and read before it reached Nancy.

> *"My dearest Nancy, I am over here in England for a board meeting, so I will take this opportunity to leave a message. If you should ever need me, my address is: 103, Paradise Bay, Northport, Long Island. Yours ever, Guy."*

He sealed the letter in an envelope and handed it to Brittany, who propped it up against the photograph.

"Did you ever speak to George about . . . what happened between Nancy and me?" Guy's tanned face flushed slightly.

The question took Brittany by surprise, simply because in the past, Guy never used to refer to George at all. "What do you think?" she asked bitterly. "Of course I didn't, don't be foolish!" She looked directly at Guy, challenging him. "It would have distressed him, you know. I didn't want to distress him. He had a hard war." Her tone of voice expressed her contempt for those, like Guy, who spent their war years behind a desk.

She tapped the letter with one finger. "Was there anything else?"

"No. I'll leave you be now." Guy smiled his crocodile smile. "Enjoy this place, won't you?" He paused in the doorway and ran a finger down the faded lemon-coloured paintwork. "I don't like this colour very much, do you? It looks kind of dowdy. I think I'll have it changed."

Brittany waited until she heard his car starting. Then she picked up the letter and carried it over to the fire.

She hesitated.

. . . *But I have to think of Nancy. I have to do this to protect her.*

She tossed the letter into the fire and stared into the flames as it burned.

* * *

"It's sad, isn't it?" said Annabel. They stood on the pavement of Barrow Road, outside the house that had been their home for three brief days. "Did you stay here long after I'd gone back?"

George shrugged and thrust his hands deep into the pockets of his overcoat. A brisk autumn wind blew dry leaves across his feet. "About a week. I couldn't stand the place any longer than that. It didn't seem right without you." He spoke sadly, but there was no reproach in his words, and he hugged Annabel to his chest. "I'm glad you're back . . ."

"Do you think anyone lives there now?"

"We could go and have a look. Up the fire-escape."

"Mrs Mather might think we're burglars."

"No, she won't, she's as deaf as a post, remember?"

They both laughed, and Annabel blushed slightly.

The iron fire-escape was damp from rain and slippery with leaves, and twice the heels of Annabel's new court shoes got caught in the lattice-work of the steps. When they reached the top, they cupped their hands against the kitchen window and peered in a little guiltily.

"My goodness, what a mess!" exclaimed Annabel. "There's obviously someone living there now. It's a terrible mess though, isn't it? I would never have let it get into such a state!"

George looked at the half-empty tins of food and overflowing ashtrays, and thought of the dismal squalor of the kitchen at Heathcote House, but he said nothing.

"How about going back to Trinity now and making some tea in your rooms?"

"With crumpets."

Annabel laughed with delight at the prospect of crumpets, and linked her arm through George's as they walked down Barrow Road. Despite high heels, a sophisticated dove-grey suit and gloves, the intensely childlike quality of her beauty shone out. Her dark hair was smoothed into a pleat at the back of her head, and tucked underneath a square-brimmed hat that made her look like a Dutch doll.

They climbed the narrow stairs to George's college room in a happy, anticipatory silence. Their relationship had settled into a formal courtship, which was not what George would have wanted, or would have foreseen as he and Annabel crouched in the candle-lit air-raid shelter in 1943. That sense of spontaneity, of urgency, had disappeared. Annabel had left Cambridge for Heathcote in August 1945, to collect Kit and make arrangements for her father's care, but she had not returned. She gave her father's declining health as an excuse. George had remonstrated but had made no progress and abandoned his attempts to understand the workings of the Steele household. For over a year there was silence between them.

Then it was Christmas Eve, 1946. George spotted Annabel at midnight mass in Nether Aston church.

She was sitting at the back, wearing a white fur hat on her chestnut hair and clutching a white fur muff. The pristine white fur had a peculiarly worldly air, and George spent the entire service staring at those two objects; the hat and the muff, and wondering where they came from. He certainly didn't remember her having them before, and they looked new, as though they might be a Christmas present. Who had given them to her? Seated next to her was her cousin, Greville Dysart. Were they from him? Were the two of them? . . . Surely not? He was practically middle-aged . . .

As they left the church he tried to catch her eye, but when she saw George she glanced nervously in Greville's direction and hurried away, her hat a blur of white in the close, black December night.

That night George had written her a note, which he slipped through the letterbox at Heathcote House when he took the dogs for their Boxing Day walk.

> *"Darling Annabel,*
>
> *The hat is beautiful, but not nearly as beautiful as the wearer. I am going back to Cambridge next week. You told me once that you would love to see the city in winter. Please come.*
>
> *GEORGE."*

He had half feared that the note would be intercepted by Patrick, but two weeks later she came to Cambridge and wore her white fur hat as they walked through the snow on the Backs. Since then she had visited him about once a month, but never made any attempt to belong to the place, and never stayed longer than a day.

Annabel sat in an armchair by the fire while George cleared all the books off the table and laid out the tea with great ceremony. Her plate was balanced primly on her knees as she ate her crumpet, but she consented to lick the butter from her fingers when she found that there were no napkins. George watched the ritual with satisfaction, then drew a small leather box from his pocket.

"Annabel . . ." he said, with the intent air of someone beginning a rehearsed speech.

Annabel continued to lick the butter from her fingers, watching him like a cat.

". . . This is my last year at Cambridge, and in the summer I'll be coming back to Somerset. I thought perhaps the time had come for us to make things official . . ." They both looked down at the box in his hand. "I suppose you can guess what this is?"

He aggrandized the banal words by flicking up the lid of the box and letting the firelight sparkle on an immodestly large diamond. "We were sort of engaged before, I wondered—"

Annabel was reaching for the ring, her dark grey eyes as wide and excited as a child's. "George, it's *beautiful*. So grand! What a lovely surprise!" She slipped the ring onto her finger.

George squeezed her hand, then began to stroke her wrist tentatively with one finger. "Will you stay tonight?"

"Yes."

He led her into the bedroom and pulled the pins from her hair one by one until it fell around her shoulders in a fine, dark cloud. She did not look like a Dutch doll now, but like a painting by Murillo. The hastily drawn curtains threw mysterious shadows onto her face, and her skin felt like skin he had never touched before.

George undressed her completely, throwing the demure suit and numerous undergarments into a disrespectful heap on the floor. Then he made love to her, enjoying the way time had made her strange to him. Afterwards they lay facing one another in the confinement of the narrow bed, and George made patterns in the red-brown hair that fanned the pillowcase.

Annabel was fidgeting. "There's something sticking into me. It must be your cuff-link."

She reached under the sheets and squinted at the object that she found there. Then she held it out to George on the palm of her hand.

It was a pearl earring.

When he seemed unsure of what was expected of him, she said quietly, "George, this isn't *my* earring." Then she got out of bed and began to dress with tight, embarrassed movements, as though she was angry that he could see her nakedness. George lay on his back and stared at the ceiling.

"Aren't you even going to tell me who it belongs to?"

"Annabel, what does it matter?" George sighed.

"It bloody well matters to me!" Annabel thrust her foot into the new court shoe.

"It was nothing. After a party . . . I'd had too much to drink. I can't even remember her name, for God's sake."

"I see. And where does that leave me?"

"It was just sex, Annabel! Nothing to do with what I feel for you."

"What about sex with me? What about what you just—"

"Well, of course I wanted to . . . but it's just not the most important thing. I feel enormously caring and protective towards you—"

"You mean you think of me as a little girl! That's how you treat me anyway. And I suppose you're going to say I'm behaving like one doing this, like they do in every rotten book, or film!" She wrenched the diamond ring from her finger and threw it onto the bed.

After she had gone, George found he couldn't move. He continued to stare glumly at the ceiling, aware of a slight cramping sensation in his arms and legs after what might have been half an hour, or even longer. The light faded suddenly. The doorway was blocked by a solid, square figure.

"They didn't tell me you were sick."

Although it was too dark to see his features, George recognized the voice immediately.

Guy Exley.

"I'm not 'sick'," said George and sat up. Guy was wearing a sports jacket of a type that George particularly disliked, and a white shirt that showed off his ostentatious sun tan.

Nobody but an American could possibly like that loathsome check . . .

He felt a sudden rush of anger towards Guy, not because he had disliked him in the past, but because his unannounced visit seemed somehow to be linked with recent events. It was as though it was Guy's fault that Annabel had gone.

"If you're not sick, then I hope I'm not interrupting something," drawled Guy, glancing pointedly to his gold wrist-watch.

"Go and wait in the sitting room, and then for God's sake, say whatever it was you came to say, because I'm sure this wasn't a social call."

Guy disappeared.

George sat on the edge of the bed and ran his fingers through his hair. Then he dressed and went into the sitting room. Guy was in the armchair that Annabel had sat in, with her empty tea-cup at his feet.

"I won't say that I was just passing, because I know that Cambridge isn't exactly the sort of place that one just passes through."

George remembered how hard Guy had always tried to understand how the English behaved.

"I came up here with the express intention of seeking you out."

George raised his eyebrows at this, but said nothing. He bent to rescue Annabel's tea-cup from its position at Guy's feet, where it seemed defiled.

"I'm over here for a meeting, and I thought that since you were graduating next summer, I'd offer you a job. It's the least I can do for my half-brother."

George stared in disbelief. Guy never once dropped the easy social manner, despite the blasphemy that was pouring forth. He felt a surge of stubbornness. "I'm not your half-brother. Jake Stein raised me, but he wasn't my father. My father was David Stein."

"I know that. OK, so Dad was your uncle. That still makes me a cousin."

"Aha!" George sat down in the shabby button-back chair opposite Guy. "This is where we came in."

"Pardon me?"

"When you first came to Graylings. Mother told us you were a cousin."

Guy laughed, but without concealing his impatience. "Let's not get side-tracked. I had a word with the directors at the board meeting, and they'd be happy to offer you an executive position in the bank. Or, if there was something else you'd prefer to do, I'd be glad to use my influence."

It occurred to George that this speech was disguising the real motivation behind Guy's visit. After all, he could have written this down in a letter. Other Americans might have gone out of their way to sightsee in a historic university town, but Guy wouldn't be that corny. And he gave the impression that there was something else he wanted to say.

"You've wasted your journey. I haven't spent four years study-

ing agriculture to work in the City, and anyway I can't think of
anything I'd loathe more.''

He suddenly felt bored by Guy's presence, and began to think
about what he would do with the diamond ring. Was it still on
the bedspread, or had it been knocked onto the floor? Should he
post it to her? . . .

''Well, how about running the Graylings estate for me? I'm
going to need someone.''

''No. I have other plans, I'm afraid. I'm sorry.'' Strange how
one always says sorry, he thought, in situations where one isn't
sorry at all.

*I really am sorry, but about Annabel. Oh God Annabel, I'm
sorry . . .*

He began to collect the crockery onto the tray, with deliberate
carelessness. Cold tea slopped over the toe of Guy's fastidiously
polished hand-made English brogue.

''OK, I'm going.'' Guy bent and wiped the toe of his shoe
with his handkerchief, using the action to avoid looking at George
as he said with enforced casualness, ''Do you know how Nancy
is?''

''No,'' lied George. ''I haven't spoken to her recently. In fact
I don't even know her address.''

He felt his old jealousy returning, and it seemed to amply
justify the lie. Guy had obviously not abandoned his attempt to
worm his way into the family circle, and George was damned if
he was going to help him.

''No,'' he repeated, ''I can't help you there.''

As an afterthought he went to the top of the stairs and shouted,
''Why not ask Mother?'' But Guy had gone.

George went back into the bedroom to look for the ring.

In the spring of 1948, Brittany was engulfed in a terrible loneliness.

Her victory over Guy had been a Pyrrhic one. She had Graylings to herself, but she could not enjoy it. George's visits in his
university vacations were fleeting and uninterested. Nancy was
completely engrossed in her new business venture and never
strayed out of London.

She found herself missing the evacuees terribly. She thumbed
through their paintings of battleships and bombers and wandered
disconsolately through the room that had been their ''dormitory'', fingering the scarred paintwork. Where were they now,
her children? Would they still remember their ''Auntie''? Per-

haps in a few years, the older girls would be married with children of their own. She even missed the dull, earnest Marion Wakeley and her cups of cocoa in front of the wireless set. Leonora was still at the cottage, but Brittany forced herself to ration her visits there, aware of the danger that she too would become dependent on alcohol.

In the winter she incarcerated herself in the upstairs sitting room, reading, sewing and writing letters. The spring warmed her blood and brought a longing for activity. She decided that she would spring-clean the house and re-decorate where necessary. But she only got as far as taking down the curtains to have them cleaned before the process reduced her to tears. What was the point of all this? Who was there to see it all, or congratulate her on her efforts in improving Guy Exley's house? The blood-red walls of Jake's library reproached her, burning the back of her eyes.

She blew her nose and went to telephone Susannah.

"Susannah, I'm fifty years old and I feel as though my life is over. God, I hate being a widow!" She burst into tears again, sniffing down the phone.

Susannah sympathized. "So do I, darling. It doesn't seem to get any easier, does it? Though they say it will eventually."

"Well, I hate *them*, whoever *they* are!"

"Can't you go to London, spend some time with Faye and Nancy? They can't be *that* busy."

"I could, but . . ." Brittany's voice trailed away.

Susannah knew what she was thinking. Graylings was like Cinderella's finery, and might "disappear" completely if she left it too long.

"You should go out more," she advised.

"If only there were someone to go out with!"

Then suddenly there was.

It was a fine day in March, with a spirited wind chasing through the trees, and Brittany climbed up the drive and took the path to the beech copse, where the bench still stood. In the distance, clean white columns sparkled cheerfully.

Valhalla, home of the heroes . . .

It wasn't a home of any sort now.

There was a movement in the trees, and a car pulled up outside the portico. A tall man got out, a stranger.

Brittany almost ran down the drive, desperate to find out who he was before he drove away.

She smoothed the wisps of hair that were escaping from her headscarf. "Can I help you?"

"I'm looking for Brittany Colby."

"That's me. Colby is my maiden name."

"Of course. I should have known that you would marry."

Brittany looked at him more closely. "I'm sorry, should I . . . ?"

"I don't know if you remember me. My name is Randolph de Beer."

Randolph . . .

If his visit had not been so startlingly unexpected, she would have known him at once. His face, although darkly tanned, was unlined, and his hair was still gold despite the layer of brilliantine. The light blue eyes still mocked slightly. How old was he now? . . . She did a hasty calculation. Fifty-six.

"Of course I remember you . . ." Brittany shook her head in disbelief. " . . . Why on earth are you here?"

Randolph started to stroll towards the lawn, looking quite as though he visited Graylings every week, and Brittany had to walk briskly to keep up with him.

"You'll remember, of course, my involvement with arms in the first war."

"Ah yes, your profiteering!"

He smiled. "My profiteering, indeed. You haven't forgotten . . . I'm still chiefly a landowner and farmer, but I also have interests in South African mines, which seem to generate an extraordinary amount of money." He laughed, as though he couldn't quite believe this good fortune. "In 1939 I invested some of that money in British munitions—"

"To help the Allied cause, of course."

"Of course! And so now these factories are no longer churning out arms they have to decide what they *are* going to do—to close, or to diversify, and so on. It seems that involves a lot of meetings for major shareholders like myself. So . . . I found myself in England for the first time in many years and I had a whim to come back to this part of the country. I thought since my meetings were all over the place this would be as good a base as any. Although . . ." he turned and smiled at her, "I couldn't quite allow myself to believe you'd still be here . . . in this place . . ."

They had come to a halt under the magnificent, brooding cedar. Brittany gestured towardss the house. "Won't you come in, Mr de Beer? Some tea?"

They both laughed.

"In a minute, yes. But first I'd like you to take me back to the field."

"*The field?* We have very many—"

"There was one particular field, where we took our picnic. We sat under a tree. Do you remember it?"

Brittany remembered. The sound of his voice, with its strange South African twang, had brought back that summer day in 1915 with all the sweetness of nostalgia. She led him through the meadows to the field with the chestnut tree that had been planted in the reign of Charles I. It was surrounded by new green spring wheat.

"We ate sherry trifle," said Randolph, "and talked about the war. I remember you lying there, stretched out amidst the corn. You were the queen of all you surveyed. I suppose you still are."

"No, not any longer."

Brittany told him then, about David, and Jake, and Guy Exley.

"So you're a widow then?"

Brittany looked up at his face and imagined him saying, *"I had hoped you would be."* But why should he say that? He was probably married himself. Dismissing these thoughts as the effects of loneliness, she led Randolph back to the house and served an English cream tea in the drawing room. She normally used the upstairs sitting room, but all of a sudden it seemed like a prison.

Nancy telephoned while they were eating, enthusing about a new line of seersucker brunch coats.

"That was my daughter," Brittany explained as she put the phone down.

"Of course, you have children. I was meaning to ask you about them."

Brittany told Randolph about Nancy and her business, and was gratified that his questions showed genuine interest rather than mere politeness.

As he stood up to go, he said, "I'm staying at the Crown in Wells. Perhaps you would care to have dinner with me?"

Brittany's heart fluttered with excitement as she prepared to go out to dinner that evening. She caught herself running up the stairs, laughing at her reflection, acting like a silly schoolgirl. Although she was not usually indecisive, she tried on several different dresses before deciding on a simple black velvet. Her jewellery case was retrieved from the safe in the library, dusted

down and plundered of an emerald and diamond necklace and
the diamond tear-drops that had been given to her mother by her
lover, Charles Teasdale. Her thick straight hair was never permed
or set, but as she pinned it into an elegant French pleat, she
found herself wishing that she had indulged in a rinse, as Susannah did, to cover up the grey. She would go into Wells
tomorrow and have it done.

During the plushy, stuffy meal at the Crown, Brittany reflected that her excitement had been justified. Randolph de Beer
was handsome, attentive and more than a little flirtatious, and
she felt so at ease with him that it was as if she had met him
every year of her life since 1915. But as soon as she was back
at Graylings, her excitement vanished and she felt crushed by
guilt.

She sat on the edge of her strawberry silk bed and rocked to
and fro, moaning, "Jake, Jake, I'm sorry."

She had not thought about Jake once until now, and she had
wanted Randolph to make love to her.

She telephoned Susannah, and asked whether she should stop
seeing him.

"Brittany, stop crucifying yourself! And go on seeing him. If
you do it often enough, maybe you'll stop feeling guilty."

Brittany went on seeing Randolph, and the weeks slowly
stretched into months.

She constantly expected him to announce his departure, but
he claimed that he was happy where he was, and continued to
rent his suite at the Crown, though he spent whole days away on
trips to factories in the Midlands.

He was having tea at Graylings on the afternoon in June when
George returned from Cambridge for good.

"I hope you didn't mind taking a taxi from the station, darling," said Brittany as she kissed her son, "but I have company
at the moment."

"You look very well, Mother," said George, and meant it. Her
figure was trim and girlish, her eyes were sparkling and she had
done something with her hair to brighten the colour. When he was
introduced to Randolph de Beer, he decided that the South African
was at least partly responsible for the transformation. A great many
warm looks passed between him and Brittany in a short space of
time.

"I hear your subject was agriculture," said de Beer, stretch-
ing his long limbs and settling back in his chair. "I'd like to

hear about it. I'm a landowner myself, so I'm on the look-out for tips. I suppose you were planning to use it on the Graylings estate?''

"Yes darling," said Brittany, peering into the tea-pot to see if it needed refilling. "You know there's a job for you here. Poor Harry's getting a bit past it."

"No thank you," said George firmly. "I've thought about it, but I don't think I could work for Guy. It just wouldn't work. I'd like to stay in the area though. I thought I'd use Father's money to buy myself a place to live, and start off by working for someone else, as an agent. It won't do me any harm to learn a thing or two before I set up on my own."

"Quite right." Randolph lit a cigarette. "Very sensible." He looked at George, who was sitting on the edge of his chair. "I expect you two would like to discuss it without me in the way. I'll go and take a look at the car, see if I can find out what's making the noise."

"That was very decent," said George after he had gone. "There *was* something I wanted to talk about." He told his mother about his estrangement from Annabel, and the broken engagement.

". . . and please don't say 'I told you so.' It *would* have worked Mother, I *know* it would!"

"Darling, I don't know what to say . . . I'm so sorry . . ." She squeezed his hand. "But surely you ought to give it another try?''

"That's just it. I want your advice."

Brittany thought for a moment, staring at the patterns of sunlight on the drawing room carpet. "I know exactly what I'd advise. Get yourself a home first. Then go to her. She won't be able to resist. Every woman wants a home of her own." Then she added: " . . . Deep down."

George sighed. "I'd better get on to it then. Will you help me?''

"Darling, of *course* . . ." Brittany could not conceal her delight at being needed again.

". . . We'll start looking tomorrow."

Nine
February 1949

AT THE BEGINNING of February 1949, Brittany found an invoice signed by Guy Exley while she was rummaging through her desk. She laughed.

Once she would have flinched and pushed it from her sight, but now it was as if Guy Exley had never existed. Since his visit in the autumn of 1947 he had disappeared from view, and did not write or telephone. Brittany had started to feel as though Graylings were hers again.

Randolph de Beer had stayed in Somerset. He claimed that his estates in South Africa were taken care of by a trusted team of foremen and managers, freeing him to spend as long as he liked taking care of his British interests. Sometimes he talked about imminent business in London, but as his friendship with Brittany deepened, she felt more and more confident that he would not leave for London without proposing first. She was privately disappointed that they had not yet become lovers, but Susannah reassured her that Randolph simply wanted to take his time and woo a lady at his leisure. Brittany refrained from asking Susannah how *she* knew about these things, feeling the rise of her old irritation at her friend's naivety.

On Valentine's Day there was no card, but Randolph telephoned to invite Brittany out for a special dinner. There was a new French restaurant in Glastonbury. Would she like to try it?

Brittany resisted the temptation to wear a pink dress, choosing instead a rich jade silk and the latest shade of coral lipstick. Her mood was colourful, positive. A Valentine's Day dinner. Surely that, of all things, was the right occasion for . . .

Randolph had offered to collect her from Graylings, but she had declined, preferring to drive herself to Glastonbury in the Citroën, which was extremely dilapidated. She had put her name down for a new car, but the waiting lists were still months long.

The restaurant was perfect: expensive, discreet, intimate, and Randolph looked ridiculously youthful in his dinner jacket. She remembered him as a young man of twenty-three dressed in tail coat and winged collar, bending over to kiss her in the moonlit conservatory. Her spirits soared.

"I've brought something to show you," she said, after the waiter had served the first course. "Do you remember this?" She handed him a small parcel, wrapped in tissue paper.

"Of course I do. I sent it to you on Valentine's Day in 1916." He held the heart-shaped pincushion near the candle, so that its satin surface glistened. "And then I never heard a word from you. Fancy you keeping it all this time."

At that moment, Brittany decided, the mood was perfect for a romantic declaration. But Randolph changed the subject.

"How are your children? Do tell me all their news."

"Well, George is still looking frantically for a job, and has one or two good ideas. There's a family of absentee landlords, called Yorke, who live in the Yeovil direction. They've said they might be able to help him. Nancy . . . Nancy, as usual, is too busy for anyone but herself. I'm sorry you haven't met her yet. I did hope she would be down at Christmas, but . . . they're always planning new designs, new lines, new materials." She laughed. "I have to confess I'm rather surprised by the way she's taken to it all. I never for one moment saw her as a business-woman."

"How did you see her?"

"As the wife of a wealthy man, I suppose. She's very beautiful."

"Is she like you were at that age?"

Brittany reflected for a moment. "I often think that the only resemblance is that we both like to get our own way. She's more self-sufficient, more secretive."

Randolph's eyes were shining, and she knew what he wanted to ask. "No, she doesn't look much like me either. She's shorter, curvier. Rather darker than I am. I've got a picture in my hand-bag—I'll show it to you."

She handed the photograph to Randolph, who nodded his approval.

After they had eaten a sentimental *coeur à la crème* and ordered coffee, Randolph said, "I have something of an announcement to make."

Brittany looked at him expectantly.

"I've made plans to leave Wells for a while and spend some time in London."

"I see."

"There are a couple of board meetings there that I can't avoid, unfortunately. But I thought I could take this opportunity to visit Nancy's shop. Have you any message you'd like me to give her?"

"I don't know, I really don't . . ." Brittany shook her head and sighed. "She'll talk to me about business, that's all. Never about herself. I think she blames me for . . . a disappointment she had."

"Trouble with a suitor?"

"You could say that."

"Well, I'm volunteering to act as your ambassador and try and make the peace .."

Brittany was doubtful. "I'll think about it."

As they walked back to their cars, holding hands in the darkness, she said, "Randolph, I've decided. I *would* like you to try and talk to Nancy. But—"

"Don't worry, I'll be discreet!" He smiled at her as he climbed into the driving seat of his car.

Brittany closed her fingers tightly around the satin pincushion, unable to quell her feeling of disappointment.

"I don't want to do it. What if she says no?"

"Just go and do it," Brittany said firmly. "Get it over with."

George hooked a lead onto the collar of Nancy's geriatric spaniel and set off towards the village at a reluctant pace. He was, at last, a man of substance and standing, with both a job and a house to offer his future wife, yet he could not stir himself into feeling anything more positive than dread.

Sir Lionel Yorke had formally offered him the position of manager on his Somerset estate, while his family occupied a still grander fiefdom in County Kerry. And in November he had attended a property auction and become the proud owner of a small rectory in Peasedown St John, to the north-east of Wells. The house had needed plumbing and had been re-decorated, under the direction of Brittany with her impeccable sense of colour, but the work was now complete and the house ready for occupation. The moment had arrived.

When they reached the stone walls of Heathcote House, the spaniel began to whine as though it shared its master's reluctance.

Annabel answered the door, a thin, wan-looking Annabel, but an overjoyed one. She flung her arms around George's neck and burst into tears.

"*George!* . . . oh, thank God . . . I prayed you would come! Have you just heard about it?"

"Heard about what?"

"You'd better come in." Annabel beckoned to George to follow her. The house was dark, with the same dead, cold smell that George remembered. They went into the dining room, which struck him as an odd choice, but the room was at least clean, if moribund. The spaniel growled and barked at an elderly cherub that frolicked mournfully over the walls.

They sat at the dining table. Annabel folded her hands and stared down at her bitten fingernails. "Father died yesterday."

George had intended to make a speech that Cicero would have been proud of, but he was so relieved that Adrian Steele's health would no longer be offered as an excuse that all he could say was, "Well, in that case you've *got* to marry me now! I've got the house and everything."

Annabel started to cry again.

"Oh Annabel, darling, I am sorry! I didn't mean to be so insensitive . . ." He stood up so that he could put his arm around her shoulders. "The circumstances aren't exactly conducive to romance, are they? But at least let me tell you about the house . . ."

He described the Old Rectory; the rosy hue of its pink Somerset stone, the large sash windows and the pretty garden with the yew hedge.

Annabel's eyes shone through her tears. "Oh, George, it *does* sound perfect! And a garden of my own . . ."

"So you'll come?"

"Please don't make me decide now. It's just that with . . . Father and everything . . . Will you wait until after the funeral please?"

After George had gone, Annabel went to find Greville.

He was in the drawing room talking to the undertakers on the telephone about "caskets" and "floral tributes". She noticed that he had already donned a black tie.

". . . Well, of course you'll do your best," he was saying in the patronizing tone he reserved for people who presented him with bills to pay. "Extremely grateful to you. Goodbye."

When Annabel told him that George Stein had proposed again, she half expected him to assume his "grave and worried" look and to warn her about Patrick's state of mind, but he broke into a delighted smile and congratulated her.

"But I just wondered . . . Patrick's not going to like it very much."

"Don't worry m'dear, I can deal with young Patrick."

"Are you *sure*? What if he tries to hurt George by telling him . . . that gossip. It's just the sort of thing he'd do."

"Annabel my dear, does it really matter if he does? If *we* heard that story as a result of village gossip, then it's quite likely to get back to your young beau—or should I say, your betrothed—anyway."

Annabel stared at him open-mouthed. There was a terrible sinking sensation at the pit of her stomach. "According to you it *did* matter an awful lot! Enough to prevent me from taking Kit and moving to Cambridge. That's one of the reasons I've been here all this time!"

"That was for your own good, m'dear."

"It's still the same person, it's still George! What's the difference?"

Humming to himself, Greville walked over to the desk and began to open a pile of condolences with an ivory paper knife. "My dear Annabel, you're really not very bright, are you? That was living in sin in Cambridge. This is *marriage* to a Stein of the Stein banking empire. I can assure you it's not the same thing at all!"

As soon as the funeral was over, Annabel moved to the Old Rectory.

"It's perfect!" she said, when she saw it. "I always imagined we'd have a house like this. And Kit's so near, he can come every day if he likes, after school."

"And we won't get married immediately, will we?" said George as he carried her cases through the front door. "To hell with people's disapproval! We'll wait a few months and see how we get on."

"How grown up and sensible we've become!" exclaimed Annabel, and they both laughed.

She did not mention Patrick, who had cursed and run out of the house when he saw her preparing to leave. At that moment he was sitting in the Lamb and Child with his third drink inside him and Greville at his elbow attempting to placate him.

"*I'm going to get that bloody George Stein!*" Drops of Patrick's beery spittle spluttered Greville's plump cheeks.

"How many times do I have to tell you, old man? This incest angle is useful, but now is not the time. It's a question of waiting for the right opportunity . . ."

But Patrick was no longer listening. He had already decided to look for an opportunity of his own.

* * *

Randolph de Beer stood in the foyer of the Crown Hotel in Wells, watching the bell-boy carry his cases to the door. He gave the boy an over-generous tip and went to the reception desk to settle his bill.

The receptionist beamed as she accepted his cheque. "I hope you'll be coming back to stay with us soon, Mr de Beer?"

"I certainly hope so," he replied, but as he walked to the waiting taxi he realised he was still unsure of his intentions. And that was as much his reason for leaving Wells as the board meeting in London. He didn't know what he wanted. He needed to get away and think. To clear his head.

As the taxi swung around the corner into the Liberty and headed for the Bath road, Randolph's thoughts were of Brittany. She was certainly as attractive as ever and they were well suited as a couple, and yet . . .

In his fifty-six years he had met many attractive women but he had never quite been able to commit himself to any one of them. He was content to toy with the idea of being married to them; that was enough. This time the idea was more appealing than ever before, and that was precisely why he needed time to think.

Randolph sighed as he looked out of the window of the taxi. He was thinking not only of Brittany but also of the photograph she had showed him.

The dark-haired, sultry Nancy had seemed to laugh at him as she looked out of the frame, and somehow he couldn't seem to get the picture out of his mind.

"At last!"

Nancy ran into the Knightsbridge shop, brandishing a newspaper. "It's over! Clothes rationing is officially over!"

"Let's see." Faye sat down at the desk and put on the spectacles that she had recently taken to wearing. She shook her head slowly, and her curtain of blonde hair swung round her face. "So this is it. What we've been waiting for."

"We're going to be rich!" shouted Nancy, throwing up her handbag so that it hit the ceiling. "All those rich women! They're going to say 'To hell with austerity' and buy loads and loads of lovely clothes."

"Do you think the shop will be big enough?" asked Faye. "Perhaps we should expand, or get something larger."

"Oh no! I like *this* shop! And we've done so much work on it."

The Stein McConnell "salon" was situated in a quiet street that led off Knightsbridge. After a great deal of argument about the most memorable, yet tasteful, décor, the girls had hit on a scheme of aquamarine, cerulean and turquoise. An art student who lived at Lindsay Place had painted a suitably mediterranean frieze around the walls, which was illuminated by concealed lights. There were racks of dresses on two sides of the room, the chaise longue from Lindsay Place (re-covered in sober grey) against the window and at the far end a heavy desk with gilt legs and a marble top, behind which the girls sat to make up bills, or intimidate loiterers. For work they wore demure grey suits and black court shoes, and Faye sported her spectacles.

"Perhaps we should just re-arrange things to make more room?" suggested Nancy, measuring a wall with her arms.

"Let's see what people want to buy first," said Faye, whose customary role was to temper Nancy's wilder enthusiasm with common sense. "People might not have more money to spend."

"Of course they will! Here, we should be able to do some sums and calculate what sort of a difference there'll be without rationing. Pass me the newspaper . . ."

While the girls were poring over their calculations, a middle-aged man came into the room and began to thumb through the racks of dresses. He spent a long time over it, examining each one with an experienced eye.

Faye beckoned Nancy into the workroom at the back. "He's been here about ten minutes," she hissed, "who's going to tackle him, you or I?"

The girls had a rota for offering assistance to browsers.

"Perhaps he's an industrial spy!" said Nancy, and giggled. "I'll deal with him."

She set her shoulders and strolled towards the man, the very high heels of her shoes making her seem taller than she was.

"Can I help you?"

He smiled at her as though they had already met. "Miss Nancy Stein . . . ?"

"Yes. I'm Nancy Stein. And you are?—"

"Randolph de Beer." They shook hands solemnly and Nancy ran an appreciative eye over the stranger. He was tall and lithe, with a very tanned skin and golden hair smoothed back from a square forehead. Nancy judged him to be about forty. He reminded her of a leopard.

"I'm an old friend of your mother's—"

"Yes, she's mentioned you in her letters," said Nancy quickly.

"And I'm here to check up on you on her behalf." There was amusement in his light blue eyes, as though he relished the idea of her as a wayward schoolgirl and himself an elderly relative. "But you're obviously too busy now. I think I could assess your welfare better over dinner. Or I've got tickets for a show. Would you like that?"

He was proffering the treat, like a bag of sweets, but Nancy found to her surprise that she did not mind this cynicism. The smart reply that usually rose to her lips would not come. She nodded.

"Well then, you had better give me your address, or I won't be able to collect you, will I?"

He came to Lindsay Place in a long, gleaming limousine with a chauffeur.

"Not what I had expected," said Nancy drily as she climbed into the back seat, "but nice for those who can afford it."

"Oh, didn't your mother's letters tell you? I am extremely rich."

This statement did not seem an aberration of taste coming from Randolph de Beer. Nancy smiled to herself as the car slid along Piccadilly, past the lights of Green Park.

"And you look extremely beautiful."

Nancy was wearing oyster satin, with a narrow skirt and décolletage, and her lustrous sable curls were piled on top of her head.

"I had somehow expected to see you in that smart little grey suit."

Nancy laughed. "Oh *no*. That's Nancy, the Little Shopgirl."

"And this is?"

"Nancy, the Woman about Town, of course!"

The car had pulled up outside the Palace Theatre. As he handed her out, Randolph said, "Well, I hope she's not such a woman about town that she's already seen Ivor Novello's latest masterpiece."

Nancy assured him that she hadn't. " . . . but as a woman about town, I shall expect to be able to tell my friends that I saw *King's Rhapsody* from the best seats in the theatre."

Randolph had rented a box.

"All to ourselves! Oh gosh, Uncle Randolph, how thrilling!" Nancy draped her fur stole over the back of her chair. "The thing I like most about this is that we can talk without everybody saying 'Sshh'. I do like to be able to talk during the performance, don't you?''

Randolph agreed. ''And rustle chocolate papers.'' He produced an exquisitely wrapped box of chocolates and handed them to Nancy.

''Good. The very noisiest sort. Oh look, the curtain's going up . . .''

Nancy was so spellbound by the musical that she forgot to talk during the performance.

''I hope your silence doesn't indicate disapproval,'' Randolph said when the lights went up in the interval.

''Oh goodness, no!'' Nancy popped a chocolate into her mouth. ''There was so much going on. Fancy the king having two mistresses! I would have thought one mistress was enough for anyone. How about you? Do *you* have a mistress?''

She raised a provocative eyebrow.

''I have had, in the past. But never more than one at a time, you'll be pleased to hear.''

Nancy was searching the programme to see who was playing Queen Elana of Murania and Marta Karillos, the royal mistresses.

''I couldn't take my eyes off them,'' she explained to Randolph. ''I know they have to wear loads of make-up, but there's something very odd about them. They look so—''

''Old? Is that what you were going to say? Look—'' Randolph pointed to their names on the programme. ''Zena and Phyllis Dare. Haven't you heard of them before?''

Nancy shook her head, her mouth full of chocolate.

''They used to be the stars of those naughty Edwardian picture postcards. Aged sixty-two and fifty-nine, respectively. Remarkable, if you think about it.''

Nancy did think about it. When the lights went down again. She stared at the stage and thought how refreshing Randolph was. If she had been with Ralph and his boring public-school friends they wouldn't have known, or cared, who Phyllis and Zena Dare were, nor would they have dreamed of letting her stuff herself with chocolates. They would have been sitting in the stalls saying ''Sshh!'' with everyone else. And they would never—*never*—have admitted to being gloriously, disgustingly wealthy.

After the show, Randolph took her to dinner at a small French restaurant in Soho, and demanded that she entertain him by telling him about her business.

"Every business has to have an underlying philosophy," he said. "You can start by telling me what yours is. I, meanwhile, will fill your glass with champagne at regular intervals, and if you acquit yourself well, I shall give you a present."

Nancy sipped her champagne with the air of a connoisseur. "You can forget the principles of honesty, integrity, and putting the customer first. Our principle is to persuade them to buy all sorts of things that they don't really need."

"And is it working?"

"Yes. We're trying to provide something that hasn't really been provided until now. Before the war, women with money to spend on clothes went to a couturier. We're making garments of the same quality, but selling them 'off the peg' like . . . like in Woolworths. People who come into the shop are at liberty to look without being pressurised to buy."

"Well, not much pressure anyway," said Randolph, remembering Nancy's appearance at his elbow.

"We offer help, of course, but the prices are on the clothes so they don't have to ask, and feel embarrassed."

Randolph poured more champagne. "Now tell me how you see the future of *Stein McConnell*."

"Well . . . At the moment we're still being cautious. We only invest a certain proportion of our capital in new stock. That means a higher turnover, but limited availability for the customer. To be really successful we would have to put our heads on the block and risk investing everything in one collection."

"Will you?"

"Perhaps. We're waiting to see how the end of clothes rationing affects the customers' behaviour. They might go mad, and buy recklessly, or—"

"Or, on the other hand, the wartime habits of thrift might have become so ingrained that they don't know how to spend."

"Exactly." Nancy drained her glass with satisfaction.

"Well, I think you've performed admirably. Ten out of ten." Randolph reached into his pocket and dropped something into her empty champagne glass. It was a necklace of freshwater pearls, with a sapphire and diamond clasp.

Nancy exclaimed over it, and then put the necklace on. The pearls nestled in her cleavage, cold against her skin.

"You must have bought it today," she said. "Before you knew anything about me."

"I bought the necklace for . . . somebody else," Randolph

sighed. "But I changed my mind. There's something I want to say to you . . ."

He paid the bill and led her out into the street. She was quivering with excitement at the pressure of his fingers. He bent his head and kissed her forehead, then kissed her hard on the mouth, and on the pale column of her throat and in the shadow between her breasts. He lifted her hands and sucked the tips of her fingers. Then he straightened up.

"Nancy Stein, you are the most exquisite, the most sensual and the most original woman I have ever met. I must, I absolutely *must* have you!"

When they lay in bed together in his suite at the Connaught, Nancy fingered the pearl necklace thoughtfully.

"If you bought this for someone else and then gave it to me . . . some people would say that you're no better than the King of Ruritania after all . . . with his two mistresses."

Randolph closed his eyes, feeling guilty. "I know . . . I didn't exactly plan things this way, I just saw you and . . . oh hell, that sounds terrible doesn't it?" He turned over so that he was facing her and ran a finger through one of her sable curls.

"Nancy, it was wrong of me to get you into this—"

"Why, because you're going back to Wells to see Mummy?" She raised one eyebrow at him, challenging him.

Disarmed by her bluntness, Randolph was silent for a moment. "I don't know. I came up here to try and decide, and I seem to have ended up making things even harder for myself, don't I?"

"But you're going to be in London for a while?"

"Yes."

"And you'll want to see me again?"

Randolph smiled. "If you give me another kiss, I'll give it some serious thought . . ."

The next morning Nancy bounced into the shop with a smile on her lips, and proceeded to imitate Faye by singing to herself as she worked.

"You came back late last night?"

There was another question lurking at the back of Faye's sleepy eyes, but Nancy ignored it. "Yes, I did rather, didn't I?"

Faye went to answer the telephone in the workroom, and after talking in a low voice for a few minutes, she called Nancy.

"Nancy, it's Ralph. He'd like to speak to you."

Nancy sauntered to the phone, still singing.

"I came over to Lindsay Place last night, to see you, old girl, but you weren't there."

"Is that an observation or a criticism?"

"I don't know."

"What would you like me to say, Ralph?"

"Where were you?"

"I went to the theatre."

"Faye says he's old enough to be your father."

"Look, if you know all about it already, why are you asking me these stupid questions? Which are none of your business anyway."

She could almost hear Ralph blushing. "Sorry, Nancy. What I really wanted to say was how about having dinner with me tonight?"

Through the shop window, Nancy could see the nose of a black limousine glide into view, sparkling in the April sunshine.

"No, I'm sorry, Ralph, I can't."

"How about—"

"Look, I haven't got time to talk now. Someone's just arrived."

She slammed the phone down and ran to the door to receive the shockingly extravagant bouquet of white roses.

A fresh spring breeze tugged at the clouds drifting over the Long Island Polo Club, and over the two young Americans who were reining in their mounts at the end of a practice session.

Guy leapt from his pony and landed in the dust.

"That was great, thanks," he said. "Great chukka, Chuck!"

Chuck Jamieson laughed his easy-going laugh. "That's the oldest joke in the book, Exley. Give it a rest, will you?"

The two men tied up their ponies at the edge of the polo ground and went to the equipment room to stow their hats and sticks. Chuck had been at Andover and Princeton with Guy, and was his "best friend", though Guy often thought that their education was all that they had in common. The amiable but dullwitted Chuck had sandy hair and freckles and a broad smile with large teeth.

"Chuck, I'm in a hell of a hurry, would you untack Gimlet and rub him down for me? As a favour? I've got to catch the ferry over to the mainland and visit the goddam office."

"Hey, I hope you're not going to be late for the party," said Chuck. "Pamela'd be awfully upset."

Chuck was holding his engagement dance that night at the Bridgehampton Country Club.

"You bet I won't be late! That's why I'm in such a hurry now. So take care of Gimlet for me, will you?"

"Sure."

"Thanks, pal. See you later."

Guy jumped into his sports car and roared down to the Jericho Turnpike, still dressed in his polo shirt and jodphurs.

On the other side of the Sound, in Bridgeport, stood Exley Engineering, the sacred calf of the formidable Hamilton Exley I. The company had started in the middle of the nineteenth century to provide wagons for the intrepid pioneers who civilized the West, and had later diversified into haulage machinery. In 1945 Hamilton Exley III had expanded the company once again, when he won a contract to make engines for battleships, and there was now an ugly new building on the wharf blazoned with the name of the subsidiary *Exley Marine Inc.*

Guy's offices were in the new building. He screeched into the car park, flung a brief acknowledgement to the receptionist and jumped into the executive lift that bore him up to the penthouse where walls of glass provided an ocean-view on every side, like a square goldfish bowl.

"Marcia?" Guy shouted, once he was in his wood-panelled stronghold.

He pressed the button on the intercom. "Marcia, come in here will you, and bring any mail I need to see."

Guy's secretary brought in his mail with glacial indifference, as though she had failed to notice that it was five o'clock in the afternoon and the president had only just put in an appearance.

Guy swung his riding boots up onto the edge of his desk and pushed his fine, nut-brown hair back from his forehead. "Right, what do we have here . . ." He flicked through a pile of letters. "Nothing here you can't deal with, Marcia. Get out the relevant files and draft some replies for tomorrow."

Marcia nodded submissively, and Guy made a mental note to add a bonus to her pay check. Marcia handed him a pile of letters to sign, and read out his diary like a machine. "Eight o'clock you have the engagement party for Mr Jamieson and Miss Whitney—"

"Yes. I'm on my way there now." Guy swung his legs down from the desk and made towards the door.

"—and Jack Badell telephoned. He wants to speak with you this afternoon."

Guy paused with his hand on the door knob. "Jack Badell?"

"The factory manager. Production figures were way down last month and he wants to talk to you about an efficiency study."

"Call him back and arrange for him to come over here tomorrow."

"He said it was urgent."

"Tomorrow." Guy slammed the door behind him.

Marcia looked at her watch. The president of the company had been in his office for sixteen minutes.

Guy ordered a mint julep and drank it in the bath.

He started to imagine what Chuck's party would be like. This was a game that he played frequently with himself, to stem the ennui generated by the prospect of Long Island's social functions. He would conjure up the details of the imaginary party, with a chronological list of events, or details. Then, as the evening progressed, he could compare his estimate with the real event and win a certain number of points.

Of course what he really wanted was to *lose* the game, to encounter an unpredictable sequence of events, or better still a degeneration into chaos. Perhaps Chuck would surprise him. Perhaps there would be a cabaret of naked women performing lesbian acts, or a re-enactment of Gettysburg, or an earthquake . . .

As he towelled himself dry, shaved, and put on his tuxedo, he listed the events in his mind. First, he would go downstairs where his grandmother would tell him not to drink any more if he was going to drive. Then she would kiss him goodbye and remind him not to be late back. When he arrived, Chuck would greet him with "Good to see you old boy" as though they hadn't met for months, and a band in rented penguin suits would be playing a treacly version of something like *Moonlight Serenade*.

He went downstairs, carrying his empty julep glass, and filled it up at the drinks cabinet with a generous helping of bourbon.

Felicity Exley was sitting in a low, white sofa wearing a diaphanous housecoat covered with purple flowers. "Guy honey, do you really think you ought to. If you're driving . . ."

Guy emptied his glass and picked up his car keys from the coffee table.

"Give me a kiss then, darling."

He kissed his grandmother on her powdered cheek.

"Now don't stay out too late, will you? You have a job to go to tomorrow morning."

Chuck met him just inside the conservative portals of the Bridge-hampton Country Club.

"Guy! Great to see you, old boy! Have a drink. Or a dance. Everybody's dancing! See there's Bitsy over there, waving to you!"

Guy went to dance with the buck-toothed boring Bitsy, consoling himself with his magnificent points average.

As the evening unfolded, he continued a run of heavy scoring. He could almost have written Charles Jamieson Senior's speech himself. Congratulations and good wishes for the happy couple disguising smug self-congratulation. Pamela Whitney was one of the richest heiresses on the Eastern sea-board, and as slow of wit as her fiancé.

"The two of you are going to be very happy," said Guy sincerely when he climbed up onto the speech platform to congratulate his friend. "You're ideal for one another."

Pamela beamed and offered a cheek to be kissed, and Chuck slapped Guy heartily on the back.

"I recommend you follow my example, Guy. Marriage is the answer, and now is the time. You're thirty, the magic three-zero." He waved an expansive hand at the dancers. "Is there any girl out there tonight who takes your fancy? Lots of pretty girls."

"Oh *Chuck*!" Pamela pouted.

"Not as pretty as you, honey."

Guy ran his gaze over the throng of debutantes. And there she was.

Nancy.

She was standing with her back to him, wearing a red dress with a full skirt, and her vivid, lavish hair tumbled over her back, begging to be caressed. Guy was just about to leap down from the platform and run to her when she turned round. And he saw that it wasn't Nancy.

Chuck's party wasn't going to provide the best surprise possible, after all. But there was more than a passing resemblance in the thick, dark brows and small mouth.

"Who's that girl?" he asked Chuck. "The one in the red dress."

"That's Missie Trowbridge. I'll introduce you. She's quite a girl!"

Trying to assess the validity of this recommendation, Guy followed Chuck onto the dance floor.

"Guy, this is Missie Trowbridge."

There was no need for him to introduce Guy. Everybody knew who Guy Exley was.

As Guy and Missie danced, he asked her questions about herself, though he already knew the answers and could quite easily have applied the points system. She liked swimming and tennis and parties and buying new clothes.

Guy just wanted an opportunity to touch her hair, to close his eyes and pretend that she was Nancy . . .

"My parents are away in the West Indies," he heard Missie's voice saying. "Do you want to come back to their place with me?"

"Their place" place was a large, opulent mansion in extensive grounds, just outside Great Neck.

Giggling, Missie dragged Guy upstairs to her cute little girl's bedroom and proceeded to make love to him amongst her dolls with an enthusiasm that bordered on insatiability.

"I love doing it, don't you?" she said as she bent over Guy's naked body. "Screwing. I just love it. I could do it all the time."

Guy didn't doubt this claim. After she had finished he felt exhausted, but a pleasant sort of peace crept over him. He hadn't thought about Nancy, as he had expected, just Missie's busy hands and greedy mouth.

"Missie, would you like to come and meet my family tomorrow?"

Her dark head shot up. "Does that mean you're in love with me?"

Guy was about to ask what the hell that had to do with it, then thought better of it.

"I suppose it must."

"You were back very late last night," Felicity Exley said over breakfast.

"I was with a girl. I've asked her here for dinner tonight." Guy scored several points for his grandparents' reaction, and even thought that his grandfather might suffer a second stroke. There was delight on his grandmother's part and suspicion that the girl might be a fortune-hunter on his grandfather's.

"Who is she, anyway?" demanded Hamilton Exley.

"Missie Trowbridge."

"Edgar Trowbridge's girl?"

"The very same."

"Ah well." A satisfied smile crept over Hamilton Exley's face. "Why didn't you say? That is a very different matter."

She's one of us, you mean.

"I can't wait to meet her," gushed Felicity. "I'll go and speak to Cook right away. Just an informal little family supper . . ."

Missie's overgrown Shirley Temple act deceived the Exleys, who commended Guy for finding a girl with such a sweet and unspoilt nature. Guy was amused. He refrained from telling them about Missie's favourite hobby and asked her out again.

But after their second strenuous bout of copulation, Guy was already wishing that he could join the ranks of the cast-off toys in her bedroom. Unfortunately Missie showed no signs of sharing his boredom and at home an invisible pressure was mounting. There were constant references to Missie, and Felicity started to issue her own invitations when she felt that Guy was not paying enough attention to his new date. He was being pushed slowly, inexorably, towards the altar.

Guy began to think about the problem constantly. If he told them all to go to hell, the pressure would only be temporarily lifted. They would soon start pushing him towards someone else. But could he really marry a girl for the sole reason that she had hair like Nancy's? What other reasons were left to him? He had promised to give up Nancy and he had done so. Now he just wanted everyone to leave him alone. Marriage to Missie would be the best bone he could throw in his grandparents' direction.

So he went to New York one afternoon and bought a vulgar diamond solitaire from Tiffany's which met with gasps of delight from Missie. Guy accepted his grandparents' congratulations with his most insincere smile.

Now will you all just get off my back . . .

The next day, he returned from Bridgeport later than usual.

Missie and his grandmother were sitting next to each other on the white sofa, poring over glossy brochures. The ceiling fans whined in chorus above their heads, and they both sipped long, iced drinks.

"You're late, darling. Come and give me a kiss. Melissa and I were just looking at these property brochures, deciding where would be the best place for you two to get a home. We thought Hampton Bays. The tennis club is wonderful, and so are the shops. Missie will have everything she needs."

"Good. I do so want my wife to be near enough to the beauty salon."

There was a tense silence.

"Why don't you fix yourself a drink, Guy, then take a shower. Guy's a little tired . . ."

Guy wearily obeyed these instructions. Felicity cornered him on the stairs.

"Are you all right?" she hissed.

"Yes."

"Well, why are you behaving so strangely then? She's your fiancée. Don't tell me you'd forgotten about it. Or have you changed your mind?"

"No. I haven't."

Guy turned away and went upstairs to his room. Clean clothes had been laid out for him on the bed. Chinos and a sports shirt. Fiancé's clothes.

He walked to the window and pressed his face against it. The sun was setting over the Sound, and its waters sighed back at him. Where was she? She hadn't written back to him. Did she even think of him? When he closed his eyes they were lying under the stars together and she was telling him the story of the millionairess who built her own air-raid shelter. Ella Marion Rowcroft. Christ, he could even remember the woman's name.

The window pane was cold and unforgiving against his skin and it took all his strength to prevent himself from crying out.

"Nancy . . ."

Brittany was on the phone to Randolph de Beer.

". . . And how about Nancy? Have you managed to talk to her again?"

"As you said yourself, she's happy to talk about business, and not much else."

"How hard have you tried?"

"I've seen her several times since I've been here in London. Quite often really."

"And how do you get on with her?"

Randolph paused for just a little too long before replying. "We get on just fine."

"Well, if you've no plans to come down here for a while, I'll just have to hang on in suspense, won't I? Goodnight Randolph."

She put the phone down and sank into a chair. This was not the first time that Randolph had been evasive about his meetings with Nancy. And he had been avoiding contact with Brittany. *And* she had told him herself how gorgeous her daughter had become.

Fool that I am . . .

Would he? . . . Would Nancy do something like that and not tell her? The little . . .

Then with a pang of shame, she remembered Guy's letter burning in the grate. She was not much better herself.

She resolved to tell Nancy about keeping Guy's visit a secret, in an attempt to promote more honesty between them. As soon as she had worked out the best way to break the news, she would sit down and write her a letter.

"That was my mother, wasn't it?" demanded Nancy as Randolph replaced the receiver. They were in bed together in his hotel suite.

"Correct. That was your dear Mama."

"It seems an odd time to ring. So late at night . . ."

She turned over in bed to face Randolph. "Randolph . . . do you remember what we talked about when we first . . . the necklace and the king's two mistresses? You and Mummy aren't—"

She was so appalled at the thought of his coming straight to her bed from the arms of her own mother that she couldn't bring herself to say the words out loud.

"Not technically."

Nancy laughed despite herself. "*Technically?* What the hell's that supposed to mean?"

"I mean that we hadn't become lovers. But I told you, I came up to London to think about it all . . . Now turn out the light, that's a good girl. As you said, it's rather late."

Nancy lay on her back, too disturbed by the discovery to go to sleep. Her mother was lonely and grieving. An old friend, who was also a charming and attractive man, had come back into her life. And she, Nancy, had the power to spoil all that. Well, she couldn't do it. Whatever her mother's failings had been, she didn't deserve to have this chance of happiness taken away. Even if she had been instrumental in Guy's departure, Nancy would show that she was mature enough to forgive. She would help Randolph make his decision. What was more, she would tell her mother why she was doing it.

She hit on the idea of writing a letter but just before falling asleep she changed her mind. At the earliest opportunity she would go down to Graylings and tell Brittany in person.

Randolph lay awake listening to Nancy's quiet breathing. He too was thinking hard about Brittany. He was *almost* sure, but the sleeping figure next to him bore witness to the fact that he had not yet gained the right perspective from which to view the problem. There was really only one way he could test his feelings.

It was time to go back to South Africa.

George Theodoure Stein and Annabel Mary Steele were married at half past three on the sixth of March 1950, at Wells registry office.

The bride wore a linen suit with matching shoes and a broad-brimmed hat, and there were only two witnesses.

George and Annabel had decided long before that their wedding would be an impromptu affair. When George found an opportunity to take some time off work they would buy a licence and go and get married, with no fuss and no announcement. They would break the news to their respective families afterwards. This was the only way they could think of to avoid unpleasantness from Patrick, who had been openly hostile since Annabel had moved to the Old Rectory, but they both felt that it was hard on Brittany, who had been very friendly towards Annabel, and visited the Old Rectory frequently.

"We'll go over to Graylings straight away," said George, as they left the registry office, "with the confetti still on our clothes."

"No darling," said Annabel. "I don't think that would be the most tactful way. It makes it too obvious that she's been left out. Drop me at home now, and I'll put some champagne to chill. Then you go over to Graylings alone and break the news in a low-key fashion, and ask her over to celebrate with us and give us her blessing."

"How clever my wife is!" exclaimed George, kissing her and brushing the petals of confetti from her hair. "That's the perfect solution."

He left Annabel in the kitchen, preparing her own wedding breakfast, and drove to Graylings, where he parked his car in front of the portico.

He pushed the front door open. "Mother!" he shouted.

He stepped onto the marble staircase. "Mother!"

Upstairs, Brittany, who was taking a nap, stirred in her sleep, but did not wake up. An unfinished letter to Nancy lay on the table beside her.

George looked in the kitchen, but there was no one there. He decided that his mother was probably visiting Leonora. Leaving the house by the kitchen door, he crossed the stable yard and climbed over the gate into the paddock, heading for Leonora's cottage. It was empty. Puzzled, George began to retrace his steps. Perhaps she was in the walled garden.

Leonora McConnell was sitting on the bench in the beech copse, with her mink coat draped over her shoulders.

She had been trying to conjure up Sandy, and relive the moment when they first met, at the dance in Yorkshire, but she found that when she was sober she couldn't even picture his face.

She didn't wear a watch, but she could tell from the position of the sun over the house that it was about five o'clock. Time for a drink. In the cottage, she had half a bottle of a rather nice cognac, borrowed from Brittany.

If she had been drunk she might never have noticed, but she wasn't, and she saw immediately.

There was smoke pouring from the house, but it wasn't coming from the chimneys, and there were flames too, leaping from the windows and bathing the white walls with an orange glow. And a terrible, deafening crackling roar . . .

Leonora began to run down the drive. She tried to run faster but her legs would not obey her terrified mind and she began to cry. There was a car parked outside the house, perhaps they could get help, unless they were in the house . . .

Leonora almost screamed with relief when she saw a man running around the side of the house. The owner of the car had escaped, and they would be able to go for help together. But the man did not go anywhere near the car. Instead he ran to the right of the house and disappeared into the shadows.

Leonora eventually succeeded in raising the alarm, but by the time the fire brigade arrived at Graylings, Brittany Stein had been suffocated by the smoke.

Ten
March 1950

AFTER THE FUNERAL, Nancy made her excuses to Susannah, who was providing refreshments for the mourners, and drove the Citroën to Graylings.

The windows of the car were open, and she was driving fast, but still she felt as though she couldn't breathe.

She had felt like that all day, on the train with Faye, in the graveyard in Nether Aston when they stood in the shadows cast by the sinister yew and laurels, and the villagers stared disapprovingly at her New Look black, and afterwards, as mousy Christina Stanwycke handed round home-made biscuits and Ralph threw her crushingly sympathetic looks and everywhere you looked there was black, black, black . . .

Nancy stopped the car and broke down and cried. She had never got round to telling her mother about Randolph. But she *had* meant to. She had even arranged to take the time off work, and then suddenly the phone call had come and it had been too late. She had been about to break down a monumental barrier, to settle the scores, perhaps even to compensate for all the time when she had been away at St Clare's, all the time during the war when her mother had been too preoccupied . . .

And now she was dead, and Nancy felt betrayed even though she had never been dependent on her mother or close to her. She had never allowed anybody to be close to her. Except Guy.

Annabel and George reminded her now of how she and Guy had been. They had a private language of looks and gestures and half-finished sentences. For that reason Nancy had refused their offer of a bed for the night, in favour of returning to London with Faye. But she wanted to visit Graylings first.

There was no flash of white through the trees any more, just a dirty smear. Nancy parked the Citroën on the gravelled arc of the carriage drive and walked slowly round the house. Where the doors and windows had been, there were gaping, charred holes. The white walls were streaked with grey.

She went inside. It was difficult to see in the hall, since the eye of the domed skylight was blackened with soot. It made an enormous difference to the room, as though someone had put a giant lid on the house. There was debris all over the floor; damp, rotting wood and drifts of what looked like brown snow. Nancy bent and picked it up with her fingers. She sniffed it and wrinkled her nose in distaste. Burnt feathers. The floor was scattered with the contents of cushions and horsehair sofas. Only the marble staircase remained unharmed, curving upwards, aloof and intact.

Nancy kicked at the wreckage angrily. Why wasn't Guy here, now that his house was burnt down? He *should* be here.

She began to imagine what it was like when the house was burning, the brilliant light, the roaring heat, the dancing flames making shadows on the wall . . . and her mother at the centre of this voracious oven, burning to death on her pink silk bed beneath the polonaise . . .

Once again the crushing weight descended, the same breathlessness that she had felt since the funeral, and it was as if she, too, were being suffocated . She ran out of the house, her chest heaving.

God, she needed a drink. Not one of Susannah's thimblefuls of dry sherry, a beverage so dry that it had almost evaporated before it reached the glass, but a real drink. Thank God for Leonora!

Leonora had not attended the funeral. She avoided large gatherings of any kind, and she claimed that this included funerals. Nancy began to run down the path that led to the cottage, wrenching her ankle on a tussock of coarse grass and cursing her high heels.

Leonora came to the door as she approached and held it open, as though she had been expecting Nancy.

"I knew someone would come," she said. "There's always someone in your family needing a drink."

The cottage was so tidy that it was almost unrecognizable. The stone floor had been swept and the rag rugs shaken. The bed was made and arranged with cushions and there was a vase of daffodils on the table.

"She liked daffodils. Your mother. I did it for her, cleaning the place up. She was always telling me off for leaving it so untidy. It was my own way of paying my respects really, and so much more useful than a funeral service."

Nancy noticed that Leonora was wearing a black dress, and was touched. There was something in this simple tribute that was more moving than the day's ceremony and ritual.

Leonora sat down. "Your mother was very good to me. The

cottage was rightfully my property, but she was the one who made it into my home for the last eight years.''

For a moment she looked as though she might cry. Then she fetched a bottle of scotch and poured two triple measures.

They drank in silence while the March wind flew through the gaps in the window frame and buffeted the daffodils to and fro in their milk bottle. It was Leonora who spoke first.

"I suppose you're desperate to know what really happened to your mother."

Nancy opened her mouth to make a contradictory reply, and then realised that Leonora had hit on the precise origin of the suffocating sensation. It came from a deep fear and mistrust; not understanding, not knowing.

Leonora emptied her second glass of scotch. "Of course, I know who did it," she said with satisfaction.

"What do you mean, who *did* it? I thought the police said it was an electrical fault. The place was dangerous. It hadn't been rewired since the 1920s."

"How would the police know? They weren't there. I *was* there. I saw what happened."

"Tell me."

"It was afternoon. About five o'clock, and I'd gone for a walk. I wandered over in the Home Farm direction for a while then I came back towards the house. I thought of going back to the cottage then, but I decided I wanted to walk for a while longer. So I went up the drive and off to the right, to the beech copse. Sat on the bench for a while, had a little think—"

"And what was happening at the house while you were doing all this thinking?"

"—Nothing. Or at least, it was, but I couldn't see it. But I'm getting to that. The fire must have already started, but up there the house looks quite small, doesn't it? Didn't really seem any different. Then I fancied a drink—"

"At five o'clock in the afternoon? That's—"

"Just a small one. I started coming down the drive and I saw the smoke, then the flames. As soon as I saw them, I began to run. And there was a car outside."

"Yes I know," said Nancy, growing impatient. "It was George's car. We know that already."

"But that was when I saw the man. I thought it must be *his* car—"

"The man?"

"I distinctly saw a man running around from the direction of the stables. But he didn't get in the car, because it was George's car and he wasn't George. Then he ran off in the opposite direction. I don't know where, because I was thinking about the house and Brittany. But I know I saw him.''

"Leonora, are you *sure* about this?" Nancy remembered Leonora's talent of old for "seeing" things.

"I *am* sure, that's the whole point. *I hadn't had a drink.* I was on my way to get one, but I was stone cold sober. Now do you believe me?''

Nancy sank back in her chair. "Yes."

"Well, aren't you going to ask who it was?"

Nancy sat up again.

"You mean you *know* him?"

"Of course. I've seen him in the village. Annabel's brother Patrick Steele.''

Nancy drove straight to the old Rectory in Peasedown St John.

Faye would be waiting for her at Bath Station, but she would just have to wait, or go on alone. She *had* to speak to George about what had happened.

She arrived before the others had returned from the funeral, and sat down on the front steps to wait. The Old Rectory was like a pink dolls' house; built in solid Queen Anne style with clematis clinging round the white front door. The garden had a wrought-iron bower and a green handkerchief of a lawn with pin-neat borders. Inside it was immaculately clean and tidy, with a lot of chintz and pretty porcelain and polished brass.

George's battered Austin pulled up in the drive. Annabel climbed out first, pale and tired. "Nancy! I thought you'd decided not to stay.''

"I'm not, I just called round . . . I thought I'd leave the Citroën here while I'm in London if that's all right.''

Nancy felt helpless. It was so difficult, with Patrick being Annabel's brother. She needed to speak to George alone. She was wondering how to corner him when Annabel announced that she was feeling unwell, and was going to lie down upstairs.

"She's tired," explained George.

"She's not the only one!" Nancy kicked off her shoes and sank down into an armchair with her eyes closed.

"Would you like a brandy or something?"

She shook her head. "George . . ." The drawing-room door was still open. Nancy stood up and closed it. "George, while we're alone for a minute . . . I want to talk to you about what happened to Mummy—''

There was a loud thump from the landing.

''What the hell was that?''

''Sounds like someone dropped something.'' Nancy opened the door. ''Oh God, George . . .''

Annabel was lying unconscious on the landing. Nancy reached the top of the stairs first and knelt to feel for her pulse. ''I think she must have fainted. You'd better ring the doctor.''

Nancy paced the landing impatiently while the doctor carried out his examination. Why *now*, she was thinking. Why does Annabel have to go and get ill now, just when I need George's attention. It's typical of *her* . . .

George came out of the bedroom and closed the door. His mouth was twitching as though he wasn't sure whether he wanted to laugh or cry.

''She's pregnant. She's two months pregnant.''

In a rush of emotion he flung his arms round Nancy and embraced her. ''Oh Nan . . . it's what we wanted . . . but of course we hardly dared hope—''

''I'm afraid it's not really the day to rush out and buy champagne,'' said Nancy drily. ''But congratulations anyway. I'm pleased for both of you. George, if we could just—''

He was barely listening. ''We can at least have a celebratory cup of tea! The doctor said I was to give her some sweet tea.''

Nancy followed George into the kitchen, scowling at his back. She couldn't possibly tell him about Patrick now. She hadn't even had a chance to talk about how she felt about their mother's death. And she *needed* to. She needed him.

''Please, George—''

He reached past her for the kettle. ''Hang on a tick. I just want to get Annabel's tea sorted out.''

The telephone rang. It was Faye.

''Nancy, *there* you are. You're supposed to be here. I'm at the station. What's happened?''

''I'll tell you later. Is there another train?''

''There's one in . . . fifty minutes. Are you coming?''

Nancy glanced at George, preoccupied with the tea-tray.

''Yes, I'm coming.''

Soon after Brittany's funeral, Greville Dysart paid an ''official'' visit to the Old Rectory.

''You're looking very smart Greville,'' said Annabel as she

let him in. She could not help feeling glad to see him, even though relations between them had been distinctly strained since she left Heathcote. Greville still claimed that he had prevented her from going to Cambridge for her own good; Annabel believed that she had exposed a blatant hypocrisy. Still it *was* good to see him. He was always so cheerful . . .

"I'll have you know this is my best suit, old girl. Wanted to make the right impression on your husband."

"I'm afraid you may have to excuse my going upstairs to rest." She blushed slightly. "I'm expecting a baby."

"Are you? My dear Annabel, what terrific news! Definitely worth a celebratory drink . . ."

Greville was wreathed in smiles as Annabel led him into the pretty, chintzy drawing room and introduced him to George.

"Hardly the occasion to congratulate you on your nuptials I'm afraid . . . Came to say how sorry I was to hear about your mother. Death-traps these old houses, aren't they?"

He noticed that George had blanched a little.

"Sorry old man . . . wasn't intending to sound so—"

Annabel came to his rescue. "A drink, Greville?"

"Mm, brandy please, m'dear. Thank you." He sat down and picked up a photograph from the table beside him. "One of your family?" he asked George.

"That's Nancy," said Annabel brightly. "Surely you remember her?"

"Well, well! I hardly recognised her. She's certainly a damned good-looking girl."

"Yes, isn't she? And very successful too. She owns Stein McConnell."

Greville looked blank.

"Haven't you heard of them? You *must* have done, Greville! They've been in all the papers! They make clothes."

"Yes, yes, of course. I'm old-fashioned, I know, but I was just thinking how remarkable it is that such a beautiful lady should be so . . . prosperous. I assume . . . does she . . . are they making money?"

"Oh yes, loads and loads of the stuff!" said Annabel. George glared at her.

"Well, I shall look forward to hearing more about her another time." Greville emptied his glass and put it down. "Once again George, so sorry about the accident. What on earth are you going to do about the damage to the house?"

It was obvious that Greville was fishing for information. Rumours of Guy's inheritance had been circulating in the village ever since his arrival at the VJ Day party.

"I'm happy to say that it's not my problem."

"Oh, really?"

"It belongs to . . . the American side of the family."

Guy Exley was staring through the floor-to-ceiling window of his office at Exley Marine Inc.

But he wasn't thinking about the magnificent ocean view. He was thinking about the cable marked "Personal" that was lying in front of him on the desk.

Marcia's voice came through on the intercom. "Mr Exley, I have your wife on the line. She wants to know what to wear to this evening's function. Should I tell her it's formal—"

"Jesus! Tell her I don't give a damn if she shows in a bathing suit!"

There was a tactful silence, then: ". . . And I have Jack Badell on the other line."

"Tell him to hold."

Guy switched off the intercom and stared at the cable. From Messrs. Jacob Stein and Company, London. "We regret to inform you . . ."

That my house is burned away to nothing. That Nancy's mother is dead. Sweet Jesus . . .

He flicked the intercom switch. "Marcia, get my diary will you? When do I have a couple of weeks clear to fly to London? Next week for example . . ."

He could hear Marcia sigh. "You have the Annual General Meeting next week, sir. You have no clear two weeks until . . ." She flicked through endless pages, " . . . until the fall."

Guy gave a heavy sigh. "OK Marcia, call my attorney in London. Guy called Gabin. Tell him to find the best fire damage experts in the country and pay them anything they like to prevent . . . demolition of my damaged property. Tell them I'll cable more instructions later."

"OK, sir. Are you ready to speak to Mr Badell?"

"Put him on."

He picked up the receiver, but he was still staring out at the glittering ocean.

I've got to hold onto that house. It's my last link with Nancy . . .

* * *

Faye noticed a distinct change in Nancy's mood after the funeral.

She had been quieter than usual after she received the news of her mother's death, but now she seemed vague and distracted. Just as she had refused to discuss Guy, she now evaded Faye's questioning. Faye began to wonder if Randolph de Beer had anything to do with her self-absorption. He had left for South Africa shortly after the New Year.

One Friday evening in May, Faye and Nancy had stayed late at the shop to calculate the week's takings and outgoings. Nancy sat down at the desk with the columns of figures in front of her, and began to punch them into the adding machine. Faye stood at her elbow.

"Wait a minute Nancy, let me get my glasses." She reached for her spectacles, but Nancy waved her aside. "It's all right Faye; I'll finish these off. You can go home now, if you like."

Faye ignored this dismissal. "What are you going to do this evening, Nancy? Are you going out somewhere?"

"I don't know yet. I might go for a walk." She looked down at the figures again.

Faye reached into her handbag and took out a bottle of crimson nail varnish. She pulled a chair up to the desk, sat down opposite Nancy, and began to paint her nails with meticulous care.

Nancy threw down her pencil. "Faye do you *have* to paint your disgusting talons here?"

"Why on earth not?"

"I can't stand the smell of that stuff. It makes me feel queasy."

Faye pushed the curtain of blonde hair away from her face and studied her cousin's expression. "Nancy, you're not?—"

"Don't be so bloody ridiculous, Faye. It would have been an immaculate conception, and even I can't compete with the Virgin bloody Mary!"

"What's all this blasphemy about?" The door of the shop was flung open and Ralph strode in, his pink cheeks shining with eager anticipation. He wore the sober pin-striped suit and polished "City" shoes like a schoolboy's uniform.

"I thought I'd drop in on my way back from work and see what you two girls were up to tonight."

Faye could see that he was looking at Nancy, so she pretended to be engrossed in applying a second coat of polish to her nails.

Nancy ignored Ralph, moving her lips as she added the figures in her head.

"*Passport to Pimlico* is on at the local. I thought we could go and see it."

"You two go," said Nancy. "I don't feel like seeing a film tonight."

"Nancy don't be such a wet blanket, old girl. It's an Ealing Comedy. You look as though a bit of laughter wouldn't do you any harm."

"No."

"Oh, come on."

"*I don't want to go to the bloody cinema! Do you understand?*"

Faye picked up her handbag and signaled Ralph towards the door.

"What the hell's got into her?" he asked as they closed it behind them and began to head up the street.

"Oh, she's just impossible at the moment. Completely unapproachable," said Faye, who was still smarting about the "disgusting talons". "I think we should just leave her alone."

Nancy sat at the desk, rubbing her eyes. She closed them, and pressed her knuckles against them. The burning house stood before her, and somewhere around its edges lurked a thin, nervous figure. A match was struck, the quick, sharp grating sound that was so tiny but capable of such massive destruction . . . and death. Was it paraffin? Or petrol . . .

With her eyes still closed, she heard a man's footsteps on the street, and the door of the shop being pushed open. Ralph, coming back to coerce her into joining them.

"Go away, Ralph!"

"Poor Ralph, to merit such treatment."

It was Randolph.

Nancy stared in amazement.

"It's half past eight and you're still Nancy the Shop Girl. Surely the transformation should have been effected by now?"

Nancy laughed. "What would you like me to be? And who are you, anyway? Randolph, the knight on a white charger?"

"Do you need one?"

"Yes." Nancy pushed back her chair and stumbled across the room, towards him, wrapping her arms around his neck and holding onto him tightly. "God, I'm *so* glad you're here," she said fiercely into his chest.

"When I got the letter about your mother, I thought I'd better come back and make sure you were all right. It . . . I was terribly shocked.''

Nancy still had her arms around him, but she was standing very still and focussing into the distance as though she had forgotten where she was. Then she stepped back briskly and began to tidy her hair.

''Well, at least now I'll be able to have a sensible conversation about it. I just can't talk to anyone else.''

She remembered how she had lain on her back under the stars and talked to Guy about their father's death, and how he had understood how she felt without her having to explain. And she had told him about Ella Marion Rowcroft . . .

. . . For a moment she regretted the candour she had shown towards Randolph, betraying the Nancy she had been then. But only for a moment. ''Where are you staying?'' she asked, fetching her jacket.

''At the Connaught.''

''Can we go there now?''

Randolph hesitated. ''Nancy . . .''

She waited.

''All right, but don't you want to change? You usually hate going out in your shop clothes.''

She shook her head.

They caught a taxi, and as it approached the hotel, Randolph took her hand in his and said, ''Nancy, I'm sorry I left so abruptly last time. But we both knew that what we were doing was unfair to your mother. I didn't feel terribly proud of myself. Being in London had only made things more complicated, so I had to get right away, all the way to South Africa, before I could see—''

''Did you decide to marry her?''

''Yes. Yes, I had decided to do that.''

Tears came to Nancy's eyes. ''God, I wish she'd known that. She would have been so happy.''

''Yes . . . Nancy, because of that I'm here as Randolph the Friend this time. Whatever happens, I'll always be a good friend to you. But since I came close to being your stepfather . . . it would probably be better if we just acted like friends.''

Nancy avoided his gaze.

Randolph collected his keys from the desk, but led the way into the dining room and asked the maitre d' for a table.

''Can't we eat upstairs, Randolph?''

''No,'' he said firmly. ''We're going to sit down here and

you're going to tell me everything that has happened to you during the last two months."

After they had eaten, and finished the champagne that Randolph still liked to mete out glass by glass as a reward for Nancy's performance as raconteur, they faced each other across the table in tense silence. Then Nancy's hand moved, quick as lightning and snatched Randolph's keys from the table.

He tried to grab her wrist, but with a peal of laughing she leapt to her feet and ran out of the dining room, pounding the carpeted corridor with Randolph at her heels. The miniature chandeliers trembled at the vibration and the desk clerk stared after them in amazement. Nancy reached the lift first, and shut Randolph out, still laughing. When he eventually reached his room, the door was open, but Nancy leapt out from behind it and locked it, dropping the key down the front of her shirt. He was trapped.

"Now I'm Nancy the Seductress."

She began to undress, removing the demure grey flannel suit, her white blouse, her stockings and suspenders and lying down on the bed in a cream silk teddy. The keys were placed on the table beside the bed.

Randolph stared at them. "Nancy, this isn't what I'm here for."

"I know, but I want you to make love to me. *Desperately*. Now."

Randolph sat on the edge of the bed and teased one of her silky curls with his fingers. "But you can't always have what you want in life."

"I can. I *always* get what I want." Guy's face was banished from her mind.

"I know you do." Randolph's fingers stroked the curve between her breasts and he bent his head and began kissing her, while she pulled at his hair with impatient fingers. "That's one of the things that makes you so irresistible."

After Nancy had got what she wanted, she felt better than she had done in weeks. She could relax. She lay back on a generous pile of hotel pillows and let her mind float off, gently, aimlessly, watching the patterns of light on the ceiling, closing her eyes to make patterns of her own.

Randolph lit a cigarette, but did not speak. It occurred to Nancy that he might be angry with her for undermining his decision. Some men thought it made them look foolish, having "no" twisted into a "yes". Should she apologize? She glanced sideways at his impassive features and decided that the time was right to offer a diversion, now that she felt sufficiently relaxed to talk about what had been on her mind for two months. She told him Leonora's story about the day of the fire, and Patrick Steele.

When he didn't reply, she asked, "Are you angry with me for getting my own way?"

He took a long drag on his cigarette. "I would never expect anything less of you, my dear. As I said, therein lies your fatal charm. No, I was wondering why on earth Patrick Steele should have wanted to do away with your mother."

"But he *didn't*. Don't you see? It's obvious."

"Is it?"

"Yes. He thought that George was in the house, because he would have seen him park his car outside and go in the front. But George went out of the back door to see if Mother was with Leonora."

"But could he *really* be so jealous that he would want to kill George?"

"Yes, by all accounts. He worships Annabel, and did everything he could to prevent her from settling down with George. But George finally won. I suppose Patrick felt he had nothing left."

"But such a crazy thing to do, don't you think? There could have been any number of people in that house. How on earth did he hope to get away with it?"

"But he has!" Nancy sat up in bed and turned to face him. Her eyes were bright. "He has, Randolph, don't you see? George is alive, and nobody had any motive to kill Mother, so the police ruled out arson."

Randolph extinguished his cigarette and began to run his fingers up and down Nancy's bare arm. "So . . . I feel like Randolph the Deus ex Machina. It's as well that I arrived when I did, I think. You're looking thin . . . Maybe I should start taking care of you again." He kissed the inside of her elbow.

But Nancy was in a more business-like mood. "Randolph, be an angel and ring room service. Ask them to send up a pot of tea . . . Jasmine . . . The point is this, Randolph, what am I supposed to *do*?—Pass me my hairbrush, will you?—I can't just forget about it, as you can see. It just plays on my mind and I can't relax. Look, already I'm un-relaxed again, and it's only twenty minutes since we—"

Randolph closed his hand over her mouth. "Sshh! One thing

at a time. Let Uncle Randolph do the talking! I quite agree, of course. You won't have any peace of mind until you do something about it. First, let's consider Leonora. Sometimes alcoholics say they haven't had anything to drink when they've drunk enough to lay you or me underneath the table. And you *certain* she can be trusted?—no, I'm not going to take my hand off your mouth just yet. Nod, or shake your head.''

Nancy nodded vigorously.

"OK. Secondly, would Annabel help you?''

Nancy shook her head.

"Too loyal?''

Another nod.

"That leaves George, and Patrick himself. George has his loyalty to Annabel to consider—''

Nancy pulled his hand away and freed her mouth.

"It's not a bloody game, Randolph! My mother is dead! Shouldn't I just go to the police?''

"No, not yet. You don't have anything, except for a story from a woman who is known to drink. You need a positive identification. I think the only thing for it is to approach Patrick yourself and see if you can force him into a confession.''

There was a knock at the door.

"That'll be room service,'' said Randolph. "Go and get it will you, and pour a cup of tea for this poor man who is feeling old enough to be your grandfather.''

Nancy had decided that there was nothing to be lost in trying to glean information from Annabel.

Accordingly she had telephoned George and asked if she might come down to Somerset and spend a few days at the Old Rectory to escape the pressure of work. Graylings was uninhabitable, and Harry Herbert was still awaiting instructions from America concerning its future.

But after two days with George and Annabel, she realised that they would be impossible as allies. They were like two doves in a dove-cote, billing and cooing and preparing their nest for the arrival of the baby bird. George was withdrawn and Annabel who was in the process of decorating the nursery, only wanted to talk to Nancy about the colour of the furnishings. Did she think blue, or pink? Or should it be yellow? Clearly neither Annabel or George wanted to be distracted from the coming birth by talk of death and, worse still, murder.

As well as chattering incessantly about the baby, Annabel irritated Nancy by constant references to her cousin, who apparently fancied himself in the role of mentor. It was "Greville said this", or "Greville told us that", and even "Greville was very interested in hearing about your business, Nancy."

But Annabel never mentioned Patrick. Nancy supposed that this in itself was a revealing piece of information.

She began to feel like a sleuth. She sat for hours in the guest room at the Old Rectory, looking out over the valley where Nether Aston lay, watching, brooding, waiting. On the third day she took the Citroën, which was now officially her car, but too decrepit to keep in London, and drove to Heathcote.

On the way she thought about the imminent confrontation, and how on earth to turn it into what *she* wanted. She did not want it to be a long drawn-out thing with endless arguments and repetition. She wanted to use exactly the right words to extract what she needed. It had never occurred to her before that the work of an interrogator was such a precise art. By the time she arrived she felt elated by the challenge.

Kit answered the door.

"Kit, what a surprise! I thought you'd be at school."

He stared.

"You remember me, don't you? Nancy Stein. You came to my VJ Day party."

He blushed, the pure crimson blush of adolescence. "Of course I remember. I often think about it, and about you." Immediately he looked worried, as though he had been too forward.

Nancy felt her heart beating very fast and she could barely look at Kit's face. "I really came here to see Patrick. Is he in?"

"No, he doesn't get back until after five and Greville's in London to see his solicitor. But you could wait."

He showed her into the drawing room, a glum, square room that appeared to have hardly any furniture in it. Nancy sat down on one of the decaying chairs and spread out her skirts.

Kit feasted his eyes on her hungrily, momentarily forgetting his role as host. Nancy Stein was sitting in *his* drawing room, and looked more like a fairytale princess that ever. Her white cotton dress was sprigged with red cherries that looked juicy enough to eat. She wore a hat with a sloping brim, like a Chinese coolie's, and her hair was twisted into a knot that rested gracefully on the back of her neck. He groped for something conventional to say, but found nothing, and instead he stared wide-eyed at her, the *real* Nancy Stein.

"Well, here we are . . ." she said. Her mouth was red too, like the cherries.

"Have you come about Annabel? There's nothing wrong, about the baby or anything?"

Nancy shook her head and smiled. "It's funny, but you mentioning Annabel made me realise something. We're related now, since the wedding. I'm your sister-in-law, or something."

Nancy's mind had been working very fast. She had a golden opportunity to snatch some inside information, but she had to make sure that Kit was on her side. If he were still that small, round nine-year-old she could have cuddled and petted him, but not now. Kit was growing up. He had grown quite tall, his sturdiness had been drawn out and honed down, and there was already a distinctly masculine line to his thighs and his back and his jaw. The expression on his face was the same, however. He still stared at her with those sad, turned-down-eyes.

Would it be too mean to flirt with him? She decided that it would. It would be best to flatter him by treating him like an adult. But she would have to draw him in very gently. If he was frightened, he wouldn't say anything at all. She leaned back in her chair and stretched her limbs like a cat.

"Yes, I often think about the party. Everyone said it was a great success, didn't they? Do you remember how you helped me with the buntings. And lighting the first firework . . ."

". . . *And* I stood up for you when you got into trouble about it with that man. What happened to him?"

"To whom?"

"The American."

Nancy's spine contracted. "He . . . he went back to America. But he still owns the house you know."

Kit fell silent. Then: "Would you like some tea?"

Nancy cursed herself inwardly for failing to lead him in the right direction.

But then he said very hurriedly, "I heard about the house burning down, and your mother and everything. I'm very sorry."

"That's one of the reasons that I'm here" She pushed her hair back so that he could see her face more clearly. It was time to tell a white lie. "Kit, the police have been in touch with me about that. Apparently they have to conduct enquiries to rule out arson. Have they been here yet, to ask you where you were on that day?"

Kit started, and flushed violently. "They don't think *I* did it?"

"Of course not. But you might help them by remembering your movements. You could have seen something, for example."

"It was the day Annabel got married, wasn't it? She rang to tell me, and it was when she was on the phone that I heard the fire engines in the High Street."

"You were on your own, then?"

"Yes. No. Greville was out. I got back from school about four, and then Patrick came rushing in the back door, in a tearing hurry. He asked me if I knew where the car keys were, then he took them and drove off in a terrible rush."

"Which way was he going?"

"Towards—"

They stared at one another in silence.

"You think Patrick did it, don't you?" said Kit at last. He looked frightened.

Nancy nodded.

"Nancy, please go. It's not a good idea, honestly. Patrick'll be getting back here, and he might hurt you. He's been even worse since Father died."

"What do you mean, 'worse'?"

"I don't know. I can't say it really. It sounds stupid." He stared at the toe of his shoe. "It's just sometimes I think he's mad."

The front door slammed. They sat in silence for a long thirty seconds.

Patrick came into the drawing room. His clothes were filthy, and he was so thin that he looked emaciated. "You should be doing your homework," he said to Kit. "And you can bloody well clear off out of here!"

This remark was addressed to Nancy. She took off her hat and laid it on her lap. *Count to ten and take a deep breath. One—two—three—four.*

"Patrick," she said quietly. "I'm here to try and clear up a few things about what happened the day my mother died. I wonder if you'd tell me what you were doing that day."

"Get out!"

Kit started instinctively to Nancy's side but she frowned at him and shook her head slightly. "Please. Just tell me where you were. You might be able to help."

Patrick looked sullen. "I was at the farm all day, as usual. I got back here at about half past five, and made myself some supper."

"Kit has already told me that you went out at about four, and

I don't think he was lying. Did you go anywhere near Graylings?''

"I might have."

He sounded defiant now. Nancy had barely dared look at him, but now she moved her head just enough to see that he was smiling. He didn't *care* what had happened. No remorse . . . And then she saw the burning house, and the burning bed beneath the polonaise with her mother's body lying immobile, on it, her *innocent* body.

She stood up. "Right, that's it! I'm calling the police."

She had barely moved when Patrick lunged across the room and grabbed the knot of hair at the back of her neck. She screamed and lashed at him wildly with her arms. Kit reached for Patrick's sleeve, but Patrick knocked him away with the flat of his hand. The next time he was ready for Kit, dragging Nancy with him to the fireplace and picking up a heavy metal poker . . .

"Kit! Keep away!" Nancy used all her strength to twist herself free and push Patrick away from her. He clung on but she used her shoe to trip him and he fell heavily backwards.

The back of his skull hit the stone hearth with a harsh, splitting sound.

"Oh God!" said Nancy.

And then there was a terrible silence as they bent over him and discovered that Patrick was not unconscious, but dead.

Eleven
May 1950

ON THE DAY after her brother's death, Annabel Stein lost the child she was carrying.

Despite long and patient efforts by the police to explain what had happened, Annabel seemed unable to see beyond the fact that Nancy had killed her brother, a fact which she repeated in shrill, hysterical screams before collapsing and being rushed to hospital.

George returned from her bedside to find Nancy waiting for him at the Old Rectory.

"What the hell are you doing here?"

He unlocked the front door and walked into the house without looking at his sister. She followed him into the drawing room, where he sank into a chair and buried his face in his hands.

Nancy was still wearing the white dress sprigged with cherries, but her hair was loose and tangled and her make-up was stale. "Your neighbour said that you were at the hospital."

He nodded. "Annabel lost the baby. The shock."

"I had no idea that Patrick Steele would be such a loss to mankind," said Nancy drily, sitting down in a chair opposite him.

"Christ, Nancy, how can you talk like that? He was her *brother*!"

"Do you think I don't know that?" she blazed. "What the hell do you think it was like for me, being there, seeing him die like that in front of my eyes? And spending half the night in police custody and the other half pacing up and down in some seedy little hotel in Wells with no one to talk to. But for God's sake, George, Patrick Steele, deserved to die. But Mother didn't! She hadn't hurt anyone, had she?"

George looked up. "Nancy, you can't go round behaving like they did in the Old Testament; eye for eye, tooth for—"

"But he started the fire, George! He as good as admitted it!"

George stood up and walked to the other end of the room. He stood at the window with his back to her and his hands thrust into his pockets, the line of his back stooped like an old man's.

When he turned to face her, his blue-green eyes were wild with anger.

"Nancy, your problem is that you're so bloody selfish! You're quite incapable of putting yourself in someone else's position. Do you think I don't know what Patrick Steele was like? He made life as difficult as he could for me, but I didn't go and kill him for it! Yes, I think you're probably right and he *did* start that fire. God knows he was sick enough! But he was also my wife's brother, and she loved him in spite of what he was. They didn't have parents to love; like you and I did. He was her protector and he bloody worshipped her. And now she's not only lost a brother but a child, *our* child, that we desperately wanted. She's absolutely distraught . . ." George took out his handkerchief and wiped away the tears that were collecting in his eyes, and the beads of sweat that were standing out on his forehead. "You should have called the police, Nancy, not just gone and hit him on the head—"

"Oh God, I don't believe this." It was Nancy's turn to grow white with anger. "Do you think I did it on purpose? I thought the police had explained all that?"

"They told me what you told them, yes."

"No . . ." Nancy shook her head in disbelief. "No. I'm not having this, George. Not from my own brother." She stood up and hurried to the door. "Stay there."

George didn't move. There was no mistaking the urgent authority in her voice.

The police told her that Kit was staying with a schoolfriend, and gave her an address in Wells. Nancy found Kit pale but composed, and he readily agreed to come back to the Old Rectory with her. George was still sitting in the same chair.

Nancy marched Kit into the room in front of her. "Okay, tell him Kit. Tell him what happened in your own words."

Kit faltered.

"Go on. Please, Kit. I'm not going to have George thinking I'm a murderess."

"Patrick told her he'd been up to your house. Graylings, I mean. She didn't touch him, or threaten him, or anything. She just said she had better call the police. But he wouldn't let her get to the door, he was pulling her by the hair, and then—"

"Don't rush, Kit. Just say it slowly."

"I tried to stop him because I knew he would hurt her. He picked up the poker to hit me, so she pushed him over. She did it to save *me*."

George stared at Kit. "Thank you," he said.

"So, do you believe me?" demanded Nancy.

Silence.

"George, why is it that you can't trust me all of a sudden?"

"I'll show you." George went to the bureau and took out an envelope, which he handed to Nancy. "This arrived just after Mother's funeral."

The message inside was made of newspaper cuttings pasted crudely to a piece of paper.

"YOU DO NOT DESERVE TO BE MARRIED TO HER. YOUR FAMILY ARE INCEST-(this last word had been crossed out). NO BETTER THAN ANIMALS. ASK YOUR SISTER IF SHE FUCKED THE AMERICAN!"

Kit and George both looked at Nancy. She was staring at the paper without speaking.

"Well?" demanded George.

"George, let me—"

"Christ, you're not even going to deny it? Then it is true! That's what—"

"George—"

"Because that's what started all this, isn't it? The fire . . . the baby . . . Patrick had it in for us because you and Guy couldn't bloody well keep your hands off each other! . . . *Get out! Go on, get out*!"

Nancy turned away from him and stood clinging to a chair, with her head bowed. When she had calmed her breathing, she picked up her handbag and her hat and turned to face him. Her voice was barely audible.

"I'll drop Kit in Wells and go and get my train. I'll leave the keys of the Citroën at the station manager's office, and I'd be grateful if someone could arrange to have it collected . . . I expect I'll see you at the inquest."

Nancy managed to keep calm for Kit's sake, but she was shaking so violently by the time she left Wells that she was forced to pull over to the side of the road. There was sweat on her palms, and running down her forehead and back. Her dress felt damp, cold . . .

She leaned against the side of the Citroën and closed her eyes as delayed shock swept over her in great waves.

Then she saw Patrick Steele's bloody, staring corpse and she opened her eyes again; gagging, retching and finally vomiting into the ditch.

My God, I killed him. I did it. Me. I killed a man . . .

She was still trembling when she got to Bath and parked the car. She rummaged through her purse for some change for the telephone.

I've got to keep going for just a few hours longer . . .

She had enough for two calls. The longing to speak to Faye was very great, but the two of them had not been getting on well lately, and she did not have enough money for a long explanation.

She picked up the phone and dialled the number of Harry Herbert, the Graylings agent, now in his sixties. "Harry, it's Nancy Stein here . . . I wondered if there was any progress about the house. Has Mr Exley been in touch with you about it yet . . . left any instructions?"

"No, Miss Stein, I'm sorry to say he hasn't been in touch direct, but I've had a letter from his lawyers, saying so much as they'll be dealing with the arrangements themselves. I expect Mr Exley's too busy himself."

"Yes, Harry. I expect he is."

The second call was to the Connaught Hotel. "Could I speak to Randolph de Beer please, in Room 315 . . . Randolph, it's Nancy . . . Please, for God's sake, don't leave London yet. You've got to stay . . . I'm coming up there now."

After Nancy had collapsed, sobbing, into Randolph's arms in the foyer of the Connaught Hotel, prompting more disapproving looks from the desk clerk, he carried her to the lift, and up to Room 315, where he bathed her, washed her hair, and tucked her up in his bed with strong, sweet tea, and a plate of bread and butter.

"It's Randolph the Angel now," said Nancy, managing a weak smile.

She told him the outcome of her trip to Somerset, becoming so agitated that he had to push her back forcibly against the pillows.

"Randolph, I'm frightened! . . . I'm so frightened . . . my God, I've actually killed someone—"

"Shhh! It's all right, darling, it'll be all right . . . Come here, let me put my arm around you, and let's talk about this calmly and rationally. Now, do you know yet if you'll have to go to court?"

"There's no one bringing charges, thank God, but it depends on the outcome of the inquest. The police have assured me that Kit's statement covers me for self-defence . . ." She shivered.

"It still scares the wits out of me even so . . . and I'm almost as worried about George."

As calmly as she could, she told Randolph about her brief affair with Guy. She waited for his reaction, and was grateful when she saw him struggle to suppress his own feelings of shock.

"I think you should telephone George. You can use the phone here if you like."

Nancy dialled, holding onto Randolph's arm with her free hand.

"George. It's Nancy."

His voice sounded faint and far away.

"What was that?"

"I said I don't want to talk to you."

"But George, please! Just give me a chance to explain!"

"I don't think there's any point. You're only making matters worse. I just want you to leave me alone."

"But we can't go on like this for ever, surely . . ."

"I think it would be better."

There was a click, and the line went dead.

Ralph stuck his head around the door of Stein McConnell. "Anybody there?"

"I'm in the back," Faye called from the workroom.

He appeared in the doorway, clutching his umbrella and brief-case, with rain running from his mackintosh in rivulets.

"God, it's disgraceful out there! I really hate these wet autumn evenings when it's pitch black and pissing down . . . Nancy not here, old girl? I thought we said six o'clock sharp."

Faye smiled her sleepy smile. "She will be, Ralph. She's rarely late."

"I haven't seen her for ages." Ralph took off his dripping coat and hung it on the back of the door. Turning back to Faye, he beamed and said, "That's a very pretty dress you're wearing. Is it one of ours?"

"Thank you. Yes it is." Faye smoothed the pale blue wool with satisfaction. Ralph had begun to pay more attention to her of late, and this was one of several compliments that he had paid over her dress-sense, on which she had always prided herself. She decided that she would wear more pale blue in future.

The door of the shop was flung open and Nancy came in with a flurry of rain, clutching several parcels and hat-boxes.

"Sorry I'm late, everyone. I was shopping, and the underground was packed.'' She took off her hat and coat and sat down at the desk, her cheeks still flushed and damp with rain water.

Ralph eyed the parcels that she had dumped unceremoniously in the corner. ''So that's what you spend the profits on! I didn't realise that we were doing quite so well.''

''They were a gift from someone,'' said Nancy tartly. ''Are we going to start the meeting then? Do you think we'll be able to fit round the desk?''

''You always say that . . .'' said Faye comfortably. She put on her spectacles and assumed a business-like pose. ''. . . and we always do.''

Ralph took out some printed sheets from his briefcase and handed them round. ''As Financial Director of Stein McConnell and Co., I would like to declare this meeting open. Take a good look at these figures, ladies. These are the estimated costs for the spring collection.''

After a moment's awed silence, Faye said, ''This is an awful lot of money, Ralph. We've come a long way from *'The Problem of Pyjamas'*!''

''Or turning your bedsock into a snazzy little hat!'' rejoined Nancy, and both girls sniggered.

Ralph's fair, handsome face coloured in irritation. ''Come on, girls, this is serious. We have to take a decision this evening about whether we're going to go ahead and do this. It's going to mean risking everything on one collection of clothes. We'll have to use all our capital, and borrow some more, so if the clothes don't sell, we could collapse altogether. It's a very big step.'' He folded his hands and adopted a look of gravity suitable to the occasion.

''There's something rather sad about expanding,'' said Nancy. ''It wouldn't just be us any more would it?''

''No, but that can't be helped, I'm afraid. That, as they say in the City . . .'' Ralph sighed dramatically, ''. . . is business. Basically we'd be moving on from being a piece goods house to somewhere with factory facilities. I've had to budget for designers and public relations people. As I said, it's a big step. Shall we put it to the vote? Nancy's vote being the deciding one, of course, since she was the one who put up the money in the first place. It's more critical for you, old girl. If we were to fail . . .''

''We won't fail,'' said Nancy slowly. Once she would have said, *''I never do''*, but now she thought better of it. ''I'm for it.''

''Me too,'' said Faye.

"That's it, then. The 'ayes' have it! Let's go out and celebrate and to hell with this foul weather!"

"You've forgotten 'Any Other Business'," Nancy reminded him.

"*Is* there any other business?"

"Yes, I have an announcement to make. I'm going to Paris at the weekend, and I shall be away for a week. Randolph's taking me."

Faye watched Ralph closely, for the disagreeable expression that always came over his face when Randolph de Beer was mentioned. And sure enough, there it was.

"I must say, Nancy, I think it's a poor show you dodging off on holiday at such an important time. If we're going to make the spring collection a success, we've got to get working on the designs *now*."

"It's not just going to be a holiday. I'm going to go to the Paris collections and see if I can pick up some good ideas."

"Right, well . . . in that case, I'm sure we can grant you leave of absence. You can tell us all about your plans for the trip over a drink."

Nancy scarcely seemed to have been listening to Ralph at all, but she turned to him now with her most blinding smile. "No, I'm sorry, Ralph. I have other plans. Now, if the other members of the board will excuse me . . ."

After Nancy had gone, Ralph exploded with anger. "Bloody hell, Faye! Who does she think she is? She really hasn't been pulling her weight lately. Always drifting off here, there and everywhere . . ."

Faye smiled to herself as she reached for her coat. She combed her straight, pale hair and pulled a blue beret over it. "Ralph, I think you're being quite unfair. A year ago if she'd gone off to Paris like that, I'd have called her a spoiled brat, but she's had such a terrible time this year, what with the fire, and that wretched inquest."

"Sorry. I'm sorry Faye . . . Ghastly . . . This business with George, is he still not speaking to her? . . . Still blames her for the miscarriage?"

"Apparently. I think it will do her good to get away."

Ralph nodded and reached for his damp mackintosh. "Once more unto the breach . . . Dinner?"

Faye nodded. "It looks as though it's just you and I again . . ."

Randolph booked a suite at the Ritz, and insisted that Nancy spend her first morning in Paris shopping in the Faubourg St Honoré.

"Well, perhaps just one or two things . . ." said Nancy.

She found them quickly: two smart alpaca weave suits, one cherry red, one mustard ("so useful . . ."), and then there was a white tissue faille evening dress that just begged to be bought ("heavenly, don't you think, Randolph? . . .") and of course some white satin shoes to match, two pairs of kid courts for everyday, and an enormous, huggable raccoon coat ("rather extravagant, but gorgeous . . .") and boxes and boxes of underwear: silk knickers and teddies, stockings and garters all dripping with lace ("even more heavenly . . .").

Nancy hugged Randolph as they walked back to the hotel together. "I feel so much better already, darling. It must be the Parisian air."

"Which is like wine, of course. Now, what would Mademoiselle Nancy, the Gay Parisienne, like to do this afternoon? We could go to Cartier and buy a few trinkets. Or have you had enough of spending my money? We could stroll in the Luxembourg, or the Bois, or just sit in a street café *'pour regarder les gens'* . . ."

Nancy chose to walk in the Bois de Boulogne.

"It's my favourite time of year for walking in parks," she explained, kicking the leaves into a spray of russet and gold. "It's Hallowe'en tomorrow. I wonder how the French celebrate it. Do you think they do? Perhaps we could roam the streets and look for somewhere that offers apple-ducking as a pastime . . ."

"Nancy, the Witch . . ."

"When I was a little girl, I used to stay awake on Hallowe'en so that I could look out of the window and see the witches riding by on their broomsticks!" She bent and picked up a handful of leaves with her kid-gloved hands and threw them in the air. They made a crackle of noise and light, drifting down to land on them both.

"I'm sure that the Parisian witches will all be very chic, and *de bon goût*," said Randolph, picking an amber leaf from her glossy hair.

"My grandmother was a Parisienne, from St Germaine des Près. She had a lovely name. Lucienne de Vesey . . ."

"Yes I know," said Randolph. "I met her once, the first time I went to Graylings. I am ashamed to tell you that it was as long ago as 1915."

"In the first war! How exciting! Were you a soldier?"

"No, I was what was known as a 'profiteer'. I sold arms. I can still hear your mother saying that word now, curling her lips in distaste. She was very idealistic."

"And what was my grandmother like?"

Randolph narrowed his eyes, and looked ahead at the setting sun. "She was a very lovely lady. Extremely beautiful. Tall, with a long neck like a swan's, and dark eyes. Beautifully dressed, of course, but with a very simple, engaging quality about her. She would have seemed naïve I think, but at the same time she gave the impression of being someone who had suffered a great deal. A sad lady."

Nancy shivered and pulled her coat around her as the sun disappeared in a burst of glorious pink. "I love the name Lucienne. If I had a daughter, I think I'd call her after my grandmother."

"Would you like a daughter?" Randolph avoided looking at her.

"Yes. I've thought about it a lot lately. Since Annabel and George lost their baby, thought about what it means. But I think I want children for all the selfish reasons. You know, so that there would always be someone who needed me. *Me*, and not anybody else."

"Ah, but they don't, do they? Children stop needing their parents. Or at least, they stop showing it. Now take your mother—"

"I know what you're going to say. She thought I didn't care. But I was going to give you back to her. It would have been the first thing I ever did for her. The first important thing. And I was just too late . . . too bloody late!"

Mention of Brittany made them both silent. They walked back in the chilly autumn dusk that stirred memories with its shadows and beckoned people home to the light.

"And what would Mademoiselle like to do this evening?" asked Randolph eventually.

"Mademoiselle would like to slip into one of her divine new negligés and consume several bottles of the finest vintage champagne that Paris has to offer!"

They got drunk: frankly, disgustingly drunk.

For Nancy, consuming champagne in Paris was like going shopping in Paris: she promised herself two glasses, but somehow there was always a reason to have another, and another . . .

Eventually Randolph staggered to his feet and drew the curtains. Nancy lay sprawled across the bed swathed in écru satin. The curtains were a soft gold, and the matching shades on the wall lamps threw a warm yellow light over the room.

"Randolph," she said dreamily, turning over onto her back, "I've been thinking about what we talked about in the Bois this afternoon . . ."

"About Hallowe'en? You thinking of hiring a broomstick, my dear?"

"No, about children. I think I'd like to have a baby."

Randolph laughed. He arranged his tall frame, clad only in a silk dressing gown, into a Noel Coward-like pose, with one arm resting on the marble fireplace. "My dear girl, what a very extravagant notion."

"Oh Randolph! . . . Listen . . . So many black, awful, ugly things have happened to me lately . . . a baby would be a good thing, a positive thing—"

Randolph had failed to notice the note of longing in Nancy's voice.

"But on the other hand it might not be," he said in Noel Coward's voice. "It might turn out to be the most perfectly horrid baby!"

"Randolph, I'm *serious*. Can we?"

"And what about a husband?"

"Well, I thought we could wait and see if there was a baby first."

"How very sensible! Very well, let us set about making one. Did your mother tell you where they came from."

"From under the gooseberry bush, silly."

Randolph dropped his silk dressing gown onto the floor and dived onto the bed. "Very well, let's start looking! Did you leave your thing in the bathroom?"

"Yes, I already thought of that."

"How very scientific of you! Gooseberry bushes indeed!"

The next morning Nancy had a headache, and Randolph was unusually quiet. She watched him shaving while she drank her tea, feeling despondent and depressed without quite knowing why.

"Randolph, do you remember what we talked about last night?"

"Yes."

"Do you remember what we *did* last night?"

"Yes." He came and sat on the edge of the bed and took her hand in his. "Nancy . . ."

"You didn't really mean it, did you?"

He sighed, and shook his head. "No, it was a lovely, drunken idea but it wouldn't be right."

"But Randolph, I thought—"

"Nancy, being childless is a great disappointment to me. But I'm too old. I'm almost sixty. And you've got all your life ahead of you. I don't want to spoil things for you."

Nancy looked away, and he saw the tears of disappointment in her eyes.

He patted her hand gently. "Come on, get dressed. It's time to go down to the Avenue Montaigne. You wanted to see those collections, remember?"

"Yes," said Nancy, but she was speaking to herself. "I'm not a mother, am I? I'm a businesswoman."

Faye was working late, and grumbling to herself as she squinted at a column of figures.

It's all right for Nancy, she thought, swanning around Paris, being wined and dined by a wealthy man . . . She sighed, adjusted her spectacles on the bridge of her nose, and turned to the next page of figures.

The telephone rang. "Faye, I just tried to ring you at the flat but there was no answer, so I thought I'd try here." Ralph sounded cheerful.

Faye smiled to herself with pleasurable anticipation.

"Did you know it was Hallowe'en tonight? . . . No, neither did I, but I thought we should do something about it. A chap at work told me about a club in the West End where they have candles and Hallowe'en lanterns and so on. I wondered if you'd like to go?"

Faye's mind was racing. "Well, it does sound a lovely idea Ralph, but I'm terribly tired this evening. But I'll tell you what . . . you haven't seen the flat yet, have you? . . . Why don't you come over and I'll cook you some supper? I've got some steak in the fridge."

"That sounds wonderful."

"I'll meet you there in about an hour."

Faye hurriedly locked up the shop, and ran up to Knightsbridge to catch a bus. A few months earlier, when Nancy's need for privacy had become pressing, the two girls had left Lindsay Place and moved into a rented flat in Kensington, near the Cromwell Road. Faye caught a bus straightaway, and jumped off one stop earlier than usual to run into the delicatessen and buy cheese, wine and vegetables.

She liked having the flat to herself, and a chance to try and stamp her own personality on it. The high-ceilinged, echoing rooms were largely furnished with pieces 'borrowed' from Graylings, including several grand portraits in heavy gilt frames, that Faye disliked. The sitting room looked out over the square gardens. It had a threadbare crimson carpet and was dominated by a huge leather Chesterfield sofa, that they had bought in the Portobello Road. Faye's contribution was a pair of cane chairs, a coffee table to match and a few pieces of modern sculpture.

Her purchases were thrown onto the kitchen table as she hurried into her room to get ready.

She flung her work suit onto the bed and started running a bath, glancing at her watch as she ran between bedroom and bathroom. Thirty minutes. She would only just have time. While the bath was running she painted her fingernails with pillarbox red polish, holding them in front of the gas fire to dry them before starting on her toenails. Nancy teased her continually about her love of nail polish, but Faye was undeterred. She loved the way it emphasised her long, slim fingers and her small, pretty feet. She washed her hair in the bath, dried it, and brushed it until the light was reflected in the smooth, honey blonde surface.

Five minutes. She hadn't decided what to wear, and Ralph was always punctual. The idea of borrowing something from Nancy was ruled out, but the contents of her own wardrobe seemed uninspiring. She chose her best black wool dress.

A little too formal, but what the hell; it's flattering.

The dress had a nipped-in waist and a full skirt that hid her wide hips. She had just fastened the last hook and eye when the doorbell rang.

"Faye, how lovely you look! That black is just right with your hair!"

Faye smiled at the compliment.

Ralph held out a bunch of white lilies. "I thought these were the sort of flowers you would like. Am I right?"

"You're a mind reader!"

Ralph made admiring noises while Faye arranged the sort of flowers Nancy disliked on the cane coffee table that Nancy despised. Faye was almost purring with delight. Not only was Ralph impressed with her own appearance, but he looked as though he had made an effort with his own. His pink skin glowed and gave off a faint smell of aftershave, and his blonde hair was damped down with water. She poured him a glass of scotch.

"Do you mind amusing yourself while I cook?"

"Can I come into the kitchen and watch?"

Faye laughed. "Of course you can!"

They maintained a comfortable silence while Ralph sat at the kitchen table, sipping his scotch, and Faye fried the steak with mushrooms and made a salad.

"We could eat in here," she said, pointing to the small, rickety kitchen table, "or take it through to the sitting room and eat it on our laps. I'm afraid there isn't a dining room . . ."

"Whichever you prefer, old girl."

"I think the sitting room would be nicer," said Faye, removing her apron and smoothing her black dress.

She fetched some coal and lit a fire in the small fireplace that faced the Chesterfield, and Ralph sat on the floor while she curled her legs up on the sofa and picked languidly at her food. The same comfortable unhurried silence was present as they ate, and Faye was glad of it. She could feel herself beginning to relax; the mediocre claret warming her from the inside, the fire from without.

Ralph laid down his knife and fork and pushed his plate to one side. "I wonder how Nancy's getting on."

Faye jumped, and the toe of her shoe knocked the wine bottle, splashing it on to the carpet. "I'll get a cloth . . ."

She ran into the bathroom and gripped the edge of the basin, breathing rapidly. The face that looked out from the shaving mirror was flushed and wild-eyed. "What's the matter with you?" she asked, staring back at it. "Pull yourself together!"

They were silent as she mopped up the wine. Ralph watched the movement of her hands with the cloth. Her scarlet nails glowed in the firelight.

"Faye, can I talk to you confidentially about something?"

"Of course." She carried the cloth into the kitchen, then resumed her position on the sofa, with her feet curled up underneath her.

"What exactly *is* Nancy's relationship with de Beer?"

"I don't know. She doesn't talk about it much, but even if she did, I suspect it would be difficult to define. He was originally a friend of her mother's. He's a mentor, and a friend, a sort of godfather figure. That's when he's here, of course. But he doesn't live in England."

"Do you think they'll get married?"

Ralph looked wistful. Faye's heart sank like a stone.

"No, I'm pretty sure that they won't. I think if they were going to, they would have done so long ago. But they . . . they are lovers, Ralph."

Ralph stared at her, as though he were so reluctant to believe what she was saying, that he would rather believe her a liar. The silence was not comfortable now. Ralph paced the room for a moment, then sat down with his back against the sofa. He held out his hands to the fire and stared into the flames.

"It's just . . . I can't get her out of my mind, Faye. I think about her all the time. All the time. I suppose that mean's I'm in love with her?"

Faye offered no comment.

"I've known her since we were children, but I think the day I first noticed her was during the war when I'd just got back from the SOE, and we came over to Graylings for the day. Do you remember? I think you were there."

"I think you were there" . . . *Christ!*

"We went riding on the Mendips, and then we played Scrabble and she was . . . I don't know, I just remember coming away thinking that she was the most delightful person I'd ever met. She was just . . . I don't know, delightful."

Delightful, and a little bitch to you, as far as I remember . . .

"Do you remember that day at all, Faye? I think I've wanted her ever since that day."

Faye remembered Ralph bending over Nancy as she played dead, cradling her head in his lap. She could even remember the shape that his dark gold hair made, at the back of his neck. Yes, she thought, and I've wanted *you* ever since that day . . .

"Anyway, I don't know what the point is in my telling you all this," Ralph said gloomily. "My case would appear to be hopeless. She doesn't have much time for me these days."

Faye wondered which would further her own cause more, encouragement, or discouragement. She didn't want to fan the fire of unrequited love. She decided to err on the side of caution. "Well, I wouldn't say that. I think there's always room for hope."

And for changing the subject, please God . . .

"I think after that truth-telling session, you deserve another drink. There's some more wine in the kitchen . . ."

"I think I'd rather have scotch."

Faye fetched his drink, and rashly poured one for herself as well, though she disliked what to her seemed a medicinal taste.

"Let's change the subject!" said Ralph after his first mouthful. Faye sighed with relief.

"What would you like for Christmas? I want to give you something really nice this year, Faye. You've been so good to me over the last few months. A real brick."

"Excuse me." Faye put her glass down and stumbled into the bathroom. As she stood up, she realised that she was slightly drunk. The face in the shaving mirror was even redder than before, the eyes were confused and the wide mouth looked a little off-centre. "So that's what I am. I'm a brick, am I? We'll see about that . . ." She splashed her face with cold water, sprayed on some scent and returned to the sitting room.

Ralph seemed quite content with the silence. "We get on really well, don't we, Faye."

"Mmm."

"I'm so glad we do. I don't know what I'd do if we didn't . . ."

Just as Faye began to suspect that he was a little tipsy too, he turned to her with a crooked smile and said, "Back's aching a bit. Is there room for two up there?"

She nodded, and he squeezed onto the sofa next to her.

"Do you mind if I? . . ." He leaned his head against her shoulder.

For a while, Faye didn't dare move. Then she wriggled her hand free and touched his hair tentatively. He didn't object, so she began to run her fingers through it, and he closed his eyes with a slightly embarrassed look on his face.

"Ralph . . . this isn't terribly comfortable. Why don't we go and lie down?"

He opened one eye. "Lie down?"

"In the bedroom." Ralph stared at her for a moment, then sat up and extricated his limbs as though he had been tainted. He looked appalled. "Faye, how could you? After everything I've just told you about my feelings for Nancy. I thought you had more sensitivity."

"Ralph, I'm sorry, it was the drink talking, just forget it please . . ."

He smiled stiffly. "Of course. I forgive you."

"There's no need to go."

"I think I ought to. I've got to get up early for work tomorrow anyway."

He kissed her on the cheek, an empty placatory gesture. Then he picked up his coat and left.

Fayed stared at the vase of white lilies, and burst into angry tears.

"Damn you, Nancy Stein, damn you!"

Christmas was celebrated in style on Long Island.

"Oh Guy, honey, it's going to be so wonderful! We're going to hire a real horse-drawn sleigh, with all those cute little bells, and I'm going to wear this white fur cape, and little white fur hat . . ."

Missie Exley was planning a retaliatory Christmas party.

". . . It's going to be *so* much better than the Jamiesons', or the O'Connors' . . ."

Guy wandered into his dressing room and stared at the racks of different coloured shirts.

". . . Guy, you're not listening to me! I was telling you about the party. Can't you even stay in the same room when I'm talking to you?"

Guy walked back into the bedroom and stood at the edge of the bed in his boxer shorts and socks. He looked down at his wife. She was lying on her side with her glossy brown-black hair sprawled over the pillow and her mouth wearing its most sulky pout.

She could not help but be moved by the sight of Guy's physical perfection; his strong, square body and his skin tanned to the same nut-brown as his hair.

She ran a finger over his stomach. "You've hardly lost your colour at all . . ." A slow grin spread over her face. "Guy, honey, come here."

She wound her arms around his neck. Her skin felt hot. She always felt hot. Her mouth was near his, her inquisitive tongue teasing at his lips and his teeth. They did not part in response, as she had hoped. Her hot little arms were unclasped and she was pushed away.

"Guy, what's the matter with you? What have I done wrong? We haven't done it for two whole days now. Don't you find me attractive any more?"

"Very," said Guy heavily, buttoning up his shirt. "It's just that I have to go to work. I have a company to run, remember, to keep you in hairdos and cute little white fur hats."

Missie was sulking again. "You never used to! When we were first married you never cared whether you got to your lousy office in time. We used to do it about seven times a day. I counted . . .''

Guy went into his dressing room and leaned against the door. To think he had got married for a bit of peace!

At least Marcia, his secretary, was pleased with the arrangement. He had to go to work now, just to get away from his wife.

He hated their house. It had been Missie's choice of course; a sugar pink mansion just outside Orient Point, with a grotesque cupola on top, a hideous gazebo and yards of wrought-iron curlicues everywhere. Inside, the whole house smelled of her perfume, and every room was littered with the clothes that she was unable to stop buying. The only things that interested Missie were clothes and sex. Guy was not sure in which order. No, there were three things. Lately she had added another to her list of hobbies. Drink. She had become very fond of drinking.

When he returned from the dressing room in suit and tie, with his shoes in his hand, Missie was sitting at her vanity unit, which was as long as most drugstore counters, brushing her hair. Her hair was so beautiful that when he saw her brushing it like that, with her back turned, he could almost . . . he could almost forgive her her faults.

She had clearly not forgiven him. ''The Hardies have invited us to West Virginia for the weekend,'' she said in a hard, uninterested little voice, brushing her hair faster. ''I don't know whether you want to go. I told Kathleen I'd let her know.''

''When?''

''Two or three weeks from now.''

''I can't,'' said Guy, sitting down on the edge of the bed to tie his shoe laces. ''I'm planning on going over to England for a while.''

Missie's eyes lit up. ''England? To London? How wonderful!''

''Missie, it's business. I'm going there alone.''

''I want to go with you. I want to go to London and go shopping for clothes!''

Missie still had her back to him, but he could see her angry pout reflected a dozen times in the yards of angled mirrors.

''It's not that kind of trip! My house over there has been badly hit by a fire, and I have to go out and sort a few things. I'm not taking you, and I don't want to discuss it either.''

Missie threw down her silver-backed hairbrush so hard that it cracked the glass top of the vanity unit.

Felicity Exley telephoned Guy at his office that afternoon.

"Missie says you won't let her go to London with you."

Guy sighed heavily. That was his grandmother's signature tune these days. *"Missie says . . ."* As soon as Missie had a grievance, she telephoned Felicity.

The voice at the end of the telephone warbled on. ". . . And she says that you're showing no interest whatsoever in the party. Really, Guy! She's been looking forward to it for so long, and it's going to be such an event. Please, for my sake, summon up some enthusiasm . . ."

Guy hated the party.

Guests took turns around the snow-clad lawn in the hired sleigh, or shivered in their furs on the terrace, where waiters were roasting chestnuts over braziers and carrying jugs of mulled wine.

Chuck Jamieson and a heavily pregnant Pamela appeared at Guy's elbow. "Guy, old fellow, this is some party! That wife of yours is quite something, isn't she, dreaming all this up? Pamela was wondering whether you two were planning on starting a family this year, weren't you, Pamela? She'd be a great little mother . . ."

Guy shuddered.

"She's so full of spirits! Why, just look at her . . ."

Missie was drunk. She had commandeered the sleigh and was driving it about the garden herself, waving, and shouting, *"We-hay, everybody! Look at me!"*

Then she started to take her clothes off. Some of the guests laughed, others clapped. Some just stared.

Guy groaned and closed his eyes. First the white fur coat was flung to the ground, the white wool skirt and the cashmere sweater . . . Missie was standing up in the driving seat clad only in her silk underwear and her hat.

The sight of her lustrous dark hair, Nancy's hair, flying out beneath the white fur, filled Guy with desperate anger. He ran across the lawn, and jumped into the sleigh, snatching the reins out of Missie's hands and driving it away from the house. He could hear the guests clapping and murmuring, *"How sweet . . . Aren't they darling?"*

"For God's sake, what are you doing?" hissed Guy. "You're making a spectacle of yourself! Not to mention a laughing stock out of me!"

"I'm having a good time," Missie smiled sweetly and started to remove her petticoat.

"Missie, stop it, please! Just behave yourself, will you! Put that thing on again!"

"What's it worth?"

Guy stared at her in disbelief. He was bargaining with his own wife to prevent her from removing her clothes in public.

"I want to go to England."

"Missie, whatever happens, you're not going to England with me."

"Say you won't go to England at all then."

The incessant jingling of the sleigh bells was wearing Guy's nerves.

"OK, you win. I won't go to England . . . *Yet!*" he added, under his breath.

"The tree looks lovely, doesn't it?" George kissed his wife's cheek. "Thanks to you."

They were sitting on the chintz sofa, contemplating the beguiling sight of the Christmas tree, and the pile of presents beneath it.

Annabel sighed. "It's a shame we can't be alone for our first Christmas together."

"You don't begrudge poor Kit house room do you? It's not even as if he has anywhere else to go, with tenants living at Heathcote."

"No, I wasn't thinking of Kit. I meant Greville."

George stood up to put another log on the fire. "I'm sorry, Annabel, but what could I do? When someone telephones like that with a tale of how they're all on their own in London for Christmas, you're put on the spot, aren't you? Anyway, I thought you were fond of old Greville."

"I am," said Annabel hurriedly. "He's always friendly and jolly and everything, it's just . . ." she sighed again, "I don't entirely trust him."

A car drew up outside. George peered through the window into the damp, grey December afternoon. "Looks like a taxi. It'll be Greville, I expect."

Annabel started to struggle to her feet, but George stopped her. "No, I'll go. You're supposed to rest."

Greville came into the house, beaming all over his chubby face, with his arms full of parcels like a jovial Father Christmas. He admired the tree, and then sat down in a chair opposite Annabel.

After consuming a large quantity of food and drink, it was

time for Greville's contribution to the evening: a collection of smutty seasonal jokes about Father Christmas and chimneys, and a bottle of port. Annabel seized the opportunity to flee.

Greville settled his portly body into his chair. "Well then, George old man, how's the life of the land agent?"

George grimaced.

"Too much like white slavery, eh?"

"Let's just say that the frustrations are many, and the rewards are few."

"You ought to go into business. Now that I'm settled in London, I'm looking for a partner myself."

"*You* are?" George could never keep up with Greville's financial schemes, which seemed to change with the seasons. "I didn't know you were going into business."

"Ah . . . I've been keeping mum, old man, until I had it all worked out. You remember at the time of Patrick's . . . accident, I was away seeing m' solicitor? Well, it transpired that old Cousin Percy had popped his clogs at last. Been gaga for years. The estate went at the end of the war—usual story . . . debts, but there was a bit of a legacy for me at the end of it all. Castle Cloud came up trump in the end!"

George stared into his glass of port. He never knew quite when to take Greville seriously and was therefore too embarrassed to look him in the eye. "Really? And what line of business will you be going into?"

"The fashion business. Like your sister."

George frowned. "What do you know about the fashion business?"

"Nothing!" said Greville cheerfully. "But I intend to find out all I need to know. Are you *sure* you're not interested in coming in with me? I know you and your sister . . . well, let's just say you haven't been seeing eye to eye, and leave it at that. What better way is there to put a woman in her place than to do better at the thing she's best at!" He laughed, as though he found this idea quite delightful.

"No thank you," said George. "I may have my grievances against Nancy, but I have no desire to change my line of work. I don't want Annabel going through any upheaval . . ."

He smiled. "We've got some good news for you. We were going to break it to you tomorrow, but I might as well tell you now. She's expecting another baby in the summer."

Twelve
February 1951

"FAYE, COME AND look!"

Nancy ran into Stein McConnell at half past eight one morning in a state of excitement. "The new shop's having its sign painted!"

They went out into the street and stood shivering in the sleet while two workmen battled to carry pots of paint up the ladder. The shop opposite Stein McConnell used to sell hand-made chocolates, but it had closed down before Christmas, and the premises had been empty for two months. Now there were signs of activity. The shop frontage had been painted a smart French navy, and the workmen were stencilling letters in gold on the blank hoarding above the shop window.

"Excuse me," Nancy asked one of them. "What sort of shop is it going to be? Do you know?"

"Dress shop, love."

"Did you hear that, Faye? A dress shop. We have a competitor on our doorstep. I'm dying to see what it's going to be called."

The painter leaned back to admire his work, and Nancy read out the extent of his efforts. "C-L-O-U *Clou*. It looks as though it's going to be quite a long name."

"They'll take all morning to finish it," said Faye sensibly, "so there's not much point standing here watching. We'll come back later and have a look. In the meantime, we've got all the new clothes to unpack."

There were only three weeks to go until the launch of the Stein McConnell spring collection, and the first deliveries of garments were starting to arrive from the factory. They all needed checking, sorting and listing.

"They're very good, aren't they?" Nancy pulled the plastic cover off a suit and laid it down on the desk, fingering the cuffs and inspecting the lining. It had a black skirt and a contrasting jacket in Prince of Wales check with black buttons.

Inspired by what Nancy had seen in Paris, and by Coco Chanel, who was their favourite designer, the girls had taken a very daring step and abandoned full, ankle-length ballerina skirts in favour of a shorter, squarer silhouette with slim-fitting pencil skirts and simple cropped jackets. It was a gamble, but their clothes would at least be different, the colours stronger and bolder than before and worn with black accessories which they intended to sell on the premises to provide the customer with a complete "look".

Nancy tried on a smart black pillbox hat with heavy veiling specked with chenille dots.

"Ladies—going to a funeral? It'll be social death for you if you're seen without a Stein McConnell hat!"

She was still laughing at her joke, and still trying to arrange the hat to her satisfaction when the telephone rang.

"Faye, it's the fashion page of *The Times*. They want to do an article on the collection. What shall I say?"

"Tell them the launch is a surprise, and we're not doing any previews. But if they'd like to come along on the day before the launch, we'd be glad to give them an interview to appear in the paper on the next day."

Nancy relayed the message, and sat down at the desk to check the delivery notice. She looked thoughtful. "Faye, I haven't seen Ralph for ages. What's he up to at the moment?"

"I've hardly seen him since Christmas myself. He's got a few weeks' leave coming up, starting next week, and he told me that he would probably spend most of it at Cleveleigh."

"But that means he'll miss the launch! I would have thought he'd want to be here for that . . . It's almost as if he's avoiding me. He doesn't like me seeing Randolph, does he?"

Faye shrugged.

"Well, he needn't worry about that. Randolph's going back to South Africa again next week." She sighed heavily, then returned to her task for a few minutes before adding, "You know, Faye, it's funny, but I really wish Ralph was going to be here for the launch. It won't feel right without him . . . Oh hell, now I've put ticks in all the wrong columns, and made it look as though we've got a hundred and fifty of the suits with the sailor collars!"

She flung her pen onto the desk and wandered over to the window. "Oh Faye, they've finished the sign. 'CLOUD COUTURE'! What a ludicrous name!"

A few days later, Nancy dragged Faye out into the street again, and this time her laughter was derisive. "Just look at this, will you? The interior of the shop. Look what they've done with it." On the other side of the glass was a shop whose interior was almost identical to their own. The colour scheme was blues and pinks, and the frieze on the walls represented a classical landscape of ruined temples and setting suns ('' 'The Temple of Lucre', presumably,'' said Faye). There was a desk at the back of the shop and a low sofa for the customers to sit on.

''What dull, derivative people they must be!'' said Nancy, clapping her hands with delight. ''They'll never be able to compete with our line though. I wonder what sort of clothes they are going to sell? I can't wait to see.''

''Oh, probably ballerina skirts and nipped-in waists and three-quarter length sleeves,'' said Faye airily. ''Not to mention padre-style hats.''

Nancy roared with laughter. For a long time afterwards she was to remember how hard she had laughed that day.

That night, Greville Dysart left his new shop in Knightsbridge armed with a set of skeleton keys that he had borrowed from a former inmate of Pentonville Prison.

He let himself into Stein McConnell and began to search through the filing cabinets, his plump hands clad in black leather gloves. When he found the sketches for the Spring 1951 collection, he laid them out carefully on the floor and photographed them. The next task was to thumb slowly through the racks of clothes, examining them and making notes in a small notebook. He scribbled furiously, as though he was excited by what he saw. Then the drawings were replaced in the filing cabinet and the door locked carefully behind him.

In only a matter of hours, the photos would be developed and the pictures would be on their way to the workshop where Cloud Couture Designs were waiting to go into production.

Ralph Stanwycke was sitting in the warm, comfortable kitchen at Cleveleigh Manor, enjoying a leisurely breakfast. The best thing about being on holiday, he decided, was not having to scramble to get to work. He could actually taste what he was eating as he worked his way ponderously through a boiled egg, and not only read the newspaper but tackled the crossword as well.

''Three down. *'Prospero's problem?'* six letters . . . Hmm . . . Incest, perhaps?''

Susannah Stanwycke stuck her head round the kitchen door.

''Ralph—telephone.''

As Ralph went to the phone, she added in a stage whisper. *"It's Nancy. She sounds upset."*

"Ralph! Thank God you're in! . . . Listen, something terrible's happened. Just too dreadful for words. Can you come up to London . . . Straightaway . . . Meet us at the shop."

Ralph arrived in London at lunchtime to find a furious Nancy and a pale, silent Faye waiting for him at Stein McConnell.

"What's up?"

"*This* is what's up!" Nancy dragged him out into the street and pointed into the window of the shop opposite. "Look! Look at that suit!"

"I'm sorry, I—"

"Ralph, can't you see? I thought we'd talked about the clothes enough for . . . it's just like one of our suits! All of the things in there, they're not identical but they're along the same lines. Short, narrow skirts. Black with everything."

Ralph looked at her helplessly. "Yes, but surely more than one shop can—"

"But they're *cheaper*, Ralph! They've cut all the corners on the finishing and made everything much cheaper than ours. People have been going in and out all morning. And right on our doorstep! I'd love to know how they got their ideas!"

"Perhaps they went to Paris too?" said Ralph unhelpfully.

They went back into the shop.

Most of the afternoon was spent arguing about what to do next.

"Who owns Cloud Couture, anyway?" Ralph asked Faye.

"Oh, what does that matter? It's too late now."

The impact of the launch was ruined, and their new "look" preempted. Ralph's suggestion that they make some last-minute changes to the garments to set them apart from Cloud Couture's brought howls of protest. But in his turn Ralph firmly resisted lowering the price of their clothes, because of the necessity to recoup their investment.

"But Ralph, what shall we do?" asked Nancy, plaintively.

"There's nothing we can do, except sit tight and hope that the clothes sell."

As he drove back to his flat, all he could hear was Nancy's voice saying, "What shall we do, Ralph?" He hated himself for it, but he was secretly willing the collection to be a flop.

The clothes didn't sell.

Ralph returned to London and started working through the necessary financial procedures with Stein McConnell's accountant, but he avoided the shop and its atmosphere of despair. The girls were well aware of the reality of the situation. Their remaining assets would have to be used to clear their debts. They were back where they started from, except that now almost all of the money that Nancy had inherited from Jake had been swallowed up.

One morning when he was at Jacob Stein and Co.'s offices in Pilgrim Street, his secretary intercepted a telephone call.

"It's a young lady, sir. She says it's a personal matter."

Ralph took the precaution of closing his office door.

"Ralph? It's Nancy. Listen, I really need to talk to you. Can you get away from work for a while? I'm at the flat."

Ralph agreed with alacrity, then felt very glad that he had closed his office door, because he was sure that he looked, and sounded, very foolish.

Nancy had left the door of the flat on the latch. She was lying on the Chesterfield sofa with a magazine in her hand, but Ralph could tell from the expression on her face that she wasn't reading it. Her mouth was set in a hard line, and for the first time in Ralph's memory her hair looked lack-lustre and neglected. A rumpled cotton skirt had twisted up round her hips, revealing her naked legs. Ralph stared at them. Stirred not by lust, but by pity.

"I shouldn't look so closely. I look a bloody mess, don't I?" She dropped the magazine onto the crimson carpet, and twisted her mouth into something approaching a grin.

Ralph was relieved. Eliciting pity was not Nancy's style. She fumbled on the table for a packet of cigarettes and lit one. "I know, I know. I haven't smoked since the war. I just feel like it at the moment." Next to the ashtray was a plate covered in crumbs of cheese and crackers, and a dirty knife. There were crumbs on the carpet. "I wouldn't make a very good housewife, would I, Ralph—for God's sake, sit down. You're making me nervous—you know, I never realised until now how much I hate being confined to a small space, being indoors all day."

"You were indoors all day at the shop."

"Ah, but that was different. I was busy. I suppose somebody else is busy there now. Has it been let again?"

"I expect so." Nancy's grey eyes were boring into his face, and Ralph began to feel guilty, as though everything that had happened was his fault. He always got that feeling when Nancy stared at him, or creased her thick, dark brows into a frown. "Let's not talk about all that, Nancy."

"But Ralph, that's why I need you! You're the only person I *can* talk to about it!"

The appeal was impossible to resist. "Well, fire away then, old girl."

"I feel totally lost without the business. I just don't know what to do with myself. And I keep thinking about how well things worked, and how many good ideas we had, and I keep thinking that surely *something* can be salvaged. Do you think I'm being fanciful, Ralph?" She stared at him again.

"Fanciful? I'm not sure I—"

"Never mind. The business. Is it possible?"

"It's always possible to start again, in theory. But you'd have to borrow money, and it would be very difficult if you were on your own. What about Faye? Have you discussed it with her?"

Nancy sighed, and extinguished her cigarette. "That's the problem. Faye says she's not interested. She doesn't want to go through the whole thing again." Once more Nancy's eyes made Ralph feel as though this was all his fault. He remembered Faye's attempt at seduction and shivered involuntarily. "Anyway, Faye's got herself a job. At the Board of Trade of all things. A nice little irony, don't you think?" She started to pick at the crumbs on the carpet. "Also, I'm practically broke, as you well know. I've got to get a job, but I just can't stand the thought of working in an office."

"I could lend you some money."

"Don't be ridiculous, Ralph! I'd rather steal it."

Ralph fidgeted in his seat. The drab atmosphere in the flat, and the tired, stale smell were beginning to affect his mood. "What about your friend Randolph?" he said more sharply than he had intended. "Can't he help you find something?"

"He went back to South Africa months ago. I could write to him, I suppose but . . ." she clapped her hand to her breast with a theatrical gesture. "Pride, you know."

Ralph put his head back and laughed loudly. "That's better. That's more like the old Nancy!" Feeling recklessly encouraged by Randolph de Beer's departure, he said, "I've got to go back to the office now, but why don't we continue this discussion over dinner tonight?"

He had tipped a fragile balance and the warm, open part of Nancy snapped shut.

"No, I can't," she said rudely, picking up the discarded magazine and swinging her naked legs onto the sofa. "I've got something better to do."

Ralph retreated, and spent several days brooding over Nancy's behaviour. She could draw him in like a fish on a line, but when he took any initiative, she pushed him away again and became aloof.

I'm wasting my time, he told himself. No more Nancy Stein. He resolved to having nothing more to do with her. The decision felt a little like turning a knife into his own side, but once he had made it, he felt better.

Then his secretary answered the telephone and announced with unprofessional glee, "A personal call, sir. One of your young ladies."

It was Faye this time.

"Ralph, it's about Nancy. She's driving me mad. Can't you do something with her?"

Ralph went straight to Kensington.

The flat was even untidier. Nancy didn't look any better, but this time she was openly hostile. "What do you want?"

"I came to see if you'd like to go riding. A friend of mine has got some horses in a livery stable near here, and we could take them out into Hyde Park. It's a lovely day . . ."

"Ralph, don't be such a bore. Just go away and leave me alone."

"I thought you hated being cooped up inside."

"For God's sake, Ralph, you're wearing a three-piece suit and a tie. Don't tell me you're just about to leap onto a horse and ride into the sunset dressed like the Young Businessman of the Year!"

"I'll go back to my flat and change first if you'll wait for me."

Ralph hurried off to change, half expecting to find Nancy gone when he returned, but she had dressed reluctantly in an old shirt and a pair of breeches, and allowed herself to be escorted to the stables, though she snapped at Ralph when he made the mistake of offering her a leg-up onto her mount.

But once she was on horseback, Nancy was a different person. She galloped down the well-beaten tracks of the Row, ducking beneath the candles of the horse-chestnut trees, and turning back to laugh at Ralph when he couldn't catch up. The sun made rainbows on her glossy dark hair, and Ralph thought it was the most beautiful sight he had ever seen.

They rode abreast for awhile, then raced to the end of the park and as Ralph's more powerful horse passed Nancy's he abandoned caution for sentimentality and shouted, ''I hope you're not going to play dead this time!''

She looked puzzled for a second, then laughed. As she caught up with him, she smiled her most shameless smile and said, ''Not now I know that it frightens you more than the entire war!''

They rode until their horses were exhausted and sweating. ''Well, that wasn't so bad after all, was it?'' Ralph asked once they were back at the stables. He helped her to lift the saddle from her horse, and this time she did not object.

''It was lovely, Ralph.'' She hesitated and then said almost shyly, ''I think I like you better when we're doing this sort of thing. It's almost as though you're different from the Ralph you usually are.''

''You mean the Ralph who wears a suit?''

''Yes, if you like.''

Ralph returned to work in a tremor of excitement and confusion. He turned Nancy's words over and over in his mind, dissecting them, giving them new meaning. If only he could be that other Ralph all the time! Perhaps he could, if she would only give him the chance. For days he longed for the chance to be on horseback again, but not daring to telephone her in case he broke the spell and turned her into the old unapproachable Nancy again.

Eventually the phone rang and his secretary announced, ''One of the young ladies.''

It was Nancy, asking if they could go riding again.

As the summer wore on, their outings gradually took on the ritual of courtship. At first Nancy only wanted to ride, and Ralph did not dare ask for more, but eventually she began to accept invitations to the theatre, and the cinema and they became, somewhat warily, a couple. It saddened Ralph to reflect that Nancy greeted this development with resignation rather than with excitement, and that she probably only saw him because she had nothing else to do, yet when he was in her presence he was filled by a reckless, optimistic happiness. All I need, he told himself as he looked in the mirror one evening, is a little more self-confidence.

I'm tall, healthy, quite presentable looking, and an average athlete. I'm twenty-six years old, a successful young merchant banker with a high salary. I have everything to offer . . .

He repeated this eulogy to himself all evening as he and Nancy dined together at *Chez Victor*, and as they dawdled over coffee and cognac, he asked her to marry him.

She smiled, but only very slightly. "Yes," she said, and added "Why not?"

Nancy Stanwycke stared out at the Tyrrhenian Sea and wished herself a thousand miles away.

She was on her honeymoon.

She and Ralph were married at the end of August, at the church of the Holy Trinity, Brompton. Nancy wore an elaborate bridal gown of ivory satin, and twisted strings of pearls through her lustrous hair. She was given away by Stephen Willand-Jones amid sighs of rapture from the hundred and fifty guests.

Annabel and George were invited to the wedding but sent a note politely declining owing to the recent birth of Matthew George Patrick Stein. Nancy took one look at her nephew's names and threw the note in the bin with a shudder.

She and Ralph were spending their honeymoon in a rented villa on the island of Capri. It was built on a rocky promontory overlooking the sea, and surrounded by flamboyant bougainvillea and delicate frangipani that gave off a sweet scent at night. Above the villa, the hill was shrouded with the silver haze of olive groves. There was a maid who bought and prepared their food, leaving Ralph and Nancy with very little to do but swim or walk on the beach.

Nancy was happier when she was walking alone, and at these moments she was acutely conscious that she had made a grave mistake in marrying Ralph. She would have been better off on her own, however bleak that option might have seemed to her once. She embroidered her footsteps in the wet sand and crouched down to marvel at sea-shells, knowing that sooner or later she was going to hurt Ralph, and she was afraid, because she would see reflected in his pain her own unhappiness and dissatisfaction.

They had been married for four days, and they had not made love once. She had allowed Ralph to kiss her on several occasions, but he was clumsy and over-eager, and she had enough experience to know that this did not bode well. When they arrived at the villa on her wedding night, she had heaved an inward sigh of relief at the sight of twin beds separated by a reading table with two lamps on it.

Ralph had looked at her longingly, and hovered near her when she went to bed, in a manner that infuriated her. She knew that he did not have the courage for outright seduction, but she also knew she would not be able to avoid the issue for ever.

Ralph had walked down to the village to have a drink at the bar.

Nancy stood on the balcony and watched the moon trembling and glittering on the black surface of the sea. The scent of the frangipani and the whine of the cicadas soothed her. She gazed up at the sky and the stars that seemed so much brighter than they were in England. *Were* they brighter, she wondered, or was she simply more aware of their presence? She wanted to reach up and touch them, to burn her fingers on their brilliance.

"All the stars made gold of all the air,
And the sea moving saw before it move, one moon-flower
making all the foam-flowers fair."

She spoke the lines of the poem out loud, sighed deeply, and then went inside to get ready for bed.

When Ralph returned, she was propped on one elbow, reading. He emerged from the bathroom dressed in his robe and began fussing around the room, picking up her clothes and folding them into a neat pile, treating each article as though he revered it. "Would you like me to get you some water, darling?"

"No, thank you."

He sat down on the edge of the bed, "Is there anything else you want, darling?"

"Honestly, Ralph! You don't have to wait on me hand and foot, just because you're married to me!"

He looked at her, but did not reply. As he stood up she slammed her book shut, switched the light off, and then lay in tense silence on her back listening to Ralph, pacing about in the dark. She felt the mattress quiver as he groped for the edge of her bed and sat down again. "For God's sake, Nancy!" he exploded. "I don't know much about this sort of thing, I admit, but enough to know that this isn't normal!"

" 'Normal'? There's no such thing as 'normal'," said Nancy wearily.

"Nancy, you know what I'm talking about." Ralph leaned closer. "All those jokes about honeymoons . . . we're not properly together until . . . I want you." His mouth searched for her face in the dark and he began kissing her roughly.

Nancy wanted to resist but she knew that it was easier not to, so she submitted to his eager, panting embrace and gritted her teeth against the discomfort she felt as he entered her. How was

Ralph to know that her moans were from exasperation, and not ecstasy? After he had returned to his bed she moved her legs uncomfortably and prayed for the oblivion of sleep.

Ralph's appetite had been sharpened. The next morning as the first sunlight was streaming through the muslin curtains he tip-toed to Nancy's bed and slid under the covers beside her. She was woken by a large, persistent hand clumsily fondling her left breast.

"Ralph, no . . ." she moved her elbow back and pushed him away.

He stroked her back, letting his fingers glide audaciously to her buttocks.

"Ralph—*don't*. I don't want it."

As he disappeared into the bathroom she resolved that in the future she would make sure to pretend she was asleep when he went to bed.

Greville Dysart sat in his office at Cloud Couture, doing his sums.

"Not too good, old man," he muttered to himself. "Not at all good . . ."

The desk was littered with invoices, final demands and wage bills. There was the rent on the shop, the heating and lighting costs, the bill from the shop-fitters . . . once he had paid them all Greville's small inheritance would have dried up.

And there was a fresh problem to face. His customers would expect the low prices and the innovation which was now associated with Cloud Couture. Ruining Nancy Stein could be justified as an act of revenge for Patrick's death, but there was no longer a Stein McConnell to plunder. And besides, stealing designs a second time was too risky. Someone would eventually put two and two together. No, there was no short cut this time. He would have to pay a good designer, or a team of designers . . .

Oh God, he thought, sometimes all I want to do is go back to Heathcote and live there in comfortable squalor, paying the odd visit to the Lamb and Child to listen, and to scheme . . . But that option was no longer open to him. Heathcote was now Kit's, and while he was finishing his education it was being let to tenants. He would just have to press on and find the money somehow. By fair means or foul.

Greville thought about Annabel. After all, he had practically arranged that marriage himself. He ought to profit a little. It wouldn't be easy though. Annabel was naïve, but a loyal wife. She would never part with money without George's knowledge. He considered asking George for a loan, but that would give George a vested interest in how the business was run, which might prove awkward later . . .

But the Stein family have got a ruddy closet full of skeletons, haven't they? Several closets . . .

What was it that he had said to Patrick about waiting for the right opportunity? Poor old Patrick. Greville sighed loudly. His death had certainly been a blow. Now there was no longer a Heathcote to run to. That particular bolt hole was sealed off. Poor misguided Patrick . . .

But in a sense they'd both got it wrong. They'd been barking up the wrong tree. Or rather, the wrong side of the Atlantic . . .

"Of course!" he said out loud, and laughed at his own stupidity. "All the ruddy money's over there!" The Americans had got Graylings, hadn't they? And that matinée idol type, Captain Exley, had turned out to be rather less than perfect. Surely "incest" was as much a dirty word in Long Island, New York as in Nether Aston, Somerset?

After a few phone calls to his contacts in the City, Greville succeeded in linking Guy Exley's name with Exley Marine Inc., Bridgeport, Connecticut. He pushed the bills to one side, picked up his pen and started to write.

Faye watched the seagulls wheel and cry over the mud flats of the Thames.

The air felt muddy too, and the water reflected a muddy November sky. When Nancy and Ralph had got married, Faye had moved back to Stephen Willand-Jones' house in Lindsay Place. She was soothed and comforted by her attic room and its view over the river. It was like coming home again.

She hadn't seen Ralph and Nancy since their wedding day, finding it easier to behave as if they didn't exist. But she knew that she would not be able to avoid them for ever. Only a few weeks ago she had received a smart new address card with raised lettering, proclaiming that Mr and Mrs Ralph Stanwycke had moved to a grand mansion block in Chesterfield Street, behind Shepherd Market.

She brushed her smooth, pale hair vigorously, dressed in her favourite black wool dress, and caught a bus to the Board of Trade headquarters on Millbank. She hung her coat on the back of her office door, put her handbag in her locker and sat down at her desk, just as she did at nine o'clock every morning.

There was a tap at the door and one of the junior girls came in carrying tea, just as *she* did every morning.

"Miss McConnell, there was a telephone call for you. A Mrs Stanwyke. She left this number, and asked you to call this morning."

"Thank you, Moira," Faye stared at the hard, white piece of paper. Then she buried her head in her hands and tried to collect her thoughts. Mrs Stanwycke. What did *Mrs* Stanwycke want? Why couldn't she have said "Nancy"?

She dialled the number, using a pencil so as not to chip her nail polish.

"Faye, I'm so glad you rang! I wondered if you'd like to come round here for tea this afternoon. It's been ages, and I so desperately want to see you."

Faye delivered a cool reprimand—"This isn't Stein McConnell you know. It's a government department. I can't just walk out when I feel like it."

"Couldn't you say you were going to get your hair cut?"

Faye could not help laughing at Nancy's irrepressible resourcefulness. "I could, but it would be a lie. Anyway, they'd notice that it hadn't been cut when I got back."

"I'll cut a bit off it here, if you like." Nancy sounded desperate.

"No, it's all right. I'll come anyway."

The flat in Chesterfield Street was modern, spacious and luxuriously furnished. The Graylings paintings, now complete with proper overhead picture lights, had been hung on white walls, and apart from dramatic touches of lilac and cornflower blue, the furnishings were white too, including—to Faye's amazement—the malabar carpet. It was tidy to the point of sterility.

Faye made the only comment she could think of. "Gosh, Nancy, you must have had fun shopping for all these things."

"Interior decorators," said Nancy drily. "Besides, when did I ever find shopping for things 'fun'? You know me better than that, Faye."

She rang for tea and it was brought on a white tray by a maid in a perfect uniform. Nancy looked perfect too, as though she had been re-designed by the interior decorators. She wore an exquisite dress of lavender silk with a pleated skirt, and spindly high heels. There was a lot of jewelery on her hands and her hair had been arranged by a professional coiffeur.

". . . That's not to say that I haven't been spending money—

as you can see," she waved a jewelled hand over the tea-pot. "There's not much else to do . . . I do envy you, Faye."

"*You* envy *me*?" Nancy seemed quite unaware of this irony, and it occurred to Faye that her own feelings about Ralph had never been investigated. Nancy was always too busy thinking about herself. Was this the moment to reveal all, she wondered? Should she change the emphasis of the interview completely by saying, *"You know, Nancy, I've always been in love with Ralph . . ."*

But Nancy was still talking. ". . . Yes, I really envy you your job. Even working in an office. It's something constructive to do."

"Why don't you get a job yourself?"

"Ralph doesn't want me to. He thinks my job is to be here."

Faye could not prevent an incredulous laugh at this statement. "If you don't mind me saying so, Nancy, that sort of consideration has never stopped you in the past. You usually go out and do just what you want. It's your hallmark."

"There's still the problem of Ralph, though. I feel I have to do *something* to please him."

Faye would have liked more time to think about what this cryptic comment meant, but Nancy was anxious to hear about the comings and goings at Lindsay Place, and they were still talking about old times when there was the sound of a key in the lock.

"That'll be Ralph. He's home early today." She greeted her husband dispassionately.

"Hullo, Faye!" he said rather too heartily. "What a terrific surprise!"

The emotion that gripped Faye when she saw Ralph was not surprise but embarrassment that she should be wearing the same black dress she had worn when she tried to lure him into her bed. He looked thinner now, and sadder.

After he had poured them all a drink he sat down and said to Nancy without looking at her, "We're going to that reception tonight, at the Mexican Embassy. You haven't forgotten, have you?"

"No, I haven't forgotten, dear," Nancy replied smoothly. "But I don't know if I want to go or not."

"I don't think it's too much to ask for my wife to attend an official function with me, do you?"

Faye was startled. She had never known Ralph to be bitter before. As she sat in her room at Lindsay Place that evening, she tried to feel angry with her cousin but she couldn't. She could only feel sorry for her, and slightly protective. At least here, in Lindsay Place, there was some peace. Who is the loser now, she wondered. Me, Ralph—or Nancy?

Guy brought his red sports car to a halt outside the Bridge-hampton Country Club.

He shivered in the autumn wind, despite his thick cashmere overcoat and scarf, and his hand trembled as he locked the door of the car. He was there for a game of racquets with Chuck Jamieson, but he didn't know how he was going to manage to play. Nor did he know how to admit to Chuck that he couldn't.

Chuck was in the locker room. He beamed, showing his big teeth. "Guy, great to see you old-boy!"

Guy mentally notched up a point. But instead of "You look terrific!" Chuck frowned and said, "You're looking thin. Have you lost weight since I last saw you? You need Pamela's cooking to fatten you up a little."

With a supreme effort of will and a cold sweat breaking out all over his body, Guy won the first game. But then he began to lose point after point, so dizzy that he blundered into his part-ner, and dropped his racquet repeatedly. Eventually he collapsed against a wall. Fragments of light spun before his eyes. Some-where—but whether it was near or far, he couldn't tell—he could see Chuck's anxious freckled face.

"Chuck . . . I can't move . . ."

And then Chuck's strong arms were around him, carrying him into the locker room where he was laid on a bench as tenderly as if he was a baby. Guy drank some water and began to feel better.

"What's up, Guy? Are you going to tell your buddy? Is it pressure at work?"

"No, everything at work's fine. Marcia seems to do most of it anyway."

"Is there something wrong at home, then?" Chuck blushed slightly and looked away. "Pamela . . . Pamela told me that Missie's gotten into the habit of going into the city and losing some money at the casino in the Café Carlyle. I wondered whether maybe—"

"I know, and I don't give a shit what she does! My marriage is a fucking waste of time!"

Chuck looked terribly hurt, as though he had been struck. He stared down at his shoes. "I'm sorry. I guess I knew that. I wonder why we feel we have to pretend all the time?"

Guy realised that he was losing points rapidly, in fact he had lost the game. Something unpredictable was happening. He had known Chuck for over twenty years, and this was the first time he had ever heard him question his own behaviour. He squeezed Chuck's arm.

"Chuck, I'm sick. Really sick."

Chuck nodded. "Shit. Have you seen a doctor?"

"Not yet."

"Well, I'm taking you to see one now. Pamela's brother-in-law's a blood specialist at the Bellevue. He's a good guy. You'll like him."

Chuck drove them to the hospital in Guy's car.

Guy was questioned closely. "Any digestive disturbances?"

"I've had bouts of nausea, and diarrhoea."

"And weight loss?"

"Yes."

The doctor shook his head slowly. "I can give you some drugs for now, but you'll have to come back and have a full range of tests. In the meantime, no alcohol."

Chuck was waiting for him outside the doctor's office. Kindly, dependable Chuck.

"Thanks for waiting. You needn't have."

"Hey, what's all this? I'm your best friend, remember?"

Guy smiled.

"Shall I take you straight back to Missie, or would you like to come home to Pamela and me first?"

Guy didn't hesitate. "I'll come with you."

Missie Exley was beginning her morning ritual. She rose from her bed at eleven o'clock, tousled, foul-mouthed and hungover. The first thing she did was to soak for half an hour in a hot bath, massage her body with scented oil and spray herself liberally with perfume. Then, clad only in a silk kimono (she never bothered to dress in the morning—what was the point?) she went downstairs and opened her first bottle of champagne.

The first glass tasted slightly sour, and slightly too cold. The second tasted like nectar and the third was even better. The maids were busy cleaning the house, so she walked out into the garden, ignoring the November frost beneath her bare feet.

She loved the look of her house, like a story-book castle. After the champagne, the virginia creeper on the balcony had a wonderful glow and an almost erotic delicacy. She fingered its auburn leaves, then danced down the driveway. On her right was a single, incongruous palm tree. "You see," she said out loud. "We have palm trees too, even here."

From the end of the driveway she could look out past the stone gateposts and onto the street. Her neighbour, Harold Sweetbaum, was unloading groceries from the back of his station wagon. The Sweetbaums were a very dull couple. They went away on holiday together and they had two perfect children, a boy and a girl. Hadn't she seen the boy around recently? . . . Yes, he was tall and dark and rather cute-looking . . .

She looked at Harold Sweetbaum with renewed interest. "Hullo," she said.

He looked up, startled by her white robe.

"Didn't I see your son the other day? Is he home from college?"

"Ritchie? That's right. Home for Thanksgiving Break."

"I wondered if he might be interested in earning himself a bit of money. The swimming pool's just been emptied, and it needs the leaves cleaned out of it. I'd give him twenty dollars."

"Sure. I'll ask him."

Ritchie Sweetbaum arrived on her doorstep about half an hour later. Missie ran a frankly appraising eye over him. Yes . . . the combination of black hair and blue eyes was delicious. The body was young, but the dark shadow on his jaw made him look older, much much older than his nineteen years. Perfect . . .

She put him to work in the garden and watched him through the window, sipping her second bottle of champagne. It was impossible to take her eyes off him. She didn't even try. She went outside. He laughed with an engaging mixture of embarrassment and youthful contempt when he saw her kimono.

"Mrs Exley, aren't you ever going to get dressed?"

"I thought you might like a drink."

He wiped his forehead with the back of his arm. "Yeah, I'd like some lemonade, something like that."

She led him to the house and poured him a glass of champagne. He accepted it, but sniffed it suspiciously. "This is a rich woman's lemonade."

"Come on, don't tell me they teach you that sort of crap at college?" She sat down next to him, so close that the silk of her kimono brushed against his blue jeans and parted to reveal her thigh. Ritchie blushed and Missie began to ache for him.

"I think I could learn to enjoy rich women's lemonade."

"I'd like to teach you." Missie's hand stole up and found its way inside his shirt to his smooth chest.

"What else do you think you might teach me?"

Missie wanted him so badly that she thought she would explode. She pushed him onto his back on the carpet and straddled his body with her legs, rubbing herself up and down him and enjoying the effect she was having on him. She hadn't felt so good in years.

"God, it's going to be good," she moaned. *"This is going to be so good . . ."*

They lay on the carpet and drank the third bottle of champagne.

"I could come back again tomorrow afternoon, if you like."

"We'll see. Sometimes my husband comes back in the afternoons. I'll call you or something."

"Mom says you drink so much because your husband's always away on business trips."

"Uh huh." Missie drained her glass.

"Maybe you should persuade him to take another trip."

"Maybe. And then perhaps you could stay over the night."

Ritchie was pulling his jeans on. He stood waiting in the doorway.

"My money. For the pool."

"Oh yes . . . how much did we say?"

"Twenty dollars."

"My purse is over there. Take fifty."

After he had visited the hospital for his tests, Guy came home to find Missie drunk. She was lying on the sofa in a pink satin negligé with her lovely dark hair sparkling round her shoulders.

"You might have got dressed."

"Have a glass of champagne."

Guy hesitated. The doctor had said no alcohol, but Christ he needed it, to cope with Missie. He accepted a glass.

The next thing he remembered was lying on his back on the sitting room carpet with Missie's face very close to his and her hot arms around his neck. Missie's voice was saying, "Guy honey, you're drunk!" in a tone of delight. Her breath stank of drink.

He struggled to his feet, rubbing his aching forehead with his fists. "I'm just tired. I'd better go to bed . . . oh and Missie, I have to go to England on business. It may be for several months."

Missie let fly the conventional tirade of shrewish objections, but Guy sensed that she was relieved, glad even. They didn't bother to pretend with one another any more. But the next morning Felicity Exley confirmed that she, at least, still believed in pretence. She telephoned Guy at his office. "Missie says you're going to England, and you'll be away for Christmas." She sounded hurt.

"Yes, it's inconvenient, but the visit's long overdue. But I hope you'll come out to the airport and say goodbye."

"No, I don't think so dear. That's Missie's privilege. The last person you see should be your wife."

But the last person Guy saw before he flew to England was his doctor.

He came out of the clinic and sat in the parking lot for a few minutes before driving to the airport. On the dashboard of his red T-bird there was a letter. It had already been opened. No sender's address, just a London postmark. Guy took it out and re-read it.

Dear Captain Exley,

It occurs to me that your family would be caused some considerable distress if they were to hear of your incestuous relationship with your half-sister, Nancy Stein. I would be glad to help you avoid this distress. If you telephone the following number immediately I'm sure we can come up with some satisfactory financial arrangement . . .

The letter was unsigned. That was to be expected. No doubt the anonymous voice on the other end of the phone would want a sum paid into some numbered account in Zurich. Only he wasn't going to call the number. If what the doctor had just said was true, it was too late to be worrying about things like blackmail demands.

He screwed up the letter and tossed it out of the open window and into the nearest garbage can.

Thirteen
December 1951

"NANCY, ARE YOU there?"

Ralph Stanwycke no longer allowed himself to assume that his wife would be waiting to greet him when he returned from the bank. Lately her restlessness had grown even more acute, and she had taken to going out for walks in the afternoon, returning long after dark. These walks rarely seemed to have a specific aim or destination. She just went out of the flat and walked, as if she were trying to get away.

He found Nancy in the bath-tub, wallowing in bubble bath and a cloud of steam so thick that her features were barely discernible.

"Oh good, you're getting ready," he said to the steam. "Have you decided what you're going to wear?"

"What for?" Nancy's voice was muffled as she sank her chin into the water.

"Nancy!" Ralph flung the evening paper onto the bathroom floor where it lay in a puddle of bath water. "Don't tell me you've forgotten. We're going to the Mackenzies' cocktail party. It starts at seven thirty."

"If you must know, yes, I had forgotten."

"I *told* you about it yesterday. I don't see what more I can do, short of getting my secretary to type up a list of 'This Week's Engagements.' Shall I run through them now for you? Monday: cocktails at the Mackenzies, Tuesday: theatre with Paul and Helen, Wednesday: office Christmas dinner at the Athenaeum—"

"I'm not going anyway. Tonight."

"Why not?"

"Because I just don't want to, that's all. I'm tired of playing Young Married Happy Families. And they're all boring anyway. All they ever talk about is their nice houses and their wonderful children and their fascinating holidays. They're boring."

"I see. And what sort of people would you like to meet? Or aren't there any good enough?"

"I don't know. *Real* people."

Ralph looked at her in disgust.

She avoided his eye. "Pass me a towel, please."

As he handed over the towel, Ralph put his hand on her shoulder. "Nancy, *please*, I hate it so much when we quarrel like this—"

"Ralph! I want to get dry!"

"Nancy . . ." He embraced her clumsily, covering her face and hair with kisses and pulling the damp towel away so that she was naked. She tried to free herself but the bathroom was so small and it was easy for Ralph to use his weight to pin her against the wall and prevent her from getting past him. The tiles were cold against her skin, and wet with condensed steam.

"Nancy, it's been an awfully long time since we made love. Come on, please darling . . ."

He was unbuckling his trousers with one hand and supporting his weight with the other as he tried to enter her.

"Ralph, for God's sake, what about my diaphragm? We can't—"

Ralph wasn't listening. He had finally managed to push his way into her and before Nancy could move he had collapsed against her, groaning.

She looked down at him with distaste. "Ralph, if you're finished, I'd like to have the bathroom to myself."

She locked the door after him.

"I suppose you haven't changed your mind about coming to the party?"

Nancy didn't even bother to answer. She climbed back into the cold bathwater and washed herself again, waiting until she heard Ralph going out of the flat. Then she hauled herself out and into a voluminous towelling robe. The flat had a delicious silence; not the gnawing, dispirited silence of the daytime but the silence of surrender. Ralph had got what he wanted and she had been given the place to herself for the evening. It had been worth suffering his seduction for a few hours of peace.

Nancy sat on a white sofa and smoked her way through half a packet of cigarettes, lighting a fresh one as soon as the old one was extinguished. For a while, her mind floated in a state of euphoric blankness. She switched on the television, but the prim voice of the BBC announcer irritated her and she switched it off again. Looking around for a diversion, she found a magazine that she hadn't read. A cigarette advertisement caught her eye.

". . . *Mellow Virginia tobacco . . . for that taste of happiness.*"

What the hell did they mean by that? How could tobacco make you happy? Irritated, she extinguished her cigarette and threw the magazine to the floor. Abstract thoughts about happiness crowded into her mind and she could not close them out; they swarmed around her consciousness like rapacious harpies. This was something that happened to her often now. Her mind was uncontrollable, and she couldn't stop it thinking. Sometimes she would speak out loud to try and silence the thoughts.

"It's because my energy isn't being used up," she said out loud. "If I were working—real, physical work—I'd be too tired to think."

Perhaps that was what happiness was, being too tired to think? Nancy closed her eyes and felt an overwhelming nostalgic yearning for the days when she walked the frozen furrows of the Home Farm clad in an army greatcoat, kicking the parsnips out of the ground.

"That was when I was happiest," she told the sterile white walls of the flat. Thinking became a pleasurable occupation now, as she remembered Greta and Maureen and their rebellious humour. The direction of her thoughts clarified. She wanted to see them again. Why *shouldn't* she see them again?

Excited by the boldness of the decision, she picked up the telephone directory and began to flick through the pages until she came to "W." *"Women's Land Army."* The organization still existed to stage reunions and put women in touch with the landgirls they had worked with. She telephoned the London headquarters, and a very dignified elderly lady told her that Maureen Studd was unlisted, but that there was a telephone number for Miss Greta Fryer, and an address in London E5.

Nancy's fingers trembled slightly as she dialled the number and asked to speak to Greta. The voice on the other end of the telephone sounded strange.

"Greta, it's Nancy. Nancy Stein. From Somerset. Do you remember?"

The strange voice assured her that she did.

"I wondered if you'd like to come over for tea tomorrow? Or does that interfere with your work?"

The strange voice said that tea would be very convenient since she was working in the evenings, and asked for the address. Nancy put the phone down and pondered over the un-Greta-like words. *"Tea would be very convenient."*

The next afternoon she was as nervous as if she were meeting a lover. What should she wear? It had better be casual, so as not to intimidate her guest. She chose a pair of ski-pants and a large patterned sweater. And no make-up. Greta would not expect her to wear make-up.

The rush of disappointment she felt when she opened the front door made her feel so ashamed that she tried to dismiss it as initial nerves. Greta looked so *small*, and so brittle. Her blonde hair was harsh and yellow under the sophisticated, modern lighting system that Ralph had installed, and waxy with hairspray.

But it's not her fault that the light was different in Somerset . . .

Next to Nancy she couldn't help but look overdressed in her cheap black suit *(a Cloud Couture original, or was she imagining things? . . .)* and seamed stockings.

They dispensed with the opening questions hurriedly. Greta had not married and was now living with her ageing mother and working in a pub. This drab fate made Nancy even more uncomfortable, and she felt obliged to place great stress on losing her inheritance in a failed business venture. Perhaps Greta would be comforted to know that her marriage was a failure, too?

". . . You've got this place set up nice, Nance. Quite the little housewife, aren't you?"

"Oh no, it's not quite like that," replied Nancy hurriedly. "There's a maid who does the housework. She's the one who ought to be proud really. I just make a mess."

"Gone back to being waited on by servants then. I suppose that's what your family was used to though, wasn't it?"

Nancy made a desperate bid to stem the tide of class differences that threatened to engulf the conversation.

"How's Maureen? Do you hear from her?"

Greta graciously accepted one of Nancy's American cigarettes in preference to her Woodbines. "Yes, we've kept in touch. We correspond pretty regularly really . . ."

Nancy quelled an unreasonable pang of jealousy.

". . . She went back to her old man at the end of the war, of course. You didn't know that? Well, more a case of him coming back to her. She's got three kids now, and another one on the way. All girls, so far."

"Still, not bad, is it? Four children in seven years. Her husband must have learnt a thing or two from old Waite."

To her relief, Greta laughed. "Or maybe she learned something from Mrs Waite. What a tub of lard that woman was! Did you ever go back there on a Saturday night?"

Nancy remembered laughing with Guy about the Waites and singing *"I've got you under my skin."* "Yes. Once. Would you like to see the rest of the flat?"

She showed Greta the dining room and the fitted kitchen, the *en suite* bathroom and the empty spare bedroom.

"Well, you've got room for a kiddie in here, haven't you?" asked Greta brightly. "I expect you'll be starting a family soon."

"I don't think so." Nancy longed for the old Greta, the one in whom she could confide. "Ralph and I don't . . . don't share the same bed."

She had expected some smart remark like, "Well, that won't get you a baby, will it?" but Greta merely looked embarrassed by this revelation, and said it was time for her to be "getting along."

At the front door she kissed Nancy on the cheek and squeezed her hand briefly. "It's been fun, hasn't it? We must do it again sometime."

Nancy closed the door sadly, knowing that they wouldn't. She sat down in the sitting room and stared at the tea-tray. What time was it? . . . Only half past four. She began to wish she had never asked Greta to come, as now it seemed even more intolerable for her to be in this flat on her own. Greta had been right to sneer at it. It was a vulgar, horrible showpiece. She hated it.

The white telephone stared at her. She rang Faye. "Faye, I feel like going out. Can you meet me somewhere, for tea, or for a drink?"

"Nancy, I'd like to, honestly, but I can't. I'm tied up with a meeting."

"How about this evening then? After the meeting."

"I'm afraid I'm going out."

Nancy panicked, "Why, where are you going?"

"Nowhere special, I'm just meeting someone." Even Faye was being evasive now. But that needn't stop her going out. She went into her bedroom and exchanged her sweater and ski-pants for a red dress and the fur coat that Randolph had bought in Paris.

Once she was on the street, a poster on the side of a bus caught her attention. Christmas shopping. Of course, it was the obvious answer. As she began to walk towards Hyde Park Corner she realised that she had come out with hardly any money in her handbag. But she kept walking. The glittering Knightsbridge stores beckoned to her.

It was only one week before Christmas and the streets were

crowded with shoppers, thronging against the coy seasonal backdrop of Christmas trees and window displays, and coloured
lights. Nancy studied the expression on their faces. Some were
excited, some just plain weary, but all of them looked different
from expressions worn for the rest of the year. It wasn't difficult
to imagine a crisp snow underfoot and snowflakes falling, in
place of this drab, damp December weather.

Nancy went limp, allowing herself to be buffeted and jostled
by the crowd. She found herself in the toy department at Harrods. The teddy bears and dolls stared out beseechingly from
the shelves, their inanimate arms outstretched. Nancy watched
parents buying them, and felt crushingly empty. She tried to
think of a present she might buy, but could only remember that
she had run out of a particular brand of face-cream. The perfum-
ery department was horribly crowded. Nancy found the cream,
but the queue for the cash till stretched for yards. I can't be
bothered to wait, she thought, but as she moved to put the jar
of cream back on the counter, she faltered and slipped it into
her pocket instead.

Horrified by what she had done she began to move quickly,
pushing people out of her way, trying to get as far away as
possible, where no one could see her. She got as far as the Food
Halls and leaned against a wall, trembling with relief.

No one had followed her! Instead of guilt and shame, she
experienced a rush of excitement that left her quite dizzy. She
had taken it without paying and no one had noticed! She wandered off into the crowd again, still dazed, pushed in one direction and then another as people bumped her with their parcels.

The jewellery department. A thousand dancing shards of light
sparkling on a thousand glittering trinkets. Nancy moved like a
sleepwalker. There was a pair of small, gold earrings on the
counter. Did she like them? She couldn't quite decide. She picked
them up, and with the blood pounding in her ears, pressed them
into the palm of her hand. The sensation of fear and excitement
was so intense that it was like being drunk, or drugged. The
sharp stems of the earrings were digging into her flesh, hurting
her, but she did not dare loosen her hold.

As she backed away from the counter, she felt very, very
frightened. Reaching the street door of the store without being
noticed she felt clever, exultant.

A hand came down firmly on her shoulder.

"Would you come back into the store please, madam? I'd like
to ask you some questions."

Nancy was looking into the eyes of a pretty woman with curly hair. Her mouth opened, but she could not speak. She clutched the earrings.

The woman held up an identity card. "I work for Harrods as a store detective. I believe you have some goods that you haven't paid for. I have to ask you to come upstairs to the office for a moment." The voice was gentle, the pressure on her arm insistent.

"That won't be necessary."

Another voice, this time with an American accent. Nancy turned round.

At first she simply thought she was hallucinating.

Guy Exley was standing behind her.

"My wife just wanted to see what the earrings would look like in daylight before she made her decision."

The woman looked sceptical. "All the same, sir, I'm afraid I have to—"

"I'm afraid I happen to be one of this store's major shareholders, and a director of the board. So if you value your job, I suggest you take these earrings back yourself and tell the assistant they weren't what she wanted after all. Good day to you."

The store detective melted away into the crowd.

"Guy . . . my God, I can't believe it's you!"

Nancy felt faint from the double shock and she could barely raise her voice above a whisper. She stood staring at him with the bright lights blinding her and the babble of voices ringing in her ears.

He stared back at her.

Then she remembered the store detective and burst into tears. "What a bloody stupid thing to do!" she sobbed. "I'm so ashamed . . . it's just, I don't know, at least it made me feel as though I was *alive*!"

Guy hugged her and kissed the top of her head. "I understand. I did it myself once."

Nancy turned her tear-stained face upwards. "*You* did?"

"In Bloomingdales. When I was about seventeen. I stole a necktie, just for the kick it gave me. Never told anyone about it."

"How on earth did you know about the earrings?"

"I spotted you in the toy department, staring at a blue teddy bear as though you wanted to murder it. Then I followed you."

"Guy, do you realise what we're doing? We haven't set eyes

on one another for six years and we're standing here talking as though we met last week."

"That's how it feels though, isn't it? We can't talk here. Let's get away some place." He led her round the corner and down a quiet side street, holding tightly onto her hand.

"Guy, are you really a shareholder of Harrods?"

"No. That was a lie." His dark, gypsy eyes looked back at her, quite unrepentant. "They were all lies. You're not my wife, for example."

Nancy held up her left hand ruefully and showed the rings. Guy preferred his own gold wedding ring. They both laughed.

"Marriage . . . what a bunch of shit it is. Who are you married to?"

"Ralph Stanwycke. How about you?"

"A girl called Missie."

"What a ghastly name! Do you love her?"

"No. I married her because I thought she looked like you. When I first met her she was wearing a red dress, just like you are now . . ." He wrapped his arms round her waist and buried his face in her neck. "Oh, Nancy, Nancy . . ."

She returned his embrace with such fervour that she thought she would break his ribs. Could he be so fragile? "You're much thinner than you used to be Guy, and not so sun-tanned."

"Old age and responsibilities! To hell with them! I'm staying at the Dorchester. And you're going to come back there with me now . . ."

The first time they made love they were desperate, tearing off their clothes, clawing at each other, trying to bleed out their passion by inflicting pain. The second time they were tender, careful, and infinitely slow. Nancy drifted to sleep in Guy's arms, and on waking to find him there behind her, she felt as though she were lying in her mother's bed at Graylings, beneath the polonaise.

But this time something was different. When she woke, she sat up in bed and waited for the cold sweat, the anxiety, the old terrors . . . but they did not come. As she looked at Guy, she realised that the difference came from him. He was calmer. He no longer emitted the electric tension that had frightened her.

She left the Dorchester at ten o'clock, applying powder to her flushed face in the back of the taxi as she tried to decide what she would tell Ralph.

Guy was also in the back of a taxi, on the way to St George's Hospital for the latest in a long series of injections.

* * *

They had three months together in the spring of 1952. Three months during which they did very little apart from eating, walking and making love, devoting themselves to the absorbing task of being happy. Nothing had changed in Nancy's feeling for Guy, yet she found him different. He was quieter, more thoughtful. When she asked him to explain why he had chosen this moment to return, he gave vague answers about wanting to check up on the work that was in progress to salvage Graylings, but he made no attempt to leave and go to Somerset. Sometimes he talked of divorcing Missie, sometimes talk of the future seemed to distress him. Nancy did not pry. She knew better, now, than to question happiness.

From the very beginning she made no attempt to deceive Ralph. Deception would have been impossible anyway. His wife was a different woman; transformed, radiant, sparkling with energy. The sulky, spoilt child had disappeared.

Besides, Nancy could lie and cheat about small matters, but never about her emotions. With stark simplicity she told Ralph that Guy had come back into her life, and that she intended to spend as much time as possible with him.

Ralph accepted her infidelity with a resignation and dignity that unnerved her. But he was very concerned for her welfare.

"Nancy, how can you do this?"

"I just can, that's all. Whoever Guy may be, I love him. That's how I can." She misinterpreted his frown. "Nobody else need know about it. I'm not going to cause a scandal, so you needn't worry."

"But Nancy darling, I *am* worried. I worry about you." Ralph clenched his hands tightly as he tried to control his distress. "What future can it possibly have? Society won't accept you, you can't possibly marry—"

"*No!*" Nancy had closed her eyes and covered her ears. "No, Ralph! No! No! No! I don't want to hear. I'm happy. That's all."

Then things began to change. Guy became increasingly evasive, going out without telling her where. He spent longer and longer periods asleep. Nancy buried her fears and clung on blindly. And she fell prey to the most superstitious fear of them all; that if she said out loud *"What's wrong?"* she would make all those other fears a reality.

"I'm a coward," she said to Guy when she was visiting him at the Dorchester one morning in April.

"Why's that, honey? You been avoiding the dentist again?"

She shook her head. "Do you remember when we went to the Lamb and Child, and we went and looked at the stars and talked about air-raids? Do you remember that night?"

"Yeah, Ella Marion Rowcroft. How could I forget her—she's been with me ever since."

"I wasn't thinking of her actually, I was thinking about my wanting to be in an air-raid, to see if I really was brave. Well, I'm not."

Guy poured himself a cup of black coffee and leaned back against the bed's sumptuous satin bolster. "You're the bravest lady *I* know, that much is for sure. Even if you do have a thing about your dentist."

Nancy laughed and smoothed the full skirts of her Horrocks' floral print dress. "Oh Guy, I'm not talking about not being scared of spiders or driving fast!" Her smile disappeared. "I'm talking about being afraid to face up to things that are happening."

She looked straight at him, but the expression in his eyes was so ghastly; so grief-stricken, so defeated, that she turned away.

"Nancy honey, I've got to be honest with you. I'm pretty sick."

"I know." She didn't turn round.

"In fact, I'm feeling pretty crummy right now. Perhaps I ought to sleep a little." Guy's voice was weak.

"As a matter of fact I'm not feeling too well myself," said Nancy. "I think it's something I've eaten." She wiped her tears away hastily before she turned round. "Why don't I go home and let you rest for a while, and then come back later?"

"OK. Sounds great!" Guy smiled cheerfully as she donned her straw hat and white gloves, but as she reached the door the smile faded. He waited until her hand was on the door knob.

"You're no coward, Nancy."

Nancy asked the doorman to hail a taxi, then wished she'd walked. The cab driver took the corners so sharply that the movement of sliding form one corner of the seat to another made her feel queasy. When she reached Chesterfield Street she let herself into the flat, went straight into the bathroom and was violently sick. She sat on the edge of the bath and waited, but the nausea persisted, together with fatigue and dizziness.

"This is no good," she muttered to herself, stumbling to the telephone and dialling the number of her GP ". . . no good to Guy if I'm ill too . . . have to get something for it."

The doctor seemed to think that a house call was appropriate, so she lay on the bed in her crumpled print frock and waited for him to arrive.

"I think I must have picked up something, Doctor . . ." She struggled to sit up as his cool fingers felt her pulse.

"When was your last period?"

"*What?*" she asked weakly.

"I think I'd better examine you, Mrs Stanwycke . . ."

Afterwards, the doctor gave her a broad smile. "You're pregnant. We'll need a test as confirmation, but I don't think I'm risking my professional reputation with the diagnosis. I'd say that you and Mr Stanwycke could expect the proverbial patter of tiny feet in five months from now."

"*I must tell Guy!*" was Nancy's first, irrational thought. As soon as the doctor had gone, she dialled the number of the Dorchester Hotel and asked to be connected to Guy's suite. The phone rang endlessly. Nancy slammed the white receiver in a panic. Then she dialled the Dorchester again.

"Hello, I'm trying to reach Guy Exley, but I don't seem to be able to get an answer."

"One moment please, madam . . ."

Nancy imagined the hand closed discreetly over the receiver, the hushed conversation in the background.

". . . I'm very sorry, madam, but apparently Mr Exley has had to go to St George's Hospital. Earlier today, I believe. Is there a message?"

Nancy didn't even wait for the lift to arrive.

She ran down the stairs of the apartment block three at a time and out into the street, where a taxi was forced to stop to avoid killing her.

St George's loomed, elegant and uncaring, above the lush spring foliage of Hyde Park. The sun blazed against its windows. Nancy ran up and down its corridors like a distracted animal, not knowing which department she was looking for, until a nurse took pity on her and found the bow-tie clad Dr Kinraid, who was looking after Guy. He stared into a folder of notes. "Are you a relative?"

Don't ask that now . . .

"My name's Nancy Stanwycke—dear God, does it matter who I am? *Please*, just tell me how he is, and what's the matter—"

Dr Kinraid looked up from his notes. "He's very sick indeed, Mrs Stanwycke. Cancer of the liver spreads very rapidly once it has taken hold." He lowered his voice to a tone of professional condolence. "I'm afraid we don't expect him to last very long."

"Long?" Nancy stared at him, wild-eyed. "What's long? Weeks, Months?"

"I'm afraid it may not even be that long."

Nancy went white.

"You did know that he was dying?"

She stood there staring at nothing, her eyes focused on some distant glimmer from the fluorescent lights at the end of the corridor.

"Yes, I knew."

Faye McConnell walked briskly along Lindsay Place, hugging a brown paper bag of groceries.

It was a fine, sunny autumn afternoon, and she felt light-hearted. She was not, and never had been, the sort of person who felt tempted to leap into piles of leaves, or kick them into the air as she trudged through them, but she smiled to herself; a sleepy, secretive smile.

She met Stephen Willand-Jones as she was coming through the front door of the house. Her truancy from the Board of Trade on two afternoons a week was a familiar ritual, and he did not ask her why she was home from work early, but merely removed his pipe from his mouth to say, "You're expecting a visitor, I see." Faye nodded, and hurried upstairs to prepare her room.

The attic floor of the house was now her private territory. She paid a higher rent for the use of a small kitchen and bathroom which, together with the bedroom overlooking the Thames, were like a small flat of her own.

Faye set about her task with a combination of haste and confidence that could only be described as "bustling". She worked methodically, but with such eagerness for the appointed meeting that she tried to do two things at once; putting the bag of groceries on the kitchen table as she pulled her arms free of her coat sleeves, filling the kettle as she brushed her hair. She decided to concentrate on the room first, and then on her own appearance.

The bed was tidied and covered with a patchwork quilt and brightly coloured cushions. A lace cloth was thrown over a low table near to the gas fire, and a tea-tray laid on it next to a plate of cream cakes. Faye arranged the latest books and magazines in a tempting pile near the hearth and filled two Chinese vases with damp crysanthemums the colour of dried blood. Her sober Whitehall blouse was exchanged for a coral-coloured mohair sweater. Make-up was applied sparingly-not as much as she would wear to go out, but enough to give her some colour. Then she sat on the battered old sofa in front of the fire and flicked through a magazine, forcing herself to look at the pictures skimming beneath her fingers in an attempt to slow the pounding of her heart. Even now, after all these months, she felt unbearably excited at the prospect of his arrival.

There was a cautious knock on the door.

She smiled as she opened it. "Come in Ralph . . ."

Their affair had been the inevitable outcome of Ralph's unhappiness. Ever since her first visit to the Stanwyckes's marital home, when she had witnessed Ralph's bitterness and pain, she had dwelt at the back of his mind as a sympathetic presence. He telephoned her the next day to apologize for his behaviour (and, in a veiled manner, for his wife's) and had given way to an uncharacteristic weakening of the stiff upper lip. When he began to cry on the other end of the line, Faye quickly suggested that he might like to talk in private, at Lindsay Place. That first meeting had been no more than a bitter indictment of Nancy's inability to love, but Faye knew that she would only have to wait.

Ralph came back. He came back time and time again, begging mutely to be taken into her confidence and, finally, her bed. He had submitted to this last development graciously, willingly, with relief, and they had been lovers since before Guy Exley's return.

Ralph sat in front of the fire while Faye waited on him. First she removed his tie and unbuttoned his collar, a ritual which confirmed that he was at home, for a few hours at least. Then she made the tea and poured a cup for him, handing it silently to him with one of his favourite cakes.

Like a geisha girl, thought Ralph approvingly . . . or a wife.

After they had eaten and drunk, Faye cleared the tea things away and returned to demand an embrace, and a first kiss. They sat with their arms around one another for a few minutes, then broke apart slightly and held hands. They always talked first, before going to bed. Ralph reached in his pocket and drew out an envelope, which he handed to Faye.

"I thought you might be interested in these. They're like gold-dust . . ."

Faye gasped with delight. Inside were two tickets for Maria Callas' debut in *Norma* at Covent Gardens. She loved opera, but far more importantly, she and Ralph were rarely able to go out together in the evening.

"Will you be able to come?" Ralph was grinning broadly, infected by her pleasure, and her appreciation.

"November the eighth . . . I should think so. How about you? What will you tell Nancy?"

"I don't know. I'll think of something though, don't worry."

Faye leaned back on the sofa, but without releasing Ralph's hand. "How is she managing with the baby?"

"Not too well. I'm rather worried about it, actually. She just doesn't seem to be interested in the baby at all. And when I try and talk to her about it, all she says is that she doesn't want to keep the baby. That she wants to leave it with me and go."

"Have you spoken to her about us?"

"No, not yet. The doctor said we should avoid putting any more strain on her at the moment. Guy's death must have been a hell of a shock . . ." Ralph sighed and moved closer to Faye. "I feel as though the whole of the last year has been a shock. I sometimes wonder what on earth you can find in me to love. I feel so bruised . . . Like an old piece of fruit."

Faye laughed and drew him into her arms like a baby. "Come on you old fruit, you . . ." She rocked him. "My little boy . . . I'm not ever going to hurt you . . ."

In the hospital room the curtains are drawn, and everything looks grey. The breeze stirs them a little and allows patches of hard yellow light to settle on a slanting axis across the room. He is talking to her, speaking softly, but with the same intonation, the same rhythms that she has always known.

". . . So maybe your mother was right to give me a verbal sock in the jaw and make sure we went our separate ways . . . it could never have worked in the way we would have wanted it to work . . . but she wasn't right to say that we shouldn't ever have let it happen . . . We showed 'em Nancy. We showed them that it was worth the pain . . ."

She sits still, not daring, not trusting herself to speak.

"I'm glad we're alone here . . . open the goddam curtains will you? I want to see your hair."

She draws back the curtains and spring light floods into the room and onto her hair. She can feel its warmth through the glass windowpanes.

"Remember old Ella Marion Rowcroft?"

She nods.

"What was it that she had written above her bed? Remind me?"

She quotes the lines for him. "Angels are watching overhead. Sleep sweetly then. Good night."

"Yes. I like that."

He closed his eyes. She looks at his fine, gypsy features and his fine, nut-brown hair, and remembers in an abstracted way how they looked when she first saw him, standing under the domed skylight at Graylings. He sighs heavily, and then lies still.

Her tears drop onto his dead face and into his hair.

"Open the goddam curtains, will you? I want to see your hair . . ."

Nancy opened her eyes. She could replay that scene at will, as though she were touching a button on a movie camera in her hand. She set aside some time to do it each day, and to think about Guy. Then she would pull herself together again and carry on with the drab, practical tasks of the day. It was a ritual for mourning, the only equivalent she had of visiting a grave and laying flowers.

Guy's family had arranged for his body to be flown back to America and buried on Long Island. Nancy didn't go to the funeral. She couldn't bear the thought of strange people staring, of some woman with hair like hers, his widow, taking *her* place behind the coffin.

She sent a simple wreath of white roses, and a card bearing the inscription. *"Angels are watching overhead. Sleep sweetly then. Good-night."*

Of course she had known that something was wrong as soon as she saw Guy in the entrance of Harrods, in the midst of those displays of material greed and ephemeral gratification, where hot air from the store blew out and cold street air blew in, and their two worlds met at last. She had known, but at first she had been too cowardly to admit it, even to herself. And she sensed that Guy wanted a peace that she could only give to him by pretending. They could not talk of marriage or of a future together, but they could enjoy the present and reminisce about the past.

And then it had simply been too late. Two days after he was admitted to the hospital, he had died.

After the initial weeks of blinding misery, when Faye and Ralph hovered ineffectually in the background and even Randolph's offer of companionship was rejected, Nancy had felt betrayed and angry. She had lived without Guy once before, but she did not feel that she had the strength to do it again. She did not want to be alone.

Nancy closed her eyes and saw the hospital room again, but this time she could only see the plastic bag suspended over the bed, dripping its contents slowly and meticulously into his veins.

Oh God, oh God . . . Guy . . .

Nancy ran through the silent flat to the little spare bedroom that had become a nursery at last. She wondered what Greta would say if she could see this perfect little palace, this haven of muslin and lace and pink satin ribbon. Surely it would live up to her expectations as the fitting backdrop for Mrs Nancy Stanwycke's foray into motherhood? Nancy leaned over the side of the crib and stared at her daughter. Lucienne.

She picked up the child and held her close. Guy's child. Guy's daughter . . .

She cradled the baby to her breast.

Then she dropped Lucienne back into her cot, ignoring her indignant screams. Of course she wasn't Guy's baby! How could she be? Guy's treatment had made him sterile. It was just a useless fantasy that she indulged in, tormented herself with. She was Ralph's daughter, and Nancy didn't want her.

She turned away from the cot and looked out of the window. It was a crisp and inviting autumn afternoon, with leaves fluttering along the pavement and a hint of frost in the air.

A beautiful day, and suddenly all Nancy wanted to do was to get out of the flat, away from the screaming child, and go and kick recklessly at those leaves. To shout out loud to the world that she didn't love her own child. Couldn't love her. She had to tell *someone* that, or she would fall apart.

Faye. She would go and see Faye and talk to her about it. Faye would understand. The nurse was here to mind Lucie. She would go over to Lindsay Place and surprise her when she got home from work. Not only would she go out, but she would get dressed properly as well. Since Lucie's birth she had been slouching around in shapeless maternity dresses. Feeling truly inspired, Nancy informed the nurse of her decision and hurried into her room to change. She wanted to look nice for Faye. She chose a mauve suit and a little musquash cape, and a pair of spindly heels that were quite unsuitable for kicking leaves.

The front door of the house in Lindsay Place was unlocked, as it always used to be, but there was no one about. Not even Stephen. But Faye would be back from work within half an hour, so she could go up to the attic and wait. She could put the kettle on, and surprise Faye by having a pot of tea ready for her when she got back. There was a kettle in the tiny attic kitchen, but no cups. They would be in Faye's bedroom . . .

As she opened the door she was aware of a movement, out of sight, between the hearth and the sofa. She only had to move one step closer and then she could see. Ralph's naked body.

And one small foot thrown over his back, with perfectly polished nails glinting.

Fourteen
March 1953

Darling Randolph,

I hardly know where to begin! There is so much to tell you since I last wrote, and also I have a specific request.

The first piece of news is that the divorce has come through. I can hardly claim to mind about it, as I told you in my last letter, but the way I found out about Faye and Ralph's affair was a bit of a shock; walking in on them like that. Chiefly it made me feel very stupid. But of course they weren't intending to deceive, simply to protect me from yet another piece of unpleasantness when I was going through such a ghastly time. I can only feel grateful to them for that. I think they will marry eventually, though understandably Ralph isn't in any hurry to put his head in the marital noose again.

I want them to be happy. Only now do I realise what Faye has been through, and when I think of how patient she has been, I feel quite ashamed. Patience is a quality that she possesses in large quantities, and I have very little of at all. However, I like to think that I am less selfish now, and more aware of the feelings of others. Faye, for example. How could I have been so blind to her feelings for Ralph, for all that time? (Mind you, she never spoke about it. The one quality we have in common is pride.)

I have decided that I don't want to stay in London. I feel I'm in a mess here. Somerset is the obvious answer, not only for myself, but perhaps for Lucie, too.

I shall be taking Lucie with me. I tried to persuade Faye and Ralph to apply for custody, but they insist that I keep her, and that once I'm out of London everything will be all right. I can't love her, Randolph. She has the wrong father. I've stopped fantasizing about her being Guy's now, but instead I just feel nothing. When I got to Somerset I'll be without any domestic help to begin with, so God knows how I'll manage.

This brings me onto my problem and my request. Do you

remember saying once that you would always be my friend? Well, I need you to be Randolph the Friend, now. Guy left Graylings to me (the estate as well) and I do so long to go back there and make it come alive again. Guy arranged for work to be started but the process has been in suspension since before his death and the house is still uninhabitable. My problem, of course, is money. Ralph was generous over the divorce settlement, but he is only a salaried employee and I have nowhere near enough to contemplate renovating a house of that size. (In fact I don't want to take Ralph's money at all, if I can help it. I got him into the mess in the first place, and I think he and Faye ought to have every penny for their own children, if they have them). Can you help, Randolph, if only through some sort of loan?

Yes, I'm being very wicked and asking for money (the sort of thing they taught you never to do at St Clare's) but I know that you are not, in the colloquial phrase, "short of a bob or two". I've seen your throw it around on enough occasions after all.

Do give it some thought, and reply as soon as possible, Randolph. I know that whatever your answer, your advice will be cynical, irreverent, and above all, helpful.

With much love, Nancy the Beggar.

Cape Town
21 March 1953

Nancy the Beggar,
How lucky it is for you that your audacity can still charm after all these years! Yes, I will certainly help with your problem, and with more than advice. I bragged to you once that I was very, very rich (with a vulgarity that would have had the doyennes of St Clare's reaching for their smelling salts, no doubt) and now I must accept the consequence with good grace.

And I shall, but first to less worldly matters. I think that divorcing Ralph promptly, but without acrimony, was the best possible thing for all concerned. I won't say that you should never have married him, because although I have never succumbed myself, I can see how easily it happens if one is vulnerable and tired of life. I blame myself for what happened, too. I should have been more assiduous in my friendship and offered support when you needed it. I should have stayed in London.

But let us stop torturing ourselves with regret. No doubt I shall come to Europe again one day, but for the moment I am quite content living the simple life of the farmer; camping out in the bush, eating fruit from my own orchards and putting my horses through their paces on the veld (the open plains, to those of you who don't know Afrikaans). You may laugh at this unworldly picture of Randolph the Farm-Boy, but I can fully recommend the outdoor life as a means of retaining one's sanity and sense of perspective.

Nothing would make me happier than knowing that you and Lucie were safely ensconced at Graylings, and I fully intend to make that possible. I may as well tell you that you are the chief beneficiary in my will, but it would be far more satisfactory all round if the money were put to good use and you avoided tiresome death duties. If you were to wait until I died, you might have to camp in a field for thirty years.

I have arranged for a large sum to be transferred to my bank in London, where your signature on a piece of paper will open the Kingdom of Croesus. If it is not enough, tell me and you shall have more.

I must confess that I am titillated by the idea of Nancy, the Renovator, and I shall find out if my old suite at the Crown in Wells will be available for an extended visit next year.

Well, my dear, I hope that this strikes you as fair, equitable and the answer to a maiden's prayer. The only thing I ask in return are frequent reports on your progress and perhaps a photograph of Lucie.

Randolph the Good.

On a warm, sultry afternoon in June, Nancy stopped her car at the bend in the lane and looked down at the house.

She was returning to her home with her child, just as her mother had done thirty years before. It was a sad sight. There was no longer a flash of white through the trees to tantalize the approaching visitor. The milk white, sugar-sweet house was grey and shrunken, hiding against against its screen of trees rather than proudly rejoicing in the contrast of white on green. The old blue cedar stood unmarked and unchanged at the left of the house, throwing its mysterious shadows over the unkempt lawn. A few wallflowers struggled bravely along the edge of the walled garden. Nancy leaned on the steering wheel and gave a deep sigh. Lucie's face crumpled and she broke into a howl. "Shut up, will you!"

Lucie cried louder.

"Damn it, Lucie, it's going to get a lot worse than this!"

Nancy had arranged for builders to do enough work to make the house habitable before she arrived. The structure had already been made safe, but she wanted them to provide water and electricity.

The house had an unfamiliar, unwelcoming smell; a mixture of plaster dust and wet newspapers. As she crossed the hall, with Lucie in her arms, a pulverized cigarette butt stuck to the heel of her shoe, making her slip and Lucie scream even louder. Somewhere out of sight a tap was dripping steadily. There was no one to greet her.

Nancy headed instinctively for the kitchen. It was stripped bare and there was no cooker, but somebody—the builders perhaps—had left a Calor gas stove. There was a note on the kitchen table.

> *Darling Nancy,*
> *Ralph telephoned and said you were coming down. He said you didn't want anyone to know just yet, but he was worried about you being on your own down here so don't be cross with him. I've left some food in the larder for you: eggs, bread, milk and some meat pasties. Upstairs you'll find a camp bed and a cot in the cleanest of the rooms.*
> *I was going to say do telephone if you need anything, but I'm not sure if the telephone is connected yet. But you'll have the car, so you can drive over to Cleveleigh at any time. Do come and visit—I'm longing to see my granddaughter again!*
> *Love, Susannah*
> *P.S. I left fruit in the larder too.*

Nancy could not help smiling at this evidence of her mother-in-law's generosity and forgiveness. Allowing her to believe that she was a devoted mother seemed a small price to pay. She carried the luggage upstairs, and washed Lucie in an enormous Edwardian bath-tub. Then she moved the cot out of the room that was to be hers and to another room at the end of the corridor. It was easy to ignore Lucie's screams as she was unceremoniously dumped in the cot. Nancy had become practised at closing the door and walking away.

But this time she found her daughter less easy to ignore. Even

after the screams had stopped, she found herself strangely aware
of the small presence behind the closed bedroom door, and she
could not sit still.

The glory of the summer's day was retreating into dusk, and
through the open windows came the scent of warm grass, jasmine and early roses, stealthily replacing the smells that had
greeted Nancy when she arrived. She wandered through the
empty rooms, leaving the lights switched off and half-closing
her eyes so that she had to feel her way, forcing herself to forget
Lucie and instead imagining how the house would be when she
had finished with it.

As she passed the drawing-room windows, something made
her gasp and turn cold all over.

There was a shape outside the window; large and dark and
furry . . . the shape reached out and knocked on the window.

Nancy burst out laughing, *"Do you want a drink, Leonora?"*
she shouted, prising open the bolts on the French windows.
"Because if so, you're out of luck. I haven't got any with me."

Leonora pulled out a bottle of claret from under her mink
coat. "It's OK, I have. I thought I'd come and say welcome
back."

"Very kind of you. Have a seat." Nancy directed Leonora
towards a packing case.

"Does George know you're back?"

Nancy shook her head. "No, not yet. The only people who
know I'm here are you and Susannah, and that's the way I want
it to stay until I've got myself sorted out."

"Well . . ." Leonora eased off the mink, though it never
entirely left her body, "there's certainly a lot of work needed.
Rather you than me."

"Ah, but I've got it all planned . . . wait a minute, there's a
corkscrew in one of these boxes . . ."

Nancy poured the wine into two tea-cups and began a detailed
account of her ideas for the renovation of the interior of the
house. She had spent three months poring over books on archi-
tecture and design, and knew exactly what she wanted to achieve.
The stuffy, heavy Edwardian furnishings would be stripped away:
all traces of velvet and candelabra and glass-fronted cabinets.
The entrance hall and the marble staircase would be the inspiration for a house that gave the impression of light and air,
combining a classical simplicity with the restrained grandeur of
a Venetian palazzo. The colours would be Tuscan; creamy ochre,
terracotta, blush pink, but with the subtle faded patination of

water-colours. Curtains would be heavy and pale and simply draped over gilded supports in the Italian manner and there would be intriguing panels of *trompe l'oeil* where they were least expected. Everything would be simple: clean, uncluttered lines and open spaces . . .

"Very nice," said Leonora and then, with her customary bluntness, "Faye told me that you have a daughter. You haven't said a single word about her. Why?"

Nancy opened her mouth to make some defensive reply but instead found herself saying, "Because I'm a bloody failure as a mother."

Leonora laughed.

"I wish *I* found it funny."

"Sorry. It's not that. I'm just remembering hearing the very same words from your mother's lips. And now you with your daughter . . . you see why I'm laughing."

"Sort of." Nancy sighed into her cup of wine. "I just wish I'd been there then. I'd have told her that she wasn't a failure. Not compared with me."

"You're probably not a failure either. Oh, listen . . ." Leonora picked up the bottle of wine, corked it and thrust it under her coat. "I didn't come here to give you a lecture, so I'd better go. But may I just use one cliché? One which I've found to be true. You can blame your children for what they are, but not for who they are."

After Leonora had gone, Lucie began to cry again. Nancy steeled herself to ignore it, but this time she couldn't. She felt herself drawn inexorably through the silent, empty rooms, to the closed door.

Lucie's legs were drawn up under her body so that her small rump stuck up in the air. The blanket was tangled around her and her face was red and wet from crying. She stopped when she saw Nancy, and stared at her.

"Come here . . ." Nancy disentangled Lucie and lifted her out of the cot. "Oh Lucie . . . Lucie, I'm sorry . . ." Her own tears fell onto Lucie's wispy dark hair. She hugged her daughter tightly.

"I'm sorry, I was wrong. It's not your fault. None of it is your fault."

Greville Dysart's desk was several inches deep with final demands and the floor of his office was crowded with hastily packed boxes of files. He looked at the chaos, shook his head in disbelief and buried his face in his pudgy hands.

He still thought that his idea of blackmailing Guy Exley had been a good one. Just singularly ill-timed. On the day that Greville had read of his death in the paper, he had been in the process of drafting a second, more urgent demand. He sent it to Guy Exley's widow instead. Her reply was on the desk in front of him: ungrammatical and badly spelled;

> . . . *my late husband left me with zero, not a cent. I don't even get to keep the house. Now I'm back with my parents so if you think I give a fuck if Guy was screwing his sister, you're wrong. And my parents don't give a fuck either, after the way he treated me. So I'd forget it, Mr Blackmailer, whoever you are. By the way, Mr and Mrs Hamilton Exley III have sold up and gone to Fort Lauderdale so you can forget them too . . .*

Greville screwed up the letter and tossed it in the bin. It was too late to save the business now, anyway. He glanced through to the shop and the "CLOSING DOWN SALE" signs in the window. Then he picked up the phone and dialled Heathcote House.

"Kit! Hullo, old man . . . Greville here . . . How are things . . . Capital! . . . I thought I might come down and stay for a while . . . What?"

Could this be his innocent little Kit talking? "Sorry, old man, I—"

"I said 'No' Greville. No, it's not convenient for you to come and stay here."

"Come, come, you wouldn't turn old Greville away . . . just for a few days."

"From what I understand, a few days can end up being a few years."

"But Kit, you can't . . . Annabel said—"

"Annabel let you get away with too much. The house is mine and I don't want any interference. You're on your own now, Greville!"

There was a click and the line went dead.

Greville shook his head in dismay. No Somerset. He had rather counted on it. Never mind, he would just have to find some cheap hotel to stay in. And he'd have to sit down and have another think. For example, there was Lady Henrietta Dysart's brother, Bertie. He'd been killed off in the Boer War of course,

but hadn't he married the daughter of some very wealthy indus-
trialist? . . .

Graylings, 19 July

> *Dear Randolph the Benefactor,*
>
> *I don't know about camping in a tent for thirty years wait-
> ing for you to die, but I certainly feel as though I shall be
> camping in the house for thirty years waiting for them to fin-
> ish!*
>
> *Seriously . . . things are slowly taking shape. The biggest
> change is in Nancy the Mother. Oh Randolph, it's so wonder-
> ful! I don't really know how it happened. Perhaps it's the
> place working its spell. I really enjoy Lucie now, and the place
> has done wonders for her, too. She seems to thrive on chaos
> (unlike her mother, who is too old to tolerate it) and is learn-
> ing to walk clinging onto buckets of plaster and step-ladders.
> She's not yet one year old—a precocious little rogue in this
> as in everything. There have already been several accidents
> with pots of my precious, Italian water-based paints!*
>
> *I am finding the whole business much harder than I
> had expected. All the work is being done by other people—
> plasterers, carpet layers, carpenters, interior designers, but
> it is essential for them to work in harmony, and co-ordinating
> all their movements is a full-time job. If I turn my back for
> five minutes to attend to Lucie, someone puts something in the
> wrong place, or an argument breaks out between the factions.
> God knows what will happen when I have to go up to London
> to order furnishings and hunt for what Mother used to call
> "objects." I think I need to employ someone just to represent
> me—*

Nancy tapped her pen thoughtfully against her lower lip. Her
letter to Randolph had inspired her with an idea. She looked out
of the bedroom window at the trees that were blowing to and
fro in the breeze, twisting sinuously like a chorus of exotic dancers. A dog barked plaintively in the distance, but the house itself
was silent. It was Sunday, and there were no men at work.

Nancy picked up a dozing Lucie, bundled her into the car and
drove into the village. The high street was deserted; the morning
services at the church long since over. She parked the car outside
the graveyard and crossed the road to Heathcote House. The
neglect and the decay that she found here was reassuring; a sign

that nothing had changed after the upheavals and revolutions at Graylings.

The door was opened by a stocky, muscular young man with mousy hair and sad eyes that turned down at the corners.

"Kit! I was hoping you'd be here. Can I come in?"

It was a few seconds before he recognised his visitor. "Nancy! My God, Nancy! Christ, what a shock! Yes, come in."

He led her into the kitchen, which had the dreary tidiness of kitchens that are never cooked in. "Tea?"

Nancy laughed. "Of course! What else would one drink on a Sunday afternoon?"

"I'd prefer scotch myself."

"My, my, Kit, you *have* grown up! All right, let's be decadent and have scotch—"

"And to hell with vicar's tea-parties!"

"Quite."

Kit put the tea-caddy back on the shelf and returned with a bottle of scotch. "And who's this little person?" He pointed to Lucie, who was crawling over the kitchen floor, fascinated by the different coloured patches of carpet.

"My daughter. I was married, then divorced."

"Yes, I heard. She's a jolly little thing, isn't she? I'm afraid I don't have much experience of children, except for Matthew."

"Ah yes, Matthew. Our mutual nephew. He must be two now, is that right?"

"Yes, and there's another one on the way in a few months' time. Perhaps you knew that."

"No. No, I didn't." Nancy stared into her glass of scotch, feeling self-conscious about her rift with her brother because it might have led Kit to revise his high opinion of her, even to condemn her.

But his smile was friendly. "Are you just passing through the area, or—"

"No, I've come back to live here. I'm renovating the house, and eventually I hope to put some new life into the estate, too . . ." she bent down to extricate Lucie from Kit's shoe-laces. ". . . That's what I came to talk to you about. What are your plans at the moment? Are you on your own here?"

"Yes, we sold the farms but kept the house." Kit noticed the expression on Nancy's face and smiled gently. "You're wondering how I could bear to live here at Heathcote, aren't you, after what happened to Patrick. It's not that bad really. I just don't think about it. Anyway, it's better than intruding on George and

Annabel's married bliss, which was the only alternative. I shall
be here for the summer, just killing time, then I'm going up to
Oxford in October.''

''Really? I nearly went there once.''

''What stopped you?''

''My own bloody-mindedness. Education never really agreed
with me.''

''You preferred to learn things the hard way, you mean?''

Nancy laughed. ''I can see I shall have to watch you, Christopher Steele! You've become far too astute. I expect you know
what I'm going to ask. Will you come up to the house and help
out?''

''Like I did on VJ Day?''

''Something like that. I need a right-hand man to keep an eye
on things. It would probably be best if you brought your stuff
up and moved in for a while. I'm not much of a cook, I'm
afraid.''

''Neither am I. But there's always scotch.''

Nancy gave him her most dazzling smile. ''Does that mean
you'll come?''

''I'd be delighted. As long as we can pin up a few buntings!''

George Stein stood near the kitchen window and watched his
wife.

She was pushing their son, Matthew, on the swing, her swollen belly projecting awkwardly as she leaned back and extended
her arms. Matthew shrieked with delight as the seat carried him
higher and higher and the breeze snatched at his chestnut curls.
Then Annabel lifted her son gently from the swing and sat down
on it herself, holding him on her lap and kicking gently with her
feet so that they swung to and fro together.

The movement seemed to bring about a communion between
mother and child and to soothe them both. Annabel wore a
dreamy smile, and she moved her lips as though she was singing. Her reddish brown hair drifted about her face like a veil
and the skirts of her floral print dress tangled around Matthew's
naked legs. George watched them for a moment longer, then
cleared the lunch dishes into the sink.

He tapped on the window. ''I'm going back to work now,
darling!''

Annabel smiled in acknowledgement and lifted Matthew off
her lap. As she stood up, she went very pale and clutched at her
abdomen, wincing in pain. George moved instinctively towards

the door, but the pain seemed to pass quickly and her delicate features relaxed as she followed Matthew down the path.

"Are you all right, Annabel? You looked as though you were having stomach pains just then."

"It's all right, it's nothing really. Just a twinge."

"Are you *sure*, darling? Ought you to check with the doctor?" Neither of them had forgotten the agony of losing their first child.

"Quite sure, honestly. I've read about it somewhere. It's just the baby's way of practising for the big day."

George smiled and pressed his hand fondly over her bulging waistline. "Two months to go yet, remember?" He picked up his jacket and bent to kiss Matthew. "I'd better be getting back to the grind I suppose. I've got the keeper to see this afternoon and the water bailiff, not to mention umpteen bloody paths that need cutting back—"

"George, wait a minute." Annabel put her hand on his arm to stop him. ". . . I do hate to hear you use that tone of voice."

"What tone of voice?"

"I don't know, so . . . . so resigned and so dispirited about the whole thing. I want to feel that you like your job."

"I *do* like it, darling, it's just frustrating working on someone's land when that person doesn't give a damn about the place. Everything could be done so much more effectively if Yorke was prepared to take an interest and make a few sensible decisions . . . it's just like banging your head against a brick wall, that's all."

Matthew ran to and fro between their feet, banging a saucepan lid against the floor. Annabel screwed up her face as though she was trying very hard to think. "Perhaps you shouldn't go on working there. Couldn't you leave and do something different? Maybe you should ask Greville if he could help—"

"Greville? Don't be ridiculous, what use could Greville be? He's nothing but hot air. That fashion business of his didn't last long, did it?"

George unwrapped Matthew's small arms from his legs. "I've got to be going now, I'm late as it is."

He reached the door, then added as an afterthought. "And if there are any more of those pains you're to go straight to the doctor. I want a nice, healthy daughter from you in two months' time!"

* * *

George left his office on the Yorke estate feeling tired and drained. He jumped into the old jeep that he used for work and braced himself for the drive back to Peasedown St John in the fading light.

Christ, I need a good, strong drink . . .

As he passed the turning to Nether Aston, he swung the steering wheel sharply to the left and turned down that road. Leonora was always good for a stiff drink, and he could use a quiet half hour before returning to the cheerful mayhem of Matthew's bedtime.

"You're after a drink, I suppose," said Leonora as soon as she saw him on the doorstep of the cottage. She shrugged her threadbare mink about her shoulders and went to fetch glasses.

"I'll go away if it's not convenient," offered George unconvincingly.

"You're drinking all my supplies," Leonora replied. "That's what's inconvenient."

"I'll bring a bottle with me next time," said George, "I promise."

He settled himself comfortably on Leonora's bed and took a first, daring gulp of the cooking brandy that they were drinking.

"I expect you'll be wanting to keep an eye on what's happening up at the house," said Leonora.

George was familiar with Leonora's unorthodox pattern of conversation.

"I take it you're referring to Nancy. She's back, isn't she?"

"How did you find out?"

"Gossip, my dear Leonora. Which spreads faster than the speed of light in rural parts . . ."

George changed the direction of the conversation, trying to quell the surge of trepidation he felt at Nancy's return, a strange bastard emotion combining revulsion and uncontrollable joy.

It was dark when he left Leonora's cottage and he found himself hurrying down the path and back to his jeep which was parked in the space where the stables used to stand. Had she seen it, he wondered? He felt like a thief, an interloper as he drove round to the front of the house and up the drive. Instinct made him stop and look back before the house was out of sight. On the first floor of the house, one solitary window was lit up.

For the next few days, George was haunted by that vision of a light at the window. Nancy was alone. And he was unable to stay away. A secretive ritual evolved, a detour on the way back from work every evening to surreptitiously examine the progress that was made on the house, to make a note of the changes that were visible from the outside. Every night he drove away with a yearning to see from the inside, and he knew that this yearning meant that he was ready to forgive.

Annabel greeted George's suggestion of a reconciliation with equanimity. He made a point of discussing his feelings at length and seeking her approval, but he met no resistance. It was as if her deepening preoccupation with her physical condition allowed her to make a generous gesture by pulling her thoughts away from the past and into an engrossing present.

George laboured over his first communication as though it were a *billet doux*. He crossed it out four times before settling on

> *Dearest Nan,*
>
> *Welcome back to Somerset! Annabel and I would be delighted if you would come and celebrate your return with us. Would dinner on Saturday (1st Aug.) be agreeable? R.S.V.P. the Old Rectory.*
>
> > *Your loving brother,*
> > *George.*

He delivered the note to Graylings by hand, and took the opportunity to go and tell Leonora of his decision.

A childish excitement overcame him as he ran up the path to the cottage.

"So you're prepared to overlook her behaviour with Guy Exley, are you?" said Leonora as they settled down with their glasses of neat vodka. "You know what I'm talking about, I presume?"

George blushed and fixed his eyes on the hideous purple velvet gas-mask case that still hung on the back of the door. "Yes, I know about that. I have to confess I was very angry with her when I first heard about it."

"But now you've forgiven her?"

George smiled. "I suppose I must have done."

"Good. Your mother forgave her, you know." Leonora's eyes clouded as though she were remembering something unpleasant or shocking. "Who knows what really happened, anyway? I believe in relying on what I see with my own eyes and not listening to gossips. You should too."

"Well, I certainly can't afford to pay attention to all the gossip about our family that goes on in Nether Aston!"

Leonora smiled. "In that case you'll ignore what they're saying about her in the village."

George's glass was suspended half way to his lips. "What do
you mean? What are they saying?"

"That she's living up there in sin with a boy half her age."

Graylings, 29 July

Dear Randolph,

Another instalment in the progress report . . .

*Since my last letter I've found the perfect person for the job
that I was telling you about. He's Kit Steele—you will remember his part in that ghastly inquest business, I'm sure. At first
I was worried that he would find it difficult, since an eighteen-
year-old does not have the authority to tell older men what to
do, but he deals with them through persuasion, and by making
them think that the ideas are their own. Clever Kit! I find him
amazingly easy to be with, but more than that, there's an
instinctive closeness between us as if a bond has been forged
by the unspeakably awful things that we went through together. He's like a younger brother of my own.*

*And talking of brothers, the other piece of news that I have
for you is that George has decided to bury the hatchet. He
has invited me to dinner on Saturday, and I have accepted. I
haven't seen him yet, but he sent a sweet note—almost like a
love-letter, I thought.*

*Things are taking shape here at last, largely due to Kit's
efforts. He's full of good ideas about where to put things and
came back from Wells yesterday with a marble bust of Marcus
Aureleus which will be perfect for the alcove in the dining
room. (Unearthed in a junk shop and bought for the princely
sum of ten and sixpence!) Also, he has a friend studying at
art college who is willing to do the* trompe l'oeil *and won't
charge a fortune, though I'm assured he's very talented. I'm
terribly excited about the* trompe l'oeil. *I'm going to have a
door where there isn't a real one, with a door knob and even
a key sticking out of a lock! I'd also like him to do a painting
on the ceiling of the drawing room, but I can't think of a
suitable subject. Not quite Nancy the Michelangelo. I'm sure
you will come up with some suggestions of your own, and none
of them serious.*

*Having Kit here has lifted a lot of anxiety from my shoul-
ders, and has given me more time to spend with Lucie. As I*

*write this she's crawling across the lawn on all fours, at the
most stupendous speed, trying to get her fat hands on the
kitten that Susannah presented us with. The poor animal is
terrified out of its wits! She (Lucie, not the kitten!) is very sly
and very naughty, but with a smile that lets her get away with
the most dreadful things. (Ah Randolph, don't think I can't
hear you saying it! Can I really have been like that once?)*

*It's a baking hot day and I am trying to absorb as much of
the sun as I can while things are quiet. We only have a couple
of men here today, so things are relatively peaceful. I imagine
the place will be fit for receiving guests in another six weeks
or so—why not book the suite at the Crown for the autumn?*

I long to see you, and to share my new-found peace.

Love,
Nancy.

*P.S. I enclose photos of the darling beast, and await your
judgement, O, Solomon!*

Nancy removed her sunglasses and stretched out in her deckchair with a deep, lazy sigh. When she opened her eyes again,
the sun was so dazzling that she had to blink hard before she
could see Lucie, a tiny, bright speck at the far corner of the
lawn. Lucie was duly retrieved and returned, protesting, to her
playpen while Nancy went into the house.

"Kit? Where are you?"

She found him sitting at a small table in the library, scribbling
on a pad of paper. Nancy blinked in surprise. His sun-tanned
torso was naked except for a pair of shorts.

"I was so bloody hot that this seemed like the best place to
be. I'm just making a list of jobs specified on the various con-
tracts which have either been omitted or not come up to stan-
dard."

"I think I must have fallen asleep out there." Nancy pulled
the strap of her bathing costume down an inch and gazed ruefully at the white stripe on her pink shoulder. "I was just going
to make myself a cold drink? Would you like one?"

On the way to the kitchen Nancy was interrupted by a knock
at the front door.

"I'll get it!" shouted Kit.

"No, it's all right, I'll go." Nancy grabbed a bath robe and
put it on over her swimming costume, still trying to fasten it as
she flung the front door open.

It was George.

After her initial surprise, Nancy was overjoyed.

"George!" She embraced him warmly.

"Hello, George." Kit appeared behind her in the doorway, the sun glinting dully on his smooth, naked chest.

George went very, very pale. He let go of Nancy as though he had been scalded.

"George, what's wrong?"

"God, Nancy. *How could you*?"

"For God's sake, surely you don't think—"

"We'd better talk about this on our own." George grabbed Nancy's wrist and pulled her out onto the portico, slamming the front door in Kit's horror-struck face.

"Is it true that he's living here with you, in this house?" he demanded, pressing his fingers into her wrist so hard that they made white marks on the sunburn.

"Yes, but only like a lodger—"

George released his hold on her and stepped back. "You always have to find some rules to break, don't you, some standards of decency to lower? Isn't incest enough for you, without child-molesting as well?"

"It's not like that George—" Nancy reached out to stop him as he ran down the steps and disappeared between the blinding white columns.

"Don't touch me! And don't come near my house, either! I don't think I ever want to see you again!"

George Stein was standing outside the estate office, arguing with Sir Lionel Yorke's keeper.

The small, wiry man listed a panoply of grievances while his small, belligerent terrier mutilated a dead pheasant, scattering the feathers at George's feet. George looked down in the dog's direction, but he wasn't watching it any more than he was listening to its owner. He was thinking about Nancy. What the hell was he supposed to think? Annabel insisted that he was mistaken and that Kit would never become involved in anything so wicked.

But George knew Nancy of old. He remembered her effortless lies as a child. Even if he went to her and asked her to explain, how on earth would he know whether to believe her or not? You just never knew with Nancy. And you could see how people gossiped about that sort of thing. It all seemed so likely. Nancy was a very beautiful, very voluptuous divorcee. Very young. Still only twenty-six. And Kit was growing into an attractive young man, certainly old enough to . . .

Try as he might, George could not dispel the sight of sweat glistening in the deep cleft between Nancy's breasts and Kit behind her with the sun streaming over his naked chest . . .

". . . So now he's telling me that he's got fifteen people coming up here to shoot in December, and I told him he's just not going to get the birds, leastways not the number he's asking for."

George was still staring at the disembowelled pheasant. He straightened himself up. "Yes, well, that's all I need to know. I'll telephone Sir Lionel myself and see if there's anything that can be done. Good day to you."

He went back into the office and sat down at his desk. A pile of unanswered letters stared back at him. The first was from a tenant who had lived in the best cottage on the estate for nineteen years, paying only a peppercorn rent, and now claimed a right to the freehold. George sighed. He would have to draft a letter giving notice of Yorke's intention to take him to court over the matter, but he found it difficult to summon the sort of forcefulness that such a letter required.

The telephone rang. "George, it's me."

"Hello, darling. Everything all right?"

"I think I've gone into labour." Annabel's voice sounded far away and frightened.

"My God, it's much too early isn't it? . . . Annabel? *Annabel*!"

The line had gone dead.

George blundered against the desk as he ran towards the door, bruising his shin, but still he went running and running, fighting to get the door of his jeep unlocked and put the key in the ignition with his trembling hands.

Oh God, I'm so stupid. I should have called an ambulance. Why didn't I call a bloody ambulance? . . .

But when he screeched to a halt outside the Old Rectory, there was already an ambulance there. They were carrying her down the steps on a stretcher and putting her inside it. She was wearing a blue gingham dress and the front of it was all covered in blood . . . the stretcher was all covered in blood and it was dripping down onto the flagstones of the path . . .

"What's going on?" he shouted, but they were all too busy to answer him and besides, it was obvious what was going on. Annabel was losing the baby. He watched them laying the stretcher in the ambulance. Her head was facing away from him and her face looked very small, and very white, as though it were disappearing.

"Wait! I'm going with her!"

The ambulanceman held him back. "You'd better not, sir. What about your little boy?"

He had forgotten all about Matthew. George raced back to the house and telephoned a neighbour to ask if she would come and take care of Matthew. Then he followed the ambulance to the hospital, trying to quell an unreasoning surge of hatred towards the people who were taking her away.

At the hospital, they wouldn't let him see her. They made him wait. A doctor came down the corridor, a small blob growing larger and larger until the bespectacled face was only a few feet away and his apologetic voice bored into George's brain. Annabel was dead.

"*. . . So very sorry . . . a rare condition called placenta praevia . . . very difficult to diagnose . . . massive haemorrhaging . . . the baby was a girl; thought you'd want to know.*"

They asked if he wanted to see her. He said no.

He closed his eyes and tried to picture her face, but he could only see a blue gingham dress covered in blood.

Nancy picked up the telephone and dialled.

"Yes?" said the voice.

"George? It's me, Nancy."

"Go to hell!" The receiver was slammed down at the other end of the line.

Nancy sighed and buried her face in her hands. Then she picked up the telephone and dialled. "Kit . . . Nancy . . . look, I've tried ringing George again, but he still won't speak to me . . . What do you think I should do about this afternoon? I really want to be there. Maybe I should just go anyway."

Kit's voice sounded thin and high-pitched, fragile. "Don't do that Nancy, please. I went over and talked to him about it, but he said he didn't want you at the funeral. If that's what he wants, I think you should respect his wishes, however perverse they may be. It's going to be distressing enough for him as it is."

"Oh God . . . oh hell Kit, this is awful . . ." She sighed. "You're right, of course. I'll send the flowers, anyway."

She put the phone down, biting her lip to control her tears. *Damn George! Damn him for judging me unworthy to mourn with him!*

A pattern had been set which continued for the next two

weeks. Every day Nancy tried to telephone her brother, and every day he refused to speak to her. She wrote him letters: they were ignored. Around her the work of the house was nearing completion, but she barely noticed it. She had her romantic colour-washed walls, her arches and alcoves and pilasters, her ottomans and fur rugs, her precious *trompe l'oeil* friezes. Outside the garden was being replanted with bay and ilex and magnolia, exotic azaleas and rhododendrons.

The house had even been re-whitewashed to assert its quiet classical superiority once more, but inside it Nancy lay awake at night, listening. It was almost as if George was emitting wails of pain and she could feel it through the few miles that separated them.

But George, I've felt it too, that stranglehold of agony that won't let you escape. I know what it's like . . .

One morning Susannah Stanwycke telephoned Nancy.

"Nancy darling, can you help? I don't know what to do. George has lost his job and he sounded so desperate when he telephoned . . ."

Nancy was trembling when she drew up in front of the Old Rectory. The pretty pink house, the perfect love-nest was now the witness of shattering loss; its prettiness rendered terrifying. She knew that nothing would have been touched, or changed. There were blood stains on the stone path, as if the end had been violent.

George answered the door.

"Please George . . . please let me in."

Nancy was crying. She was crying before the door was opened. George buried his face in her shoulder and wept like a child.

They went together into the drawing room, and Nancy forced herself to repress a shudder at the filth and the clutter; the dirty plates and empty bottles. Matthew was sitting on the floor and eating macaroni out of a tin.

George lit a cigarette with trembling hands and started talking very quickly. "Nancy, I'm sorry, I've been taking it all out on you, stupid really . . . I was jealous . . . I suppose I've always been jealous, ever since we first met Guy . . . I felt as though I'd lost you, or you had changed, or something. Do you think you can forgive me?"

Nancy took her brother's hands in hers and kissed them. "No, can *you* forgive me?"

"For everything, even for Guy. You loved him, and he died.

That's simple. I understand that now." His blue-green eyes, swollen and bloodshot, were far away. "I suppose I knew that Annabel might lose the baby, after the last time . . . but I never once thought that *she* would die. You don't, do you? . . . I don't know what to do with myself. I daren't touch anything, but I'm afraid to go out . . . look at those flowers—"

He pointed to the piano where a vase of rotting roses stood, the petals wrinkled, brown and yellow. "She did those the . . . on the day she died. I can't stand the sight of them, but I daren't throw them away either. It's as if I'm hurting her . . . being heartless . . . cruel." He wept again then took out his handkerchief and blew his nose. His voice changed. "It's this bloody house, Nancy. I can't bear this house!"

"I think you should leave it. Sell the house and bring Matthew to live at Graylings for a while . . ." Seeing the relief that crept over his eyes, she went on quickly, "Harry Herbert's retiring and I need someone to look after the estate. I'm going to do a lot of work on it, improving properties, putting the land to better use. I think you ought to help me. I may be the one who won the prize in the grand draw, but really Graylings is your home too."

He shook his head. "No, I can't do it, I can't start all over again."

Nancy grabbed his hand. "Look George, we've both suffered terribly, but we've still got Graylings! I was in such a mess until I got back here, but then things started to improve. For God's sake, George . . . we're both so young, there's so much still ahead of us. Let's *use* Graylings! I don't want us to treat it like a beautiful museum and just sit there and vegetate like Darby and Joan! Let's fill the house with people, throw parties, *live* . . ."

George managed a smile. He squeezed her hand tightly.

"You're right, Nan. I think I should come home."

Epilogue

September 1955

As the sun began to sink lower over the horizon the white-washed walls of Graylings faded from gold to grey and wood pigeons called in the fading light.

George Stein was standing at a first floor window, watching the lengthening shadow of the cedar tree. There were voices in the garden below him; the murmur of conversation punctuated by an occasional burst of laughter. And now Nancy was coming out of the house to hand round a tray of drinks. He could hear the ice cubes rattling in the glass jug, and the little scraping noises that her stiletto heels made on the flagstones of the portico.

Further down the corridor, in adjoining rooms, the children lay sleeping. Matthew was curled up tightly in a ball, with only his hair showing. George kissed the top of his son's head and replaced the covers on his three-year-old niece who lay spread-eagled across the sheets. Then he went down to join the cocktail party.

Most of the guests were grouped on the portico. Leonora was there, with her mink draped over her shoulders and a glass in her hand. And Nancy, beautiful in a pale, gauzy dress. She was holding court to a group of enraptured young men, but as George passed their eyes met and she gave him a special smile.

He watched her for a few moments, and then moved on.

About the Author

Caroline Bridgwood was born in Cheltenham, Gloucestershire, in 1960. As the daughter of a diplomat, she lived in Norway, Israel and Laos. She was educated at Badminton School, Stowe and Oxford, where she read English. After graduating in 1982, she worked in London for two years before turning to writing full time. Her first novel, *This Wicked Generation*, to which *The Dew of Heaven* is the sequel, is also available from Charter Books.